Ranger
Dietrich Stogner

ISBN: 8-9930287-0-5

ISBN-13: 979-8-9930287-0-5

This book was outlined, plotted, drafted, written, edited, and proofread

without the use of AI. No AI was used in the creation of the cover.

Edited by Cameron Montague Taylor

Sensitivity reading provided by Rebecca Thorne

Cover design by Mellody Stout

Audiobook narration by Cassie Corbin

Author photo by Nephi Niven

Contents

To my friend.

Thank you for listening to me stress about this world, these characters and these stories.

Thank you for always being one of the first to read these books.

Thank you for insisting that I tell Jaina and Antoinette's story, and that I do it right.

And thank you for always being there when I needed you.

Dedicated to Toni Snyder.

(... how's that for cheese, you butt?)

2,902 Hours

There was a certain joy to be found in monotony. Jaina Creighton had been at the forge for six hours, pausing briefly to drink water at the exhortations of Master Mikel Georges, the smith under whom she'd apprenticed for the six years since her thirteenth birthday. In that entire time, she'd done nothing but hammer out one horseshoe after another, setting them aside on a battered and scorched wooden table to be inspected by Georges. The older man had left a half hour ago to deliver an order, so the pile awaiting his practiced eye had grown to a substantial level by the time he returned.

"You're falling behind, old man," she called out as she saw him walk back up toward the forge. "I'm getting faster, and it takes you long enough to squint at each one and pretend like I haven't had this down for the last two weeks."

"Jaina." His tone stopped her hammer on the downstroke, and she turned to look at him with a frown. He ran his hand over the liver spots dotting his bald head, his wrinkled face creased with worry. "You need to go home."

"What? Why?" Her eyes widened. "Dad?"

"No, everyone's fine," Georges said, shaking his head. "Your brother. He got his marker."

She shut her eyes for a moment. "Okay. I, uh... I haven't finished. We need eight more for the order."

"I think I can manage." He waved his hand. "Go. Be with your family. This is always hard."

Jaina nodded, untying the heavy cowhide apron she wore and hanging it on an iron nail. "Thank you." She jogged out into the Autumn Market, the year-round outdoor market that filled the main square of Lofland Fork. It was late in the year, the forests surrounding the sprawling city surrounding the crossroads of the Duke's Road long having since given up golden leaves as the first frost appeared, but there were still dozens of vendors shouting at anyone passing their stalls. Several waved at Jaina as she passed, and she offered a half-hearted nod without pausing to say hello. As she walked past a weaver's booth, she saw an older couple weeping, a younger man not much older than her sitting before them, clutching a bright red stick. Her stomach tightened, and she quickened her pace.

You knew it was coming. You all did.

The Oak's Shade was the largest inn in the city, a pair of three story buildings straddling the northern stretch of the Duke's Road as it came into the city. A skybridge spanned fifteen feet above the cobbled road, lamplight filtering through the alder lattice, and she could see several people talking and eating at the tables within. She darted underneath and headed to the back patio. She knew that her parents wouldn't want the guests to see them upset.

Joran was standing by the cluster of outdoor ovens. Her older brother had always been tall and gangly, and he was folding his arms and unfolding them repeatedly, as if unsure what to do with his hands. Her father was sitting on one of the several benches lining the patio's edge, his head buried in his hands. Gail Creighton stood over him, hand on his shoulder, and glanced up as she saw her daughter approaching.

"Didn't expect you until dinner," Gail said. "Mikel said something?"

"Of course he did." Jaina stopped a few feet away. She started to raise her arms for a hug, but none of them were looking at her. She turned to her brother. "When did you find out?"

"Hour ago." Joran shrugged, and held out a hand, showing a slip of pine painted red. "Always figured it'd be me."

"It was an even chance."

"Yes, but I'm prettier than Jak. Figures they'd want me."

"You're twins, you idiot," she said.

"Really, Jaina?" She turned as her father looked up from his hands, his eyes red. Paul Creighton rose to his feet, and came over to hug her. "You always pick the right thing to say, Cricket."

"I'm too old for you to call me that," She hugged him anyway, leaning into his chest, the scent of apples and spices filling her nose. "Apple tarts today?"

"Too late in the year for most other fruits." He smiled down at her, but it faltered right away. "I'm glad you're here."

"Yeah." Jaina looked over at her mom. "I saw the Pages. Devin got his chit too."

Gail started to nod, but stopped, frowning. "That can't be right. Ryder left last year."

"I don't know what to tell you, but his parents were in tears." Jaina looked back to Joran. "Least you'll know someone."

"Devin's an ass."

"Language," Gail admonished.

"I'm a soldier now," Joran said. "Soldiers curse."

"What?" They turned to see Jak Creighton walking towards them, carrying a crate loaded with sacks of flour. His eyes fell on the chit in his twin brother's hand, and his face fell. "Shit."

"Language!"

"Sorry, momma." He swallowed. "Thought it'd be me. I'm the pretty one."

"Do we have to joke about this?" Paul snapped. "This isn't funny."

"It's okay, dad," Joran said. "We knew it was going to happen sooner or later. Gods, we've been eligible for two years. Lasted longer than most." He nodded at his father. "You did your five. You were fine."

"I spent the entire time at the cookpot. Never got near the front lines." Paul shook his head. "Most aren't that lucky."

"Maybe I will. I know how to cook."

"You're a terrible cook, dear," Gail said gently. "There's a reason that we have you working front of house." She gripped her husband's shoulder. "You're right, though. We knew this was coming, and..."

"Creighton?"

The door to the back of the inn had opened, but the man who came out wasn't familiar. The military uniform he wore was. He had a sheaf of papers in his hands, squinting down at it. "Is this the Creighton family?"

Paul scowled at the man. "Things were more organized when I wore the colors. You people have already given my son his chit."

The soldier shook his head. "We don't do duplicate chits."

Joran held the painted wooden chit up as he stepped forward, handing it to the man. The man glanced at the numbers stamped on the cheap pine, comparing them to the papers in his hand. Finally, he shook his head, handing it back.

"That one's for Joran Creighton." He held up the one in his gloved hand. "This one's for Jak Creighton."

***

Jaina's father had a booming voice that could carry through the din and clamor of the crowded inn's dining hall, but even Paul's shouts didn't deter the soldier, who had stubbornly refused to leave until Jak had made his mark confirming receipt of the summons. Even after the door had closed behind them, the big man stalked back and forth across the stone tiles of the patio, muttering to himself while the rest of the Creightons sat in stunned silence. It felt as if they'd been in an accident. None of them knew what to do next.

"How..." Jak cleared his throat, and glanced at his brother. "It's not that I was hoping you'd be chosen and not me. But they never said that they were pulling more than one from each family."

"It's happened before." They all looked at Gail, who took a deep breath and smoothed her skirts. Paul glared at her, but she didn't quail before his stare. "You know it has, love."

"Not for a long time. Not since..." Paul's voice trailed off.

"Since when?" Jaina asked. Her parents exchanged a long look before the response.

"It was before my time. I was still young, maybe five or six," Paul said, his voice thick. "It was when the eastern duchies made that play for independence."

"The rest of the dukes allied together, called up as many men as possible for the rebellion," Gail said. "It ended up not mattering. The dukes backed down fast."

"I haven't heard about anything like that," said Joran. "And we'd know. If we got as many tips as we did gossip, we'd both have a seat on Vetticci's table."

Gail shook her head. "There haven't been as many border squabbles in the last year. Everything's been quiet."

"Then why are we both going?"

Jaina didn't want to say the thought that had popped into her head while they were talking. It felt like speaking it aloud would somehow bring it to life, but the fear felt alive, as if it would eat her if she didn't say it. "Is it Cicerone?" She tried to keep her voice steady. She knew she wasn't successful. "Is it the Confessors?"

She waited for her father to scoff, to dismiss the idea as childish or impossible. But the patio was silent.

***

Master Georges jumped when the door of the forge rattled open, resting a scar-covered hand on his chest, his eyes wide. "Gods, Jaina. I didn't expect you this late."

"Sorry," Jaina said. She pulled the heavy cowhide apron off the wall. "I didn't mean to startle you. I just wanted to finish the order."

Her teacher gestured at a pair of crates. "It's done. You'd finished all but the last batch, and I do remember the process." Georges shook his head. "You shouldn't be here. You should be home with your family."

She didn't meet his gaze, but could hear the raw sympathy in his voice. "You heard."

He nodded. "I did. It's not just your brothers, either. Apparently, it was every boy in town within the age range. A few that were a bit outside the age range, too. The Loughlin boy got a chit. He's only sixteen."

Jaina stared at the crates loaded full of iron horseshoes. "Do we have anything else I can work on?"

"Jaina..."

"I've been home," she said dully. "I've sat and listened to my dad stomp around, my mom try not to cry. I've heard my brothers make jokes about how easy this will be until I wanted to punch them. There's not a gods-damned thing I can do at home. So please, let me be useful."

Georges nodded. "Okay. We got a shipment of stock delivered. It's out back. Bring it in, sort it, and finish cleaning up. Also, Shakkar's going to be here tonight to pick up the shoes. He's already paid. Can you help him get loaded?"

Jaina nodded. "I can do that."

The old man hung his apron and gloves up, and gave her shoulder a squeeze.

"Are you going to tell me it's going to be okay?" she asked, not meeting his eyes.

"No. Wouldn't really mean much if I did," he said, not unkindly. "Things are going to happen how they happen. But your brothers are strong, and if there's a silver side to this mess, they'll be together. They'll have each other."

She didn't know how to respond to that, so she said nothing. He gave her shoulder one more squeeze, and left.

Jaina spent the next hour carrying in bars of stock steel from where they'd been left behind the forge. The first time Georges had tasked her with bringing in the stock, she'd been sore for days, her arms trembling whenever she tried to lift them. Years of swinging a hammer had made the task a bit easier. She'd hoped that the repetitive, heavy task would block out the parade of scenarios that her imagination kept conjuring, each more awful than the next.

Jaina tried to imagine the brothers who had played with her, teased her, always been around her, wearing the Dominion uniform. Marching with a Dominion army. The picture wouldn't form. But when some particularly nasty part of her imagination suggested what they'd look like with blood soaking the cheap grey wool that soldiers wore, that image came to the front of her mind far too easily. She tried to think of other things, but it was like a piece of gristle stuck in her teeth.

As she set down the last bar, a knock sounded at the door. "It's open," she called out.

She turned to face the man who stepped through, a genial smile on his face. Edmund Shakkar was not a big man. He peered up at her as he stepped forward, a full handspan shorter than her. His arms and legs were thin, and his fingers long and spindly as he stuck his hand out. "Got a message. Said my order was done."

Jaina gripped his hand. The ranger's handshake was always limp, as if he were afraid to squeeze. "Master Georges finished the last few tonight." She gestured at the pair of crates. "You sure you don't want me to split them up into smaller batches? He said it was fine, but that's a lot of weight."

"Will the crates hold?" She nodded, and Shakkar shrugged. "Should be fine, then." He walked over, wrapped his arms around the box, and lifted it with no apparent difficulty. Her eyes widened briefly as he walked towards the door, pausing just long enough to tilt his head. "You mind? Rangers don't generally get issued an extra arm."

"Sorry." She jogged over and held the door for him.

"Appreciate you." Jaina held the door as he came back in to get the second crate, watching him load it in the back of a wagon, the wood creaking under the weight of over two hundred steel horseshoes. When he was done, he came back over, counting a handful of Dominion marks from a leather pouch. "Here."

She shook her head. "Master Georges said you already paid."

"For the shoes. Not for the courtesy." His hand remained outstretched. When she didn't reach for the marks, he offered a kind smile. "Heard about the news. That's a hard one."

Reluctantly, she accepted the coins. "Thank you." She glanced at him. "Don't suppose the rangers know why..."

He shook his head. "We have nothing to do with ducal affairs. They don't share anything with us we don't need to know."

Jaina nodded. "Is your family... I mean, do you know anyone who was called up?"

"I'm an only child," Shakkar said. "My father died a long time ago. I have an uncle, but he's too old. Not that it'd matter anyway."

"What do you mean?"

"Ranger families are exempt. From conscription, I mean." He shrugged. "One of the rare fringe benefits." Shakkar walked back to his wagon. "Please give Master Georges my thanks. We'll have a new order in the spring, and if I have any say, we'll bring you our patronage again."

He turned to leave, but stopped as Jaina stepped forward. "Wait."

Shakkar glanced back. "I forget something?"

She shook her head. "No, I..." Jaina swallowed. "No one in your family has to serve?"

"Like I said, not much of a family to include, but that's the rule." His eyebrow lifted slightly. "Oh. Jaina..."

"What are the rules? About who can join?"

Shakkar shook his head. "Jaina, you're upset."

"That's not an answer."

He sighed. "No record of malfeasance. No significant debt. No one from the military or any mercenary guild. Basically, we don't want crooks and we don't want soldiers. Past that, you need a nomination from an active ranger."

"Women?"

"We have quite a few women rangers."

"I'm not a crook," Jaina said. "You've known me my whole life. Clearly not a soldier. I'm strong. You know that."

"That doesn't matter." Shakkar rubbed his forehead. "Look, Jaina, if this were any other day, I'd be eager. You're right. I know you well. You're a good person. More than anyone else, that's what we look for. But this isn't any other day. This isn't something you've decided after due consideration."

"The rangers are honorable. They're respected," Jaina replied. "You're telling me that I can serve my people, serve my community while also keeping my brothers safe? Not sure that the timing makes that anything less than a good idea."

He was quiet for a few moments, then sighed. "It wouldn't happen right away."

"That's okay."

"You'd have to go through the ritual. And complete a one-year novice period. Only then could we issue the writ of exemption." Shakkar stared at her. "This isn't a small decision, Jaina. The oath is for life. You don't get to change your mind. You don't get to decide in a year when they're back home that you made a mistake."

Jaina folded her arms. "If it brings them home, it's not a mistake."

Shakkar ran his fingers through his thinning hair. "I'm not saying yes."

"But you're not saying no, either."

"No, I'm not." He shook his head. "You need to sleep on this. Talk to your family. Really consider the scope of what you'd be giving up. No husband."

She raised an eyebrow. "Really? That's your argument?"

"No wife, then. No children." She started to respond, and he held up his hand. "I'm not going to swear you in tonight, an hour after you got this news. Three days. If you don't come to your senses before then, if you still think this is what you want, you can come find me."

Jaina nodded. "Three days. I'll find you." She took a deep breath as the smithy door closed behind him.

I can fix this.

2,884 Hours

F ish swam in lazy circles beneath Antoinette DeLuca's feet. She watched as a pair of silver fish danced around each other through the lazily waving seaweed.

"It really is extraordinary, isn't it?" She looked up at the voice, meeting the smiling face of the man looming over her. Antoinette wasn't exactly short, but this lanky gentleman was another head taller. He bowed deeply. "I know it's not quite the focus of tonight's event, but I understand you're responsible for the aquatic marvel we all stand upon."

Count Lamon. 68 years old. Claimed family holdings, 54 million ducats. Actual family holdings, 1.4 million ducats. Antoinette selected the correct smile for this interaction. *He's important, but not so important that you need to show genuine interest. Just basic courtesy.* Tilting her head, she said, "Thank you, Count..." She shook her head. "My apologies. It can be difficult to keep track of so many people."

"That's quite all right, my dear. Bryan Lamon, and I am very much at your service."

"Count Lamon, of course. How impossible of me to forget."

"If I may ask, how do you keep the fish alive?" He gestured down to the labyrinth of interlocking tunnels and chambers beneath the translucent quartz floor upon which the room full of notables was standing. "I assume the glass is actually shifted quartz, very impressive that, but every time we try to keep Rainnell Silvers alive in our family aquarium, they die within days."

Good thing this party only lasts eight hours, then. "I'm afraid that's outside my expertise, Your Excellency," Antoinette said. "I simply carved the base for the exhibit. The rest was assembled by artificers from the College." A soft bell chimed from the center of the room. "Forgive me, Your Excellency. I believe I might be needed for this part."

"I should say so." Lamon bowed. "Mistress DeLuca."

Antoinette weaved through the crowd, offering nods and greetings when each was appropriate. At the center of the crowded room was a space clear of people, everyone keeping at least ten feet away from the table sitting in the center with the exception of one older man who held the chime that he'd just rung.

At first glance, it would be easy to mistake the table for something natural. It was in the shape of a massive tree stump, ivy covering the outer bark. A small salamander looked as if it were crawling up the outside, the bright reds and blacks in sharp contrast to the bark beneath. Each ivy leaf was a deep green, tiny and delicate. Staining them all had taken weeks.

The room fell silent as Antoinette approached the gentleman. He wore a simple grey tunic, dotted with paint stains carefully placed to create the appearance of accidental. The wire rimmed spectacles on his nose glinted as he made several notes on the writing board in his hands, and on his breast was the insignia of the College of Artisans.

Antoinette came to a stop in front of him, and bowed. The first time she'd done this, she'd kept her hands under a shawl so as not to betray how much they'd been shaking. *Things change.* Her hands were steady as she spoke in a clear voice that carried through the room. "Master Chicane. It is my honor to present the College of Artisans with this work, in the hopes that my handiwork is worthy of their consideration and traditions."

Chicane nodded. "Antoinette DeLuca, Mistress of the DeLuca family, do you swear this work is yours and yours alone?"

"I do."

"Who witnesses the creation of this work?"

"I do." Every voice in the room fell silent. Every eye in the room turned to the older woman who stepped forward, hands folded before her, eyes hard and unblinking. "Toni DeLuca, Madame of the DeLuca Family, member of the Vetticcian Peerage, and grandmother to Antoinette DeLuca."

Chicane bowed. "Madame DeLuca." Raising his voice to carry through the room, he said, "In the judgment of the Vetticcian College of Artisans, this table is a true work of art, a representation of the talent, vision, and imagination of Antoinette DeLuca. We deem it worthy of inclusion in the guild archives, and name it masterwork." Stepping forward, he handed Antoinette a small rosewood box, the lid open. Sitting inside was a small bronze coin with an oak leaf engraved on the surface.

The room erupted in applause and cheering as Antoinette accepted the box. Master Chicane leaned in to speak through the din. "Well done, my dear. This is your third, correct?"

"My fifth," she said. "I'm grateful you were able to take the time to view the work."

"He'd better, considering how much we donate to the College." They both turned to the burly man who'd just spoken. Count Dominic Merino grinned broadly as he reached out to grasp Antoinette's shoulders. Toni DeLuca stood silently a few steps behind him, watching. "We're going to miss seeing you around the estate, my dear. I have half a mind to adopt you."

Antoinette blushed. That had taken her some time to learn to do on command. "Your Excellency is too kind. It was a pleasure to get to spend time in your beautiful home. I'm just happy you're pleased with the commission."

"Pleased?" Merino rapped his knuckles on the driftwood table. "I have an original DeLuca, and I'll be hard pressed to imagine you surpassing this, even considering your formidable gifts." He pounded the table again, and Master Chicane winced visibly. Merino laughed. "Calm yourself, sir. I have no intention of damaging this piece. I paid enough for it." He nodded down at the table. "A single piece of oak. Can you believe it?"

"Even more than its beauty, the technical difficulty was the primary factor in our consideration," Master Chicane said. "I'm not a sculptor, but I didn't think it would be possible to achieve that level of detail, particularly without compromising the strength of the piece. Particularly the leaves. How many are there?"

"Six hundred twenty-two, Master Artisan," Antoinette said. "It took some time."

"I should say so. The patterns on each one appear to be unique. That's an attention to detail most wouldn't notice."

I certainly hope not. Antoinette knew that even if Merino or his staff had noticed the patterns on the leaves, the code was indecipherable. But it was best that they remain blissfully unaware of the messages hidden within their new table. "You're very kind, sir. I just wanted to be sure Count Merino and his very welcoming family felt this piece deserving of their lovely home."

"It's going in my library, and there it will stay," Merino said. "There are pieces you display for the world, and there are those that are simply for my own enjoyment. Have you completed your sketches for the Archives, Master?"

"Nearly, sir," Chicane replied. "I will finish after the celebration tonight."

"Please, take your time," Toni DeLuca said. "If you both will excuse us, I'd like a moment with my granddaughter. She's been away for some time."

The two women wove through the crowd, exchanging nods and pleasantries as they made their way to the doors at the end of the long banquet hall. Stepping through, they found themselves on a balcony overlooking a sprawling garden. A couple was leaning against the iron railing, whispering to each other, but as they met Toni DeLuca's stare, they both stammered out apologies and fled inside.

Only once the doors closed did they speak. "Well done." Toni began tugging off the pale linen gloves she wore. "It's too warm for all this nonsense."

"I should have stretched it out longer," Antoinette said, gripping the railing and staring down at the pair of peacocks bobbing slowly across the manicured grass. "If I'd slowed down, I could have been there another week, maybe two."

"And it might have raised the Count's suspicions." Toni shook her head. "You spent three months in their home, and you got plenty. Pushing things too far is rarely wise, Antoinette."

"Yes, Grandmother."

"The trick with the leaves..."

Antoinette nodded. "One of his sons slipped up the second day I was there. Mentioned something from one of my letters home. I don't think they could have found anything in them, but it felt best to record what I learned in another manner."

Toni didn't look at her. "So you thought it wise to leave a permanent record of your espionage. On a piece that a member of the Table will keep in his personal library for decades."

Antoinette felt her stomach clench. "He doesn't know the cipher. He couldn't possibly..."

"Be very cautious making assumptions about what people are and are not capable of, my dear," Toni said. "A seat on the Table doesn't guarantee intelligence. But Merino is a shark, and not to be underestimated. You could have accomplished the same by simply modifying the progress sketches. Those leave with us."

"I was trying to improvise."

"You were showing off." Toni shook her head. "There will come a day where your duties take you much further from home. You'll need to show more discretion."

"I'm sorry."

Toni glanced at her and nodded. "The cipher key has been destroyed. There's no record of it anywhere. So we'll call it a lesson well learned, and speak no more about it." She watched a pair of gulls wheel past. "Anything else I should know? While the experience is fresh?"

Antoinette nodded. "He's quite pleased with the new loans to the Dukes up north," Antoinette said. "It's a lot of money, but he doesn't seem concerned."

Toni snorted softly. "Never doubt Merino's ability to turn a profit. He's a pompous ass, but the man could squeeze ducats out of a dead fish. Plus, the Dominion is always a safe investment. They'll pay back five times the loan's value in grain and meat."

"But why are they borrowing so much?" Antoinette asked. "Six of thirteen dukes have taken out major loans."

"Nine." Toni raised an eyebrow at Antoinette's surprised expression. "Merino's far from the only one offering them terms. Don't lose track of the ocean for the drop."

"Nine, then." Antoinette shook her head. "They've spent the last ten years pulling away from us, ever since the bridge was done. Why now do they suddenly want our money?"

"An excellent question. And one I'm looking into finding an answer soon." She said nothing more.

I suppose we're done speaking of that. "What next?"

"I'm not certain," Toni said. "Several houses have offered residencies, but I'm waiting on another possibility."

Antoinette tried to keep the dismay from her voice. "A proposal offer?"

She clearly hadn't been as successful in hiding her emotions as she'd hoped. Toni arched an eyebrow. "No. But that's coming. You're eighteen years old, and that is a card we are going to play one day. You're our only female heir. The future of our house lies with you, and it's best you come to terms with that."

"Yes, grandmother."

Toni eyed her for a moment, then nodded, satisfied. "Not a proposal. Something else. We'll speak soon."

2,849 Hours

J aina wordlessly finished sorting the stock in the dark and quiet
  smithy. During the hour, she kept returning to her conversation
with Shakkar, turning and inspecting it in her mind. It kept the ugly
thoughts of her brothers carried home at bay.

She thought about following Shakkar to the small flat he stayed in
above a bakery, knocking on the door until he understood how certain
she was. Instead, she doused the pair of oil lamps that threw weak
flickering light across the smithy, and headed home.

It was only a few short blocks to her home. The moonless sky
offered little light, but she knew the route by heart. Somewhere out in
the darkness, the watchmen cried out the time, and she nodded. Her
family would all be asleep by now. To be certain, she walked quickly
past the dark dining room and turned down the short alley that led to
the paved patio lined with ovens. She eased open the back door and
stepped into the kitchen, slowly easing the door closed as quietly as
possible.

"We need to talk, Jaina."

She whirled, heart hammering in her chest. "Gods! Dad, you scared
me half to death!"

Her father was leaning up against one of the long wooden tables
that ran the length of their kitchen. His face was shadowed, but she

could read the expression, and Jaina swallowed. "A lot of that going around," Paul said. "Care to tell us about your evening?"

"Paul, there's no need for games." Jaina turned to see her mother walk into the kitchen, followed by her brothers.

"I didn't mean to wake you all up," she said.

"Please," Jak said. "We were trying to be dramatic. Ma and me waited in the dining room, Dad and Joran were supposed to be waiting in the kitchen."

"Jak."

"Come off it, dad." Her brother rolled his eyes, and turned to Jaina. "Mikel came by an hour ago. He forgot something, went back to the smith. Heard you and the ranger talking."

Well. Shit. "So he came right back to tell you."

"Of course he did," Paul said. "Known the man for forty years. Gods, he grew up next to your mother. You don't think he's going to do the right thing by telling us when our daughter's about to light her entire godsdamned future on fire?"

"Paul, this was meant to be a conversation," Gail said.

"She's not doing it!"

"Good conversation," Joran said. "I know personally I always respond with delight to people bellowing orders at me in a dark kitchen."

"Can I speak?" Jaina asked. "You know, given that this is my decision?"

"Not much of a decision to make. You're not doing it." Her father's voice was getting louder. Gail came and rested her hand on his arm.

"Can we all just calm down? Gods, we're supposed to be the ones who get into trouble." Jak and his brother had moved, positioning themselves between Jaina and her parents. "Just feels unnatural to not be the one getting yelled at."

"Why would you even consider..." Paul didn't get the chance to finish before Joran cut him off.

"Dad. Stop it. Why would she consider doing something to protect us?" He glared back at his father. "Are you actually asking that question? I think she's gotten enough shit at this point."

"It's not too late," Paul said, acting as if his son hadn't spoken. "Go find Shakkar. Tell him you changed your mind. Tell him it's against your religion. Tell him you're allergic to ranger juice. Tell him anything."

"And then what?" Jaina was horrified to feel tears spring to her eyes, and wiped them away angrily. "I'm supposed to watch my brothers carted off? Go back to the forge, not think about all the things that could happen over the next five years?"

"Yes, you idiot!" Jak snapped.

"Jak!"

"Sorry, momma, but..." He turned back to his sister. "Everyone does this! Conscription is mandatory for every man in the Dominion! We were always going to go."

"At the same time? Like this?" Jaina shook her head. "I've lost count of how many families I've seen panicking in the last day. They're taking everyone. Someone told dad that there are thirty wagons waiting to take all the conscripts north. This isn't the same. If it was one of you going, like it was supposed to be, that's one thing, but both?"

"You have to admit, it's strange," Joran said, glancing back at his parents. "And the rumors..."

"Are only rumors. There are always rumors," Paul said. "Last week that idiot Marc Pellen told us the Imperial Chorale was opening a guild house here in town. Before that, it was drought out east, or pirates near McElroy. Just because someone says it..."

"I'm not an idiot," Joran said. "But if this kind of conscription is happening in other cities... Westcott, Havensport..."

Jaina spoke. "That's thousands of new soldiers. That's a lot of food, a lot of money. Why would the Dukes be doing that if Cicerone wasn't acting up?"

The room fell briefly silent at the name of the Confessor nation. Several decades earlier, the religious faction known as the Confessors had declared the province of Cicerone their holy land, and seceded from the Dominion. Rather than risk war with the entire church, the Dukes who ruled the Dominion had let them go. For years, the church of the Confessors had been shrouded in mystery and rumor, none of it good.

Jaina seized on the brief moment of silence, doing her best to keep her voice even. "I was never going to work the inn. We've known that for years. You two are supposed to take it over, to keep it in the family. I'm not. So whether it's in Master Georges' forge or with the rangers, it doesn't matter to me. But this way, you two get to stay home. Permanently."

"You've worked for years," Gail said, the desperation bleeding through her voice. "There are two smiths in this entire town. What, maybe fifty, sixty in the entire Dominion? Another year, you'll be a master. You'll make more money than this inn brings in. You'll have choices. You've worked so hard, Jaina. And you love being a smith."

"I do." She didn't look at her brothers. "But it's not worth losing these two idiots."

"It's five years." Her dad shook his head. "I don't want them to go either. Particularly not like this. But five years, we would have all been together again. Maybe a few more scars, but if you do this..." He looked up at her. "Jaina. This oath is for life. You don't get to go back to the smith. Depending on your orders, you might never get to come back home."

"You don't know that." Jaina shook her head. "Rangers come through here all the time. Shakkar even lives here."

"Shakkar has only been the ranger in this city for five years. Not likely he'll be replaced soon," Paul said. He scowled. "Too bad he'll never get to eat under our roof again. Bastard."

"This isn't his fault," Jaina said. "Gods, he wouldn't even let me make the decision tonight. Said I had to sleep on it."

"See? Even he thinks it's a bad idea!" Paul slowly pounded his big fist on the wooden table. "It's five years, Jaina."

"Five years, unless the Confessors come across the border," Jaina shot back. "How am I supposed to spend my days making horseshoes and nails, wondering if I traded a bed and a job close to home for one of my brothers' lives?"

"That's a bit dramatic, Jaina."

"Yeah?" She glared at him. "Then tell me this. Honestly. If Shakkar had come to you. Told you that if you handed the keys to this place to these two, and walked away with him, that they'd get to grow old here. Wouldn't have to go away, wouldn't have to put on that itchy uniform you've always said you hated, wouldn't have to march off every time Duke Gaile gets cranky with one of the other dukes, would you do it?"

Paul opened his mouth, but didn't answer. Before he could say anything, Jaina turned to her mother. "Would you?"

"Jaina…" Her mother shook her head.

"And how about you two?" Jaina said, spinning to face her brothers. "If either of you could be a ranger to ensure the other stayed safe? How fast would you make that choice?"

"Is that an option?" Joran said.

"Gods, it's fucking spreading," Paul said.

"Language, honey."

Jaina shook her head. "You've both been called up. You technically become part of the ducal army the moment you're handed that chit. We all know that. Shakkar said that they won't allow soldiers to join." She looked at her parents. "Not a single one of you wouldn't at least give it some serious thought if you were in my place. So how can you sit here and tell me not to do this?"

The room fell silent. Jaina looked back and forth between them all. "Being a ranger... it's honorable. It's a good calling, a good life. It's even possible I'll end up close to the city. There's nothing that says I can't come visit." She offered a weak grin. "I'll get to rub it in their face every time I see these two getting fat and lazy at home."

"You don't even know what you're signing up for," Paul said. Desperation had begun to bleed into his words. "Shakkar's the exception, you know that. Rangers almost never stay in one place. They sleep in the dirt. They deal with bandits and deserters. You'd be cold, and alone, and never knowing if the next place you go doesn't hide someone looking to put steel in your belly. And you'll be doing that for the rest of your life."

"And honey..." Gail stepped forward, taking her hand. "You won't be able to..." She cleared her throat. "You know the oath they take. No husband. No children."

She nodded. "I know. But I never wanted kids. And even if I did..." She flushed slightly, glancing down at the rough wood floor.

Jak shook his head. "Definitely not the right angle to take." He came to stand next to Jaina, nudging her with his shoulder. "You're upset. Maybe not the best time to make a decision like this."

"When do you have to decide?" Joran said.

"Three days."

"So we have three days to talk you out of this idiocy." Her father was biting off his words, anger still flushing his cheeks. "I don't care what your argument is. I don't care whether you think this is what you need to do. This isn't happening, Jaina. You're not walking away from us, not on the off chance that you lighting your entire future on fire might help your brothers."

"Last I checked, I'm over sixteen years old," Jaina shot back. Despite her best efforts, she could hear the frustration riding the words out of her mouth. "The choice is mine."

"It's not HAPPENING!" Paul roared. His fist pounded against the table, and before anyone could react, he stormed out, the door to the dining room slamming behind him.

"Well." Gail shook her head. "How do we think that went?"

"He's being unreasonable," Jaina said, angrily wiping away the tears.

"He's being a father." She sighed. "Look, Cricket, I get why you want to do this. I do. And your heart's in the right place. But you always do this. You try to fix everything, even if it's too big. Too much."

"So, what. If you do this, we just... don't go?" Joran asked.

"Seriously?" Gail said, staring at him.

"I'm just asking the question!"

"No, it won't happen right away," Jaina said. "I have to go through some kind of ritual, I think. I'm guessing that's my training. And something called the novice period. Shakkar said probably a year."

"Gods, a year," Jak muttered. "We'll barely be out of drill. After which our baby sister gets to spend the rest of her life paying for four years of ours." He shook his head. "Your heart is in the right place, Jaina, but your head... You can't fix everything. Not by yourself."

She shrugged, offering him a smile. "Kind of seems like I can."

***

The western gates of Lofland Fork barely deserved the name. The city didn't have walls, didn't have the palisades that surrounded communities closer to the border with Cicerone, or even another Duke that might cast an ambitious eye toward a mine or mill. Instead, the road leading to the capital of Westcott was flanked by a tannery on one side and a shop that sold honey and jams on the other. Today, it was also flanked by hundreds of families, all with a dark cloud hanging over them.

"Have you ever seen this many?" Joran asked his father, quietly enough that Jaina had trouble making it out.

Paul Creighton shook his head. "I knew they'd taken quite a few, but this..." He nodded towards a weeping couple not far away. "The Briersons don't have a son. They must have recalled Timothy."

"They're recalling people, too?" Jak swallowed, fidgeting with the collar on his new uniform. He wore the same tan cotton tunic that hundreds of other young men now wore, absent any decoration. A few soldiers with rank slashes on their sleeves were moving through the crowd, marking names off on sheafs of paper far too thick for anyone's comfort.

Paul and his wife exchanged a dark look, and Gail said, "This isn't right. Feeding and boarding this many people, it's going to cost a fortune. Why are they doing this?"

A voice boomed from some distance away. Jaina couldn't make out the speaker. "Five minutes! Load into the wagons, we leave in five minutes!"

The lump that formed in Jaina's throat felt as if it were going to strangle her. She swallowed several times, trying to push it down, watching as her older brothers folded their mother into their arms, murmuring into her soft brown hair. Gail kissed them both on the cheek, and smiled up at them through eyes that were brimming.

"Be safe. Stay together, and take care of each other." Reaching up, Gail cupped both of their cheeks. "You come home. Just as soon as you can."

Jak and Joran nodded down at their mother. "Love you. We'll be fine," Jak said.

Gail nodded, then stepped to the side as her husband came forward to crush his sons into his arms. One by one, he grasped them by the shoulders, trying to give what he thought was a stoic nod, but tears streamed down Paul's face. "Listen to your sergeant. Keep your gear in good condition. And don't volunteer for anything. Just..." He shook his head. "Just be smart."

Jaina stood behind her parents, wringing her calloused hands and popping her knuckles. Part of her was desperately willing her parents to take longer to say goodbye, to stretch out this moment until someone came running up to announce that there'd been a mistake. When Joran stepped over to her, she felt her eyes burn as the tears she'd been trying to deny for hours came smashing through.

"Hey." Joran pulled her close, hugging her so tight she thought her ribs would snap. She desperately wanted him to hug her tighter. "It's okay. You can't get rid of us this easily."

"Better not." Jaina mumbled into his shoulder. She saw Jak standing just behind his brother, and broke free to go hug him. "I'm bringing you two home. I promise. Just stay safe. Stay together. I'm bringing you home."

Jak shook his head, but said, "Spent three days trying to talk you out of it. You're as stubborn as we are. Just…" He gave her a squeeze. "Just be careful."

Another shout, and he let her go. "That's us," Joran said. The pair nodded at their family, and turned to join the stream of young men walking towards the hundreds of waiting wagons.

They watched Jak and Joran climb into their wagon. They watched the convoy slowly, one rattling wagon at a time, pull onto the road and head west. They watched until the last wagon disappeared around the curve in the road. They were not alone. Countless families stood and watched their sons vanish into the distance, and every single one had the same shameful thought.

Theirs, not mine. Please.

Gail Creighton was one of the first to head back. Paul and Jaina stayed a bit longer, silently staring into the distance. Finally, her father spoke. "I shouldn't have yelled. When you told us. I'm sorry." He didn't look at her as he spoke.

Jaina nodded slowly. "It's okay."

"It's not." Paul shook his head. "Your mother always said my temper was going to cause me problems. Gods know if she ever turns out to be wrong about something, it won't be that. Same thing happened when you were younger."

Jaina frowned. "What do you mean?"

"When you came to us, told us you didn't want to work in the inn anymore."

She nodded. "You were upset. I don't remember you yelling."

He chuckled. "You have no idea how hard parents work to keep their children from knowing how human they actually are. You were eleven years old. I waited until you were tucked in bed to let anyone see how angry I was." He cracked his knuckles as he spoke, pops rattling off from his big hands. "Thought you just wanted to leave. Thought you couldn't think of anything more than getting out from under us. Your mom calmed me down. She always does. Helped me see that you just wanted a different path."

"Dad..."

Paul continued as if she hadn't spoken. "Getting you that apprenticeship... it wasn't easy. Or cheap. It took quite a bit before Mikel took you on."

Jaina closed her eyes for a moment. *Gods. No matter what I do, someone gets hurt.* "I didn't know that."

"Of course you didn't. But it's okay. That's what parents do. It might have taken me a bit to figure out why you wanted an apprenticeship, but once your mother helped me connect the pieces, we knew we had to see it done. We do what we can for our children. It's our job." He shook his head. "I'd hoped you'd know that for yourself one day. But doesn't look like that's in the cards."

Jaina reached out and took his arm. He didn't resist. "Dad, please. I'm not doing this to get away from you and mom. I need you to understand."

He patted her hand. "I understand what you were thinking, but..." Paul cleared his throat. It was hoarse, from the yelling or the crying, Jaina wasn't sure. "Do you remember when your brothers were sick?"

"What?"

"When the well got tainted. Do you remember?"

"Uh, I think so? They were in bed for weeks, right?"

He nodded. "They were. The entire hall stunk. Your mom was so exhausted from taking care of them she fell asleep at a table in the dining hall."

"I don't remember that," Jaina said, still staring out at the cloud of dust slowly settling in the distance.

"You were five, maybe six?" Paul said. "You came downstairs, found your mother asleep. Put a blanket on her. Threatened the handful of people eating breakfast not to wake her up." He chuckled. "You were quite fearsome."

Jaina shook her head. "I remember them being sick. But not much else."

"You were so desperate to do something, to help. It was early, but you realized your mom hadn't lit the ovens out back. So little Jaina decided to go do it herself."

Her eyes widened. "Oh. I do remember that. I didn't realize it was the same time."

Paul nodded. "We lost three ovens. Had to repaint the entire north side of the building. It was the gods' own luck that you weren't hurt."

"I was six."

"But you're still doing the same thing, Jaina." Paul finally turned to face her. "Trying to fix everything yourself. So determined to save everyone that you don't think."

She shook her head. "I'm not a child anymore. And I know what I'm doing."

"You're nineteen."

"Exactly."

He exhaled slowly, holding up his hands. "Look, I'm done trying to get you to see reason. I don't want to fight, Jaina. Not now. Not with everything. But I'm afraid. I'm afraid that there's going to come a day when you realize how much you paid to save your brothers three, four years in uniform. And when that happens, I don't know who you'll be more angry at: yourself or them."

"Dad." Jaina took a deep breath. "I'm doing this for us. For our family."

"I know, Jaina." Paul smiled sadly. "I just hope this is really what you want. Because if it's not, the road ahead of you is so much harder than I ever wanted for you."

2,688 Hours

The charcoal danced over the paper, spilling leaves and branches onto the white page. Antoinette's fingers were nearly stained completely black, the only part of her outfit that was not immaculate. She sat on a stone bench, eyes darting between the sketch in her lap and the split tree that sat in the middle of the garden. The storm that had rumbled through last night still left the scent of rain and ozone lingering in the air, competing with the charred smell of the wood shattered by the lightning strike that crashed down. It was unique. Antoinette collected unique.

"Something for a current project?"

Antoinette didn't react. Her grandmother didn't approve of her being startled. Toni DeLuca didn't approve of anything that showed vulnerability. Instead, she said, "Something for a possible future project, perhaps." Antoinette finished the stroke she'd just begun, and set the paper down, rising to face her grandmother. "We don't see many lightning strikes in the city. Seemed a shame to waste the opportunity." She gestured at a bowl of water on a nearby table. "May I?"

Toni nodded, and as Antoinette washed her hands, drying them with a strip of white linen, she picked up the sketch, considering it with a practiced eye. "Your shading has improved. Good." She nodded at a nearby house guard, who walked briskly over from his post at the entrance to the garden. "Go see this placed under glass. I need to speak with my granddaughter, and I won't see her work damaged should the rain come back."

"Madame DeLuca," he replied, bowing. Taking the sketch, he disappeared into the huge house.

"I could have done that myself," Antoinette said, tossing the stained cloths back into the water.

"I should hope so." The table had a pair of chairs, carved to look like vines had grown into the shape of the seats. It had been one of Antoinette's projects last year. Toni sat in one, and gestured towards the other. "Independence is a fine thing. Wasting time is not."

"Yes, grandmother." Antoinette didn't allow the flash of annoyance to reach her face.

From inside her shawl, Toni withdrew a rolled piece of paper. She handed it to her granddaughter. "Your thoughts, please."

It took Antoinette a few moments to read the message, her frown deepening with each paragraph. "Have we verified this?"

Toni nodded. "From three of our people in Westcott, and two in Lofland Fork."

"If these numbers are correct, that's two separate dukes raising thousands of soldiers for conscription," Antoinette said. "Are the other dukes doing the same?"

"Walshire, Breguet, and Elloway have been confirmed. We haven't gotten word from the other provinces yet, but I can't imagine we'll hear different." Toni raised an eyebrow. "Thoughts?"

Antoinette rolled the paper up, and handed it back to her grandmother, who dropped it into the bowl of water. It immediately began to dissolve. "We've seen buildups before, usually before one of the dukes starts an incursion with another. But that doesn't seem to be likely here."

"Why?"

Antoinette could feel her grandmother watching her. *Always a test*. "It's always been reactive in the past. One duke begins building up his army, the neighboring dukes find out, they do the same to deter an attack. But this suggests both Duke Gaille and Duke Westcott began their conscription efforts within days of each other. Do we know when the others began?"

Toni nodded. "Conscription notices in all five provinces went out within a week of each other."

"That's coordinated," Antoinette said. "It's also expensive. Which explains the loans." She glanced over at her grandmother. "When did they arrange for the loans?"

"Negotiations with the families began four months ago."

"So they've been planning this for a bit. That's another point of confirmation. If we can find out which dukes took out loans of that size, we can know how many are rearming."

"Not all the dukes need that level of funding. After five years, the Vorchese Ranch is at full operation again, so Snowsill has all the money he needs. And the mines out west are producing well. But yes, most would need the Bank's assistance," Toni said. She withdrew another piece of paper, and handed it over. "Every province. All thirteen appear to be mobilizing large groups of conscripts."

Antoinette looked over the paper. "This is millions in loans. That almost doubles their debt to the Bank."

"It does." Toni tilted her head, and held up three fingers. "Three questions."

Antoinette did her best not to let her irritation show. This was one of her grandmother's favorite exercises with her. "Yes, grandmother."

"What does such a mobilization indicate?"

"Either they're afraid they're about to be attacked, or they're planning to attack someone else."

One finger dropped. "Of the two, which do you believe more likely?"

Antoinette considered. If she was wrong on any one question, it meant hours studying and pages written to illustrate that she wouldn't make such a mistake again. More than one, and she wouldn't be permitted to sleep until her grandmother was satisfied.

"I think it more likely that they believe they're about to be attacked."

A pause, and a second finger dropped. Antoinette exhaled in relief. "Why?"

"There are only three possible targets," Antoinette said. "They have no reason to attack us. We may not have as many trade deals with them as we used to, but there's still a lot of money that flows north. Even if they considered it, they could never get through the Myre."

"Be careful to assume that someone won't do something simply because it's foolish," Toni said. "History is littered with the graves of those who chose the stupidest possible path." Even so, she lowered the third finger.

Antoinette nodded, exhaling slowly. "I understand, but I still think it unlikely. The second possibility is that they plan to retake Cicerone. But the dukes are terrified of the Confessors. They've taken every possible step not to anger them. I have trouble seeing them get from there to massing for an invasion."

Toni gestured for her to continue, and Antoinette said, "Invading the Empire has the same challenges as invading us. That bridge is the only way across the Breaking, and they've established hundreds of lucrative trade deals with the Empresses. Their relations with the Empire have been nothing but good since the bridge was finished." She shook her head. "I don't see them attacking anyone."

"So you think they're fearful of an attack?" Antoinette nodded, and Toni asked, "From whom?"

"Not us. We don't have the soldiers, and Vetticci has never had a taste for conquest. We hit the Myre, and stopped expanding."

"The Myre Wood works both ways," Toni said. "Doesn't matter from which direction you approach, it's impassable. What about the Confessors?"

"That's hard to say. Nothing comes out of Cicerone but missionaries and the occasional shepherd. They don't trade with anyone, they don't send envoys or diplomats, nothing. I can't imagine them attacking the Dominion, though. It's... what? Five, six times their size?" Antoinette shook her head. "I think they're worried about the Empire."

"Why?" Her grandmother's face was, as usual, unreadable.

"A few reasons," Antoinette said, knowing every word she said was being judged. "The Imperial family spent two hundred years conquering every square inch of soil above the Breaking. They've only been at peace for a few decades. Plus, with everything we know, the original intent for building the bridge was to open up the Dominion to invasion."

"You're leaving a fairly large element out of that argument."

"The coup. I know." Antoinette shook her head. As long as she could remember, this had been her relationship with her grandmother. Quiet interrogations, tests to see how much of the lessons that defined her childhood had taken root. No matter how much she studied, how much she learned, there were always gaps in her knowledge, gaps her grandmother never failed to discover and dig into. *One day, you won't find any. One day, you'll see I'm ready.* "The new government has spent every day since the bridge was finished saying exactly the right things to the Dominion, everything needed to convince them that they aren't bringing the Imperial cavalry south. But two hundred years of conquest... I'd be shocked if it hasn't been considered. If I'm the Dominion, I might be thinking about at least being able to demonstrate a unified front."

Toni nodded. "It's not the worst reasoning. But if they are raising a national army, the costs are exorbitant. Even with the loans they took out, they could only afford to maintain such a force for twelve months at the most."

Antoinette frowned. "Maybe they think just demonstrating they have the ability to raise an army of that size will be a deterrent."

"But if that's the case, why are they not building forts or other fortifications south of the bridge?" Toni asked. "Construction like that would be impossible to keep quiet."

"Too provocative?"

"It's impossible to say. There are too many unknowns, and unfortunately for us, the only people who know for sure what the Dominion is doing are the Dukes."

The gate to the garden creaked as one of their stewards carried a silver tray out to them. The pair fell silent as he set the tray down on their table, chunks of ice clinking merrily in the chilled tea, bright blue blooms bobbing on the surface. He poured them each a glass, and disappeared as quickly as he'd appeared. Only when the gate closed did Antoinette speak.

"We may have to wait and see," she said. She took a tip of the fruity and spicy tea. "Unless we have sources close to one of the dukes."

"I have ears in some of the smaller houses," Toni said. "But we need a sense of what Snowsill, Walshire, or Westcott are thinking. Their duchies are the largest. Those three have to be driving any decisions, particularly if the other dukes are going along."

"So how do we find out?"

Toni DeLuca took a sip, eyes fixed on her granddaughter over the rim. Only when she set the glass down did she respond. "That, my dear, is going to be your job."

***

It was late when the knock came on Antoinette's chamber door. She glanced over at the water clock built into the wall over her fireplace. She pulled a shawl over her shoulders, and called out, "Come in?"

Antoinette and her younger brother Mattia could not look more different. Her hair was the inky black of a midnight sky, her features and build slender and delicate. The shock of bright red hair atop his head and the dusting of freckles clashed horribly with the black tunic and breeches he wore. He was also slender, but his tight sleeves showed the lean muscle the young soldier had developed in the years of training he'd begun before his twelfth birthday.

"Tell me it's not true," he said without any greeting.

"You'll need to be a bit more clear than that, little brother." She raised an eyebrow. "Is that always how you enter a woman's room?"

He glanced around, and only then seemed to notice his sister was in her nightgown. "Sorry. I didn't mean..."

"It's not the first time I've gone on assignment, Mattia." Antoinette pulled the shawl tight around her, and gestured at a plush chair. "Sit down."

"I'm fine." Mattia began pacing. He always did that. It was as if he had too much energy bubbling up inside him. "This is different."

"It's a commission. I've done seven in the last four years." She sat down on the edge of her bed. "I've been gone far more than I've been home."

"And every one has been in Vetticci. And you've had guards. And there have still been problems." He shook his head. "I knew you might take commissions outside the city, but I assumed you'd be bringing a staff."

I did too, little brother. Antoinette had been somewhat surprised when she was told she'd be going alone. She hadn't been completely successful in masking her apprehension from her grandmother, but Mattia had never been as observant. It was important that he not see the doubts. "If the point is for Duke Westcott to let down his guard around me, that might prove a bit difficult if I'm surrounded by house guards." Antoinette paused as she noticed the linen bandages on his wrist. "What happened?"

Mattia glanced down at the wound, and made a face. "I don't want to talk about it."

"I thought you were still training with dulled blades."

"Not for six months. But this isn't from the master-at-arms."

She reached out to take his hand. The bandage was clumsy, stained red. "You didn't see the anatomist?"

He yanked his hand back. "Wasn't an anatomist available. It wasn't during training. At least not my training."

It took a moment, but when she realized the truth, she couldn't help the grin that spread over her face.

"It's not funny."

"It's a little funny."

"She's a gods-damned menace."

"You're the one who volunteered to train her until she was of age."

"That was before I knew how crazy she is. Little piranha hides knives like most kids her age hide candy." He shook his head back. "Stop changing the subject. This is not a good time to be traveling the Dominion alone."

"Please, brother, tell me something I don't know about the Dominion. Or any other topic for that matter." She raised an eyebrow. The DeLuca family was one of the oldest in the city. It was also one of the last to follow the old ways, the matriarchal structure that defined the first few centuries of the city. As the only female heir, Antoinette held a position of power exceeded only by her grandmother, and while she didn't relish reminding her younger brother of that fact, his impulsiveness made it necessary at times.

"I didn't mean..." He scowled. "You're my sister. I'm supposed to watch over you."

"I've managed quite well. And your job isn't to question grandmother. Or me, for that matter." Antoinette kept her voice even, not wanting to come down too hard on him. "The agreement's been signed. I'll be staying in the ducal palace. With dozens of guards between me and any fool who thinks harming a DeLuca is a good idea."

"Dominion soldiers," Mattia muttered, his tone the same as if he'd scraped something off his shoe. "A joke." He took a deep breath. "I live to serve the family. If this is what she wants, this is what happens."

"As it always is," Antoinette said. "The contract has been signed. I leave in the morning."

"What if I come with you?"

"You?"

"I'll try not to be offended by your incredulity," he said. "I'm your brother. I could come along and assist you. Hold your brushes or whatever."

"It's an engraving job."

"Then hold your chisel. I don't know. But I promise I can keep you safer than those amateurs wearing the Westcott sigil."

"Yes, nothing fosters a relationship between a man and woman better than her brother glowering at him over her shoulder," Antoinette said.

He shook his head. "She can't expect you to..."

"She expects me to do my duty, whatever that may be," Antoinette said. "But I don't think it's worth worrying about. The Duke is married. They're quite traditional about that sort of thing."

"So what's the problem?"

Antoinette reached out and squeezed his hand. "I appreciate the concern. I do. But I have my job. And you have yours."

Mattia's jaw worked. "I just don't want to have to do my job because something happens to you."

"If you do, I have no doubt you'll leave our mark," she said. "But I suspect I'll be fine. Grandmother had one demand regarding my protection. I'll have a personal escort."

"A personal escort? What difference does that make?" Mattia's eyes widened. "Oh. You mean..."

"Yes." She stood up. "I have to get ready. I do appreciate the concern, brother. But I think a ranger should be able to keep me quite safe."

2,653 Hours

Even after she had signed all the places she was meant to sign, even after she had said goodbye to her parents, trying to ignore the mixture of grief and disappointment on her father's face, even after she'd gotten a few tips on riding from Shakkar and they'd begun their journey south, Jaina still felt as if nothing had changed. The older ranger had said little on their trip, only telling her they were meeting someone for her to take the oath. It was very different from the controlled chaos that had whisked her brother and every other young man in Lofland Fork away, and finally she had to ask.

"Ah... Master Ranger?"

Shakkar glanced over at her, a bemused expression on his face. "We don't do that."

"Excuse me?"

"The 'master' thing. Rangers don't really do that," he said. "You can call me Shakkar. Or Edmund. But no one really calls me Edmund."

Jaina frowned. "You don't have a rank?"

He shook his head. "Nope. Ranger suffices quite well for all of us. Not all that many of us, anyway."

"Then how do you know who's in charge?"

"Why would we need one of us to be in charge?" he asked. "We're rangers. We do what's needed. We'll help guide you through the first year or so, but once you finish your novice period, you'll be equal to any of us."

A clicking sound echoed out of the treeline they rode along. It wasn't the first time that Jaina had heard a strange sound issuing from the Myre Wood. The pair had ridden south from the city until reaching the point where the Duke's Road joined the Myre Road, the long stretch of paved road that was the only path through the Myre to Vetticci. But instead of riding in, they'd turned east, and rode along the edge of the woods.

She did her best not to stare for too long into the dark, twisted forest. Stories about the Myre Wood were a mainstay of quite a few of the stories her brothers had told her when she was far too young. The smell coming off of it was musty, thick with decay. The tree trunks were wrapped in vines and damp patches of moss. Even if she'd decided to ignore the warnings of all of her brother's tales and attempt to venture in, she had yet to see a spot where the growth thinned out enough to allow a horse. But the strange clicking and other eerie sounds were more than enough to convince her to stay well outside.

Once the clicking faded, Jaina turned back to Shakkar. "Okay, uh, Shakkar. I have a few questions."

"Seems like the proper time to ask those would have been before signing the pledge to join." In contrast to his words, his tone was casual, not critical.

Is this a test? Jaina considered her next words as carefully as she could, but in the battle between curiosity and caution, caution was hopelessly outmatched. "You didn't ask me much. When I offered to join, I mean."

He shrugged. "We needed a new ranger. One of our number retired. I've known you and your family for a while. Seemed a good fit. Plus, you were motivated." Shakkar waved a dragonfly that buzzed around his head away. "Did my duty, made you take a breath or three before saying yes. In any case, you aren't really committed. Not yet. Until you commit to the ritual, you can go back home."

Jaina shook her head. "No, I want to do this."

Shakkar just grunted.

"So no ranks. No commanders. How do you know what you need to do? What your assignment is?" she asked.

"We get requests from local communities. Sometimes from the dukes. If they're within our purview, we help," he said. "If they're not, we don't."

"Who decides if they are?"

"We do," Shakkar said. "Each ranger chooses whether to take on a request. Otherwise, you patrol your area. Walk the land. Make sure the people are safe."

"Do we have a book of rules? Something governing our conduct that I need to know?"

He frowned. "Do you have difficulty telling right from wrong?"

"No, but I..."

"Then why do you need a book to tell you what to do?"

Jaina tried not to let her frustration show. *This has to be a test.* "Okay. When does my training start?"

"Yeah, we don't really do that."

"We don't..." She stared at him. "You're not going to train me?"

"I'm just bringing you to the monks."

"Are they going to train me?"

"No, they're going to conduct the ritual."

"And after that?"

"You'll get your novice assignment, and you'll go do it."

Jaina stared at him. "My brothers just left for the army. They're going to have three, four months training under a master-at-arms before they go to their unit."

Shakkar made a face. "That sounds miserable. Not to mention boring."

"But if I'm not getting any training, how..." She trailed off, taking a deep breath. "I don't know anything about being a ranger."

Shakkar nodded gamely. "We know. That's why there's a novice period. For you to figure that out."

"So someone's going to teach me during the novice period?"

"Usually. Might be different now." He shrugged. "Not my decision. I'm sure it'll all be sorted."

Jaina rubbed her forehead, trying to reconcile this utter vacuum of useful information with all she knew about the rangers. She'd grown up hearing the same tales, playing the same games pretending to be rangers fighting off bandits or protecting people from wolves. *Amazing how little any of that seems to matter once the particulars become important to you.* She pulled her mount to a stop, which took a moment. She still wasn't all that steady as a rider.

"Shakkar." The older man turned his horse around to face her. Jaina took a deep breath, and said, "I just signed my life to you and yours. I'm going to be a ranger for the rest of my life. I know, everyone knows, there's no walking away from this, not until I'm too old to do it anymore. But I thought... I thought it would be like joining the militia, or becoming a sheriff. That I'd be taught what I needed to know, that I'd have people to give me commands and..." She waved her hand. "Stuff."

"Stuff?"

She scowled. "You know what I mean."

"You know, I'm not quite sure I do."

"I don't need you to tell me everything. I just want to know what it is I signed up for."

He shrugged. "You're going to be a ranger. We walk the land, and we protect the people." Before she could respond, he held up his hand, and she fell silent. "I know you want more answers. Pretty sure I did too." He paused for a moment, and asked, "You know what the withering pox is?"

Jaina nodded. "It's a sickness that some children get. Came from tainted water. No one really gets it anymore."

"No one gets it in Lofland Fork, or Westcott, or any of the big towns," Shakkar said. "But in some of the outlying settlements, it pops up every now and then. I was six when I caught it."

Jaina frowned. "I thought it was usually fatal."

"Usually is. Guess I was lucky. It only crippled me." Shakkar shrugged. "One of my legs was pretty much dead. Couldn't take my weight. I was ten. Had to wait eight years, but me, my parents, everyone knew what I needed to do. Joined as soon as I could."

"Wait." Jaina shook her head. "How did the rangers fix your leg?"

Shakkar shrugged. "Don't know. I took the oath, did the ritual, and a few days later, my leg started hurting. Hadn't felt anything in it for years. By the end of the week, I was walking. End of the following week, I was running. Don't know how, don't much care. Rangers gave me back my leg. All I have to do is protect people and walk this land. Seems a good trade."

He nodded at her. "Look, I get why you joined. You want your brother home."

She was still trying to wrap her head around the story about his leg, but she glanced up at that. "Brothers."

"What?" Shakkar raised an eyebrow.

"They took them both," Jaina said.

"Oh." Shakkar shook his head. "Shit thing to do. So you want your brothers brought home. That's fair. Only thing the rangers ask in exchange is to walk this land and protect the people. Think that's a good trade?" Jaina nodded, and he continued. "Okay then. I don't have a lot of answers for you. But I promise, you'll figure it out. We all did."

He pulled his horse around, and resumed riding. She clicked her tongue, and her mount fell in beside him. She mulled over what he'd said, and finally asked, "Can you tell me about the ritual?"

Shakkar chuckled. "You just don't stop, do you?"

She thought about arguing, but honesty seemed the better route. "Not really, no."

"Fine. But no, I can't tell you about the ritual. Not because I'm not allowed to, not because I don't want to. But I don't remember it. None of us do," he said. "And before you ask, no, I don't know why."

That did little to settle the pit of unease that had begun to form in her gut. *Gods, please don't let dad be right.* Jaina opened her mouth to ask another question, but Shakkar interrupted her. "Look, I'm not the one to talk to about this. The monk will tell you what you need to know."

Jaina sighed. "Notice you didn't say what I want to know."

"Yeah, well," he said, shrugging. "I think it's important to couch expectations."

***

"Let me guess," Brother Fillias said as they watched Shakkar ride back the way they'd come. They'd met the monk standing a few hundred feet out of the Myre Wood, a few hours after they'd left the main road.

Shakkar had taken her horse, leaving her on foot. "He wasn't the most talkative companion."

Jaina shook her head. "Not really."

Fillias chuckled. He was plump, a full ten inches shorter than Jaina, and had the kind of face that looked as if he'd need to sprain several muscles to stop smiling. "Sounds like Edmund. Even when he came for his ritual, he didn't have much to say. Just asked if we had food."

"So it's okay that I have questions?" After her experience with the ranger, Jaina was still a bit hesitant to ask.

"Gods, of course it is. Thought it was a bit strange that he didn't, to be fair." Fillias beckoned. "We can talk as we walk. And in case you and he do have more in common than might be apparent at first glance, yes, we do have a meal waiting for you."

She started to fall in beside him, but quickly came to a halt when she realized the direction they were headed.

"Problem, my dear?"

"We're not going in, are we?" She gestured at the treeline of the Myre Wood.

"Not too far, but yes, we are." He grinned at her. "It's all right. We've done this more times than you can imagine. It's safe."

"Everything I've heard about the Myre says otherwise."

"We have done a fine job of making sure no one wanders in, haven't we?" Fillias said, looking very pleased with himself. "It's true, entering the Myre Wood is a lovely way for most people to relieve themselves of that pesky breathing habit. But there are places that the Sylvan Order can safely go." He nodded at the tangled woods. "This is our home. Where the Sylvan Order of the Rangers was born."

Jaina swallowed. *Dad would be screaming at me right now.* She stared at the treeline, every story she'd ever heard telling her what a bad idea this was, but she took a deep breath. "All right."

"See? You're doing wonderfully. First test passed!"

"That was a test?"

Fillias shook his head. "A bad joke. There aren't any tests. Just the ritual." The pair stepped into the woods, and began walking along a narrow pathway that wove between drooping cypress trees coated in moss. Jaina hadn't been able to see it from outside the woods. She realized that was the point.

Her feet sank into the damp soil as they walked, her nose full of the rich smell of rain and decay. Buzzing insects howled their song from every direction at a low hum, and she fell in behind Fillias, the path too narrow for them to walk side by side.

"Shakkar said that I wouldn't be able to remember the ritual."

"True, true," Fillias said. "A necessary step, I'm afraid. The ritual is our most closely guarded secret. Only way a secret stays a secret is if no one knows the secret."

Jaina frowned. "But you know what it is. The monks, I mean."

"When we need to, yes." Fillias stepped over a puddle with bright red insects skating along the surface. "Right now? Not a clue."

"That..." The monk was doing little to keep her stomach from twisting. A wailing sound drifted from somewhere deep into the woods, but was cut short with a wet crunch. "What the gods was that?"

"I'm guessing an animal."

"What kind?"

"A slow one, from the sound of it."

Gods. She tried to focus on the path in front of her. "Okay, you don't remember the ritual except for when you need to? How does that work?"

"Shakkar really wasn't being intentionally obtuse," Fillias said. "There's much about the rangers that we don't talk about, not because we don't want to, but because we really can't. But I can tell you this much. The ritual does two things. First, it judges you. Determines if you're of the right temperament to join the rangers."

Jaina came to a stop, and he turned to face her. "You mean I might not be accepted?"

He nods. "Unfortunately, it happens. Should you wake from the ritual without having changed, we'll give you dinner, some coin for your trouble, and arrange transportation back to your home. You'll return to your life, and that will be that." At her stricken expression, Fillias said, "Try not to worry too much. That used to happen quite often, but our rangers are more careful about who they bring as candidates. Shakkar has known you and your family for some time. He wouldn't have agreed to bring you if he thought you wouldn't be accepted."

If I have to go home, and all this was for nothing... Jaina pushed the thought away. *Dad will be happy. At first. But every day that goes by with Jak and Joran gone, every day without knowing if they're dead or alive...* "Is there anything I can do to make it more likely that I'll be chosen?"

Fillias shook his head. "There isn't. But as I said, it's not as common as it used to be. Plus, as there's nothing to do, that's a worry you can leave right here." He pointed at a mossy patch. "There. That's a good spot."

"For what?"

"To leave your worries!" The monk offered a toothy grin, and Jaina stared at him for a moment. When she didn't laugh, he shrugged, and kept squishing through the wet moss that carpeted the trail they were following. "Sorry. I don't get out all that much. Usually just when we have a new novice."

Most important day of my life and he's making jokes. Bad ones, too.
Jaina gave her head a quick shake, and said, "Um, do you know where I'll be assigned?"

"Not really," Fillias said. "We leave that mostly up to the rangers. I know Iro patrolled up north, along the Breaking."

"Who's Iro?"

"Ranger that just retired. Nice man. Likes lime candy." A large beetle landed on Fillias' bald head. The monk took no action to shoo it away. "Maybe you'll take his route. Maybe someone else will, and you'll go somewhere else. It's all very exciting."

"I was hoping I could stay close to Lofland Fork."

"Why?"

"I grew up there. I have family there. It would be nice to go see them."

"Okay!" Fillias nodded, and the beetle lost purchase on the smooth scalp, tumbling to the forest floor.

Jaina straightened up, her eyebrow lifting. "So I can stay in Lofland Fork?"

"I have no idea. We leave that mostly up to the rangers." He shrugged. "But if you want to go visit them, go visit them. I'm sure it would be fine."

"Okay, can we stop for a moment? Please?" Jaina knew her hours-long battle to keep her frustration from her voice was coming to an unsuccessful end. She reached out to lean against a tree, and pulled her hand back at the feeling of leathery bark pulsing warmly beneath her hand. "What kind of tree is this?"

Fillias came to a stop, and turned to face her. He glanced at the tree. "A brown one, I believe."

"That's... okay." She took a deep breath. "Brother Fillias, I mean no disrespect. But I gave up a lot to come here. I thought serving with the rangers is for life, but you just talked about a ranger retiring. I don't know how being a ranger works. I don't know who I report to, where I'm going to be serving. I don't know how much I get paid, how I get paid. And both you and Shakar are very kind, but you're not really all that helpful in me getting those answers so I know what I'm about to pledge my life to. I just want to know the plan."

She fell silent, and felt the flush to her face as she realized how loud she'd gotten. To his credit, Fillias made no attempt to stop her or interrupt, he simply listened until she was done. He tilted his head. "You make a lot of impulsive decisions, don't you?"

Jaina didn't really have a good answer to that. "I know why I'm here."

"And none of it has to do with actually being a ranger," he said. "If it did, you would have asked how being a ranger works. Who you report to, where you were going to be serving, how much you get paid. But you didn't ask any of that. You pledged your life to something you know nothing about, and gave it... what? Two, three weeks thought?"

She swallowed. "Three days."

He nodded. "That's not very much time."

"I know." *I'm blowing this.* "I'm not..."

He held up his hand, and she fell silent. "Jaina, I'm not really judging. I don't know how to do that, honestly. Pretty sure I used to, but that was a long time ago. Look, I've done this..." Fillias frowned for a moment. "A lot. I have trouble remembering how many. But a lot. And I promise you, people come here for all sorts of reasons. They got sick. They don't have anywhere else to go. They want power, they want revenge, they just want to be stronger than everyone else. And they go into the ritual, and many of them wake up no different and are sent home."

"You think that's going to happen to me, don't you?" It wasn't really a question.

"You?" He shook his head. "No. You came here impulsively, that's certain. But you came here for someone other than you. You came here out of a desire to make someone's life better. That's the right kind of reason. That's what the ritual is, you know. It's to look to see what kind of person you are, what you'll do if you get the blessing. Whether you'll make the right choice, not for you, but for someone else. That's what being a ranger is. Making the choice, every time, to stand with those in need. We choose those who will make that choice.

"But you don't know what kind of person I am," Jaina said, her voice quiet.

Fillias nodded. "We don't. But we will." He reached out and took her hand. "Rangers are just that desire given form, Jaina. A desire to do what you can for those who need it. A desire to make things better any way you can. We live in a broken world. This continent is split in two to remind us of that fact. And no one person can change that fact, but any one person can make a choice to stand when others would run. The first ranger that stepped out of these woods did so for someone other than her, and we've followed her lead." He gestured. "We don't want to be late."

They resumed their walk, and he kept talking. "We don't report to the dukes because we can't know that the dukes will do what's best for their people instead of themselves. We don't report to the Ducal Army or militia for the same reason. We aren't here to change the world, to wage war, to lead governments. But as broken as the world is, it gets a bit less so when people act to protect others. We find those who want to do that, people who act to make the world a bit better." He turned, walking backwards as he grinned at her. "Even if they don't think before they do so. We look in their heart, and if they are who we hope they are, we give them our blessing to walk this world and protect, to aid."

"Don't you need to watch where you're going?"

"Not really," Fillias said. "Our pay comes from a trust set up by King Ammon, who helped found the Sylvan Order two hundred years ago. It moved to the Bank of Vetticci, and is managed by a bursar there. We'll have it sent to you. It's not a lot, but you won't go hungry. We'll give you a mount, a weapon, and a task. And we'll have faith that you'll go forth and do it as best you can."

Jaina shook her head. "But how do you know that you can trust me?"

"Honestly, that's a bit of an absurd question. Either you're someone we can trust, in which case I don't have to ask, or you're not, in which case there's no point in asking," he said, nimbly stepping over a gnarled root. "But we will know you, Jaina. Before you get the blessing, we will know you. Now. Then. And in the future."

Something about his eyes made her realize he was telling the truth. *Where in the gods am I?*

To her relief, he spun back around. He'd shown no difficulty in navigating backwards, but the sight had been unsettling. Fillias kept speaking. "Rangers can retire. Once they've fulfilled their purpose, once they feel their watch is done, they can take a well earned rest. But the oath you will take? That's for life. You will bear no children. You will take no husband, no wife, no love of any kind. We hold no illusions that risking your life for someone else is an easy choice, but that choice becomes virtually impossible when you have a family, people who depend on you. Your family will be those you protect. You will dedicate yourself to the people of this nation, and you will lay down everything else in that purpose. And you will find joy in that purpose."

"How do you know?" she said, so quietly that she thought he might not hear her.

"We'll know." He said that as if it answered all her questions. "Tea?"

Fillias had come to a stop between two trees. As she drew up behind him, she saw the clearing. The small patch of relatively dry moss barely deserved the name, but the thick canopy that had blocked out most of the light had a gap, and dappled sunlight danced over the rich emerald ground. In the center, there was a small table, painted the color of a pumpkin. Sitting in the center was a single glass mug, filled with a dark amber liquid that steamed in the air.

Jaina came to a halt, and stared. Tangled woods surrounded them. The trail came to an end at this mossy clearing, and she could see no path out except the way they'd come. There was no one else there, nothing to indicate anyone had ever set foot in this place before a monk and a frightened and confused young woman. "I don't... What is this?"

"It's the last chance." Fillias sat down on a fallen tree, and gestured at the table. "That's your oath. If you drink, you're pledging your life to us. You're promising the strength of your back and your character to those who need you. You will close your eyes, and you will wake a Ranger of the Sylvan Order." He pointed to the path they'd taken in. "Or you and I can leave, and I can see you back home."

She couldn't take her eyes off the table. "Where did this come from?"

"The Myre."

"I..." Jaina swallowed. The air was humid and thick. "I still have questions."

"I know you do. But I'm afraid the only answers you'll find are at the bottom of that cup." The forest had fallen silent, the only sound the breeze rustling the leaves and his voice. The trees seemed to loom overhead, and it felt as if she was being watched from something deep within the verdant darkness. "Drinking it is an accord between you and an order that's so much older than you know. You will give us your life. You will give us your future. You will give us your vow to spend the rest of your days choosing to carry those who cannot walk, to lift up those who cannot stand, and to fight for those who cannot endure. And in return, we will give you our strength, our will, our eyes, our ears. You will be one of us."

She looked at him. He was not looking at her.

Jaina walked slowly towards the table. *This is crazy. I don't know this man. I don't know this place.*

She found herself standing before the table, looking down at the mug. She heard her brothers laugh, saw her mother's face as they disappeared down the western road.

For the rest of her life, Jaina wouldn't remember drinking the tea. She would only remember setting the empty mug back down, and the sounds of the forest growing more and more faint, the dappled sunlight fading into darkness, and hands catching her as the world spun and came to a quiet halt. She blinked once, then twice, and when she opened her eyes a third time, stars twinkled overhead.

Jaina was laying on a blanket arranged on soft grass. A fire crackled nearby, four skinned rabbits roasting over the flames. A big man crouched next to them, his back to her, sprinkling some kind of herbs over the meat. He spoke without looking.

"Welcome back, Ranger."

***

Jaina tried to scramble to her feet, but a rush of vertigo drove her back down to a seated position on the blanket.

"Best not to rush this," the man said. "Takes a few to get your bearings. You've been unconscious for almost five days." His voice had an odd throaty quality to it.

"Five days?" Jaina said, and winced. Her throat was raw.

"Water next to you."

Glancing down, she saw a canteen next to her, but she made no motion to reach for it. "Who are you?"

"Veres Martine." He put the cork back into the small glass bottle of herbs, and stuffed it into a pack. Rising to his feet, he turned to look down at her. "I'm the ranger patrolling the road between Westcott and Lofland Fork. I'm here to help you get your feet under you."

Jaina stared up at him, pushing herself a bit more upright. Something about him seemed familiar. "Have we met?"

"Not as such." He sat down on a log about six feet away.

"I thought Brother Fillias would be there when I was done."

Martine chuckled. "You've met Fillias when you have your wits about you. Think he'd be any more help when you're a bit off?"

"So he's always like that?"

"All the monks are. Comes from not really talking to anyone more than two, three times a year."

Jaina coughed, and Martine pointed to the canteen. She hesitated for a moment, but finally picked it up and took a long drink from it. She emptied half before she took a breath, wiping her mouth. "So you're my... what? Boss? Instructor?"

"More of a guide," Martine said, shrugging. "We don't really do the whole command thing in the rangers."

"So I've been told."

"Yeah, that threw me off when I did the ritual too," Martine said. "Kept waiting for someone to tell me what to do. No one did. They just had me follow this sixty year old ranger through the Sagebrush Moors. I kept waiting on her to tell me what to do. She spent most of her time telling me the proper way to prepare rabbit." He shrugged. "Did that for five years before I realized that was all the training I was going to get."

Jaina finished the canteen, and Martine picked up another, tossing it to her. She snagged it out of the air. "Thanks. So that's what's going to happen to me, too?"

"Nope." Martine shook his head. "Normally, you'd shadow me for at least a year. Probably longer. But circumstances are a bit different with all that's going on." He sniffed the air. "We can eat while we talk. You haven't done that in nearly a week. Pretty soon, your stomach is going to remind you."

She slowly stood up and stretched as he went to pull the crackling meat from the fire. Her joints popped in quick succession, and while the vertigo nudged at her for a moment, it passed fairly quickly. She turned to see if he needed help, the fire popped, and Jaina nearly screamed.

The pop thundered in her ears, louder than the boom of thunder. Her hands flew up to her ears, and she stumbled back. Far faster than she thought possible, Martine was next to her, his hand on her shoulder. "It's okay!" he said, locking eyes with her. "You're okay!"

"What the fuck was that?!" she shouted, staring wide-eyed at the fire. As she stared at it, every crackle, every shift of a burning log, came into sharp relief, louder than it possibly should have been. A chirp the volume of a baby's scream echoed from the night, and she spun to find the source. When her eyes turned away from the fire, the darkness seemed to peel back more and more, as if hazy grey light was spilling out from where she stood, revealing every blade of grass, every stone, every shiver of the brush and whisper of the wind racing along the plains upon which they stood. She could see everything as if it was bright daylight, but when she turned her eyes to the sky, an impossible number of stars gleamed against inky black.

"Jaina." Martine's voice brought her back, and she found his grey eyes locked on hers. "Deep breath. It takes a bit to get used to it. Like waking up to bright sunlight. Burns your eyes at first, but you'll get used to it."

"Get used to..." The fire popped again, and Jaina winced. "It's so loud. Everything is so..." She shook her head sharply. "What's happening?"

"You're a ranger," he said. "Jaina, there's a reason I chose this spot. It's quiet. I'm speaking as low as I can. Your hearing, your sight, even your sense of smell, they're stronger. They're going to keep getting stronger over the next few weeks. You'll adjust, learn to filter it out. I promise."

She stared at him for a moment. There was a steady thumping sound. She realized she could hear her heart pounding. She also realized she could hear his. "Okay..." Jaina took a deep breath, and lowered her hands, wincing at the cacophony that rolled in from the grass. "What do I do?"

"Just breathe." He squeezed her shoulder. "Sit down. We'll eat, talk, give you a chance to get your feet under you."

Jaina nodded, and walked over to a log next to the one Martine had been sitting on, wincing at the crack of grass beneath her boots. She sat down. A few moments later, he was offering her a pair of roasted rabbits on sticks. "I don't know if I can eat that much."

He grinned. "All four are for you. Along with the other new features, being a ranger comes with an outsized appetite. Trust me, once you start eating, you won't want to stop."

Chewing proved to be a bit of a ghoulish experience, as Jaina quickly came to miss the benefit of not being able to hear every bit of chewing and swallowing. As he spoke, she did her best to focus on his voice.

"Oh. By your pack."

She looked behind her, finding the worn canvas pack her father had given her long ago. Laying on the ground next to it was the strangest staff she'd ever seen. It was as long as she was tall, carved from inky black wood, and about as big around as her wrist. She reached back to pick it up, and her eyes widened at its heft.

"Blackthorn," he said. "We issue them to every ranger. Staff, or staves, or a cudgel. Just depends on what the monks can harvest."

"It's too heavy," she said, setting it back down. "I can't carry that thing around. I'd be exhausted in a half hour."

"Give it a day or so," Martine said. "You might be surprised."

Doubtfully, she set it down, and returned to her food.

"All right." He settled back down onto the log. "A few things. Your abilities are going to take a few weeks to really settle in. You're going to feel sore for a few months, like you've been lifting a lot of heavy things. You were a smith, correct?"

Her mouth was full, so she just nodded.

"Good. You'll know the feeling. It's at its worst in the morning, but you should feel better after a few hours," he said. "You need to work with your strength. Lift things, heavier and heavier. You've spent your entire life being this strong." He held his hand out flat to the ground at the level of his belly button. "You know how to interact with the world being this strong. You don't know how to interact with the world being here." His hand rose past the top of his salt-and-pepper hair. "You walk through your front door right now, you're liable to tear the door off the hinges. You need to get used to it. It's going to take some time."

The rabbit was still steaming hot. Jaina couldn't stop eating it. Between bites, she said, "You can help me with that, can't you?"

Martine shook his head. "You'll have to navigate that yourself. It's why we usually send new rangers to a fairly isolated region to shadow a senior ranger for the first five or ten years. Gives them a chance to adapt. Not an option for you."

"Why not?" Jaina said, her mouth full. She swallowed. "Sorry." Focusing on his voice seemed to help tune out the rest of the sounds.

"Once in a while, we get a request to help support a community when their sheriff or militia captain is unavailable. Maybe sick, maybe dead, maybe retired and they haven't found the time to appoint someone new," he said. "Makes them feel better knowing we're about. Normally, we're handling two, maybe three requests like that." He picked up a twig and began fiddling with it. "We've got eighty-six at the moment."

"Why so many?"

"Why do you think?" Martine said. "Damn dukes are calling up everyone who can find their way around a longbow. And if you're young and healthy enough to serve in the militia, you're damned sure young and healthy enough to march in the ducal army. So we've got whole villages without a stitch of protection. Add into that the risk of deserters, people are asking for help. We can't really say no."

Even among the cacophony that she was trying to adjust to, that registered. *It's not just Lofland Fork. It's everywhere.* The thought did not make her feel better. Jaina swallowed, set down the bones of the first rabbit and reached for the second, wiping grease from her mouth. "Deserters?"

Martine nodded. "Plenty of men don't feel too happy about being called up. They've got arrest notices out on them, and they're desperate. We've seen theft and assault ticking up quite a bit. Point is, we don't have enough numbers to cover every place shouting for a ranger while watching over you at the same time."

Jaina took a deep breath, trying to wrap her head around everything he was telling her. "So is that where I'm going? To help out a village?" *I know absolutely nothing about how to do that.* She tried to keep the thought from reaching her eyes. "If Lofland Fork needs coverage, I'm willing to..."

"I know where you're from," he said. There was no animosity in his tone, just a simple statement of fact. "And no, we're not sending you on patrol. A novice, on her own, around possible deserters is a recipe for the kind of mess I don't much enjoy cleaning up."

Jaina exhaled in relief. "I don't know that I would have felt good about that kind of assignment."

Martine nodded. "We have another job for you. Escort. Vetticcian noble coming up on some kind of art commission for Duke Westcott. The duke wasn't too fond of her bringing half their household guard into the palace for the four or five months the job's going to take. Vetticcian family wasn't too happy about her coming up unguarded. Compromise was suggested. Ranger makes a halfway decent bodyguard."

Jaina frowned. "You just said novices were normally shipped off to the middle of nowhere, shadowing a senior ranger. You want me to spend the next few months alone in Westcott? In the Ducal Palace? That doesn't make a lot of sense."

"Best of a bad situation. Should be an easy job," Martine said. "You'll be in the palace, surrounded by the duke's guard. You'll watch some artist do her..." He waved his hand in the air aimlessly. "Art. When she's done, you'll escort her back down to the border, hand her over to her family's household guard, and you're done."

Jaina chewed slowly as she considered what he'd said. "This seems as if it would be a better fit for a more senior ranger. Someone who knows what they're doing."

"We don't have a senior ranger available. We have one novice." He shrugged. "This should be an easy assignment. Secure location, no real travel necessary. Normally, we wouldn't contribute a ranger for something like this, but it happened to coincide with you joining us as a novice. The stars aligned."

"You say Vetticcian noble. Do you mean her family sits on the Table?" *Great. He was worried about you breaking a door. Now you might cause a diplomatic incident.*

Martine shook his head. "No, but that doesn't mean she doesn't have pull. Hear of the DeLuca family?"

"I don't think so." She paused. "Wait. Yes, I do. Don't they own several guild houses in Lofland Fork?"

"Be surprised if they didn't. They have a long reach. Small family, but old. Claim to be descended from the original founders of Vetticci." He snorted. "Of course, they all say that. But her grandmother, Madame Toni DeLuca? She's richer than any four dukes combined, and if half of what we hear is true, she's got ears in every house south of the Breaking. Her granddaughter is the artist. Next in line to take over the DeLuca family, so she's important. If something were to happen to her, Madame DeLuca would make her displeasure very clearly known."

Jaina stared out into the night, eyes locking onto every bit of movement. She saw a rabbit burst from a clump of grass, bounding over the ground. She saw the hawk stooping, plummeting down at a steep angle, only to pull sharply up as the rabbit vanished into its warren. "I know you said this should be an easy assignment, but if she's this important." She looked back to Martine. "I don't want to cause a problem. It's really important that I do well, that I finish my novice period."

He nodded slowly. "I know about your brothers." She looked up sharply, and he said, "Far as reasons to take the vows, I've heard worse. If I could, I'd send the exemption to the Duke now. But you have to finish the novice period. It's the only way."

Martine leaned forward. "I'll make you a deal. You watch over this Vetticcian, keep her happy, keep the duke happy, and see her back home when she's done doing whatever he's paying her far too much to do, and we'll call your novice period done. Turn a year into at most five months. I'll stop in as often as I can, check in on you, and when she's done with her work, I'll draw up the exemption. It'll be in the duke's hands within a day or two of her heading back home."

Jaina stared at him. *That fast... They'd barely be out of training. Can it really be that simple?* "I don't... Why would you do that?"

"Ranger's supposed to help those who need help. Nothing saying the people we help can't be one of our own," Martine said. "You're with us for the rest of your life. We show you we're an order worth serving, worth dedicating yourself to, I figure that shows you that this life you chose is worth living." He extended a hand. "We have a deal?"

She gripped his hand tight, and he raised an eyebrow. "Might want to make sure that's the last time you squeeze when you shake someone's hand. I can handle it. Most won't."

"Okay." Jaina nodded so fast she felt like her head was going to tumble loose. The vertigo was gone, and for the first time since Master Georges came to deliver the worst news, she began to hope. "I'll see it done."

2,491 Hours

T he DeLuca family carriage was a masterwork of craftsmanship. Everyone who saw it marveled at the mother-of-pearl inlay on the outside, the gleaming silver trim, the witchwood polished to nearly a mirror shine. Few knew that craftsmanship extended to the construction in ways they couldn't imagine, for which Antoinette was grateful.

The Myre Road was the only passage through the dense woods surrounding Vetticci, and the artery through which every bit of trade upon which the city lived. The Five Families who sat on the Vetticcian Table, governing the massive city-state, spent a fortune maintaining the road, replacing paving stones that had cracked and digging up roots that threatened to encroach upon the trade route. Their efforts were nearly enough to keep up with the wear caused by the constant hooves, boots, and wagon wheels each doing their best to grind the road back into the dust. Many merchants who made their living traveling north and south on the Myre Road joked that ten trips were enough to rattle the teeth out of one's skull. Most knew it wasn't really a joke.

The wagon was flanked by four DeLuca house guard, two on each side. Another four followed in a somewhat less well-designed wagon, and Antoinette could hear the wheels rattling from inside the family carriage. For her part, the surface of her tea barely moved as Andreas handed her yet another sheet of paper.

"More balance sheets?" Antoinette asked. *Please no.*

The attaché shook his head. "These are the latest reports from our people in the Ducal Army. They haven't been able to get too much, but we've got a sense of the numbers they've managed to conscript to this point."

Antoinette took a sip of the spiced tea, glancing down at the cup. "I doubt I'll be able to find this in Westcott. I should have thought of that."

"There are two casks in your luggage. And please, Mistress, this is important."

Without looking up at her family's long-time attaché, Antoinette said, "With the updated numbers out of the McElroy, Gould, and Snowsill duchies, the ducal forces have exceeded two hundred thousand conscripts. Desertion rates have been held low, less than one percent. "

Andreas blew air through his drooping grey mustache. "You might have told me you'd already seen this one."

"Andreas, with all respect, I've done nothing but review these reports for five days," Antoinette said. "I'm dreaming in crop projections and ledger balances, in desertion reports and warrants. I've read the dossiers we have on all the high-ranking deserters, the materiel supply lists... Gods, I read a breakdown of what kind of horses the army has access to. I have six more precious hours until I put on my face and don't take it off again for almost six months. May I please just have a bit of time to enjoy my tea?"

"Mistress, I had no idea," Andreas said. "Please, enjoy your beverage."

"Thank you."

"Would you like a scone?"

Antoinette set her cup down, glaring at him.

"Perhaps a massage, or a dip in a lavender bath?" Andreas patted the black coat he was never found without. "I'm all but certain I put it next to my very tiny harp upon which to play a mournful song accompanying your tale of woe."

"You're fired."

"Only your grandmother can do that."

Antoinette slid the window open. "Doug!"

"Mistress?" One of the guards on horseback brought his mount closer.

"I need you to messily execute Andreas."

"Of course, Mistress." Doug leaned down, peering inside. "Andreas, mind popping out so I can do a quick murder? Won't take but a moment."

"Pencil you in for tomorrow, guardsman."

"I'm getting new trousers tomorrow."

Antoinette slid the window back shut. "This is mutiny. I'll see you all hanged."

"Very good, Mistress," Andreas said. "While we all await the gallows, could you grant an old man's last request and please review your objectives for me?" Antoinette held up several fingers in a rude gesture. "We'll call that an ancillary objective."

She couldn't help but grin. "Why can't you come with me?"

"Because you don't need me," he said, not unkindly. "You've been ready for this for a very long time, Mistress. And this is not going to be the last time you leave home on a job. You knew that the first time you picked up a chisel."

No one lets me forget it. "I know." Antoinette took another sip. "Primary objective: identify the driving force behind the Dominion military buildup."

"Whether defensive or offensive," Andreas nodded. "Particularly if they are casting an eye on Vetticci."

"If that's the case, I do believe I'll come home as quickly as possible." Antoinette shifted in her seat for a moment, smoothing the velvet of her dress. "I know we think it unlikely that they're hostile towards Vetticci, but if that's the case, are we worried about the dukes seeing me as a possible hostage?"

Andreas shook his head. "That's very unlikely. The fact is, the bulk of the Dominion's wealth is still with the Bank. Detaining a DeLuca would immediately result in those funds being frozen. The entire country would be crippled overnight," he said. "And, not to put too fine a point on it, that would result in a visit from your younger brother and his colleagues."

"The Di Ombra are secret."

"A badly kept secret," Andreas said. "More than enough stories to make anyone think twice before laying a finger on Vetticcian nobility."

She nodded. "All right."

"Secondary objectives?"

"Gather and communicate any intelligence on ducal army organization, equipment, and deployment," Antoinette said. "That part will be difficult. Wherever the army is staging, it's not in Westcott."

"You're going to be working directly with the staff of the most powerful duke in the Dominion," Andreas said. "You may not find the actual army, but you should be able to collect enough tidbits on supply routes or the like to give us an idea."

"Send details the usual way?"

He nodded. "In addition, our contract with Duke Westcott includes a requirement for sketches to be taken and sent back to the College of Artisans on the progress of your work. He agreed. I suspect he likes the idea of a documented masterwork adorning his throne room."

Antoinette nodded. "Will the Duke be present for the work?"

"Doubtful," he said. "He's the most influential member of the Ducal Council, and whatever is going on, it's big. There's little chance he won't be directly involved. Most likely, you'll be dealing with the head of his house guard, Ethan Poole. He's worked for the Westcott family since he was young. Lost his left arm in a border skirmish between Westcott and Snowsill saving the Duke's life. He's had a place in the palace ever since then."

"Loyal?"

"Extremely. Very low potential as an asset. Poole will be the one watching the most closely, so be aware."

Antoinette finished her tea. "I'm now annoyed you were joking about the scones."

Andreas reached into a basket at his feet, and pulled out a small plate wrapped in a violet linen cloth.

"You're joking."

"I have never made a joke in my entire life. Anyone who suggests otherwise is a scoundrel and a charlatan, and should be hung on general principle."

The scones were cold, but still delicious, flavored with lemon and herbs, with flecks of cured whitefish throughout the crumbly dough. She took delicate bites, setting the scone back down and swallowing before speaking again. "The last time I checked, we didn't have much information on my babysitter."

"Ah. There, we do have some news." He pushed the papers he'd handed to her around, and plucked a page from the bottom. "See what happens when you ignore me?"

"A thousand apologies."

"The rangers are spread thin. They don't have the manpower to assign an experienced ranger to, as you so delicately put it, babysitting duty. So they're sending a novice," he said. "Jaina Creighton. 19 years old. No royal connections. Family owns a large inn in Lofland Fork, but their liquid holdings are fairly meager. She has two brothers, and her parents are both alive. Trained to be a smith until she recently decided to join the rangers."

"Why?" Antoinette said, her eyes darting over the page.

"We don't know. But she's young and inexperienced," Andreas said. "That's an opportunity."

"You think she could be an asset?"

"Doubtful, and I don't really think it would be wise to try. Too many ways that could go sideways on us. But those lacking experience often don't know the value of silence, and we know very little of the rangers as an organization."

"What do we know?"

It was Andreas' turn to look uncomfortable. "Well... nothing certain, in point of fact."

Antoinette looked up, surprised. "Nothing?"

He shook his head. "It's not for lack of trying. But as far as we can tell, they have no command structure. No supervising officer or lord. They don't report to the Ducal Council. They almost all operate on their own, taking assignments as they're requested. We think there are between 150 and 200 rangers, but if there's a roster kept somewhere, no one seems to know where it is."

Antoinette didn't know what to say. One of the few certainties in her world was the fact that her grandmother, and by extension the family attaché, had ears and eyes in every corner of the continent south of the Breaking. The Empire was the only significant blind spot for the family, a fact that was a constant source of irritation to her grandmother. "I can't remember the last time we've had that kind of gap in our knowledge," she said. "Must drive grandmother crazy."

"She's not fond of the fact, no," Andreas said dryly. "But the rangers seem to have an infuriatingly cavalier approach to their duties."

She shook her head. "But people talk about the rangers like they do the kaviaks of the Empire, or even..." Antoinette trailed off as Andreas' eyebrow climbed. "Well, you know."

"They do. The stories we hear about rangers seem half rumor and half mythology. We know they're strong. Whether that's from their training or something else, we don't know. We know there are stories about them not needing sleep or seeing in the dark. Depending on who you talk to, they're possessed by demons or the unnatural result of humans crossbreeding with bears."

Antoinette giggled. "Was the bear the mother or the father?"

"Either possibility doesn't bear thinking about."

"You did that on purpose."

"I have no idea what you're talking about, Mistress. I told you, I never joke," Andreas said. "But that's our point. Do I believe the rangers are half ursine demons? Of course not, but we have as much evidence supporting that as we do any other theory."

The attaché began ticking items off on his fingers while they spoke. "We know they're beloved by the people. They've reached almost folk hero status. We know there have been rangers since before the dukes decided to relieve the king and most of his family of everything north of the collarbone a century and a half ago. We're fairly sure they don't leave the Dominion."

Leaning forward, he said, "What we do know is that when the duke proposed a ranger escort for you, he proposed that in lieu of a dozen DeLuca household guards. That speaks volumes to what they believe this woman to be capable of. Most of what we know is most likely nonsense, but they believe them to be formidable. This is an opportunity we have never had, and you have the chance to actually get us some answers."

Antoinette nodded slowly. "All right. I'll try. Anything else?"

"Do try to get a bit of sculpting done while you're there, if you have the time."

She smiled. "Grandmother always said if you're only doing one job, you're not doing enough."

"She's sentimental that way." Andreas smiled at her. "You're going to be fine. You've done this before. I'll be waiting when you're done."

***

"Feel better now that we're in a proper city, milady?"

Antoinette had spent many years learning how to keep her face steady, no matter what thoughts were bubbling in her head. As she looked around the streets of Westcott, she found herself calling on every lesson. *Playing it a bit loose with the word "proper", aren't we?* She smiled at the Dominion soldier. "Much, Sergeant. I'm sure I'm going to feel right at home here."

She'd said goodbye to Andreas and the rest of the household guard at the Vetticci-Dominion border, where the Myre Wood gave way to the rolling fields and pastures of the Dominion. They'd been met by an escort of ten Dominion soldiers, there to see her safely on the day's ride to Westcott. The road ran parallel to the Myre, drifting north for a bit but always returning. They passed several small settlements, clusters of homes surrounding mills and granaries, but most of the land was filled with densely packed crops, neatly planted rows of trees for lumber, and herds of goats.

The contrast to what she'd known her entire life was disorienting. Antoinette was very aware of her place in Vetticcian society, about the value of the privacy and space she'd grown up enjoying in the massive city-state. But she'd never known a land to simply sprawl like this one. It seemed as if she was staring out over a verdant ocean that stretched impossibly far, past the horizon, and while she knew the Dominion had millions of people calling it home, they all seemed to get lost in the green and lovely expanse.

Her escorts had not been shy in answering her questions. Indeed, it seemed the sergeant in command of the soldiers was desperate to ensure that Antoinette's every need be met, to the point that it became a bit exasperating. Still, even as he chattered on, she did her duty, smiling, laughing at his terrible jokes, and playing every bit the part of the overwhelmed socialite, all while filing away every word he said that he probably shouldn't.

As they approached Westcott, the traffic on the road began to thicken. Convoys of wagons loaded with grain and vegetables rattled past on the poorly maintained road. Hundreds of people on foot walking in and out of the capital, burlap sacks slung over their shoulders and babies in their arms. Every eye followed her as she passed. Those that came too close or stood in their path found a mounted soldier staring balefully down at them, hand on the hilt of the short swords they all had sheathed at their waist. Antoinette did her best to smile at everyone who caught her eye. Her escorts did not.

They'd passed through the gate without being stopped, the guards posted at the entrance to the walled city waving them through without fanfare. Westcott was large for a Dominion city, with a thirty foot stone wall surrounding it. The buildings were nestled tightly together, though nowhere nearly as cramped as the tangled chaos of the lower parts of Vetticci. Antoinette frowned as she looked at the charred exterior of the first few buildings. "Was there a fire?"

Sergeant Milla shook his head. "No, milady. It's to protect the wood inside. They char the outside of the buildings, paint it with a resin from some tree. Hardens, keeps the wood dry. Lasts longer. Most of the buildings here use it." A cluster of people filled the road up ahead, gathered around a fruit cart set up on the side of the road. Milla frowned. "They shouldn't be blocking the way."

"It's all right, Sergeant. They're not hurting anything."

If he'd heard her, he didn't show it. Instead, he clicked his tongue, and rode forward, shouting, "Move! Get out of the damned street!"

The people immediately began to scatter, pushing against each other to get out of the mounted soldier's way. The horse whinnied at the sudden surge of motion, stepping back, and bumped into a woman trying to make her way past. The woman stumbled, catching herself, but as she did, she collided with the little girl whose hand she'd been clutching tightly. The child spilled to the ground, her knee skidding off the cobblestones, and she gave out a piteous wail.

"For all the gods," Milla muttered. "Pick her up and move, woman!"

Antoinette was already climbing off her horse, shouting, "Sergeant!" She rushed over, glaring up at the soldier. "She's hurt!"

Milla's face scrunched up as if he'd tried to scowl and smile at the same time. "If she'd cleared out of the way..."

"Do you have any bandages?"

"Pardon, milady?"

"Bandages, soldier," Antoinette snapped. Milla nodded, and began fishing in his saddlebags as Antoinette approached the sniffling child. The mother looked up, her face drawn and fearful, and her eyes widened as she saw Antoinette's clothing. Antoinette smiled, holding up her hands. "It's all right. I just want to make sure she's okay."

The little girl sat on the pavement, tears streaking down her face. Her knee was scuffed, tiny drops of blood welling up from the abrasion. Antoinette lowered into a crouch before her. "That looks like it hurts," she said. "Are you all right, little one?"

Tears forgotten, the girl's eyes widened as she looked at Antoinette. Sniffling, she said, "You talk funny."

"Lila, don't be rude," her mother said, her eyes wide with horrified mortification.

"It's all right," Antoinette said, smiling at the mother to reassure her before looking back at the child. "I'm not from here. I come from Vetticci. Your name is Lila?"

Lila's eyes darted between her mother and Antoinette, but finally she nodded. "Yes."

"Milady?" Antoinette looked back over her shoulder, and took the wrapped linen from Milla.

"I'm Antoinette, Lila. And I'm very happy to meet you." She pointed at Lila's scraped knee, which had already stopped bleeding. "Do you have an anatomist you can take her to?" she asked, handing her mother the bandage. "I'm sure she'll be all right, but someone should clean that."

The woman shook her head. "Only a few in town. Can't afford nothing like that."

"Sergeant?" Milla stepped forward again, and Antoinette said, "Is there someone close who can see to her?"

"There's an anatomist down the street. Mostly does teeth and boils, but I'm sure she could sort the girl out."

Antoinette nodded. Turning back to the mother, she said, "What's your name?"

"Aubrey." The woman glanced up, saw the expression on the soldier's face, and hurriedly added, "Uh, milady. Aubrey Cole."

"Aubrey, I'm sorry that Lila was hurt. If you like, one of these soldiers will take you and your daughter to get her bandaged up."

"Milady, I'm sorry, but I can't..."

Antoinette shook her head. "It's all right. Any cost will be taken care of." She looked back to Lila. "You have a lovely name. I'm sorry you took a tumble."

Lila considered her, and said, "Are you really from Vetticci?"

"I am."

"Oh." She shyly smiled up at Antoinette. "I like the color on your mouth. And that's pretty." She pointed to the emerald necklace hanging at Antoinette's throat. "It looks like a bird."

Antoinette smiled. "It does, doesn't it? You're very sweet." She stood up, and turned back to Milla, who'd motioned over one of the other soldiers. Lowering her voice, she said, "Have the anatomist bill my family for any costs. Once she's taken care of, see them safely home, and give them this." She reached into the folds of her cloak, and dropped a small stack of coral coins into his hand.

"Milady, that's..." Milla cleared his throat. "That's quite a bit of money."

"Thank you, Sergeant. I'm quite able to count." Reaching up, she unclasped the necklace and dropped it next to the coins. "Give this to the child."

The soldier nodded, and Antoinette watched them walk down the street, Lila craning her head back to stare at her. Once they were out of earshot, Antoinette said, "Sergeant."

"Milady."

"I'm going to be here for five, maybe six months. I understand the value of punctuality, but if being a bit late means we don't knock children down in the street, I find that a fair trade, don't you?"

He dipped his head. "Begging your pardon, milady. It won't happen again."

"I know."

The rest of their trip to the center of town was a bit slower, but much less eventful. They stopped to allow milling crowds to pass, people staring up at Antoinette as she smiled and nodded. When they reached the massive wooden doors of the Ducal Palace, a small group was waiting for them.

Standing at the front was an older man with a thick, heavy beard. The sunlight glinted off his bald head, and his sky blue tunic was immaculate with the exception of the left arm, pinned up at the shoulder. A thick tanned leather belt held a scabbard on his left hip, the hilt of a longsword visible. He stepped forward, and bowed deeply.

"Mistress DeLuca, welcome to the Dominion, and welcome to Westcott. I am Ethan Poole, captain of the Westcott militia, captain of the ducal palace guard, and aide-de-camp to Duke Bryan Westcott, lord of the Westcott Duchy and commanding general of the Ducal Army." Poole's voice was rough and cracked, rumbling up from somewhere near his boots. "It is my honor to offer you shelter and hospitality during your stay in our home."

Antoinette dipped her head, holding her hands out palms up. "Captain Poole, I am Antoinette DeLuca, Scioness of the house of DeLuca, and artist of the Vetticcian College of Artisans. I thank you for your shelter, and offer my talents as recompense. My hands are yours for so long as I call your roof my own."

"Now that that's out of the way." The tall thin man who stepped past Poole wore a neatly tailored military uniform, the breast covered with several medals Antoinette recognized, and a dozen she did not. Duke Bryan Westcott grinned, showing a row of bright white teeth as he stuck out his hand. "Can't tell you how excited I am to have you here, Madame DeLuca."

I read every bit of detail we have about your military service. All two pages of it. I'm fairly sure those medals aren't worth the metal they're made of. Antoinette took his hand, and winced at the tight grip. Extracting herself, she said, "The honor is mine, Your Grace."

Poole leaned forward, whispering something in the duke's ear. The duke scowled. "Mistress DeLuca, not Madame. As if it matters worth a damn. I've been trying to get you to come out and do some work for us for five, six years. Ever since you got that first leaf. Been to Vetticci several times," he said, puffing his chest. "Saw The Lily the first time I went down there. Have to see it to believe it, isn't that right, Poole?"

"Yes, Your Grace." Poole's voice hadn't changed, his expression flat.

"Poole saw it. Gods, I made every member of my staff take a look."

"That's very kind, Your Grace. I'm grateful my schedule allowed me to come spend some time in your lovely city," Antoinette said. *This one's a talker. Poole isn't. I think Andreas was right. Not much to grip there.*

Westcott nodded, his head bobbing up and down. "Truly wish I could stay, watch you at work. Kicking myself for missing the opportunity. But too much to do, too far to travel. Going to take me at least three weeks to get there."

Years of practice kept the dismay from her face. *He's leaving so soon?* She considered what he'd said. *Three weeks of travel time. With the kind of escort he'd travel with, that's not much more than a hundred miles per day. 2100 miles puts him either on the eastern coast, up near the Breaking, or on Cicerone's northern border.* "Will Your Grace be back before I finish the project? It would be an honor to present the finished work directly."

"His Grace's travels are unpredictable," Poole said before the duke could respond. "It's impossible to say."

She didn't look at Poole. She knew he'd be watching for that. "Hopefully, this gives you something to anticipate on the way back, Your Grace."

"Maybe I'll invite that ass Snowsill back with me," Westcott said to Poole. "Show him how a royal is supposed to do things."

"Perhaps I could show the Mistress to her quarters. Let her see where she'll be working." Poole's inflection still hadn't changed.

"What? Oh, yes, yes." Westcott nodded. "Looking forward to the results, Madame. Let Poole know if you need anything, he'll see to it." He turned and walked back into the palace, several retainers trailing after him.

Poole waited until he was gone before speaking again. "The Duke will unfortunately most likely be away for the duration of your work. However, I run the palace, and I will never fail to be nearby should you need for anything."

Translation: I'm watching you.

"I look forward to our close collaboration, Captain." Antoinette smiled at him. He did not return the expression.

"You'll get to know the rest of the house staff quickly, I've no doubt. They've been instructed to afford you every consideration during your stay." Someone cleared their throat behind Poole, and he nodded. "Yes. Mistress DeLuca, as an expression of the esteem in which the people of the Dominion hold your house, may I introduce your escort for your time here. Jaina Crofton of the Sylvan Order of Rangers."

Antoinette had to stop herself from correcting him, instead turning her attention to the woman stepping forward. She wore no uniform, only a simple cotton tunic and breeches, with heavy leather riding boots. Her sandy blonde hair was cut close to her head, and her eyes were a deep green color Antoinette had not seen before. The sleeves of her tunic were cut at the elbow, and the muscles of her forearms were thick and defined. She stood nearly a head taller than Antoinette, and offered her hand. "It's Creighton, actually. Jaina Creighton."

Antoinette hesitated for a moment, then took the woman's hand, bracing for a grip worse than the duke's. It took some effort to keep the surprise from touching her eyes when the ranger's hand barely squeezed, the handshake limp and delicate.

One thought swam to the top of her mind. *Oh, my dear. Bit of a lack of confidence. This is going to be easy.*

She smiled.

2,448 Hours

One thought swam to the top of her mind.

For all the gods, Jaina, don't crush this woman's fucking hand.

It had been seven days since she woke up next to the fire. Seven days since she began the ride to Westcott alone, thoughts swirling through her head. It had been five days since she woke up one morning, began packing up camp, and picked up the staff, not realizing until a moment later that it felt lighter. It had been two days since she stumbled while looking for a secluded cluster of trees off the road to relieve herself, stumbled, and tore a two-inch branch from a tree while trying to catch herself.

As she had stared at the thick wooden limb in her hands, a familiar voice came from behind her.

Thank god you're not a man. Taking a leak would be terrifying with that kind of grip.

When Jaina was five, she'd been hiding from her parents after breaking a crystal goblet, one of a pair they saved for visiting dignitaries. She ran nearly three blocks before finding a small hollow in the ground at the base of an abandoned tannery. She had no way of knowing that was the only visible part of the sinkhole that had led to the building to be abandoned. By the time she realized her mistake, she'd fallen deep into the black pit, finding herself pinned between several rocks.

It had taken her parents nearly eight hours to find her, and another ten for the dozens of guards and neighbors who gathered to find a way to safely bring her to the surface. To help her stay calm, her mother had tasked her brothers with lying on their bellies next to the pit, talking to her while the adults frantically argued behind them. Their voices had kept the tears at bay.

But in the days and weeks that had followed, Jaina was gripped with moments of terror. The memory of the crushing black and steady, unrelenting pressure on her body would come pouring back, and she'd fall to her knees, gasping for breath and sobbing. And when those moments came, it was her brother's voices that brought her back, whether they were there or not. She would imagine Jak or Joran there, unseen, but teasing her, reminding her that even if they weren't there, she was never alone.

It had been a long time since she'd found their voices in her head. But she could practically see Jak staring at the mangled wood in her hand, shaking his head.

I've outgrown this, Jaina thought, gritting her teeth.

You would think so, wouldn't you? But here we are.

I can't believe they're just going to send you off into the world like this. Joran's voice added to the conversation. *You're going to hurt someone. Or yourself.*

"Thanks for the vote of confidence."

Hey, we're in your head. If anyone's not confident about their lot in life, it's not us.

Maybe she's rethinking the wildly impulsive decision she made? Jak mused.

Shut up. Jaina had shaken her head sharply, and they were gone. But more and more, she found herself imagining their voices in her head, and whether she wanted to admit it or not, it helped keep the fears at bay, just as it had when she was in that dark, deep hole.

They were always there when she woke up after sleeping on the ground. Mornings found herself waking to a dull, throbbing ache throughout her body, but after a few hours, it faded. Martine had taught her several breathing techniques when the onslaught of stimuli became too much. They helped. She learned the importance of focus, of choosing what she wanted to zero in on, and when she did, Jaina was stunned how far she could see, how clear sounds from impossible distances became.

She'd barely been in Westcott for a few hours before a messenger came to the quarters she'd been assigned, letting her know that DeLuca and her escorts had been in the city. She followed the young man to the front gate, where several people were assembled. Poole had been the first to greet her, shaking her hand, and introducing her to the Duke.

For his part, Duke Westcott had not seemed impressed. He'd simply asked, "You're the ranger?"

"Yes, Your Grace."

He looked her up and down, and grunted. "Poole's in charge. Do as he says." He turned away from her before she could speak.

Well. He's a delight. Jak made a face. *Too bad we're not in the inn. He's got a face absolutely begging for a lapful of hot soup.*

Poole leaned in, his voice low. "He doesn't mean any offense. He's on a tight schedule today, and the Vetticcian woman is running late. Some nonsense delay in the city."

"Is she all right?" *Blowing the job before I start the job. That'd be a good story to tell Martine.*

I'm sure you'll find plenty of ways to screw up, but I really don't think they can blame you for anything that happened before you got here, Cricket.

"She's fine." Poole glanced up at the cluster of mounted soldiers that came around the corner, approaching the gate. "Excuse me."

Jaina watched as he moved to the front of the group, but as the escort dismounted, her eyes fell upon the woman at the center. She had long inky black hair hanging down between her shoulder blades, and wore a deep red dress that moved like water, clinging tightly to her slender form. Her skin was dark and flawless, her eyes a brilliant blue. Jaina watched as she was greeted by Poole, saw the duke impatiently shifting until he couldn't wait any longer, bulling forward to shake her hand, and Jaina saw the briefest flash of discomfort dart across those delicate features.

She thought back to the mangled remains of the branch from a few days ago, and her stomach dropped two feet.

Realizing that too, eh, Cricket? She could practically hear Jak grinning. *If you did that to a tree branch, what do you think you could do to the hand of a famous artist?*

Don't forget rich.

Thank you, Joran. Yes, a rich and famous artist. That's whose hand you're about to shake.

Jaina tried to keep her face impassive as the panic grew within her. *Why didn't I practice? Ask for some duck eggs or something, learn how much pressure I can apply without mangling the woman I'm supposed to protect?*

I think we've established that common sense isn't one of your strong suits.

Poole was speaking now, and Jaina prayed she wasn't sweating as he spoke her name, gesturing towards her. She stepped forward, feeling far too big for this moment, and stared down at the extended gloved hand of an artist her country was paying a fortune to be here. Some part of her brain registered Poole mispronouncing her name, and she stammered out, "It's Creighton, actually. Jaina Creighton." She shook, as carefully and as quickly as she could, and saw the ghost of a smile play across Antoinette's face.

Well, at least I did that part right.

"I'm at your service..." Jaina trailed off, frowning.

"Is something wrong?" Her voice had less of an accent than the Vetticcians that Jaina had come across in Lofland Fork, just a slight lilt to it.

"No, I just..." Jaina cleared her throat. "I'm realizing I don't know the proper honorific for someone of your status."

That ghost of a smile bloomed to full life, and Jaina felt her mouth go dry. *Shit.*

Already? Jak rolled his eyes. *You always were a sucker for a pretty face.*

"Well, technically I'm a scioness, so the generally accepted term is Mistress," Antoinette said. "But I'm to understand we'll be working quite closely together. So why don't we see how things go?"

Jaina didn't quite know how to respond to that. She glanced back at Poole for a moment, but the captain's face may as well have been carved from stone.

I think that's your cue, Cricket.

"I'm looking forward to it, Mistress," Jaina said, "Captain Poole will be responsible for security in the actual palace, but I've been assigned as your escort. I'll remain by your side for the duration of your stay in the Dominion."

"So I've been told." Antoinette's eyes took in all of Jaina in a few quick scans. "You're a ranger, correct?"

Jaina nodded. "I am."

Joran snorted. *Barely. I think I've got pimples on my ass older than your career in the rangers.*

"Well, ranger, why don't you show me where I'll be working?"

Poole stepped forward. "Our porters will place your things in your quarters, mistress. Creighton here knows where they are, so she can show you there when you're ready."

"All but the two witchwood chests," Antoinette said, nodding. "Those have my tools. They'll go to the worksite."

"I can take those," Jaina said quickly.

"You'll want some help," Antoinette said, shaking her head. "I didn't know what I'd need, so I brought pretty much everything."

"It's all right." The chests weren't particularly large, each about the width of Jaina's shoulders. They were immaculately crafted, and her stomach lurched as she did a quick calculation of the value of each chest.

As funny as it would be if you dropped the extremely expensive tools in front of all of these people laboring under the assumption that you're a professional, perhaps it would be best to let the porters handle it, Cricket? Joran had always been the more pragmatic among the two.

Jak, however... *Gods, no. I want to see how much she can lift.* Jak gestured at the chests. *Come on, baby ranger. Let's see what you got. Show this Vetticcian woman how strong you are.*

There were deep inset handles in the side of each chest with plenty of room to get a good grip. Jaina lifted the first, setting it carefully on top of the second. They'd been designed so the pair nested together neatly, and she crouched, picked up the pair, and her eyes widened. *Well. Shit.*

The chests felt as if they were empty. As she shifted her grip, she could feel the weight shift back and forth, and knew they were full, but they felt like a bundle of reeds, light and delicate.

Turning to Antoinette, she said, "If you'll follow me, mistress?" She tried to keep her face even, ignoring the stares from the porters and guards.

That's good. Act casual about it. Act like someone who's not shocked more than they are that worked.

Antoinette blinked several times before responding. "Ah. Well, yes. By all means."

The pair walked past the rest of the guards and house staff, who all stepped nimbly aside for the ranger and the artist. Antoinette fell into step next to her. "I... I trust your trip up here was comfortable?" Jaina said, peering over the top of the upper crate.

"Reasonably so," Antoinette said, still eyeing her. "Those crates really are quite heavy. I have to admit to being taken aback to no small degree."

Shit. Was I not supposed to show my strength? Jaina went back and forth with several possible answers, each of them more stupid than the last. "I, uh, I'm a ranger."

Erudite as always.

Antoinette glanced at her, smiling again. "So I've been told."

"We're pretty strong, mistress."

"So I can see." Antoinette shook her head. "It took two of my family porters to lift those into our carriage. I'll be delighted to inform them that one solitary woman managed both at the same time."

"I'm sure they did their best, mistress." Jaina spotted the step in their path just in time.

Would have been a fitting capper on this conversation to fall face first on top of the rich girl's toys. Do try to watch where you're going.

She could feel Antoinette's eyes on her as they navigated through the hallways. Westcott Palace was inaccurately named. While tapestries on the walls and sumptuous rugs did their best to bring a bit of warmth to this place, this was a fortress, built early in the border conflicts that raged between the dukes just after the fall of the royal family. There was little elegance to the construction, no sweeping woodwork, no glazed or stained windows, simply heavy slabs of rock piled atop each other in the most sturdy way possible.

Bringing an artist to this place feels kind of like adding a bit of filigree to an axe, Jaina thought. *Might be pretty. Definitely out of place.*

Jaina reflected that described her new charge, as well. She'd realized fairly quickly how good her peripheral vision was, which came in handy now as she did her best to surreptitiously glance over Antoinette. Every inch of her was immaculate. The cut of her dress was perfect, clinging to her body like a second skin in some places, loose and flowing to maintain decorum in others. The fabric looked as if it had been cut from some kind of liquid, the embroidery glinting in the light in a way that argued that it might indeed be silver thread. Her face was painted, not excessively, but highlighting everything that should be highlighted, and her hair looked as if someone had taken the entire scalp aside and informed them, in no uncertain terms, the dour fate that awaited any strand foolish enough to fall out of place.

She stands out. Jaina had realized that the moment she'd laid eyes on Antoinette, but it rang even more true now. *She's clearly not meant to be here.*

Neither are you, Cricket, Joran pointed out.

They emerged into the throne room, the heavy banded oak doors propped open, and Jaina whispered a silent prayer of thanks that she'd remembered the way Poole had so quickly shown her. The room was huge, stretching nearly eighty feet in length, wide enough to hold

hundreds of subjects. Today, it was empty of both people and fur-
nishings. Six huge stone columns were regularly spaced, and the only
part of the room that wasn't the same slabs of granite were the walls.
Thick paneling of white oak had been affixed to every stretch of the
walls to the left and right of the dais at the end of the hall, eight feet
tall. The heavy boards were unfinished, but the seams between them
were barely visible.

"You can set those down here..." Antoinette paused, and glanced
over at her. "Is Ranger your title? What do I call you?"

Jaina felt a flash of panic as she realized she didn't really know the
answer. She set the crates down where Antoinette had indicated, her
mind racing. They'd always called Shakkar by his name as long as she
could remember, but she didn't know if that was due to familiarity or
some other reason.

*You cannot tell this woman you don't know what she's supposed to call
you.* Joran said emphatically. *You absolutely, definitely cannot.*

"You can call me Ranger. But, uh, my name is Jaina. You can call me
Jaina. Or Ranger Jaina." She blanched. "No, not that."

Nailed it.

Antoinette considered this, and said, "Jaina. It's a pretty name."
She knelt, fiddling with some mechanism at the front of one of the
chests, and the top unfolded in several segments, the trunk splitting
and opening up like a blooming flower. There, held in precisely carved
insets, were countless chisels, knives, and other tools. Antoinette selected a small brass hammer, and rose to her feet. "We're going to
be around each other quite a bit. Would you be willing to call me
Antoinette?"

*Martine really did a bang up job preparing you for this, didn't he?
Are you even allowed to call her that?*

"I'm not sure, mistress..."

"If I'm going to call you by your first name, I think it's only fair for you to do the same."

Well. Shit. Jaina tried to think of a way out of the corner she'd very neatly painted herself into, and came up empty. "If you insist."

"I do."

She watched Antoinette walk up to the wall, and tug off one of her gloves. Her fingers were long and delicate, but Jaina could spot countless tiny scars dotting the bare hand. Antoinette ran her fingers over the heavy wood paneling, pausing after a few steps to tap the hammer gently against the wall, listening intently.

"Is something wrong?"

Antoinette held a finger to her lips. "If you don't mind." She continued slowly walking the perimeter of the room, pausing every few steps to tap the wall. Twice, she reached somewhere into the folds of her dress and pulled out a slender stick of graphite, marking the wall.

She's focused. Jaina watched her as she meticulously examined every inch of the room, only speaking once she returned to the spot she had begun. She crouched down, returning the hammer to the tool set. Finally, Jaina asked again, "Is everything all right?"

"What?" Antoinette glanced up, and nodded. "Oh, yes. I sent very specific directions on how the room was to be prepared. I just needed to know that they'd followed them. If they hadn't, I couldn't have started until we tore all this out and started over again."

"And did they? Follow directions, I mean?"

"Well enough." Antoinette rose to her feet. "There are a few spots that I'm not thrilled about, but I think I can work around them."

Jaina turned slowly, looking around the room. "May I ask what it is you're doing? The job, I mean?"

"A relief carving," Antoinette said. "Documenting the history of the Westcott family. They sent us the paintings from which they wish for me to pull inspiration. A bit exaggerated, but they do give me plenty to work with."

Jaina frowned. "That's a lot. You really think you can do that in five months?"

"That eager to spend more time with me, ranger?" Antoinette smiled. Before Jaina could stammer out an answer, she said, "I plan my jobs carefully. I'll have a schedule. If we stick to it, it shouldn't be an issue."

"All right." Jaina looked down at the tool chests. "Will you get started tonight?"

"Yes, but not here." Antoinette smoothed her skirt. "It's been a long day. If you don't mind, I think I'll make changes to the planning sketches in my chambers."

"Of course." Jaina nodded at the chests. "Want me to bring them with us?"

"If Captain Poole can't secure a pair of tool chests in the throne room of the nation's capital, I will suddenly become much less confident in the security of this place," Antoinette said. "I trust they'll be safe here."

Jaina motioned. "This way."

As they walked, Antoinette asked, "Are you from Westcott?"

"No, mist..." Jaina cleared her throat at Antoinette's tiny twitch of an eyebrow. "Ah, Antoinette. No, I'm from Lofland Fork. My family is." She glanced around. "My first time to the capital."

"So my bodyguard is as familiar with this place as I am."

Jaina shook her head, a little too enthusiastically. "No, I've been here a bit. I made sure..." She trailed off as Antoinette shook her head.

"I was teasing," she said. "I'm sure this place is very secure, and I'm sure you're quite qualified to watch over me as I spent ten hours a day in the same room." She paused, and pinched the bridge of her nose.

"I'm sorry. That was..." Antoinette smiled up at her. "As I said. It's been a long day. I don't mean to question your capabilities."

Probably best if she doesn't also realize that you have no idea what you're doing.

"No apologies necessary." They came to the end of a long hallway. At the end were two wooden doors, one to the left, the other to the right. Jaina pointed to the one on the right. "This is yours." She opened the door for Antoinette, who stepped through.

The room had two windows, but they were narrow and tall, barely as wide as her shoulders, more slits filled with shifted smoked quartz, the whorls of grey glinting in the lamplight. The room was already appointed with a large, four poster bed, and Antoinette's luggage was arranged next to a suite of dressers made of polished rosewood and cedar. There was a fireplace on the far wall with a large painting over it, a picture of the glimmering waters of Pallia Bay dotted with countless ships. The painting felt almost ethereal.

Jaina pointed to it. "Suppose they put that to help keep you from being homesick."

Antoinette glanced at it, and shook her head. "The duke is showing off."

"What do you mean?"

Antoinette walked over to one trunk, opening it up. "The painting. It's mine."

"You brought it from home?"

"No." Antoinette gestured back to the painting. "Look in the bottom corner."

Jaina glanced over, her eyes finding the thin black signature quickly. "Oh. It really is your painting."

Antoinette frowned. "You can see that? From across the room?"

"Just an educated guess." Jaina tried to change the subject. "It's beautiful. But I thought you were a sculptor."

"I am now. It's been at least six years since I did any serious painting."

"Six..." Jaina frowned, and stared at the painting. "You did that when you were thirteen?"

"Nine."

"Oh." *Gods. So she's not just a pretty face.* "That's kind of amazing."

"Thank you."

The silence that followed was deafening. Jaina didn't know how to break it, but finally cleared her throat and said, "Well. I'm right across the hall. If you need me."

"I'm sure I'll be fine." Antoinette smiled. "Thank you, Jaina."

"You're welcome, Antoinette."

2,437 Hours

Antoinette stared at the door for a long few moments after it closed. *Well. She's not quite what I expected.*

She opened a trunk, pulling out a large stack of bone-white paper lashed to a drawing board. The top few sheets were covered with sketches, numbers scribbled next to them, and she sat down on the bed, flipping through them until she found what she was looking for. She began making notes on one section, the sharpened tip of the graphite dancing over the page as her plans shifted in light of the unexpected.

Antoinette lost track of how long she'd been working. That had always been the case. Her life had never been entirely her own, but when she was focused on a project, she was the one making the choices. She was the one in control. It was often hard to pull herself away from that, but she did. Every time.

Once she'd finished making the adjustments needed, she moved over to the cedar desk they'd placed for her. Antoinette pulled out an inkwell set from her bags, along with some stationary, and sat down. The set had two inkpots, visually identical. She dipped the nib in the pot on the left, and began writing.

Grandm ther,

The trip here took place without i cident. The duke et up a proper gree ing for my rrival, and while he offered a our of the city, I declined in f vor of inspec ing the work s te. The wo d is of acceptable quality, and only mi imal adjustments need to be onsidered. I'll be starting t morrow mor ing, and don't an icipate any del ys in the project. Please o give Mattia and Lorenzo my aff ctions, and know that my family is in my thoughts always.

It had taken her some time to get accustomed to leaving out letters while she wrote, but after hours upon hours of practice, no one watching could tell anything was amiss unless they looked at the page. She filled several pages, and once she'd signed her name in the precise script she'd learned, Antoinette put that nib into its proper slot, picked up a second, and dipped it into the inkpot on the right.

One by one, she filled in the missing letters. The ink had an odd shimmer to it when wet, but as the pulp of the paper slowly sipped in the black ink, the letters settled into place, indistinguishable from those next to them.

On station. Contact made. Reports to follow. Duke is leaving. Not expected back during job.

In one of her bags was a vial of perfume, a wonderful concoction that smelled of woodsmoke and honeysuckle. It was one of only ten vials of its kind in the world. Eight of the remaining vials were locked away in the DeLuca estate. The ninth was with her brother. When dabbed on her wrist and blown in the direction of the letters, those written with the right inkpot's contents would develop a slight halo, a faint outline barely noticeable unless you knew what you were looking for. Satisfied, she dusted the page with a drying agent, and left it to sit overnight.

As she changed into her small clothes to go to sleep, she found herself glancing at the door. *She's definitely new. Seems unsure of what she's doing, what she's allowed to say. Could be useful.* She laid down, staring up at the ceiling. *Need to be careful. Mattia wasn't wrong. No quick rescue here.*

I'm all alone.

Antoinette had left home before on jobs, but this was her first time in an entirely different country. Before, her grandmother, her brothers, all the trappings of home had been less than a day away. But here, she was truly on her own. She had thought that idea, once she allowed it to realize fully in her mind, would be accompanied by apprehension. But as she repeated it in her mind, Antoinette felt only a surprising sensation of relief. She let out a long, slow breath, whispered, "I'm alone," and shut her eyes.

***

The morning sun had yet to peek through the windows in her room as Antoinette pulled on her boots. She had spent a few moments lying in bed, listening for the sound of the staff going through all the steps to ready the castle for the day, but other than the occasional bootfalls of a watchman, she heard nothing. As she got dressed, Antoinette considered the possibilities afforded by being unattended for a short time, but when she opened her door, sketches tucked beneath her arm, Jaina was waiting, hands clasped before her. A long black staff was tucked under her arm.

"Good morning."

Antoinette nodded at her. "I'd not expected to see anyone up at this hour."

"I heard you moving about. Thought you might be getting an early start."

Did I make that much noise? "I like getting started early in the day. Less chance of being interrupted."

"I can understand that," Jaina said. "Need to bring anything with you?"

Antoinette shook her head, and they began walking together down the hall. "I will need to find my way on the right side of a cup of tea before too long," she said. "I brought a spiced mixture from home that I quite enjoy. You'll have to try it."

"Never had much of a taste for tea," Jaina said. "Didn't much see the point of drinking dirty water."

"What a thoroughly unpleasant way to describe one of the true highlights of life."

Jaina grinned. "I'm sure your tea is much better than what my father served."

"By your tone, I'm not sure that counts as a ringing endorsement."

"It's not." They reached the throne room. The doors had been shut sometime during the night, and Jaina stepped forward to pull one open for Antoinette. "If you didn't find some debris floating in your mug, it was a surprise for everyone."

Antoinette made a face. "I would never think to impugn your father's capabilities, but perhaps tea should not be on his menu."

Jaina raised her eyebrow. "How did you know my father ran an inn?"

Careful. "I didn't, although that's funny. I simply meant his personal menu." She raised an eyebrow. "Please don't tell me he serves this beverage badly masquerading as tea to his guests."

"Most of his guests prefer ale. A handful will buy demitasse when he has it, but that's not often."

Antoinette shook her head as she opened both the trunks. She pulled out a hair clip and began fastening her long black hair behind her head. "So instead of tea, they like bean juice."

Jaina held up her hands. "I don't like either, so at least it's equal." She glanced around the room. "So are you going to start carving today?"

"Gods no," Antoinette said. "It's going to take some time to finish sketching the outline. But fear not. While that step may be long and tedious, it makes up for it by being extremely boring to watch." She glanced back at Jaina. "Truly a thrilling assignment you've received."

Jaina didn't quite smile at that, but Antoinette could see the corners of her mouth twitch slightly. "I think I'll be able to manage," Jaina said. "Besides, the point isn't to watch the work, it's to watch..."

"Me?"

"To watch for anything that might be a threat." A bit of color in the ranger's cheeks.

"Ah." Antoinette nodded. "Well, given we're inside the throne room of the main keep of the most secure castle inside the walled capital city of the Dominion, I would think that threats will be few and far between." She pulled several graphite sticks, wrapped in rough cotton and dipped in wax, from the tool chest.

"Are you suggesting I'm unnecessary?"

"I'm suggesting that you might find yourself acting as companion rather than bodyguard." Antoinette glanced back, smiling. "Not the worst thing, I hope."

"Believe me, I'll be quite happy if this job passes without incident."

"Mmm." Antoinette pulled out a canvas apron, and tied it around her waist, tucking the graphite sticks into pockets sewn for that exact purpose. Reaching in, she pulled out a squat jar, and unscrewed the lid, pulling out a gummy substance.

"What is that?" Jaina asked, leaning to the side to see better.

"Pine sap." Antoinette stood up, and brought the sketches over to the wall. She made a tiny ball of the sticky sap, and pressed it to the wall. She then firmly pressed the first sketch to the sap, sticking it to the wall. "Just need to be certain to clean my hands before I use a candle. Burns hot." She glanced back. "Ask you a question?"

"Depends what it is."

"You didn't have that staff yesterday."

"No. Captain Poole didn't like the idea of me meeting the duke with a weapon."

Antoinette nodded. "If you don't mind me saying, it didn't seem like the duke considered you a close friend. Have you two met before?"

"Not until yesterday." Jaina shrugged. "Maybe he doesn't like rangers."

"I thought the rangers were quite popular in your country," Antoinette said.

"The rangers are the only people in our country that don't report to the dukes," Jaina said. "We all thought that was pretty exciting when I was a kid."

"The way the handful of Dominion visitors we've received back home talk about them, they sound like folk tales. Most have to be nonsense, of course."

"What do you mean?'

Antoinette paused, and turned to face her. "Well. I know that you're quite strong. But I don't believe you could lift a carriage with a single hand."

Jaina shrugged. "Probably not. Haven't tried."

"I do believe that would be the first thing I would try, if I were a ranger."

"Really?" Jaina said, raising an eyebrow. "First thing you'd do after waking from the ritual is to go chasing after the first wagon rattling past, asking if they wouldn't mind if you gave them a quick lift?"

Ritual. Interesting. Antoinette wanted to push on that more, but her grandmother's voice swam up. *Never push too hard too fast. Everything they tell you must be their idea.* "Well, maybe not the first thing. I'd have some tea first."

"Of course, only thing that makes sense."

Antoinette resumed sticking up the sketches, talking as she went. "Can you see in the dark?"

"Not as well as I can in the daylight."

"Jump over a house?"

"How big a house? My dad built a little house for our dog when I was a kid. It fell over pretty quickly, but I think I could have cleared it."

"Why did it fall down?"

"Remember how bad I told you he is at making tea?" Antoinette nodded, and Jaina said, "He's even worse at carpentry."

Antoinette was surprised at the laugh that slipped free of her lips. She hadn't intended it. *She's funny. More so than she realizes, I think.* "You're an inexhaustible font of useful tidbits about rangers."

"Here to serve, mistress," Jaina said. "May I ask why you're so curious?"

"We don't have rangers in Vetticci. We have quite a few things you don't have up here, but rangers and elbow room are strictly the province of the Dominion." She glanced back. "Have you ever been?"

"To the city? Gods, no," Jaina said, shaking her head. "Never had cause, and certainly never had the coin."

Antoinette finished sticking up the last page, and went back to the tool chest. Pulling out a small stitched notebook, she made a quick note to herself, then returned to the first section. As the graphite began scratching over the surface of the wood in quick, sure strokes, she said, "You said your father owns an inn, right?"

"He does. Inherited it from his father, who got it from his father, who…"

"I think I can guess."

Jaina nodded. "Five generations. Each one adds more."

"You didn't want to take it over?"

"Never was the plan for me."

"So what happens when your father is ready to hang up his ghastly tea skills?" Antoinette wasn't looking, but when an answer didn't come immediately, she glanced back toward the ranger. There was an odd look on Jaina's face.

Clearing her throat, Jaina said, "One of my brothers will take it over. Most likely both. They do everything together." Before Antoinette could respond, she said, "If you don't mind, I'm going to check the grounds. I won't be gone very long. I'll post a guard outside the door should you need anything."

Poked something sensitive there, didn't you? Might be worth digging. "Of course." Antoinette watched the big woman walk out the room, her head bowed.

2,431 Hours

There was a mixed blessing to being busy. Jaina's long ride to the capital had given her ample time to think, and that was not something she enjoyed since watching her brothers disappear over the horizon. Thinking gave her brain far too many opportunities to point out how many ways this all could go wrong, how many mistakes she'd made in her frantic rush to do anything to stop it from happening. Once she'd arrived in Westcott, things happened very quickly, and she'd had little time to think.

Antoinette had given her that time.

She'd left a guard posted outside the throne room, and found herself walking around the outside of the ugly castle. *Too long. This is going to take too long.*

"Ranger?" When she turned, she saw Captain Poole walking towards her. "Everything all right?"

"It's fine. I'm just checking the grounds. Making sure everything is... You know, checked." She winced as the words tripped over each other coming out of her mouth. "It's fine."

An absolute font of professionalism, you are.

He nodded, considering her. "You know that palace security falls under me and my people, right?"

"I know, and I didn't mean to insinuate that you weren't doing your job."

"It's okay," Poole said. "Mind if I ask you a question?" Jaina nodded, and he asked, "This is your first assignment, isn't it? As a ranger?"

Jaina hesitated. *Am I supposed to be telling people that?* She couldn't think of a way around it. "It is."

"Thought so."

"Am I that obvious?"

He grinned. "Definitely. That's not a bad thing. And it makes sense. Everything going on in the country, we don't need a seasoned veteran on this post. It's a good one for you to cut your teeth on."

She nodded. "Not really sure what I'm supposed to be doing. Feels like I'm standing around, waiting for something that's not going to happen to happen."

"Probably ought to switch that mindset right now," he said. "Graveyards are littered with those who were certain nothing was going to happen. And that's what jobs like this are. Ninety-nine days out of a hundred, they're boring. One day out of a hundred, they're not, and you need to keep ready for that day."

She chuckled.

Poole raised an eyebrow. "Something funny about that?"

"No, it's just..." Jaina shook her head. "That's the best, and only real piece of advice that I've gotten about this job."

"Ah." Poole nodded. "I've worked with rangers before. They're a bit odd, aren't they? Present company excluded, of course."

You've only just met her. Give it time. She's plenty odd.

Shut up, Jak. "They weren't what I expected, to be sure," Jaina said. "I thought I'd have a commander, or mission orders, or rules telling me how to actually do this. Instead, I'm wandering around the outside of a castle because I have no idea what I'm supposed to be doing."

Poole leaned back against the stone wall. "Well, if it makes you feel any better, you wouldn't have any idea what you're doing even if you had someone hovering over your shoulder telling you which foot to move next. That's the nature of jobs like this. You can be told over and over what to expect, but reality never quite looks like what you thought it would."

"So you think their approach is the right one?"

"Gods, no." Poole shook his head. "But the rangers have always done things their own way. One of the many reasons the dukes don't much care for them."

She nodded, and after a moment's hesitation, said, "You've been a soldier for a long time, right?"

"Ayuh, that's a fact. Started as a pikeman in the duke's army. Not this duke, his father. Conscription ended, and I decided to stick around as part of the regular army. Did that until I lost the ability to clap."

"Can I ask you a question?"

"If it's about the arm, I'd really rather not."

"It's not."

"In that case, ask away."

"How long does training take? For the army, I mean. How long before someone actually ends up holding a longbow or pike and marching off to fight someone?" She tried to keep her voice level as she spoke. She knew she wasn't all that good at it.

Poole considered her for a bit, then nodded. "Makes a bit more sense now. Brother? Father?"

Jaina took a deep breath. "Brothers. Twins."

"Took 'em both?" She nodded, and he shook his head. "Bad business, that. Only serves to make the people panic, and it's going to leave a lot of farms short staffed." Poole thought for a moment. "You're from Lofland Fork, right?" She nodded, and he said, "Duke Gaille, then. His troops have always been fairly well trained. My guess, your brothers will spend at least two months drilling before getting assigned a unit. Maybe three."

Jaina mentally adjusted the countdown that had begun in her head weeks ago. "Okay. That's something, anyway."

"You joined the rangers for the exemption?"

Jaina nodded. "You disapprove?"

Poole snorted. "Your business is your business. Rangers earn the exemption. You'll be tromping through these hills and pastures for the rest of your days. Least we can do is make sure you have a family to visit every now and then. Seems like a steep price to pay, though. If they were with Snowsill or McElroy, sure. They both do ten year conscription periods. But Gaille still does five." He raised an eyebrow. "Lifetime for five years is a hell of a trade."

And a stupid trade to boot, Joran muttered. *The man knows what he's talking about, Cricket.*

"Four," she said. "Exemption isn't issued until after I finish my novice period."

"That's shit," he said. "Not like you can quit. How long's the novice period?"

"Normally a year. For me, it ends when Mistress DeLuca heads back down south."

"Well, here's hoping the Vetticcian works quickly."

She nodded. "Do you know? Why both Duke Westcott and Gaille are conscripting so many soldiers?"

He chuckled. "I'm an old grunt in a sunset posting. If it's not part of my job, they don't tell me." Poole considered for a moment, and said, "It's not just Westcott and Gaille. From what I hear, it's all the dukes."

Jaina hesitated. "Is it the Confessors?"

"Gods, I hope not. The dukes would have to be insane to want to retake Cicerone." Poole shook his head. "My guess is the domino effect. One duke starts raising troops, his neighbors get nervous and do the same, and it spreads. Might be good for you and yours, though."

"How do you mean?"

"You don't attack an enemy when their fists are balled and their blood is up," Poole said. "You hit them before they know they're in a fight. If every duchy is ready to dig in and bite, there's a good chance the dukes bluster at each other for a bit and let the whole thing wind down. No one wants to lose. Makes it a hell of a gamble to step into the fight first. That's what happened when the eastern duchies started making noise about secession. Whole lot of thunder, not a lot of lightning."

He straightened up. "I'm not going to tell you not to worry. Not much point to it. But if you'll take a bit of advice from an old soldier?" She nodded, and he said, "Do your job. Whatever happens next, it's out of your hands. Most likely, your brothers will drill until they spill their lunch on their boots, spend a few weeks sleeping on the ground, and then get a letter telling them to get their asses home."

"I hope you're right."

"I'm always right. Thought I was wrong once, but that was a mistake." Before Jaina could point out what he'd just said, Poole said, "Hard part's going to be what comes after. Once your brothers are home safe, and you've got nothing left to worry about except for the rest of your life paying for something that's already happened. Hope you're coming to terms with that, because that day's coming."

After which you get to grow slowly more and more bitter at us for the rest of our lives. Jak scowled. *It's not a fair trade.*

That's not true.

I hope you're right.

"Thank you, Captain," she said.

He started to walk away, then paused, turning back. "Offer you one more piece of advice?"

Jaina nodded. "Of course."

"Don't trust the DeLuca woman," he said. The warmth had vanished from his voice, and his words were hard as the granite slabs of the castle. "Dealing with Vetticcians is always dicey. They'll shake your hand with their right while hiding a dagger with their left. That goes double for the families. Never trust anyone who's got enough money and power to stay far away from consequence. People like that will never see the world like you and I do. Far as they're concerned, we're nothing more than pieces on a game board." He gestured back in the general direction of the throne room. "She's young and pretty and says all the right things. But I promise you, she didn't come up here just to carve a few flowers on a wall. Your job is to keep her safe. Do that, and nothing more. Get her back to that cesspool she comes from, and bring your brothers home. You get me?"

Jaina nodded, but found herself struggling to reconcile the captain's words with the woman she'd met earlier. *Maybe. Maybe not. You just met her too, Captain.* "I get you."

Poole considered her for a long few seconds, then nodded. "Hope so." The soldier turned and left.

***

Less than an hour had passed since Jaina had left the throne room, but when she came back, she came to a halt almost as soon as she walked through the door. "Gods," she said, louder than she had thought.

Antoinette had divided the wall into ten sections, five on each side. She was currently crouching next to the third section, intently focused as the graphite in her fingers darted over the wood. Jaina could see two discarded graphite pencils that had broken or grown too short to handle tossed aside on the ground.

When she had left, the only markings on the first panel had been rough shapes. Those shapes remained, but layered atop them were more and more details, revealing the beginning of a garden. Lilies and blue ferns clustered before willows, and while the only markings on the wall were graphite, Jaina could see the way the light filtered through the drooping branches, shadows dappled over the details.

She stepped closer, eyes darting over the sketches, finding more and more detail with each passing moment. Jaina was still absorbed in the sketch when Antoinette spoke.

"I didn't mean to upset you. Earlier, I mean."

Jaina turned, and Antoinette had stood up. Her fingers were stained black from the graphite, and a strand of her hair had fallen free and curled across her forehead. Her expression was difficult to read. Jaina shook her head. "You didn't, I promise." Before Antoinette could say anything else, she pointed at the sketches. "These are astonishing."

"Those?" Antoinette shook her head. "They're just guide sketches. I'll use them when I begin carving. Usually no one sees this part."

"I'm glad I did." Jaina shook her head. "I've never seen anything like them."

"Hopefully, no one has," Antoinette said. She walked over to the trunk, and pulled out a linen cloth, wiping the graphite from her hands. "I'm hoping to earn another leaf."

"A leaf?"

Antoinette nodded, and pushed up her right sleeve. A delicate vine was tattooed around her wrist, with a tendril climbing up her arm. About three inches above her wrist, an ivy leaf hung from the branch, struck through with colors that could never be found in nature. "We get the vine tattooed when we're accepted into the College of Artisans. When one of our works is accepted by the College as a masterwork, we add another leaf."

Jaina nodded slowly. "We have something similar." Pushing up her sleeve, she showed the solid band tattooed around her forearm. "Nowhere near as beautiful, though."

Antoinette's eyes widened. "You have a mastery ring!"

"Just the one," Jaina said, pushing her sleeve down. She was surprised how self-conscious she felt.

"What's your trade?"

"Smithing. Smithing was my trade before I joined the rangers." Before Antoinette could ask another question, she pointed at Antoinette's wrist. "How old were you when you got it?"

"The vine? I was thirteen. My first leaf took four years, though."

"Thirteen..." Jaina shook her head. "You were accepted to the College when you were thirteen? And wait, your first leaf? How many do you have?"

"I'm hoping this will be my fifth."

Jaina stared at her for a moment. "I have to be honest, I don't really know how to respond to that."

Antoinette frowned. "What do you mean?"

"You're a genius. An actual genius," Jaina said. "I've never met a genius before. My instinct is to compliment your work, but I'm going to guess that you've heard that more than a few times."

Antoinette tilted her head. "Not from you, I haven't."

Jaina's mouth went slightly dry. "Oh." She glanced back at the sketches on the walls, and said, "I don't know art. Not much of it in Lofland Fork, unless you count the boar heads my dad put up on the wall of the dining room." She looked back at Antoinette. "But that's beautiful."

Antoinette smiled. It was as if the sunlight dappling those graphite flowers had burst through and lit up every inch of this room, and Jaina felt as light-headed as she had waking up next to that fire. "Thank you, Jaina. I'm excited to show you the final result."

"Me too." Jaina glanced at the wall again, hoping the flush she felt in her cheeks wasn't visible. "But if I'm honest, I think this is what will stick with me. It's a bit sad that it will go away."

Antoinette shrugged. "Art is creation and destruction, over and over again, until you can't find anything else to change. It's all part of a process."

"I suppose," Jaina said. "But I still think it's beautiful."

2,379 Hours

S leep didn't want to come for Antoinette. The first night, she had worked very hard not to let anyone see how much the travel had impacted her, and she had fallen asleep as soon as her head hit the pillow. Tonight was more difficult.

She's talking to me, but not about the rangers. Not about anything valuable. The torchlight outside threw glittering patterns onto the ceiling, the clouded glass adding a haze to the lights she stared up at. *But she is talking. More than she should.*

Antoinette tried a breathing technique she'd been taught as a child, something to slow her heart rate and help her find the sleep that was eluding her. Unfortunately, this technique required that her mind be clear and still, but her mind kept returning to the puzzle that was Jaina Creighton, again and again.

Finally, she sat up, running her fingers through her hair. Antoinette glanced through the window, trying to gauge what time it was, but this room was absent any water clocks, and the windows made it impossible to see the position of the moon or stars. It was dark, though, and quiet.

She glanced at the door at the sound of boots on stone. There was no knock, but as she listened, she heard the door across the hall creak shut.

Maybe it's time for a little push.

She quickly dressed, putting on a simple dress and bundling her hair up behind her head. Pulling on her slippers, Antoinette gathered up a thick sketchpad and several charcoal pencils, and eased the door open. She'd taken less than a step out into the hallway.

"Can't sleep?"

Antoinette clutched the pad to her chest, whirling to face Jaina, who was sitting on the windowsill at the end of the hall, hoping her expression of surprise looked natural. "Gods. I thought... You nearly made me jump out of my skin."

"Sorry." Jaina unfolded her legs and hopped down. "I didn't mean to startle you."

"What are you doing awake?"

"I could ask the same about you," Jaina said, glancing through the open door. "Is everything all right?"

Antoinette nodded. "I sometimes have trouble sleeping the first few days away from home. Thought I would take a walk. One of the chambermaids told me about a lovely view, at the top of the north tower. I thought I'd take a look."

"At this hour?" Jaina frowned. "It's going to be pitch dark."

"The sun will be up in a few hours." Antoinette held up the sketchpad. "No artist worth their pencil will ever miss the chance to see a good sunrise."

Jaina didn't look convinced. "I don't know that it's such a good idea for you to be wandering the castle at night."

"Are you telling me I can't go?" Antoinette arched her eyebrow.

"No, I just..."

"Listen, if you're that concerned about it, come with me," Antoinette said. Before Jaina could respond, she turned and began walking down the dark hallway. Moments later, Jaina fell in beside her.

"I still feel like this is a bad idea."

Antoinette shrugged. "Sometimes bad ideas lead to the best moments. I'm an artist. The whole job is to preserve those moments."

"Thought the job was the throne room."

"If you're only doing one job, you're not doing enough."

It took them a few wrong turns before they found the parapet staircase, a narrow spiral wrapped around a thick central column. Antoinette took the first few steps up, but came to a halt as she stared up into the pitch black stairs. "This could be a problem."

Jaina came to a stop next to her. "It's almost like we're not supposed to go up there at this hour."

"It's not locked behind a door," Antoinette said. "We'll just go slowly."

"I'm not letting you break your leg because you wanted to see a sunrise."

Antoinette turned, raising an eyebrow at her. "You're going to stop me? Not sure that's in your job purview."

Jaina scowled. "I didn't..." Sighing, she said, "Just wait here."

Before Antoinette could respond, Jaina melted into the darkness, her steps echoing down the stairs as she ascended. Antoinette leaned forward, and heard the light clinking of glass and a scratching sound. Moments later, flickering orange light spilled down the stairway, and Jaina's head poked back around the center column. "Okay. I can light the lamps as needed. We can go."

The parapet was tall. Four separate times as they ascended, the light from the last lamp faded behind them and they found themselves in darkness again. Each time, Jaina would vanish into the dark, and moments later, the next lamp would flicker into life. By the time they reached the top, Antoinette was puffing, her heart beating quickly in her chest, her legs burning from the climb. She glanced at Jaina as the ranger opened the door at the top of the stairs for her, who seemed unaffected.

They stepped through the door. The balcony on the parapet wasn't large. Two strides brought Jaina to the railing at the edge. As she peered over the edge nervously, Antoinette glanced back at the door. The latch was a simple mechanism, with a small pin inserted to keep it from locking. Antoinette had seen the type before, and a faint smile crossed her face.

"This is really high." Jaina was still staring out over the edge as Antoinette plucked the pin out of the mechanism. As she came over to stand next to Jaina, the door slowly shut with a definitive click. Jaina spun, eyes widening. "Did that door just lock?"

"It was unlocked when we found it," Antoinette said. "I'm sure it's fine."

Jaina stepped over and tried the handle. The door didn't budge. "I think it's locked." She jiggled the handle several times, her expression darkening. "Definitely locked. Why did it lock behind us?"

"Maybe you can only open it from the inside?"

"Godsdammit." Jaina winced, glancing back at Antoinette. "Sorry."

"For what?"

"I'm fairly sure I'm not supposed to curse around you."

Antoinette smiled. "I'm fairly sure that if I spent three days and three nights researching in the College Library, I could not possibly find something that bothered me less."

Jaina turned to face her. "You don't seem worried. Are you not worried?"

Antoinette shrugged. "There are guards that patrol this castle. I'm sure someone will be up to check this door soon. Besides, once they see that the lamps are lit, they'll figure it out."

"I suppose." Jaina stepped back to the railing, and looked out over Westcott. The city was dark, but dozens of tiny dots of light flickered throughout, dotting paths for the streets and shops.

"Speaking of the lamps." Antoinette came over to stand beside her. "You can see in the dark?"

"Oh. I mean, they did show me around the castle before you got here. Maybe I just have a really good memory for... lamp placement."

Antoinette shook her head, smiling. "Yes, I've heard of lamp savants with your gifts. It must have been difficult growing up with such an awe-inspiring talent for remembering where the lights are."

"Thankfully, I had my family to keep me grounded." Jaina nodded out over the city. "Not much to see."

"I'm willing to bet that you can see a bit more than I can."

"I suppose it's possible."

"Besides, look." Antoinette tilted her head up to the sky. The moon was huge and bright overhead, nearly full, spilling silvery light down upon them, and countless stars glittered in the black sky. "You have lovely skies up here. I would have been sorry to miss this."

Jaina looked up at the sky. "You don't have stars in Vetticci? That seems horrible."

"We have stars. And every once in a while, the smoke from the canneries and forges and factories and cook fires and chimneys clears up enough that I can see one or two of them."

"You're taking some of the romance out of Vetticci, you know." Jaina stepped forward and tried the handle again.

"Did it unlock itself while we were talking?"

"It did!"

Antoinette looked at Jaina. "Wait, really?"

"No." Jaina scowled at the door.

"You're a ranger. Can't you break it down?"

Jaina rapped her fingers on the wood. "This is solid oak."

"So that's a no?"

"That's a 'this is an expensive door, and I'm pretty sure demolishing entire sections of the ducal palace isn't in my job description'."

Antoinette smiled. "So you could break it down."

"Maybe. But unless you're in actual danger, I suspect our hosts would prefer that I didn't."

"So we wait. I have enough moonlight to sketch, and the sun will be up soon." Antoinette walked over to the railing. She set the sketch board on the rough iron of the rail and began to draw, eyes glancing up to take in the faint details of the sleeping city far below. "May I ask you a question?"

"Does it have to do with whether seeing the woman I'm supposed to be protecting leaning on a railing over a several hundred foot drop makes me nervous?"

"Nope."

Jaina sighed. "Sure."

"Where are you going after this job is done? Once you've successfully held the rampaging horde at bay and seen me safely back to civilization?"

"Rampaging horde?"

"Ethan seems as if he could do some rampaging."

"The kitchen boy? The one who brings the meals?" Jaina asked. "The seven-year-old?"

"Full of menace, his eyes. And did you see how he brandished that pepper mill?"

"He definitely seems the type, but I'm fairly sure I can hold him back."

"Your valor will be remembered forever," Antoinette said. "But once you've defeated the sixty-pound child in single combat, what does your future hold?"

"I'll go wherever the rangers send me, I suppose," Jaina said. "Most likely walking some part of the Dominion that doesn't have a sheriff or a town militia. Watch over the people there."

"Alone?"

"I mean, there will be people there. I'm allowed to talk to them."

"No, I mean will there be another ranger with you?"

Jaina shook her head. "Not enough rangers for that. I'll be alone."

Not an exact number, but their numbers are low. On the page, the pencil twitched, leaving a slight variation in the line. It had taken nearly three years of practice before she could add the code markers into her sketches without it disrupting her process. Now, it was as easy as breathing, and the variation was joined by several other minuscule points. "You're lucky," Antoinette said.

Jaina lifted an eyebrow. "Am I?"

Antoinette nodded. "Solitude is probably the most sought-after luxury in Vetticci."

"From what I've heard, your family is not lacking in luxuries," Jaina said, and immediately looked abashed. "That came out wrong."

"It's all right," Antoinette said. "You're right, my family is... comfortable."

Jaina chuckled. "Comfortable. I've never been to Vetticci. Neither have either of my parents. But even we've heard the name DeLuca. Your family is rich, richer than anyone north of the Myre will ever be."

"Well, yes, we have wealth," Antoinette said. "I'm much more fortunate than most in that regard." Her pencil paused as she looked over at Jaina. "Did you ever play outside as a child? By yourself, I mean."

Jaina nodded. "Sure. Usually with my brothers, but sometimes I'd see what kind of trouble I could get into."

"Ever do something to upset your parents?"

"More times than I can count," Jaina said. "Still am."

Interesting. Antoinette filed that away, and said, "That's the luxury I'm talking about. To do what you want, when you want. To be alone with your thoughts." She stopped sketching for a moment, and turned to face Jaina. "I've had people around me since I can remember. Telling me what every moment of my day will be. What I eat, when I sleep, what I study, what I wear. Every moment of my life has been planned out like a war campaign. This assignment is the first time I haven't had family guards and aides surrounding me."

Antoinette nodded down at the sketch pad. "I know you didn't want to come up here. But moments like this, they're the only time I get to make something that I haven't been tasked with making. Where I get to make something entirely for myself." *Not entirely true, though, is it?* Every one of these sketches would go to Andreas, who would pick out the tiny messages hidden within. "Moments like this, when things are quiet? When I get to be alone? They don't come along that often."

"Being lonely can be hard," Jaina said.

"Never getting to be lonely is harder," Antoinette replied. "Yes, my family is wealthy. But growing up like that comes with its own restraints, its own limitations. Even here, even now, I don't have a choice. I'll never have a choice." She fell silent, realizing that she hadn't meant to say quite so much. *She's easy to talk to. Maybe a bit too easy.*

Uncertain what else to say, Antoinette returned to her sketch. Jaina didn't say anything for a while. Antoinette could see the indecision on her face, and stayed silent, the only sound the pencil dancing over the smooth paper of the sketch pad. *Don't force it. Let her come to you.*

Finally, Jaina spoke. "The ranger thing. It's for life."

"Pardon?"

"When you join the rangers, it's a lifelong oath. I can't leave. Can't go back to the forge, or work in my family's inn. As soon as I woke from the ritual, my life was set."

Antoinette stopped sketching, and nodded. "I'd heard rangers served for life, I think. It must have been a hard decision to make."

"It should have been," Jaina said. She shook her head. "I don't regret joining. I know why I did it, and it was the right reason. But I can understand the way it feels not to have a choice. There is a difference, though."

"What's that?"

"When I leave this place, I won't leave anything like this behind." Jaina nodded at the sketchbook. A stylized rendition of the silhouetted buildings and walls of Westcott had burst into life. "What you can do... I've never seen the like. And I promise you, the countless people who set foot in that throne room once you're gone will know without a doubt that you were here. You create something everlasting. Beautiful."

Antoinette smiled. "You're very kind."

"No, I'm just not blind. Between a pair of functioning eyeballs and the ability to hold the rampaging hordes at bay, I don't know what you'd do without me." Jaina smiled.

It was the first genuine smile that Antoinette had seen on this woman's face since they had met, and it transformed Jaina's face. The moonlight glinted from her eyes, and while it was most likely only moments between when the ranger smiled at her and when Antoinette collected herself enough to speak, it felt like hours. She felt her cheeks heat, and swallowed. "I'll begin drawing up the orders for your commemorative statue to be drawn up immediately."

"Now that I know how good you are, I'm going to insist that you be the one to sculpt it."

Antoinette laughed. "I'd be honored. But my grandmother handles the contracts, and she charges quite a bit for my services."

"No price is too high."

"The duke is paying half a million ducats."

"I would like to immediately and enthusiastically retract my previous statement."

"I thought you might."

"Well, maybe a tiny statue," Jaina amended. "Something you can put in your pocket."

"Mine? I thought this was your statue," Antoinette said.

"I mean, I know what I look like. And this way you'll have something to remember me by."

"I can promise you, that won't be difficult." The words were out before Antoinette could stop them. *Why did you say that?* The flush bloomed in Jaina's cheeks and the smile spread across her face once more. *Oh. That's why.*

Antoinette looked back down at her sketch.

Well.

This is a problem.

2,117 Hours

I t had taken another hour before a confused guard had discovered the lit lamps and locked door. When he did, he found Jaina and Antoinette deep in conversation. In the weeks since that day, Jaina had made some effort to keep a gap of professional distance between herself and her charge. She was also increasingly aware of how miserable a job she was doing at just that. Antoinette was kind, funny, and easy to talk to, and more and more, Jaina found herself stepping out of the role of bodyguard and just trying to find ways to make her smile.

Even when it's actively burning your hands.

When she was very young, Jak had told Jaina that rangers were impervious to pain. As she tried to find the best grip on the steaming mug of tea she held in her hands, she chuckled softly to herself, muttering, "Wrong about that one, weren't you, Jak?"

Maybe other rangers are just tougher than you, Cricket, he said. *What in the gods is happening with your hair?*

Jaina's hand reflexively went to the top of her head. *Shut up.*

How many times? How many times did ma beg you to brush your hair, to detangle that weasel nest you carried around with you? Turns out we just needed to bring a pretty artist from Vetticci around and you'd be up with the latest styles.

She could practically hear him grinning at her. *Hair done. Clean clothes. And you brought her tea. Smitten is a new look for you, Cricket. I think I like it.*

Before she could reply, the door opened, and Antoinette stepped out. She saw Jaina waiting, and smiled. "Good morning." Her eyes fell to the steaming cup of tea, and she said, "Did the kitchen send that up?"

Go ahead, tell her you brewed it yourself.

"I, uh, I went and got it for you. Wasn't sleeping anyway. Thought it'd help start your day," Jaina said, wincing internally at the way she tripped over her words. She held out the mug, the handle facing Antoinete.

"How are you not burning your hands?" Antoinette said, carefully taking the mug.

"I'm a ranger, remember? It's not as bad."

Gods, you're a terrible liar.

Shut up. "Shall we?" Jaina asked, gesturing down the hall. Antoinette nodded, and they headed towards the throne room.

"So what are the rules about me getting some time away from this place?" Antoinette blew on her mug, carrying it carefully as they walked.

"Away from where? The palace?"

"It's not that this place doesn't have its charms," Antoinette said. "But it's been two weeks, and I'm beginning to forget what the sky looks like."

"Big, blue. Lousy with birds," Jaina said. "Not sure it'd be your thing."

Antoinette smiled through the steam. "I'm willing to take the chance. Besides, I need to get my carving tools honed. And a new kiff."

"You didn't bring a kiff?" Jaina said in disbelief, holding the throne room door open for her. "I thought you were a professional. How could you not bring a kiff? You won't be able to do a thing without a good, flaky, well-seasoned kiff."

"Jaina?"

"Yes?"

"Do you know what a kiff is?"

Jaina nodded. "I think it's definitely a type of pastry."

Antoinette patted her on the arm. "Maybe stick to rangering."

"That's not a word."

"And a kiff isn't a pastry." Antoinette crouched down next to her tool chest, and pulled out a slender piece of blackened steel, about half an inch wide and four inches long, handing it to Jaina. The end came to a hooked point, but the tip was snapped off. "It's a marking knife. Mine broke on the way up here. I'm just hoping to find someone who can make one that'll work for me."

Jaina inspected it. "This is a terrible pastry."

"Well, you're not wrong."

"Can you work without it?"

"I can, but it's one of my favorite tools. Having a new one will make things easier."

Jaina nodded. "I'll speak with Poole, but I think we can take a walk through town tomorrow. I know they have a trade district. I'm sure we can find something that will work for you."

Antoinette selected a few other carving tools, and went to the first section of the wall. Jaina watched as she sat on the ground, tucking her skirt beneath her and shifting position until she was comfortable. The wood paneling was now covered in detailed, complex sketches, small scribbled notes in different places. She ran her fingers over the wood slowly and carefully, focused. Finally, she picked up a sharp blade and pulled it over the surface, a tiny strip of oak curling up and falling to the floor. Antoinette picked it up, and said, "If you don't mind. On the top shelf of the chest, there's a small empty glass vial."

The tools and supplies were carefully organized. It took Jaina no time at all to spot the vial. She brought it over. "What's this for?"

Antoinette dropped the curl of wood in the vial. "Old tradition. One of my teachers taught it to me. Once you put blade to wood, there's no going back. You can never return to the pristine blank space," she said. "I used to be terrified to get started, knowing that. Master Tellour told me to embrace the fear, remember the moment that I took a breath and made the first cut."

"Does it make it any less frightening?"

Antoinette reached up and pushed a curl back from her forehead. "Not yet." She bent her head, and began to work.

The room fell silent, other than the occasional crackle of flame from an oil lantern and the low hiss of the blade biting into the oak. Jaina had seen Antoinette work enough now to appreciate the way she fell into a kind of trance, her breathing slow and even, every bit of her focus zeroed in on the work in front of her. Jaina watched her for a long while.

Watched her. Not her work, her brother pointed out.

She gave her head a brief shake. *I'm doing my job.*

Jak snorted. *Oh, sure. That's why you're checking the doors, watching the exits, doing all the things that a guard does when they're, you know, guarding someone. Face it. You can't stop watching her.*

I'm supposed to be a ranger, remember? I can multitask.

Oh, well excuse me, warrior of the wilds. Here I thought you were just falling ass over eyebrows for the worst possible person to fall for at the worst possible time to fall for them. She could see his grin. *Seriously, you really do make the worst decisions. Someone should study you. They could write a book. Get accepted into one of those colleges down in your sweetheart's hometown.*

Jaina's jaw worked. *I swear to the gods, if you were here...*

Well I'm not. Isn't that why you took your little swamp nap? Another top notch decision, by the way. Drinking weird tea brewed by a strange bald monk. That can be chapter four in your book. Also, you never denied it.

"You can talk, by the way." Jaina blinked, pulled from her reverie by Antoinette's words. She hadn't looked back or paused in her carving, but she said, "It can't be that entertaining, sitting there and watching me do very slow work."

"I didn't want to throw you off."

Antoinette chuckled. "Most of my clients don't leave me alone to do my work. They all want to talk, all want to ask questions about my grandmother and the family, gossip about the scandal of the week. I learned to work while talking a long time ago."

"I mean, just because you can, doesn't mean that you like to."

Antoinette glanced back over her shoulder. "I like talking to you."

Oh, you're done, Jak chuckled.

Jaina held no illusions as to whether or not the flush that heated her cheeks was visible. "I..." She swallowed. "I like talking to you too."

Antoinette smiled. "So tell me something." She turned back to her work. "Tell me about growing up in an inn."

Jaina shrugged, instantly realizing Antoinette couldn't see the motion. "It was good, I suppose. Comfortable. The Oak's Shade is the biggest in Lofland Fork. Probably not as big as the ones in Vetticci."

"You'd be surprised. Not much room in Vetticci for buildings of that size. Only people who can afford them are the families, and they're not building inns."

"Oh. Well, it had twenty guest rooms. Most of them were usually full, so there was always work to be done," Jaina said. "I always volunteered to clean them."

Antoinette glanced back, making a face. "Why would you volunteer to clean?"

"If I wasn't cleaning, my parents either put me to work in the kitchen or in the dining hall. Cleaning happens mostly at my own pace. But the kitchen is hot and fast, and the dining hall is loud and fast," Jaina said. "I always did better working at my own speed."

That's a really interesting way of saying slow.

Shut up, Jak.

"So you cleaned most of the time?"

"Not really," Jaina said, grinning. "I said I volunteered. Most of the time, my parents put me in the kitchens anyway."

"Really? Does that mean you're a master chef? Are gourmet meals part of your duties as ranger?"

Jaina snorted. "I'm fairly sure me cooking for you would be considered an act of war. No, I washed dishes, or cleaned. Any task that wouldn't involve me preparing anything someone would put in their mouth."

Antoinette paused in her carving, and turned to face Jaina. "Do you miss it?"

"Working in the kitchens? I haven't done it in a long time." A memory swam up, crouched over a tub of soapy water as her brothers brought out armfuls of tankards, dumping them in and splashing her. Jaina could remember her outraged squawk and their giggles as she splashed them back. "I guess I do. I always smelled like the soap my parents got. It would make my hands red and cracked, so my mother would use this ointment on them. It smelled like lavender, like she always smelled. I used to complain, but I liked it." Jaina realized

Antoinette was watching her, and cleared her throat. "Sorry. I'm rambling."

"Don't apologize." Antoinette tilted her head as she smiled.

"Do you have brothers or sisters?"

Antoinette nodded. "I have two brothers. Lorenzo and Mattia. I'm the middle child."

Jaina grinned. "I think I'd at least prefer that to two older brothers. Do you get to give them as much grief as my brothers give me?"

How dare you. We're a delight.

Antoinette's smile faded. "No, I don't…" She paused for a moment. "I don't really know my brothers all that well."

Jaina frowned. "How far apart in age are the three of you?"

"Two and three years." Antoinette fiddled with the carving knife in her hand. "We had expectations. All of us. But theirs were different from mine. Lorenzo's my older brother. He manages our family's shipping and fishing interests. Mattia… Mattia has his own training. But I was always busy, studying with grandmother or one of my tutors. And once it was decided that I would be an artist, I was rarely home. I spent most of my time at the College or on residencies."

"Oh." Jaina didn't know what to say. "Maybe when you're older, you can get to know them better?"

Antoinette's face was unreadable. "Maybe."

"May I ask you something?"

"Of course."

Jaina paused, briefly debating if it was okay to ask this, but decided to risk it. "You talk about your grandmother a lot. But…"

"I don't mention my parents." Antoinette nodded. "My parents are gone. My mother died when giving birth to my younger brother. My father passed during a grey fever outbreak a year later."

"I'm so sorry."

"It was a long time ago. I don't remember much about them. My grandmother raised me."

"What's she like? Your grandmother, I mean."

Antoinette considered this for a long few moments. Finally, she said, "She's Toni DeLuca. I don't really know what else to say." She nodded back to the wall. "I should..."

"Of course." Jaina fell silent as Antoinette returned to her work.

***

It was cool enough outside that Antoinette had ducked back inside to get a cloak, rich wool the color of a stormy sky. She fastened it around her shoulders as she glanced around, feeling the autumn wind slip between buildings to blow through her hair. There weren't many trees inside the city of Westcott. The roads were paved with cobblestones, and most of the greenery had been torn up when the city was created. But the few trees that remained were already scattering golden leaves on the cobbles to be crunched beneath their feet.

It had taken a few days to arrange this trip. Poole had not been thrilled with the idea, and reminded Jaina several times that he didn't have enough men to send a detachment of guards to escort them. Finally, Jaina had pointed out that Antoinette was not a prisoner, and that they really had no control whether she left the castle or not, and Poole had reluctantly dispatched two guards to come with them. One was well into his sixties, the other missing several fingers on his left hand.

"Name is Meyers, milady," the older guard said, offering Antoinette a bow. "Young pup here is Boyajian. We'll be keeping the two of you company this fine day."

Antoinette dipped her head. "I appreciate your company, gentleman, but I'm certain our ranger friend here will be more than sufficient. I assume you have other duties."

"Begging your pardon, milady, but the captain felt different, and while I don't wish to offend, he pays our coin," Meyers said, grinning. A scar traced a path from his right cheekbone down through his lips. The effect was somewhat disconcerting. "Won't even know we're here. Practically invisible, we are. Ain't that right, Boyajian?"

Boyajian blinked.

"He's a quiet one, on account of being mute and all, but take my word, milady, that was the most enthusiastic assent you'll be seeing today."

Jaina and Antoinette looked at Boyajian, who blinked again.

"See what I mean?" Meyers said cheerfully. "Now where would milady care to visit today?"

"I need to see a smith," Antoinette said. "And if there's a vendecolori, that would be welcome as well."

Jaina frowned. "What's a vendewhatzit?"

"A vendecolori? A colorman?" Antoinette looked back and forth between the blank expressions on Meyers and Jaina's faces, and sighed. "I need ink."

Boyajian blinked again, and Meyers snapped, "You did not know what she meant." He turned back to the pair. "Boyajian thinks the apothecary would be the best bet for that, milady."

"He does?" Jaina asked.

"Ayuh. He's a bit of a showoff sometimes. Don't let it offend," he said. "We'll take point. Just follow us, if you please."

Jaina fell in beside Antoinette as the two guards walked ahead about twenty feet. They couldn't make out what he was saying, but they could tell Meyers was chatting animatedly to his colleague. "I can't decide if Boyajian would be the best or worst conversation partner," Jaina said.

Antoinette giggled. "He seems to be a good fit for this pairing." She glanced over at Jaina. "Thank you for arranging this."

"Of course." Jaina felt a twinge of pain in her head, and did her best to keep it from her face. She was apparently unsuccessful.

"Are you all right?"

"I'm fine." Antoinette didn't look convinced. Jaina said, "I promise. Just a bit of a headache."

For weeks, the pair had lived in the castle, splitting their time mostly between the throne room and the residencies. Jaina really hadn't appreciated how quiet the castle had been. But stepping into the street was quickly becoming overwhelming. There were at least two dozen groups holding discussions, and Jaina could clearly hear each of them, her focus shifting from one to another. It was as if her brain couldn't decide where her attention needed to be, and the conflict was disorienting. "My hearing, it's..." Jaina swallowed. "It's a bit more sensitive since I became a ranger. I didn't realize how off-putting it would be to be around so many people."

"Do we need to go back? I can send a messenger to get what I need."

"No, thank you. I think I need to get accustomed to it. Just didn't realize how quiet it had been."

Antoinette didn't look convinced, but she nodded slowly. "If you're sure."

"I am." Jaina smiled at her. "Thank you for your concern, though."

"You're not wrong. I've worked a lot of jobs, but I've never had one that's this quiet," Antoinette said. "This is the palace in the capital, and the place is almost empty. My family's home is big, but it's not a castle, and we have thirty, forty staff on the grounds at any given time.

If we're hosting someone, even more. But I don't think I've seen more than a dozen guards and house staff since I've arrived."

Jaina shrugged. "The duke's away. I just figured he took most of his staff with him."

"Maybe. But look at this." She nodded at the street. The city of Westcott was arranged with two main streets intersecting at the palace, one of which they were walking through. These streets were the center of commerce for the city, shops lining both sides of the cobblestones. "It's early afternoon. Why isn't it more crowded?"

Jaina rubbed her temple. "Feels plenty crowded."

"You're overwhelmed. But take a moment, and look." Antoinette took her arm, and Jaina felt a shiver run up her bicep where Antoinette's fingers touched her skin.

Gods, Jak was right. You really are cooked.

Jaina scowled. *Shut up.*

She's talking to you, Cricket. Might want to pay attention.

"Sorry, what did you say?" Jaina tried to ignore the fluttering in her stomach.

"I would just expect there to be far more people than this. I've seen streets in Vetticci in the middle of the night with more crowds." Antoinette slid her arm through Jaina's. Jaina glanced down, and Antoinette said, "Is this all right? You are my escort, after all."

"No, it's fine."

I'll bet it is.

Jaina swallowed, and said, "Uh, Vetticci is a lot more crowded than any other city. I wouldn't think Westcott would have anything on it." She looked around, all the while being hyperaware of Antoinette's hand on her skin. To her surprise, it helped ground her, and the headache began to ebb. "You're right, though. It's a bit sparse."

Jaina had grown up near the Autumn Market in Lofland Fork, a public market that in stubborn defiance of its name remained open all year. She was used to the dull roar of merchants shouting the virtues of their wares to anyone who crossed their field of vision. The shops here were open, but few merchants stood outside, and while there were people on the streets, it was far from what anyone would call crowded. In addition...

Not a lot of men, are there?

Her eyes darted from person to person. She saw a woman with two children, each of them carrying baskets full of carrots and lettuce. She saw a group of kids, running and swerving around anyone in their path, shouting and giggling at each other. She saw a trio of women arguing over a blanket draped over a rack in a weaver's window. But the only men she saw were the two guards in front of them.

Antoinette squeezed her arm. "Hey. Are you all right?"

Before she could answer, Meyers interrupted. "I'm telling them, I'm telling them," he snapped at Boyajian. "No need to jump down my throat." He pointed at a red door. "Boyajian says this is the best apothecary on this block."

"Are there other apothecaries on this block?" Jaina asked.

"No, but this one doesn't require lots of walking, which in my mind, endorses their talents tremendously." He held up his hand when Antoinette began to walk to the door. "Begging milady's pardon, but Boyajian's going to go in first. Make sure there aren't any Suievian sea lions in there."

Antoinette raised an eyebrow. "Sea lions."

"Ayuh. They grow to the size of houses, I hear."

"They're also famously native to Suiviev," Antoinette said. "Which, if I recall, is about two thousand miles that way." She pointed north.

"Sneaky bastards, though. Never can tell." Boyajian came back out, and nodded. Meyers grinned. "See? Now you can peruse the paints and whatnot without fear of sea lion attack."

"Thank you, guardsman." Antoinette shook her head, and she and Jaina stepped through. Antoinette released her arm to step forward to speak to the woman behind the table, and Jaina felt a twinge of disappointment that she pushed aside. Antoinette and the apothecary spoke for a few minutes. Antoinette counted out some coins, handed them to the grateful woman, and came back to Jaina.

"That was fast," Jaina said. "You didn't buy anything."

"She doesn't have the ink I want in stock, but she knows how to make it," Antoinette said. "She's going to deliver it to the castle." She looked at Meyers. "A smith?"

"That I definitely can help milady with," Meyers said. "My nephew's apprenticed to the best smith in the Dominion."

Boyajian blinked.

"Well, the best in Westcott at least."

Boyajian blinked.

"Okay, the best on this street."

All three turned to look at Boyajian, who shrugged.

Jaina smelled the forge before she saw it, and moments after the scent of hot iron and sweat filled her nostrils, the steady ringing of steel on anvil brought memories of her life before rushing back. It wasn't so far away. Less than two months before, she had stood over the anvil, a piece of glowing steel gripped tightly in tongs, sweat on her brow as the familiar ache slowly bloomed in her arms from the tenth, fiftieth, thousandth swing of the hammer. It was hot, hard work. It was happy work. Less than two months had passed, but it felt like a lifetime.

She felt an odd pang of fear when she saw the open door of the forge. It wasn't the place she'd learned to shape metal, but it was close enough to remind her of all she'd given up. *Two months shouldn't be enough to wipe out that life I was supposed to have.*

No one took it from you. Joran's voice was mournful. *You did what you always did. You try to fix the world, even if it means burning your own in the process. And you don't wait. You rush, and you stumble, and your knees are bloody and your eyes wet, and the world is still broken. It'll always be broken, Cricket.*

The lump in her throat was choking her. *You're going to come home. I'm going to bring you home.*

You will. And what a cost you will have paid.

"Jaina?"

She blinked, and was horrified to feel the sting of tears. Jaina turned away, hand coming up to her eyes, clearing her throat and shaking her head sharply. "Sorry. The smoke. My eyes are sensitive."

Antoinette took her arm. "We can go."

"No." Jaina shook her head, wiping her eyes. "Just a bad moment." She offered a smile, knowing that it wouldn't fool a blind man. "Let's go."

The smith didn't turn when they walked in. He was an older man, past his sixties, his head bald and a long drooping mustache hanging far past his chin. He was intent on his work, hammer drumming out a rhythm that beat the steel into a wicked point. Only when he paused to hold the spearhead up to the light did he realize he was no longer alone. He turned. His eyes found Antoinette. Jaina expected a reaction, but he offered the slightest bow. He looked impossibly tired.

"Forgive me, miss. My ears haven't been what anyone would call good for a long time. Sixty winters in this world haven't helped. Master Evan Lee, at your service."

"Milady," Meyers corrected. Antoinette held up her hand.

"It's all right, guardsman." She smiled at the smith. "I didn't mean to interrupt. If you're busy, I can come back another time."

"Now or then, I'll be busy, milady. Don't really know any other way to be." He gestured towards the spearhead in his tongs. "I need to get this in the quench, and I can be right with you."

"May I?" Jaina asked. Lee raised an eyebrow, and she pulled up her sleeve, revealing the mastery ring tattooed on her forearms. "Jaina Creighton, at your service, sir. I studied under Master Georges in Lofland Fork."

"You apprenticed with Mikel?" He grunted, but handed her the tongs. "He's slow, but he knows his trade."

"He does, sir."

"Quench is back by the rack."

Jaina walked over, leaning the blackthorn staff against the wall, and lowered the still glowing steel into the barrel of oil. It hissed briefly, streams of bubbles pouring off the surface, flame bursting to life before sputtering out. It felt good. Natural. *I've spent the last few months feeling like a child playing at dress-up. This, I know how to do. I belong here. But that?* She glanced over at the staff. *I wear the clothes, but it's not me. I don't know if it'll ever be me.* She pushed the thought aside. As the hissing died down, she could hear Antoinette speaking to the smith.

By the time she returned, Lee was already shaking his head. "I truly wish I could help, milady. I do."

"If it's a question of payment..."

"Forgive me. I've no doubt you could pay. But I've an order from the duke. Not the kind I can put off." He nodded back at the quench. "That's the twentieth I've done today. I've sixty more to finish before the end of the week. And if the pattern holds, those that come to pick up this batch will have another order for me."

"This is apprentice work," Jaina said. "A master smith shouldn't be doing this."

He nodded slowly. "Ayuh, it's been more than a few years since I spent my time on spearheads. But my sons are my apprentices, all three of them. They got their markers last month. Now I'm alone, and the work hasn't changed. Truth be told, it's worse."

Antoinette frowned. "This is a big city. Surely you can find someone..."

"Look around, milady. They've taken everyone who can hold a bow." He shrugged. "Five years, and I'll have enough help to make you anything you need. Of course, I'm guessing you won't need it by then." He ran his hand over his shining scalp. "I'm truly sorry."

Antoinette shook her head. "Don't be. I hope your sons find their way home soon."

Meyers and Boyajian led them back to the castle. As they walked, Antoinette looped her arm through Jaina's again, but it was different this time, almost as if she was holding Jaina up. "Your brothers?" Her voice was low.

Jaina said nothing for a bit, but finally gave a short nod. "Two months ago. Both of them." She shook her head. "Not supposed to happen. They're only supposed to take one from each family. Service is mandatory, we knew they were going to have to go, but not both. Not at once."

Antoinette squeezed her arm. "That's hard. How long after you joined the rangers were they called up?"

"Not how it happened." Jaina saw a cluster of three young men step to the side as Meyers gently told them to stand aside. The three watched the pair pass. They looked impossibly tired, their faces dirty, their eyes blank. "After I found out what happened, I joined."

Antoinette stared at her. "But... why would you do that?"

"The families of rangers are exempted from military service. I join, finish my novice period, and they get to come home." Jaina realized what she'd just said, and closed her eyes for a moment. "Not sure I was supposed to tell you that."

Antoinette shook her head. "Jaina, you're my age. I didn't really think you were a veteran ranger. I don't care about that." She glanced back at the trio watching them walk past. "Why are they staring? Do I need to be worried?"

"Them?" Jaina shook her head. "They look like they haven't slept in days. Probably just hungry. And they're staring because you're beautiful."

The words had left her mouth before she could stop them. Everything seemed to stop. *What did I just say?*

She could practically see the grin on Jak's face. *What you've been wanting to say for a bit. About time, too.*

Antoinette smiled but said nothing. Jaina opened her mouth to apologize, but before she could, her amplified hearing caught Antoinette's heartbeat quicken, and the soft exhalation as the woman on her arm let loose a breath.

See? The world didn't end.

Her brothers were still gone. She was still far from home. But in this moment, in the cool evening air, Antoinette laid her dark hair on Jaina's shoulder, and everything was all right.

2,116 Hours

*P*rogress.

The scope of the conscription is so much larger than we thought. Irresponsibly large. They've taken tradesmen. We spoke to a smith today whose apprentices have been called up as bowmen. That conflicts with everything we've heard about the shortage of skilled tradesmen in the Dominion. And the shortages are plain. Westcott feels hollowed out. The people are walking around as if in shock.

It won't take long before the lack of skilled workers begins to cause real pain for this country. That means one of two things. Either the dukes really are so shortsighted that they'd gamble their country's future on this military buildup, or they believe it won't last long enough to have too much of an impact. I don't have enough insight into the thinking of the various dukes, but I've seen no sign of discord, heard no whispers of disagreement between them. If they're all in agreement, they must believe what they're doing to be valid.

The ranger...

Antoinette's pen stopped. She stared down at the page for long enough that a drop of the custom ink fell from the tip of the nib, splashing on the corner of the page. Muttering a curse, she dipped a linen cloth in a small vial of wood alcohol, dabbing up the expensive ink. Shaking her head, she dipped the nib and continued writing.

The ranger is confirmed to be a novice. She's here for her family, to take advantage of a benefit offered to rangers that will exempt her brothers from military service. Given the lifetime commitment, that's a significant sacrifice. May indicate she has a better idea of where these troops are headed. I will continue to develop our relationship and provide updates.

Antoinette felt a wild urge to tear the paper in half, again and again until it vanished into fragments small enough to disappear on the wind howling outside the window. The storms had arrived an hour before, rain lashing at the cloudy glass as if trying to break through. The walls of the castle were thick enough to muffle most of the sounds, but the rumbles of thunder were easily heard. She realized she was clenching her fist, and forced herself to relax.

She glanced back at the door, and swallowed. Taking a deep breath, Antoinette stood up. She didn't know what she was going to say to the ranger, but she knew she needed to say something. She opened the door, and froze, eyes widening in surprise.

"Everything okay, milady?" Meyers was leaned up against the far wall, a chunk of bread smeared with butter in his hand. His words were muffled around the bite he'd been chewing, and blanched when he realized, his hand coming up to cover his mouth. Antoinette glanced to the right. Boyajian was standing silently ten feet away, and he dipped his head in her direction. After swallowing, Meyers asked, "The storm bothering you? She's blowing, that's for sure."

"No, I..." Antoinette paused, and said, "I needed to ask the ranger a question."

"Ah. Sorry, milady. She stepped out. Asked us to keep an eye open. Something we can help you with?"

Antoinette shook her head. "Thank you, but no." She closed the door, and leaned forward, pressing her forehead against the wood as she muttered, "What in the gods are you doing?"

The only answer came from the wind and thunder outside. Letting out a long exhalation, Antoinette walked back to the desk, folded the letter, and sealed it in an envelope. Walking back to the door, she poked her head out. "Actually, there is something you can help me with." She handed Meyers the letter. "Could you see this reaches the next convoy bound for Vetticci?"

Meyers touched two fingers to his forehead. "One leaving in the morning, milady. I'll see it done."

"Thank you. Both of you."

Antoinette closed the door. She changed for bed, and laid down, trying to ignore the pit in her stomach. Antoinette had grown up listening to spring storms drum their staccato rhythm onto the roof of their estate, hearing the distant rumble of thunder. Usually storms helped her sleep. Tonight was different.

***

She didn't get much sleep. The storm died a few hours before the sun sent light dancing through the window, but Antoinette had tossed and turned most of the night. It took her a bit longer than usual to wake, but she stirred for the soft knock at the door that meant her tea was here. She wrapped a robe around her shoulders, and padded to the door, rubbing eyes she knew would be red from exhaustion.

When she opened it, her stomach sank to see Meyers still standing there. "Jaina..." She pressed her lips together, cursing the slip of the tongue. "The ranger still isn't back?"

If the guardsman caught the misspeak, he gave no indication. "Came back a few hours ago, but had to head right back out. Asked us to give you this along with your tea. We'll be your shadows today, milady." He held out a tray with a steaming mug, a small box, and a folded note.

"Thank you, Meyers. Have you both eaten?"

He nodded. "Kind of you to ask, milady. They sent food for us not long ago."

"Good. I'll be ready in an hour or so." He closed the door behind her as Antoinette carried the tray back in, setting it down on the small table next to the bed. She picked up the note.

Antoinette, forgive me for not being here this morning. Needed to follow up on a favor. I should be back by this evening. These two should be able to keep an eye on you.

Also, I told you I knew what a kiff was.

Jaina

The box was a simple pinewood box, seven inches long and two inches wide. Antoinette lifted the lid. Inside, nestled in some shredded straw, was a kiff. The steel was a deep blue, with ripples running through it like water, the end sharpened to a gleaming point. The handle was wrapped in leather, burnished to a sheen. Burned into the leather were the initials AD.

"Gods," Antoinette breathed, running her fingers over the tool. The steel was still shining with oil.

She sat for a long time, staring at the gift, trying to reconcile the dozen thoughts clamoring for attention in her mind. Finally, she put the kiff back in the box, replaced the lid, and got dressed. When she opened the door, smiling at Meyers and telling him she was ready, the box was still sitting on the table.

Antoinette worked as the two guards stood by the throne room entrance, listening to Meyers chatter on and on to his silent companion. She did her best to focus on what Meyers was saying, and every twenty minutes or so, a snippet would catch the part of her brain that had been trained since she was a girl.

Complaints about the lack of horses for the patrols that roamed the forests surrounding the city. *They need the horses elsewhere.*

The price of grains climbing. The price of fresh fruit dropping. *Demand for quickly perishable food is falling. Demand for easily stored food is climbing.*

The Confessors relinquishing ownership of the Vorchese Ranch. *Cicerone pulling back its influence in the Dominion.*

Each tidbit was like a puzzle piece. Until all the pieces were arranged on the table, and one could see how they clicked together to form a full picture, they meant nothing. Antoinette knew she wasn't responsible for seeing the picture. She was just one of countless people sending the pieces back to her grandmother. An image swam into her mind: Toni Deluca, in a dark room, illuminated as she towered above an impossibly large table, staring down as the picture became clear.

But she does need my pieces. She set down the tool, flexing her hand as she called out, "Meyers?"

He paused in the middle of a sentence about pickled pig feet, and walked quickly over to her. "Something I can do for you, milady? Need anything?"

"I'm fine, thank you," she said. "Just needed a break, and wanted to ask a question."

"You're in luck. They call me the Almanac of Westcott," he said.

"They do?" She couldn't see Boyajian's face, but she somehow knew exactly the expression she would find on his face.

"Well, they should, milady. Like a sponge for knowledge, I am."

"How fortunate," Antoinette said, trying her best not to roll her eyes. It took a great deal of effort. "What can you tell me about rangers?"

Meyers grinned. "Oh, I have a hundred and a hundred stories about the rangers."

"And I'm sure they're all worthy of inclusion in the Literary College stacks, but I'm more looking for facts," she said.

"Ah. Well, that's a bit trickier," he said. "There aren't many of them, and they aren't the chattiest sort. But of course, you know that. Been thick as thieves with one for more than a few weeks now, and I'm willing to bet an aggressively small amount of money that you're asking me because she's about as talkative as my colleague."

"Hence, why I'm speaking to the Almanac of Westcott."

"I told you it would catch on," Meyers shouted at Boyajian, who shook his head. Turning back to Antoinette, he said, "Most of what I know for sure is pretty common knowledge."

"To you, perhaps. But we don't have rangers in Vetticci," Antoinette said. "Anything you can tell me would be helpful."

He nodded. "Well, everyone pretty much agrees on a few things. They're stronger than they should be. Saw that with her carrying that trunk. I tried to lift it one day. Needed to lie down for six days and eight nights. Faster too, though I've not seen that myself. But I've heard people talk about seeing them run as fast as a horse at full gallop."

Antoinette raised an eyebrow. "You believe that?"

"I do. Man who told me not the type to tell tales," Meyers said. "Supposed to be able to go days, even weeks without sleep, walk for five hundred miles without a rest. I know they can see in the dark. Seen your companion walk these halls on a moonless night without a lantern."

Frowning, Antoinette said, "If it was that dark, how do you know it was her?"

"She's not exactly the stealthy type, milady. The house staff are asleep at that hour, and the few of us guards who are still here are all old hands at moving about all quiet-like. Could hear her thumping her way through the halls at an hour that should be illegal." He shrugged. "Past that is just stories. Some say they can turn into wolves. Given we haven't seen a wolf in this country since long before I was born, I find myself doubting that one."

Boyajian turned and blinked.

"No need to shout, I was just getting to that," Meyers said, glaring. He turned back to Antoinette. "Beggin' your pardon for the interruption, milady. No manners on that one. So, ah, rangers can heal."

"I don't follow. They can heal people who are sick?"

He shook his head. "No, they can heal from getting hurt. Cuts, bruises, all gone in days or hours, depending on who you ask. Not just new injuries, either." He looked uncomfortable for a moment, and fell silent.

"Meyers, I promise you, anything you tell me will stay between us."

"Just..." He shook his head. "I don't mean to eavesdrop, milady. But it was our job to keep an eye on you the other day. Heard bits and pieces of your discussion."

Well. I need to be a damn sight more careful. "It's all right. I've nothing to hide."

"Heard her say she trained as a smith, am I right?" Antoinette nodded, and he said, "You ever met a smith whose hands don't look like they stuck them in a bag of glass and loose nails? Burns, cuts, I think there's more blood in half our steel than anything else."

"It's a hard trade," Antoinette said. "I'd guess it'd be impossible to avoid."

"Ayuh, and that's a fact," Meyers said, nodding. "But you notice the hands on our ranger friend? Not a mark. No scars, no cuts, looks like she's never touched a tool in her life."

Not as simple as you seem, are you, Meyers? "I hadn't thought about it, but I think you're right."

"I'm always right, milady. It's why everyone loves me," he said. "Past that, anything else I could say is just guessing. Like I said, they're quiet. Show up when they're needed, move on when they don't. 'Less you find yourself on the wrong side of an angry ranger, you'd never know they were anything special. If you do find yourself on the wrong side of an angry ranger, well..." He shrugged. "Not likely that you'll know much of anything at all after that."

Antoinette tried to imagine her quiet companion angry. The picture wouldn't form. "So who's in charge of the rangers? The dukes?"

Meyers snorted. "Rangers are the only ones who don't have to pay the dukes any mind. They're independent."

"How is that possible?" Antoinette already knew the answer, but she wanted to keep Meyers talking. *Not that it's going to be difficult.*

He shrugged. "Part of the founding charter. Back when King Pavati wore the crown, before the dukes took over. He signed the charter, tasked them with walking the land and protecting his people. And he apparently made it clear as a spring lake that they did not owe fealty to the king, the dukes, anyone. Only thing the dukes do is sit in judgement if a ranger breaks their oath or a law. Past that, the rangers do what they were created to do. They walk the land. They protect people."

"I'm surprised the dukes are okay with that."

"Don't really think they are. But don't think they've that much of a choice. Half the stories told in the Dominion are about rangers. Children here grow up pretending to be rangers. The people love them.

The few times a duke has tried to lay down the law, tell the rangers which way to go, they just... leave," Meyers said. "And the people get really gods-damn salty. It's not worth the headache. Rangers don't interfere with the dukes, dukes do their best to ignore the rangers."

Antoinette nodded, considering Meyers. *Smart, thoughtful. A possibility.* "Do you mind if I ask you a personal question?"

"All right with me, milady. Appreciate you asking first."

"Why are you here?" she asked. "You're clearly good at your job. You know what you're doing. Seems like every man your age has gone off to serve in whatever's happening."

The smile that seemed a permanent resident of the guardsman's face disappeared, and his eyes fell. Quickly, Antoinette said, "I meant no offense, I promise. I'm not questioning your..."

"No, it's all right, milady." He chewed on his lip for a moment. "I, uh, I have a thing." He pressed his fingers against his belly. "Don't know what it's called. Duke Walshire was kind enough to have an anatomist sent from that big place down south. Can't remember the name."

"Pallia Clinic?"

"Ayuh, that's the one. She called it a mass." He shrugged. "Said a lot of other stuff that I didn't really follow. But if we're being honest about it all, only one thing she said I needed to follow."

"What's that?" Antoinette asked.

"Less than a year."

"Oh." She reached out and squeezed his arm. "I'm so very sorry."

"Don't be, milady. It doesn't pain me most days. Besides, I spent eight years serving the duke. Never got so much as a scratch. Knew I had to be cashing in all my good fortune early, so this makes sense. And Captain Poole's a good man. He asked what I needed, and I told him I just wanted to keep busy. Stay with my friend, be useful." Meyers smiled, and to her surprise, it wasn't forced. "I've got a bed to sleep in, and people to watch over. A man could do worse."

"Well." Antoinette didn't know what to say. "I'm glad you're here."

"Of course you are, milady. No finer guard south of the Breaking." He lowered his voice, and said, "And if you'll forgive me, milady, I do know one other thing about rangers you may want to keep in mind."

"What's that?"

"Their oath is for life. And a big part of that oath is that they'll take no spouse."

She kept her face even. "I believe I knew that."

"Thought it might be useful. Not that it's any business of mine." He shrugged. "You get a chance to find a bit of happiness, seems you ought to grab hold like your life depends on it."

Antoinette took a deep breath. "Thank you, Meyers."

"Milady." He touched two fingers to his head, and left her to return to her work.

2,098 Hours

It was late in the evening by the time Jaina returned to the castle. She saw that the lanterns were still lit in the throne room, proof that Antoinette had not finished her work for the day. She started to head towards the doors, but paused, looking down at her dirty hands.

Yeah, you're going to want to knock some of the sweat off of you first.

Not as much an issue, Jaina thought. *Seems a bit difficult for me to sweat.*

Jak snorted. *Sweaty or not, you still look like someone who just spent almost twenty-four solid hours working at a forge. Take a moment, clean up first.*

She sighed, but turned right, heading towards her quarters. Once she got inside, she had a chance to look in the mirror leaning up against the stone wall, and winced. Her clothes were covered in soot, and when she glanced down at her sleeves, several burn marks marked spots where errant sparks had landed. Quickly, she stripped out of her clothes. There wasn't a tub in the room, but there was a bucket of soapy water to wash her hands, and she dipped a cloth in and scrubbed herself as best she could, making note to arrange for a proper bath before the end of the day.

Fresh clothes made a world of difference, and she stepped out into the hallway as she heard Jak speak. *You going to tell her what you did?*

She knows what I did. I made her a kiff.

You also made the rest of that smith's order of spearheads. Worked for a full day, barely stopping to drink some water. Jak chuckled. *Real shame about the whole ranger thing. You'd be a devil in the kitchen now. Washing dishes for days on end with no breaks, a titan of domesticity.*

Shut up. Jaina headed down the hall. *She doesn't need to know about that.*

So you save the day for some poor soul, but don't tell the woman you're fluttering for what an amazing thing you did. If I worked for more than three hours straight, I'd be hiring a crier to tell everyone within fifty miles.

Oh, I know. You never shut up about helping dad install the new bartop.

Hey, that took almost a whole weekend. And you and Joran didn't help at all.

We were sixty miles away, picking up the cider order.

Still, could have picked up a hammer.

Jaina got to the door, and Boyajian looked up as she approached, touching two fingers to his forehead.

"Any issues?"

He shook his head.

"Thank you for covering. Meyers inside?" He nodded, and she opened the door and stepped through.

"... sixteen wagon loads of dead snakes. We had to get shovels to handle them. It was terrible," Meyers finished saying to Antoinette, whose practiced expression of polite kindness was clearly reaching its breaking point. He saw Jaina come in, and brightened up. "Ranger! Welcome back. We kept those sea lions at bay, we did."

"Your service will be the stuff of legends, I'm sure," Jaina said. "All quiet here?"

"Just doing my duty to provide hospitality and enrichment to our guest from the south."

"I appreciate you two keeping watch while I was unavailable. By my count, you two have been awake for nearly twenty hours. Go get some sleep."

Meyers frowned. "I hadn't finished the story."

Antoinette spoke up. "I'm very certain we'll have time to reach the thrilling conclusion later, Meyers. Please, go get some rest."

He gave her a short bow. "Milady." He headed out the door, Boyajian falling into step behind him.

Once the doors had closed, Jaina turned to Antoinette to find a scowl on her face. "I was a bit dismayed to find out my ranger companion had chosen to abandon me."

Jaina began to panic until she saw the crinkle at the corner of Antoinette's eye. She bowed deeply at the waist. "I have failed you. I will resign my position effective immediately and go walk into the sea." She turned towards the door, saying, "I think if I hurry, I can catch Meyers so he can finish his story…"

Antoinette's hand closed on her arm, pulling her back as the Vetticcian let a giggle slip through. "Don't you dare. Besides, rangers can't resign."

Jaina turned back. "I should have told you before I left."

"I was in good hands. Chatty hands, but good hands."

"Yeah, Boyajian really does go on and on."

"It's a bit much, honestly." Antoinette smiled at Jaina. "Thank you for the kiff. It's beautiful. A bit too beautiful, honestly. The rest of my tools will look a bit drab alongside them."

Jaina nodded. "It was my pleasure." She glanced down at the tools arrayed on the floor and frowned. "You're not using it?"

"You never use a gift until you've thanked the person who gave it properly. Is that not a custom here as well?"

Jaina shook her head. "If it is, I've never heard of it."

"Well, my family takes custom and propriety very seriously. And in that spirit..." She stood up on her tiptoes, and kissed Jaina on the cheek.

Jaina's heart was hammering so hard in her chest it seemed as if it would burst through, and the heat that rose in her cheeks was intense enough to erase any question of whether or not her blush was visible. But past her own pounding heart, she could hear the way Antoinette's heart was racing, and the way her breath caught in her chest as she pulled back, watching Jaina for her response.

Swallowing, Jaina said, "Custom and propriety, huh?"

"Well, custom." Antoinette reached up with her thumb and wiped her lipstick from Jaina's cheek. "I've always been bad at the latter."

Any words that might have been said were strangled in Jaina's throat. Antoinette grinned, and gestured to the wall. "I want to finish the section I'm on. I know you haven't slept much, but are you all right to spend a bit longer with me before we go to bed for the night?"

Well THAT was boldly phrased. Joran said. *Not much for subtlety, is she?*

That's not what she meant. I'm nowhere near the type of person she would... "I'm fine to stay as long as you like."

I love you, Cricket, but you're an idiot. She's clearly interested.

Antoinette nodded. Someone had brought a wooden box in for her to sit on. A blanket had been folded atop for her comfort. She sat down, and began her work. The petals of a rose had emerged from the wood, and as she sent more curls of wood tumbling to the floor, she said, "You told me you'd trained as a smith. I have to admit, I assumed you were talking about an apprenticeship or the like. But you're quite gifted. That kiff is genuinely beautiful."

"That's very kind, but it was fairly simple. I just wanted to be sure you had something that would last."

You going to tell her how many you scrapped before being satisfied?

"How long did you study?" Antoinette asked.

"My dad got me the apprenticeship on my twelfth birthday," Jaina said. "I'd already been helping Master Georges a bit. Sweeping up, bringing in stock bars and coal, that kind of thing. I'd told them I wanted to learn from him, but he's one of only four smiths in town, and the only one that was doing the kind of work I wanted to learn. I didn't think it would happen. Dad was so pleased when he told me."

"It's not easy. We have a lot more smiths in Vetticci, but we also have a lot more people. Even the families can struggle to get a child placed," Antoinette said, pausing to blow a piece of errant wood shaving free. "He wasn't upset that you didn't want to work in the inn?"

He cashed in every favor he had to get you placed there. Can't have been too much of a surprise that he wasn't happy about you giving it up.

"I think he knew my heart wasn't in it." Jaina stared down at the stone floor, the guilt thick in her stomach. "He's like that. He's got a temper, sometimes speaks before he thinks, but give him a bit, and he'll spend every minute he has finding a way to make us happy. When I made journeyman, he..." She cleared her throat, trying to move past the lump. "It was six months ago. He bought the lot next to the inn. Don't know where he got the money. Wasn't like we ever had all that much. Said he was going to spend the three years building me my own forge so he could come over and have me make him tankard handles anytime he wanted."

He was proud of you.

"He was proud of you," Antoinette said.

"Yeah." Jaina picked up one of the graphite pencils, fiddling with it. "They both were. I made them new rings for their anniversary a few years back. They showed everyone. I don't even think they were all that good, but it never mattered." She shook her head. "He was so upset when I told him what I'd done. Not just angry, but... sad. Sadder than I think I've ever seen him. Kept trying to figure out a way to fix it. Told me over and over that it wasn't too late to change my mind."

Antoinette looked back at her. "Did you ever consider it? Changing your mind, I mean."

"About a thousand times on the first day."

"Why didn't you?"

"I don't know." Jaina paused, and said, "That's not true. I know why. Once I heard about the rule for rangers, once I knew that the option was there, it was all I could think about. I saw my mom and dad's faces while they looked at Jak and Joran both holding those gods-damned markers. Saw the worry that had taken root in their heads, worry they were going to carry around with them for every minute of every day of every one of those five years. And then someone walked up to me and said that if I did something that most everyone I know thought was noble and worthwhile, I could pull that worry out of their heads and strangle it."

She raised her eyes, and could almost see her brothers standing silently, watching her, their faces impassive, each clutching that red marker. "And over and over again, I knew I could go back to that ranger. Tell him I was wrong, tell him I didn't know what I was agreeing to, and he would have been okay with it. He would have gotten on his horse and ridden away, and I would have spent five years waiting."

"For what? For them to come home?"

"For someone to walk into our home and tell my parents that if I'd just kept my word, if I'd just done this noble and worthwhile thing, their sons would be home with them right now, but since I didn't, one of them would never come home again," Jaina said, so quietly she didn't know if Antoinette could hear her. "And it would be my fault. They wouldn't say it, and maybe they wouldn't think of it most of the time, but every now and then my mother or father would lay in bed and wish they lived in a world where their daughter wasn't a coward, and their sons were home safe in their beds."

They wouldn't have thought that, Cricket.

Jaina swallowed. *You sure about that? Not once?*

"You made a choice," Antoinette said. The woman was blurry through the tears Jaina had to wipe away.

"I did." Jaina nodded. "I can live with my mom and dad being disappointed in me for however long they are. I can't live with..." Something inside her reached up and strangled the sentence before it could be real.

Antoinette was quiet for a long time. It was late, and the silence seemed to stretch through the room, filling up every space until that quiet was the biggest thing in the world. Finally, she stood up. She picked up her tools, and walked back over to the chest, carefully placing each in its designated spot. "I'm going to have to have an insert made for your gift," she said.

Somehow, that idle comment was exactly what Jaina needed to hear. It gave her permission to exhale a long, shaking breath. "Can't help you there," she said, offering a tired grin. "I've always been hopeless with wood. I do know a ridiculously gifted sculptor, though."

Antoinette shook her head. "She's way too expensive." She shut the trunk, and came over, looping her arm through Jaina's. "You need rest. To be fair, I do too."

They walked back through the empty halls, past flickering oil lamps and tapestries. They said nothing, but Jaina found herself willing the route back to their quarters to have somehow stretched, to give her just a bit more time with this woman on her arm. When they reached the door, Jaina cleared her throat, and said, "Good night."

Antoinette let go of her arm, and turned to face her. She looked up at Jaina, her eyes bright, and said, "I think I'm very glad that I met you, Jaina Creighton."

"Me too." Jaina felt her cheeks heat. "I thought you were going to be different. I couldn't have imagined..." The distance between them was so close Jaina could hear every inhalation, every thump of this woman's heart. "I'm glad to have met you, too."

For a moment, she was sure that Antoinette would come up on her toes, her lips coming up to find their way to Jaina's. There were a long few seconds where they said nothing, just stared at each other. But between heartbeats, something changed in Antoinette's eyes, and she stepped back. "Goodnight, Jaina." Her voice was even, and Jaina could read nothing in her expression as she turned, walked through her door, and closed it.

***

Jaina didn't know how long she'd stood there, trying to wrap her head around what had just happened. Finally, she turned and walked into her room.

So how do YOU think that went?

Shut up. She could almost see the bemused expression on Jak's face. *I just... Shut up.*

Well said. He snorted. *I swear to the gods, Cricket, you can lift a carriage but you can't pick up a hint. Why didn't you kiss her?*

Jaina sat heavily on the padded bench that sit on the edge of the bed. *Off the top of my head?* She began counting things off on her fingers. *She's basically Vetticcian royalty. Worth more than everyone in our home town put together.*

Seems like a positive for me, but go on.

I'm supposed to be protecting her. It's my job to protect her.

Not really seeing why you can't protect her from inside her bedroom.

Jaina scowled. *That's not funny.*

It's a little funny.

It's against the law.

He snorted. *What law?*

My oath? You remember, the one I swore so that you two could find your way home? Jaina balled her fists. *I don't know the consequences for breaking that. I don't know if I'll end up in shackles, end up at the end of a rope. But I'm gods-damned certain it will mean the end of my novice period, which means you two don't come home.*

We will come home, Cricket. Joran spoke up. *We'll come home the way dad did. The way Master Georges did, the way everyone does. We'll do our time, serve our five, and we'll come home.*

You don't know that!

None of us do! None of us know whether we'll get the grey fever tomorrow, whether we'll fall and break our neck. None of us know what's coming down the turn for us. And you turning your back on someone that makes you smile in a way we've never seen is not going to change our fates.

She and I can't work. We don't have any future together.

So? Jak said. *Let's say you're right. Let's say that in a few months, she heads back down to Vetticci and you head off to wander the land and save the world by lifting heavy things and putting them down again. If you're right, if nothing can change that, then whether you spend these next few months happy or miserable won't change it either.*

Joran spoke. *If you go back across that hall, if you knock on her door, there are possibilities. If you sit here and sulk about how unfair everything is, there are nothing but certainties. That's what all of this has been about. That's why we all got so upset with you for doing this, for taking all the possibilities that your life had and throwing them away. Don't do it again. Give yourself a chance to smile. She makes you smile.*

Jaina stared at the floor. *She could have kissed me. She didn't.*

You could have kissed her. You didn't. He shrugged. *You can't change what she does next. But you can change what you do next.*

She looked at the door for a long few moments, and stood up. Her hands were shaking. *I don't know if I can.*

Three soft knocks.

Looks like someone decided they could. You gonna leave her to stand out there?

Jaina swallowed, walked over, and opened the door. "I'm glad you..." Her words died in her throat.

Veres Martine smiled at her. "Hello, Jaina."

***

After a long few moments of stunned silence, the veteran ranger chuckled. "I know it's late, and I know this is a bit unexpected, but may I come in? I wouldn't hate sitting down for a few minutes."

"Of course!" Jaina gave her head a quick shake, holding the door open as Martine stepped through.

He looked around, nodding appreciatively. "I have to say, I'm a bit concerned this is setting a bad precedent for you. Rangers don't usually get to stay in places this nice." He pointed at the chair at the end of the room. "You mind?"

"No, please. Make yourself comfortable," Jaina said. "I can send for some tea or food if you like."

Martine waved his hand, plopping down in the chair. "I'm sure whatever staff are still in the palace went to bed hours ago. No need to wake them." He leaned back, his spine popping as he arched it against the wooden back of the chair. Jaina winced, and he chuckled. "Been on horseback for almost fourteen hours. My age, that takes a toll, ranger or no."

Jaina walked over to the small table next to the bed. There was a pitcher of water and a few mugs. She filled one and brought it to Martine, who accepted it gratefully.

"Many thanks." He took a long drink, then wiped his mouth. "The Vetticcian asleep for the night, I assume?"

"She usually stays up for a bit to write to her grandmother. Sends the letters out in bundles once a week."

"Isn't that sweet." It was not a question. "Woman didn't strike me as the sentimental type."

"You've met Antoinette DeLuca?" If Martine noticed the pause between the first and last name, he gave no indication.

"No, I mean her grandmother. Haven't met the granddaughter, but if she's anything like that barracuda in high fashion, I can't imagine your time here has been all that pleasant."

Jaina shook her head. "No, actually, Mistress DeLuca has been uncommonly kind. She's a very gifted artist who's been nothing but gracious to the staff here."

Martine nodded. "I'm glad to hear that. I felt a bit guilty about sticking you here alone with her. Not that we had much of a choice. But all the better if it's going smoothly."

"Is that why you're here?" asked Jaina. "To check in on me?"

"Mostly." He finished the cup, and pointed at the pitcher. "You mind?" When she started to rise to her feet, he waved her off. "Sit, sit. I'll get it." He loped across the room, and as he refilled his cup, Martine said, "I think I told you before. We usually have a senior ranger shadowing a novice. Keep an eye on them while they find their footing. Haven't been able to do that here, and I didn't feel great about it. But mostly I wanted to give you an update."

Jaina raised an eyebrow. "Is something wrong?"

"Not a whole lot right, to be honest." He sat back down, shaking his head. "Things have only been getting worse. The dukes have snatched up everyone fit to hold a bow." He looked up at her. "They tried to call up your father."

Jaina was on her feet before the thought fully penetrated. "What? No!"

Martine already had his hand up. "It's all right. Shakkar shut it down. Told the conscription sergeant that we'd already filed the exemption papers, that he wouldn't even have the chance to reach his unit before they'd have to pay to send him home. They didn't like it, but they accepted it. Left him be."

"Gods." Jaina ran her fingers through her short hair, trying to convince her heart to slow down. *Dad, too?* "Thank you. Thank you so much."

"We take care of our own," Martine said. "But it did put us in a bit of an awkward position. See, rangers take great pride in our honesty. Didn't sit right that we'd lied, so I figured I'd just make it a slightly delayed truth."

"I don't understand."

"I signed your exemption papers last week, Jaina. Soon as I heard what happened with your father."

Jaina opened and closed her mouth several times. She didn't trust herself to speak without tears. For his part, Martine just drank his water and let her come to terms with what he'd said. "I thought..." She cleared her throat, blinking quickly. "I thought I had to finish this assignment."

He chuckled. "Not sure if you've noticed, but we're not all that formal in the rangers. I stopped by the throne room. The Vetticcian is making fast progress. Neither she nor her grandmother has sent letters of complaint to either the dukes or myself. Given what we know about that family, that's about as high a mark of success as we could have asked for. I could wait until it's official, but in the long run, us moving a bit more quickly makes no difference to anyone." Martine shrugged. "Except you and your family, and that's all upside. Seemed the right decision."

Jaina nodded. "Thank you," she whispered. "Thank you." *You two are coming home.*

"Don't thank me quite yet." Martine shook his head. "I have to deliver the papers to the commanding duke, and, well..." He looked a bit uncomfortable. "I can't find him."

"You can't find the duke?"

"I can't find the army," Martine said. "The dukes let us know the three staging areas they were bringing conscripts to for training. They needed to, with the numbers of deserters they've been dealing with. We've probably caught over two hundred, and we've been bringing them to the army for trial and punishment. But I just came from the second of two staging areas I checked. They're not there. Soon as I leave here, I'll go check the third, but I'm not optimistic."

Jaina frowned. "So what happens next?"

"I'll find them. At this point, the army is huge. Hundreds of thousands, the biggest that the Dominion has ever fielded. Force like that isn't exactly stealthy, and I have a suspicion where they're headed."

"Where?"

"West." Martine looked grim. "We've gotten reports from the handful of rangers we have up and down Cicerone's border. They've spotted groups of soldiers. Can't tell how many, but the Confessors have definitely been building up forces. If I had to guess, the dukes got wind, and they're moving the army to deter the Confessors from coming in."

For the first time since she'd seen the marker in her brother's hand, Jaina felt a new fear at the thought of banners with shepherd's crooks flying outside the walls of her home. For long before she'd been born, the Confessors had been the nightmare no one wanted to see realized. The idea that it might happen left her skin cold. "Do you think..." Martine was shaking his head before she finished.

"It's a long border, but there are only a few places that the Confessors could bring any substantial force through. With the sheer number of Dominion soldiers, any invasion would be a disaster for Cicerone, and open them up to a counterattack. I don't think they'd risk their holy land like that," he said. "Best guess, there might be a few skirmishes at the border, but neither side will want to field an army for that long. It's going to get awfully expensive, and fast."

"Okay." Jaina nodded slowly. "So you think you know where they are?"

"Not exactly, but like I said, it shouldn't be hard to find them. Once I do, I'll run my way up the chain of command until I find someone senior enough to accept and take action on the exemption. They'll grumble about the expense, but I'll escort your brothers back myself. Make sure they get home."

Jaina took a deep breath. "I don't know what to say."

Martine shrugged. "Unfortunate reality of a job like this is the fact that we don't always get clean answers to the problems we encounter. You're at the beginning of a long career of protecting people, and that's rarely an easy or simple matter. When we find a way to make someone's life a bit better this cleanly, it's an easy call." He smiled. "You're one of us. We look out for our own."

"I'm grateful. More than I can say." Jaina thought for a few moments, and asked, "Have you thought more about where you'll send me once Mistress DeLuca heads back to Vetticci?"

"That's the other thing I wanted to talk to you about," Martine said. "Even after the armies turn around and go home, things along the border are likely to be fairly tense for a while. We're already planning that it's going to take a fairly substantial ranger presence to keep things from boiling over just due to corn-fed idiocy."

"You're going to send me to the Cicerone border?"

"What? Oh, gods no." He shook his head vehemently. "We need people who have connections and experience. Rangers who have had ten, fifteen years to get used to their abilities, dealt with more than a few scrapes. Appreciate the work you've done here, but that's not you. That being said, Edmund Shakkar is from Pevitt Mill. Right on the border. Knows the people and the land. We're going to be sending him out there. Which means that Lofland Fork will need a new ranger." Martine tilted his head, grinning. "Interested?"

Her eyes widened. "You're joking."

"Granted, I'm very funny, but in this case, not really," he said. "You've done a good job here. See it done, and you'll be a full fledged ranger. Same reasoning for us sending Shakkar out west applies to you. You know the community in Lofland Fork. You have deep roots, people who will talk to you. You'll still be unseasoned, but it's an established city with a dedicated and trained militia, which means you'll have support. Plus, you'll be happy there. We do try not to go out of our way to make our rangers unhappy."

Jaina's head was spinning, but she couldn't help the grin that crowded onto her face. "I'm going home?"

He nodded. "That's the plan."

"I don't know what to say." Jaina let out a relieved chuckle. "I've spent so much time being terrified I was going to mess things up, fail my novice period, I didn't even think about what might come next."

"I wasn't worried. We almost never wash out someone from their novice period. We're pretty good at making sure we've picked the right person," he said.

She glanced at him. "Can I ask what would have happened? If I had bungled this? Failed the novice period?"

Martine nodded. "Every novice asks that sooner or later. It's not a conversation we're ever all that eager to have." He took a sip of water. "Jaina, the vow is for life. But that's not just a rule, it's baked into the ritual. It's part of what was done to make you what you are. That process, it can't be reversed. Long ago, we realized that there might occasionally be cause to have to discipline or even imprison a ranger who violated their oath. But that's not..." Martine looked up at her. "The type of person that could take the steps necessary to deal with a ranger's punishment is miles away from the type of person we want in our ranks. So in that unlikely event, we hand the ranger over to the dukes for judgement and sentencing."

Jaina paled slightly. "The dukes hate the rangers."

"Probably a bit too strong a word, but they're not our biggest supporters. I don't think they'd be particularly gentle." he said. "I suspect for you, however, the biggest cost would be the loss of the exemption. Even if your brothers had found their way home, they'd snatch them back as fast as possible. Most likely would be a bit bitter about how things played out, so it's good for everyone you've done the job you have." He raised an eyebrow. "That question was hypothetical, right? There's nothing you need to tell me?"

"Completely hypothetical," Jaina said, a bit too quickly.

Oh, yeah, that was super convincing.

Jaina ignored Jak. "I think I've just been very aware of everything riding on this. Takes my head to the worst case scenario."

"Well, hopefully I've put at least a few of your fears to rest." He stood up. "Just keep doing what you're doing. I'll do my part, and make sure your brothers beat you home." Martine thought for a moment. "Actually, our route back will probably take us through here. If we can, I'll see if we can't stop for the night. Let you see them before they head home."

He stuck out his hand, and Jaina shook it. "Are you leaving already? There are plenty of rooms here. You can rest before you go," she said.

"Thanks, but I'm more comfortable if I'm not surrounded by walls," he said. "I'll head out, find a place to camp and some game to cook."

"Anything else I need to know?" Jaina asked.

"One thing," Martine said. "I don't expect that you two are traveling much outside the city. Am I right?"

Jaina nodded. "We've barely left the castle. Went into town to get some supplies for her."

"Good. Keep it that way," he said. "I mentioned deserters earlier. It's getting to be a problem. A lot of soldiers weren't happy about being recalled, and more than a few of them decided to run rather than return to the field. Given the penalty for desertion, not to mention the reward offered for anyone who turns them in, they're desperate, and not too shy to reach for a weapon. Best to stay in the city until it's time for the good Mistress to head back south."

"Understood," Jaina said. "But as I said, I don't have any plans or need to leave."

"Easy enough, then." He touched a pair of fingers to his forehead. "Much appreciated, ranger. Good luck."

2,086 Hours

She hadn't been able to sleep. Antoinette had laid in bed for hours, feeling the weariness of the day drag at her eyelids, but every time they shut, she saw Jaina's eyes, inches from her. She had felt their proximity, and every inch of her body had been aware how simple it would have been to close that last distance, somehow impossibly vast and unbearably close at the same time.

It's my job.

She kept repeating those three words, over and over. She was a DeLuca. Born and bred to do anything it took to advance the family legacy. Jaina was a potential source, a way to illuminate one of the biggest blind spots her family had within the Dominion. Her grandmother had never been satisfied with rumor and story, and had made the importance of cultivating that source as clear as crystal.

It's my job.

She was free of the complications that could ensue, as well. It was always questionable to use sex or romance to develop a source. Feelings emerged, ideas about what the future might look like, and those ideas bore no resemblance to reality. But Jaina was temporary, bound by oath and commitment to walk away. In a few short months, it would be done, nothing but a memory.

It's my job.

Antoinette had seen the look in Jaina's eyes. It had told her that had she leaned up, let her lips brush against Jaina's, the ranger would be undone. It was all right there. But Antoinette knew that if she'd been able to see her own expression, it would not have been much different. She wasn't thinking of how best to collect the names of the rangers, their deployment, the depth of their abilities. In that moment, she knew that she could have everything she wanted from Jaina if she kissed her.

It's my job.

She knew every reason that she should have kissed Jaina.

There was only one reason she chose not to.

Gods.

I think I'm in trouble.

When she was fourteen, Antoinette had been given her first residency assignment. It was less than an hour's ride away, but the prospect of being away from home terrified her, and she'd told Andreas that she couldn't do it, that she didn't want to take the assignment. He didn't argue, but instead turned and left. When Toni DeLuca arrived in the room minutes later, Antoinette had braced herself for anger, but instead, her grandmother sat and spoke to her.

"Do you know what we trade for this estate, child?"

Antoinette had shaken her head.

Toni DeLuca never looked away, her grey eyes fixed on a nervous child. "This home, this staff, the power we can leverage on those near and far. You were born into luxury that most will never even imagine, but it was not given to you freely. The moment you drew breath, you entered into an accord with every woman who has borne our name since this city was nothing more than huts on a beach. You live among the wealth and influence to which each DeLuca woman has contributed, sacrificed her wants, her desires, her fears. You want for nothing, because your wants are nothing."

She had shaken her head at Antoinette's dismayed expression. "It's the same accord I've lived in every moment of my life. It's the same accord that wouldn't allow me the luxury to drown in the grief I felt when my only daughter bled out in the birthing bed. Such are the luxuries of those who live for themselves alone, but we live for something more. Something so much bigger. We live for the dozens of women before us that fought and fucked and bled and wept for every spare ducat, who gave up their dreams and their loves and their fears to build a world in which DeLuca women will never be victims, never allow an outsider to dictate our fate, a world of which you and I stand as stewards. We live for the dozens of women who will come after us, who will take the DeLuca family beyond the boundaries of this city, across the massive farms and fields of the Dominion, even across the Breaking itself. They gave us everything, and in return, we give them everything."

Toni DeLuca had stood, staring down at the teenage girl. "Your wants, my wants? We sold those generations ago. We live and serve something bigger than us. In exchange, we are DeLucas. Do you feel that a fair trade? Or will you cast away the work of generations because you don't want to?"

Antoinette had never questioned her grandmother again. But now, as she lay in bed, remembering her grandmother's words, she whispered to the ceiling, "It's not a fair trade. It's never been a fair trade."

Sleep didn't come that night. She got up before the sun rose, and sat at the desk, quill scratching over the page.

Jaina Creighton is not a viable source. She is a novice, far too new to have any information of value. Her motivations are too closely tied to family, and she has no vulnerabilities based on financial gain or compromising information. She is a good woman doing a hard job as best she can, and I will no longer focus my efforts on developing her as a source.

The pen stopped, and she stared down at the words she wrote, trying to imagine her grandmother's expression as she read it. Only four sentences, but it was the closest she'd come to defying her grandmother, her family, since that day. She let the ink dry, dusted it, folded it carefully, and sealed the message with wax, setting it atop the rest of the messages going out in a few days.

***

As she had for dozens of days before, Antoinette walked to the door of her quarters in the morning, and opened it. As had been the case for dozens of days before, Jaina was waiting. But something was different.

Antoinette had expected different. What had happened last night was undeniable, and while she had judged it a possibility that both would pretend as if it hadn't happened, she was certain the energy between the two of them would have changed. But she had not been prepared for the odd flat expression on Jaina's face.

"Good morning," the ranger said, offering a slight nod. "You ready?"

"I am." Antoinette frowned, but recovered quickly, shutting the door behind her, and falling into step behind Jaina, who wasn't looking at her. They walked quietly through the halls, Jaina's boots seeming disproportionately loud in the vacuum of conversation. It was only once Antoinette had begun selecting her tools for the day's work that Jaina finally spoke.

"I had a visitor last night."

Antoinette paused, turning to face Jaina. "I'm sorry?"

"A visitor. Late. After you went to bed."

"Who in the gods would be disturbing you at that hour?"

"Veres Martine," Jaina said. "The ranger responsible for my novice period."

Antoinette felt her stomach drop, and worked to keep her face even. "Ah."

"Yeah." Jaina ran her fingers through her hair. "That was basically my reaction."

"Was he... I mean, is he unhappy with your performance?"

Jaina chuckled. "Not exactly." She sat down heavily on one of the stools in the room. "He's very happy. Happy enough that he's already drawn up the exemption papers. He's on his way to find my brothers and bring them home."

Antoinette's eyes widened. "Jaina, that's wonderful!"

"It is."

Tilting her head, Antoinette said, "You don't seem to believe that. Do you think he's not telling the truth?"

"I'm getting the sense that lying isn't really part of the ranger lifestyle." Jaina shook her head. "This is everything I've been hoping for. More, too. I'm going to be assigned to Lofland Fork after this job. I get to serve from my home."

"Then why do you look as if he told you the world was ending?"

Jaina glanced at the closed door. Finally, she said, "Antoinette, what happened last night..."

"Nothing happened last night," Antoinette said, a bit too quickly. Taking a breath, she said, "Nothing happened. You didn't break any rules. Neither of us did."

"Am I wrong in thinking we were close?"

Antoinette shook her head. "No, you're not wrong."

Relief and dismay fought a pitched battle for position on Jaina's expression. "Yeah." She looked down at the floor. "Antoinette, you know that we can't..." She cleared her throat. "Rangers aren't allowed to be in relationships. It's kind of one of the biggest rules. If I cross that line, it would undo everything. I'd be stripped of my title, packed off to face the tender mercies of the dukes, and the exemption would be null. My brothers would be taken right back, and if Martine is right about the Confessors threatening the border, that's..." Jaina looked up. "I can't let that happen."

"It won't." *Confessors at the border?* Antoinette felt a brief flash of anger at how quickly her brain latched on to the tidbit of information in the midst of this discussion. "Jaina, it won't. We didn't cross any lines. Nothing happened. I thanked you for the gift, and we said goodnight."

"Antoinette, I'm sorry."

"Don't be." She came over, and sat on the stool next to Jaina. Taking a deep breath, she said, "I've told you before that in my family, women lead."

"I remember," Jaina said.

"I don't have sisters. My mother died in childbirth. I'm the only daughter in our family. Which means that when my grandmother passes, leadership of the DeLuca family passes to me," Antoinette said. "I've known this since I could talk. And that means that in a few years, she'll choose a husband for me."

Jaina was altogether unsuccessful at keeping the stricken look from her face. "Oh," she said. "I'm guessing that same sex relationships are frowned upon in Vetticci."

Antoinette shook her head. "Not really, no. Honestly, the Table approves of relationships that adopt rather than adding another hungry mouth to the population. City of four million people, there's more than enough who need a home. But the family needs a daughter, and her claim will be stronger if she's mine."

Jaina frowned. "So you don't have a choice? At all?"

"We have wealth. Comfort. Power. Asking for choices as well seems a bit greedy."

"It doesn't seem fair."

Chuckling, Antoinette said, "My grandmother finds that the most pointless word in existence. I'm not quite as calloused as she might be, but whether fair or not, that's the way the winds blow for me." Looking down at her hands, she said, "I'm not going to pretend that I don't see you in a certain light." A smile ghosted over her face. "It would be impossible not to. You're an amazing woman, and I'm so glad that I've gotten to spend this time with you. But there was never a future in which I didn't go south, and you didn't stay north, and that this time was anything more than a memory."

She didn't want to look at Jaina's face. There were a thousand possible expressions that could have greeted her if she looked up at the woman who'd managed to occupy every square inch of her mind, and she didn't know which she was hoping for. But she heard the stool squeak as Jaina stood up, slowly looking around the room. "You're making good progress," she said. "That day's coming sooner rather than later."

Antoinette was spared from having to answer. The doors to the throne room crashed open, and they both spun to see Meyers and Boyajian run in, breathing heavily. They both were filthy, streaked with soot and sweat, and Meyers gasped out, "Fire. At the smith."

Jaina stepped forward, eyes wide. "How bad?"

"Bad," he said. "We're trying to contain it, but there aren't enough people who…" He gripped his stomach and winced, doubling over. Jaina and Antoinette rushed over, and he waved them off as Boyajian gripped his shoulder. "Captain Poole sent me. We need you, ranger. We have sand, but the barrels are too heavy to bring closer."

Jaina looked back and forth between him and Antoinette. "I can't leave her unattended."

"Meyers, you stay here. Collect yourself, and stand guard here," Antoinette snapped out. "Jaina, please, go do what you can. I'll be fine."

Glancing down at Meyers, Jaina still looked uncertain, but he straightened up, taking a deep breath. "I won't leave her side. You have my word."

Her jaw tightened, but Jaina nodded. "Let's go." She and Boyajian ran through the doors out into the early morning.

"You need to sit." Antoinette took Meyers arm, and led him over to one of the stools. "Were you hurt? Did you inhale too much smoke?"

"No, milady, I..." He grimaced again, shaking his head. "It was already a bad day. Some are worse than others. Running around didn't help." He shot a worried look at the door. "I should be out there."

"You're right where you need to be. I believe my orders were very clear."

Meyers managed a half-smile. "All respect, milady, but I don't work for you."

"I'll have you know, I'm a scioness of Vetticci," she said, pouring him a cup of water and handing it to him. "A member of one of the oldest families to grace this continent. I am very used to getting my way, and I'll be extremely cross should you not stay here with me to defend me against the hordes of sea lions."

He took a sip, nodding. "We can't have that, can we?"

"We certainly cannot." She squeezed his shoulder. "Your duke signed an agreement that I would be protected at all times. You're simply honoring his agreement and doing your duty. Now tell me. What can I do for you? How can I help?"

"You can get behind me."

The timbre of his voice had changed completely, all humor gone, and his eyes were locked on something behind her as he rose to his feet, his hand falling to the hilt of his short sword. She turned, and felt the temperature in the room drop as she watched the four men step through the door, fanning out to block the exit. The two in the center had heavy iron banded cudgels gripped in their hands, while the two to the flanks held longbows, arrows nocked.

Meyers pushed her behind him, stepping forward, the oiled steel of his blade whispering against the leather scabbard as he brought it into the light. "Who are you?"

"Makes little difference," the tallest one said, hand flexing around his cudgel. "We don't want trouble. But she's coming with us."

"She's not. You have one chance to turn and walk away."

"Checking the count, I'm not seeing much incentive to do that." The man shook his head. "Last warning."

Meyers dropped his voice, low enough that only Antoinette could hear. "If you see a chance, run. Scream for Jaina. She'll hear you."

"I'm not going to leave..."

He glanced back. "Milady," he said, and then he moved.

Meyers made it nearly fifteen feet before the first arrow punched into his belly with enough force to double the man over, but he staggered forward, roaring with rage, and kept moving, closing the distance faster than she would have ever thought possible. Antoinette screamed as a second arrow tore across his face, the arrowhead glancing off bone. Through the spray of blood, she saw the bowman to the left desperately trying to fit another arrow when Meyers reached him, the gleaming steel of his blade blurring through the air. His slash tore through the side of the bowman's jaw, tearing it clean off, and Meyers reversed into a second strike, cutting a bloody path across the man's belly, his guts spilling to the floor.

The two men armed with cudgels charged in at him, and Meyers spun, blood fanning from both his blade and his face like water off of a dog's tail, managing to block the first strike. The heavy cudgel smashed into the sword, glancing off and hitting Meyers' knuckles, and the man grunted as the sound of cracking bone reached Antoinette. The blade clattered to the floor, but the old guard reached out with his other hand, grabbed the back of the man's head, and drove his forehead into the man's face, spitting his nose in two. The man staggered back, blood pouring from his face, but the tall man's cudgel came down onto Meyers' shoulder, driving him to his knees as the heavy weapon smashed down again and again.

"STOP!" Antoinette screamed. She reached down and grabbed her kiff, and ran forward. The remaining bowman tracked her with the point of his arrow, but didn't loose, and she brought the kiff down onto the tall man's back. It didn't punch through the leather jerkin he wore, but he spun and knocked her to the floor, the tool clattering across the floor. He stepped towards her, but roared in pain as Meyers pulled a dagger from somewhere on his person and raked it across the back of his thigh.

The remaining bowman crashed into Antoinette as she sat up, bearing her down to the floor, pinning her hands to the ground as she fought. He wrapped his arm around her from behind, and she sank her teeth into his forearm. Shouting, he released her, and she snapped her head back, hoping to hit his nose, but her angle was wrong, and her head collided with the point of his jaw, pain blooming in her skull bright and hot. He stumbled back, falling onto his ass, and as she started to clamber to her feet, she saw the tall man bring the cudgel down on Meyers' hip with the sound of a watermelon being crushed underfoot.

He raised it again, and looked back at her. "Stop. Now."

She froze, eyes darting between him and Meyers. The guardsman was struggling to stand, his leg not responding, his belly a mass of blood, the arrow still jutting out. His face was a mask of rage and pain.

"Come with us. Now, and we'll leave him. Like this. Maybe an anatomist can help him." The tall man stared at her with hard eyes. "Otherwise, I'll beat him to death while you watch."

"Don't you fucking dare, milady," Meyers raged, blood painting his lips. "I swear by the gods, I'll tear you both apart." He lifted himself a few inches up, and collapsed back down, face now white.

"Last chance."

Antoinette looked down on Meyers, feeling tears sting her eyes. She nodded slowly. "Leave him, and I'll come." She stepped forward, staring into the man's eyes. "Leave us both, and maybe you'll be the only member of your family to die screaming."

The man's eyes widened, but he said, "Bind her hands."

2,085 Hours

S he ran.

Jaina had no idea how fast she was going, how she managed not to smash through one of the people crowding around the smoldering ruin of the smith. From the moment Poole ran up to her and spoke those two words, she just ran.

"She's gone."

She hadn't really had a sense of how much of Poole's guard force had been cannibalized by whatever insanity had gripped her nation. But even now, in the midst of what could only be described as a disaster, fewer than seven guards were milling about the throne room. Jaina shouldered past one, and knew that her push had sent the man sprawling. Part of her brain suggested she stop to see if he was hurt, but she couldn't stop.

Boyajian was sitting on the ground, Meyers' head slumped back against his shoulder. His face was twisted with grief and fury, and he had his hands wrapped around the chest of the older guard. Meyers' face was whiter than Jaina thought possible, the red dots on his lips the only color, and tears streamed down his cheeks as he gasped in deep, whooping breaths. Jaina dropped to her knees, and he grabbed her sleeve.

"I tried," he choked out in a sob. "I tried to protect her. I tried, ranger. I did."

"I know," she said, clutching his hand. "Who were they?"

He shook his head. "Don't know. They were just here." He coughed, and pain wracked his body, as he let out a shuddering groan. "It hurts. Gods, it hurts so bad."

Jaina wanted to grab him, wanted to shake him until he told her where Antoinette had gone, but she knew there was nothing left in the old soldier. She held his hand and Boyajian hugged him as he sobbed.

"Not fair. I didn't…" He choked, more blood staining his teeth red. "I was supposed to have more time. I don't want to go." Meyers clutched at Boyajian. "Don't let me go. Don't…"

The pain in his eyes broke, giving way to emptiness. Jaina heard his heart stutter and fall silent, and Boyajian let loose a low, broken moan.

Jaina's hands were shaking as she set his hand back into his lap. "Did…" She cleared her throat. "Did he say if she was hurt when they took her?"

Boyajian didn't answer, but another guard whose name she couldn't remember nodded. "Said her hands were bound, but she walked out with them. Three of them. Fourth is there." He pointed at the bloody corpse lying on the other side of the room.

Poole crashed through the door, his chest heaving. He saw Meyers, and his jaw tightened. "Godsdammit."

Jaina came to her feet. "She was still alive when they took her. We have to go after her. Now."

"Take a breath, ranger. We need a plan."

"The plan is to run those bastards down and bring her home."

"We don't know how long they've been gone, how far…"

For the second time that day, Jaina didn't remember moving. But somehow, she had Poole's tunic in her clenched fist, his back against the wall, his feet four inches off the ground. She could hear shouting, hear blades coming free from scabbards, but she only had eyes for the captain she had pinned against the wall. "There's no time!" she roared.

Poole brought his hand down, shouting, "Stand down! Now! All of you!" He looked down at Jaina, and in a quiet voice, said, "This isn't helping her. This isn't helping you. If we rush off, if we spend six hours racing around in the wrong direction, she's lost. We have to think. Take a godsdamned breath."

Jaina couldn't even feel his weight. He was the only target for her fear and anger, but she knew he wasn't the right target, and she choked out, "She's my responsibility."

"And Meyers was mine. We both fucked up. Let's work together and figure out how to make it right."

Calm down, Cricket. You know he's right.

She let him go. Poole stumbled slightly when his feet hit the ground, but he straightened his tunic as if nothing had happened. "I want the grounds searched. Every room, every inch. If you find a twig out of place, I want to know about it. I want the horses counted, and I want a headcount on every person who's allowed to be here. Move, people."

Everyone but Jaina, Poole, and Boyajian scattered, running out of the room to begin the search. Poole turned to Jaina. "If they wanted her hurt, they would have killed her here. You and I both know what this is. Her family has more money than any three dukes combined. This is a ransom."

Jaina swallowed. "Few days ago. When we were in town. I saw three men. They were staring. I thought they were staring because she was so out of place, but..." Her fists clenched. "I should have told you."

"Nothing I could have done if you had," Poole said. "Staring's not enough to make a fuss. Besides, you don't know that..."

"One of them is dead on the ground right over there."

"Ah." Poole walked over and crouched next to the man, lifting the bloody hem of his tunic. "This is army issue. Dominion."

"My senior ranger came through last night," Jaina said. "He mentioned deserters. Do you think it's possible that's who this was?"

"I think it's pretty godsdamned likely," Poole said, straightening up. "If it was a crew from Vetticci, I don't think they would have been likely to leave a witness. The dukes haven't exactly been gentle with conscription. There are a lot of angry people out there."

"Then why go after Antoinette? She has nothing to do with this."

"She's rich. Money can buy a lot of options." He took a deep breath. "Look, I think I might know where they went. If they are deserters, they don't have many options. South takes them to the Myre, and no one's stupid enough to try to hide there. They'd want to stay off the roads, and hiding in a city or town is a non-starter. But there's a forest, about twenty miles east of here. We've had reports of bandit activity on the roads passing near there, and we're pretty well convinced there's a group hiding out."

Jaina frowned. "If you're so sure there are deserters in there, why haven't you sent men to clear it out?"

"What men?" His frustration broke through. "I should have had at least twenty guards on station. This place should have been so secure that a battalion couldn't have breached its defenses. Instead, I've got so many holes in my perimeter that four armed men were able to reach the fucking throne room. I've been bled white."

"Okay, so let's go. Now," Jaina said. "You can show me where, and we can track them..." She trailed off. Poole was already shaking his head.

"I told you. I don't have enough men to secure this city as it is. I'm pretty sure that fire was started as a distraction, but I have to do everything I can to keep the lid on this place. I can't dispatch what few guards I have left to chase down a theory."

Jaina opened her mouth to shout again.

He's not telling you this because he wants to, Cricket. He's not who you're angry at.

Her fists were tight at her side, but she took a deep breath and said, "I'll go. I'll do the search. I just need a horse, and someone who knows the way to guide me."

Poole looked surprised that she wasn't shouting. "Horses I can do. We have twenty waiting for pickup by couriers. As for a guide..." He glanced over. "Boyajian. Want to help the ranger run these bastards down?"

Boyajian nodded, his jaw set, his eyes hard.

"Right." Poole turned back to Jaina. "The courier for the horses is supposed to be here tomorrow afternoon. That's going to be the first opportunity I have to send a message about this mess. I would really prefer that message to end with us getting the Vetticcian back safely, because if word gets back to the city that one of their family daughters has been taken in the Dominion, we're going to have ten thousand guild mercenaries racing north to tear Westcott apart looking for her. But if we don't hear from you by the time those couriers get here, I have to send word to both the Duke and Madame DeLuca, and once that happens, we're all fucked."

"I'll find her," Jaina said. "I have to."

Poole nodded. "Good hunting."

***

Ever since she had woken next to that fire, Jaina had worked to try to dampen out the cacophony of input that hammered against her perception every moment of every day. It had taken weeks, but she'd learned to tune out the beating of her own heart during the rare moments she was able to sleep. She'd learned to focus on what was right in front of her, ignoring the orchestra of chaos that had become her world. Even now, she realized that her world was masked off, except for the thunder of the hooves beneath her and the road spilling out in front of her.

That's not going to do it this time. Joran's voice was always serious, but it had an edge to it now. *A smith's apprentice can't find her. It's time to be a ranger, Cricket.*

Boyajian rode ahead of her, head down. Jaina had been tucked in behind the silent soldier since they'd ridden out the city gates. In this moment, she took a deep breath, and tore down the walls that had been keeping everything at bay.

The world erupted around her.

Insects shrieked from all directions, the wind whipping past her ears sounded like a tornado. Her eyes darted from point to point, every shiver of a leaf drawing her attention like a bursting firework. She could see everything, the distant curve of the hills snapping into sharp relief, details impossibly far away now as plain as the rising sun, and the familiar pain came howling back into her head as Jaina tried to brace herself against the onslaught.

She gripped the reins tightly, feeling every grain in the leather, every imperfection in the cuts. The heart of her horse thundered beneath her like a kettle drum, the hoofbeats sounding as if they were cracking the world in two, and for a few terrifying moments, the overwhelming flood threatened to drown her, to swallow her world in chaos and confusion.

Here. Lock in on me. Listen to me.

Her eyes snapped back open. Joran's voice was the same. It was even, steady, just as it had been since she could remember, and it didn't howl, didn't shriek into her ears. He wasn't there, he was just the memory of the boy who had always been her rock, and Jaina locked on to that memory and held tight as she immersed herself within the storm.

Breathe. Remember what Martine told you. It's like waking up to a bright light. It's blinding, overwhelming, but your eyes adjust. You adjust. And once you do, you can see.

Patterns began to emerge from the torrent of input. Sounds fell into their proper place, and soon Jaina let out a long slow breath, and began to see.

The road they were on was muddy, soaked from the rains a few days prior. She could see the way hoofbeats had torn up the packed dirt, the individual bootprints on the side where people who lacked a beast to ride walked. Her ears picked up rapid heartbeats, too fast to be human, and her eyes tracked the squirrels and birds darting from tree to tree. Jaina began scanning, slowly letting her eyes and ears sweep over the terrain as they rode, trusting her new senses to spot anything that might tell them...

"Boyajian!" she shouted, and the soldier craned his head to look back at her. Jaina thrust a finger towards the treeline. "On me!"

He nodded, and the pair pulled their galloping mounts to the right. They rode to the edge of the forest, where the tangles of ivy became too dense to risk the horses, and she jumped off, boots thudding into the dirt. As Boyajian secured the horses, she ran forward, eyes locked on the glint that she'd seen from so far away. Crouching, she brushed aside the leaves and picked up the button, brass polished to a mirror shine.

Boyajian came up behind her, and she held it up. "Not army issue. Too expensive for most. It's hers."

He nodded, and began scanning the treeline as he pulled a longbow off his shoulder, nocking an arrow. Poole's longsword was scabbarded at his hip. The captain had given it to Boyajian before they'd left. Boyajian pointed at his eyes, and then pointed deep into the forest. Jaina looked where he'd pointed, and immediately spotted the bootprints and broken branches.

"They were in too much of a hurry to move carefully," she said. She started to rush forward. Boyajian grabbed her arm. Jaina looked back at him, and he shook his head sharply. He flattened his palms towards the ground, and took an exaggerated slow and deep breath.

Gods. He's right. I need to calm down. "All right. Do you know how to track?"

Boyajian nodded.

"Okay. You take the lead. I'll follow you. Tell you if I spot something."

The pace at which they moved through the woods was interminably, infuriatingly slow. Jaina did her best to push aside thoughts of what Antoinette might be enduring. Her mind kept returning to their last conversation.

Stop that, Cricket. It wasn't your last.

If something happens to her...

It won't. This is why you're here.

I didn't tell her. Jaina gritted her teeth. *Told her everything else. Didn't tell her how I feel.*

You had your reasons.

None of them good enough. None of them seem to be all that important right now.

Jaina froze, her hand darting out to grab Boyajian's shoulder. Her eyes were locked on a cluster of elm trees half a mile deep into the woods. Light dappled in between the leaves, dancing over the man leaning against tree next to a heavy spear. He held a longbow in his hands, and as he looked in their direction, Jaina's heart drummed out a steady frantic rhythm, but his eyes slid past them. She pointed, and Boyajian squinted, shaking his head for a few seconds.

Too far, Jaina thought. *It's why he didn't see you.*

She stepped close in behind Boyajian, resting her arm on his shoulder, her index finger extended past his face. Understanding immediately, he brought his cheek in tight to her arm, eyes locked in the direction she indicated. It still took nearly twenty seconds, but the soldier in the distance moved, fiddling with something on his belt, and she heard the sharp exhalation from Boyajian.

He looked back at her, and pointed to the ground once, then twice.

"You want me to wait?" she whispered, and he nodded. He pointed to his chest, and then traced a large semicircle in the air, tracing an arc that swung wide to the right.

She frowned. "What if you need help?"

Boyajian shook his head, and put the tips of his thumb and middle finger together, bringing them to his lips. Jaina was confused for a moment, and he repeated the gesture, blowing softly, and her eyes widened. "You'll whistle."

He nodded.

Jaina scowled. She didn't like it.

He knows how to do this, Jak said.

And I very much don't. She took a deep breath. *I need to follow his lead.* Jaina lowered into the smallest crouch she could manage. Boyajian silently turned and began moving through the woods, each step careful as he began moving wide to the right of the man watching for them, his steps slow and silent.

The waiting was agony. Every fiber in her being wanted to charge in, get her hands on the man, squeeze until answers spilled out. It was taking too long, not happening fast...

Her ears caught the whisper of something cutting through the air. Her eyes locked on the shaft darting from Boyajian's bow, eating up the distance in half a heartbeat. And Jaina heard the flesh tear, bone crunch, and blood drops spatter over the leaves as the arrow punched through the man's temple and burst free from below his cheek. Without uttering a sound, the unnamed soldier collapsed into a boneless heap, and Jaina heard his heart give one last whimpering beat before stopping forever.

Jaina hadn't eaten since the evening before. This proved to be a blessing. Her stomach seized up at the second dead body she'd seen in the last few hours, and she gagged, dry heaving and coughing. When she lifted her head back up, Boyajian was staring at her as he crouched next to the body. He pointed at her and gave a questioning look. She waved him off, nodding, and jogged forward as he began searching the body at his feet.

As Jaina got closer, he held out his hand. Lying in his palm was a red marker, a twin to the ones held by her brothers mere months ago.

"Poole was right," she said, keeping her voice down. "Deserters."

He nodded.

"Do you know what direction they went?"

Boyajian shook his head, but pointed to the southeast. They were near the top of a ridge line, and in the direction he'd indicated was a shallow valley. A stream glinted as it wound through the densely packed trees. Boyajian looked back at her, and mimed taking a sip of water.

"You need a drink."

He shook his head, and pointed, first at the body, then at the stream. He held his hands over his head, and then took a drink.

"Oh. They'd need cover and water if they're sheltering here."

He nodded.

"So what, we follow the stream?"

He nodded, and pointed in the direction of the ridge line. He made walking motions with his index and middle finger, pointed at her, to his eyes with two fingers, then back to the valley.

"Okay. We make our way along the ridge line, and I watch for signs of people." She nodded, trying to avoid looking down at the body. "Let's go."

***

It didn't take long for Jaina to be grateful for Boyajian's presence. She didn't know much about the guard's background and training, but it became very clear very quickly that this was not his first time stalking an enemy through the wild. Jaina thought his movements loud, but as she learned to adjust to the constant din that now pressed in on her, she realized his footfalls were no louder than most of the ambient sounds of the forest.

Her boots, on the other hand, were nowhere near as quiet. It didn't help that she had to actively restrain herself from breaking into a sprint. Had she been alone, Jaina was fairly certain she'd have given away their position in an instant. Boyajian kept them at a steady and quiet pace, his bow in his hand, eyes scanning down into the base of the valley.

It took nearly an hour of that infuriatingly slow pace before she finally spotted the curl of smoke, right next to a small waterfall. She whistled, and Boyajian froze in position. Jaina stared at the smoke for a long few seconds before she whispered, "I think it's a fire. Maybe. I don't see the flames, but there's definitely smoke." As she spoke, she saw movement, and her eyes widened. Two men were tucked back in the brush near the smoke. Even with her eyesight, they were almost impossible to see until they moved.

She could hear Boyajian's heart accelerate and knew he'd spotted them as well, but to her surprise, he immediately began scanning the other side of the narrow stream, eyes darting over the hillside leading up from the burbling water. He paused, frowning, and pointed.

Once she knew the direction, she spotted the hidden man immediately. He was tucked back into a shallow cave, only his face and the front of a crossbow visible, branches piled up around to keep him hidden. It took her a moment to realize that all three were watching the trail running alongside the stream, but from two different angles.

God, Martine, you couldn't have taught me anything? Her heart was hammering in her chest. *I've been pretending to know what I'm doing since I woke by that fire, pretending like I knew what being a ranger actually godsdamned meant. But pretending's not going to work here.*

Boyajian considered the situation, and turned to her. He pointed to her, then to the two men sitting at the fire on the east side of the stream. He pointed at himself, then to the man tucked away into the hillside. Holding up both hands, he counted down from three, two, one, then made a pair of fists simultaneously.

Well. Shit. Her hands were shaking. She hoped he hadn't seen. *The waterfall's making a lot of noise. Maybe I can get close enough before they hear me. Maybe.*

Jaina took a deep breath, and nodded at Boyajian. Satisfied, he began to creep down the hillside, doing his best to move into position for a shot. Jaina examined the terrain, and moved twenty feet to the other side of the ridge they'd been walking along, letting the slope of the hill hide her from view as she moved to above where she'd spotted the smoke. As she got closer, the acrid smell of burning oak stung her nostrils, and she could hear the churning roar of the rapids. Dropping into a low crouch, she crept to the top of the ridge, looking straight down the hillside.

She'd judged the distance well. They were about two hundred feet below her. At this vantage, she could see the flames. They'd dug a pit, about a foot deep, and a small fire flickered within, invisible except for someone staring straight down. One of the men sat by the fire. The other was standing, leaning against a tree. As she focused in on them, she realized that they were talking, and the more she listened, the more she was able to filter out the churning water and the constant drumming of her own heartbeat.

"... twelve hours is bullshit." The standing man scratched his face. Jaina could hear his fingernails scrape against two days of unshaven stubble. "Dovetailing watchpoints is overkill. No one's coming."

"Saksel says different." The crouching soldier fed a few twigs in the fire. "Besides, not much else to do but wait. Gonna be a while before word comes back."

"Easy for you to say. You can sit without your balls feeling like they're going to fall off." The standing man shook his head. "Thought the Vetticcian bitch was secure. Wasn't even a point to it. She knew she couldn't run. Just kneed my bits out of spite."

Your girlfriend's not making their life easy.

She's not... Jaina shook her head. *I have to get her.*

You're not doing anything until you deal with these two. Boyajian's going to wait to take the shot until you move, you know that.

Jaina looked at the spear held by the soldier with the bruised balls. The point was blackened steel, but the edge gleamed silver in the light coming through the trees. *I haven't been in a fight in six years.*

To be fair, Toby had it coming. And you kicked his ass.

He was thirteen. And he didn't have spears and short swords.

And you weren't a ranger. Joran's voice was hard. *Go get your gods-damned girl, Cricket.*

Jaina took a deep breath, and leapt.

She had reasoned that the steep hillside leading down to the two men favored speed over stealth, which, given her lack of ability in moving quietly, worked in her favor anyway. She'd ran less than ten feet when her brain registered her error. The steep terrain was covered in roots and fallen branches, and the patches of moss dotting the ground were slick as ice. Jaina stumbled once, managed to catch herself and keep from falling, and then stumbled again. The second time was worse, and she pitched forward with a loud squawk, tumbling over and over, the blackthorn staff flying from her hands.

The world spun around her, the ground coming up again and again to smack into her hip, shoulder, back, and she struck something yielding, a loud curse sounding in her ear. She scrambled to her feet, realized she was facing the wrong way, and turned to see two things. First, she'd collided with the man crouching next to the fire, and spilled him into the dirt. His arm had gone into the fire pit, and he was rolling on his back, cursing and shaking the singed limb.

The second thing she saw was that blackened spearpoint, in much greater detail than before, blurring towards her chest.

Jaina didn't have time to think. She threw herself backwards, falling back onto the hillside, desperately hoping that she would fall under the thrusting spear. It half worked. The sharp point didn't punch through her unarmored chest. It raked across the side of her jaw, a sharp bloom of brilliant pain marking its path, and drove deep into the dirt next to her. Flat on her back, staring up at her attacker, Jaina did the only thing she could think of. She lifted her leg and kicked as hard as she could, striking the soldier in the hip. The angle was bad, and the kick wasn't well delivered. It didn't matter.

The soldier flew off her heel as if he weighed nothing, spear falling from his hand as his body folded around her kick and tumbled through the air. He struck a thick oak tree trunk ten feet away with a sickening thud, and collapsed to the ground, unmoving.

Jaina didn't have time to be shocked. Both she and the other soldier were scrambling to their feet at the same time, but he'd already pulled the short sword from his hip, and lunged forward, slashing the blade down towards her. She managed to dodge the first, but he reversed the stroke in a practiced motion and brought it back up, and the point raked across her upper arm, the spray of bright scarlet painting his enraged face.

Jaina screamed in shock and pain, stumbling forward, balling the fist of her left hand and swinging a wild haymaker towards the man. He didn't have time to block, and her knuckles struck him just below his mouth, tearing the jaw completely from his skull. Teeth and bone pattered across the forest floor as his eyes went wide, a horrible gobbling sound emerging from the ruin of his face. Somehow, he managed to swing the sword again, less a conscious attack and more an instinctive motion, but before he could get halfway into his attack, Jaina stepped in close and buried her fist in his stomach.

It was like punching rotten fruit. Ribs caved around her balled fist like uncooked noodles, and something swollen burst on her knuckles as her punch drove nearly all the way through his body. He just fell, sliding off her gore-soaked hand and bonelessly crumpling to the ground.

The sound of the waterfall was gone. The noise of the forest was gone. All that thundered in her ears was her own heartbeat and the blood rushing through her veins. She couldn't blink, couldn't look away from the ruined pile of broken bones and meat that used to be a person, someone she'd heard talking and complaining moments ago. Her hands were shaking so hard that blood spattered off like water from a dog trying to dry itself. Jaina lifted her eyes, already stinging with tears, to the man she'd hurled into the tree. His eyes were open and staring at nothing, his back twisted at an impossible angle, and she let loose a choked sob before falling to her knees and vomiting.

She didn't hear Boyajian sprint up to her, barely registering as he skidded to a stop, clutching his short sword. His wide eyes took in the abattoir he'd found himself in, and he looked at Jaina with an expression that was a mixture of awe and horror. Boyajian's eyes fell to her shoulder, and he reached into a pouch on his belt, pulling out a roll of linen.

Jaina didn't react as he bandaged the deep cut on her shoulder. The pain was there, it just felt very far away. She wanted to look at anything but the ruined bodies lying on the ground in front of her, but her eyes kept returning to them, as if insisting on reminding her of precisely what she'd done.

Boyajian snapped his fingers in her face, and she looked dully up at him. He took an exaggerated deep breath once, then twice, gripping her shoulder, staring at her intently.

Listen to him. You need to breathe.

She reached up a shaking hand, touching the spot on her face where the spearpoint had ripped across her jaw. There was blood, but the pain wasn't as bad as she expected. "Thought it would be worse," she said aloud, and Boyajian looked up at her. He reached up and gently took her jaw, turning her head to look, and shook his head, giving her a thumbs up. He pointed at her, raising a questioning eyebrow.

"What?"

He pointed at her again.

"Oh." She realized her voice was off. It felt like someone else was speaking. "I don't know. I tripped coming down the hill. Don't really know what happened." Jaina looked down at the tight bandage he'd tied around her arm. "Doesn't hurt. Not that much."

His brow furrowed, he stared at her for a long few moments, but pointed downstream. When she didn't respond, he took her forearm and pulled, trying to get her to stand.

She nodded. "Okay." She fell in behind Boyajian, leaving the carnage she'd caused behind, and knowing she'd never stop looking.

2,083 Hours

Initially, they hadn't bound Antoinette. She had gone with them quietly, offering up silent prayers that Meyers' injuries weren't as bad as they'd seemed. Once they'd cleared the city, the value of her compliance had vanished, and she'd begun making a nuisance of herself. It wasn't until she'd kneed one of the men in the groin when he'd grabbed her arm that they finally tied her wrists together, and lashed her to an iron bolt fixed to the side of the covered wagon in which they'd stashed her.

Even when she'd attacked that man, they'd been very careful not to hurt her. *They want me alive.* She began cycling through possibilities, trying to figure out who they were. *Definitely Dominion. Hair, clothes, accent, none of it Vetticcian. Could have been hired by Vetticcians, but not many would be willing to risk grandmother's irritation.*

They had traveled by wagon for nearly an hour before pausing. A group of six men were waiting next to a dense forest. One of them stepped forward, frowning. "Where's Evan?"

The tall man who'd led the four that had kidnapped her shook his head. "Didn't make it, Sergeant."

The sergeant muttered a curse. "Let's move."

Not all of them came along. The one whose nose she'd broken climbed up and drove the wagon onward. Antoinette watched him go with a sinking feeling. *Even if they track the wagon, there's no way to tell they stopped here.*

The man they'd called sergeant stepped forward. "Mistress DeLuca. I apologize for this. It's necessary. We don't mean to harm you, and I give you my word, you'll be comfortable while you're our guest. But we need to travel for a bit." He glanced down at her bound hands. "If I untie you, do I have your word that you'll behave?"

Antoinette let her hands tremble, and she nodded.

"Do it."

Another soldier came up and began unfastening the ropes binding her wrists together. She winced at the swollen red marks, and said, "Thank you." Without hesitating, she drove her forehead forward as hard as she could, smashing the man's nose and feeling the hot spray of blood paint her face. He staggered back, and she threw himself at him, hand scrabbling at the hilt of the short sword he carried.

Two other soldiers grabbed her, yanking her back and pulling her hand away from the weapon. She thrashed around, hoping that in the chaos, they wouldn't notice the button she'd pulled loose. It fell to the ground, lost among the leaves, as the soldier with the broken nose stumbled forward. "Vetticcian whore," he snarled.

"Enough!" the sergeant barked at the man. "You've had worse." He turned back to Antoinette. "I thought I had your word."

"Oh, I'm sorry, did my impropriety offend you?" Antoinette asked in as pleasant a tone as she could manage. "You failed to provide a properly vetted contract specifying my behavior before you abducted me."

He gritted his teeth. "Bind her. We have to move."

Even after she'd broken her second nose of the day, they were surprisingly gentle with Antoinette. They moved at a quick pace through the woods, but were careful to help her avoid roots and debris that she might trip on. One of the men kept a firm grip on her arm the entire time, but never so tight that they might do harm.

Not looking to hurt you. That's something at least.

By her best estimate, it was nearly four hours before they reached the camp. They'd traveled along a narrow trail for nearly a mile, passing several concealed soldiers on watch, before they reached a small clearing nestled at the heart of a dense copse of oak trees. About a dozen men had bivouacked there, with nine cheap military shelters set up and a fire pit in the center, the logs cold and dark beneath a large battered steel pot.

They brought her to the largest tent. Inside was a cot, several battered wooden chairs, and a table with a bowl, several blank pieces of paper, and a quill. They sat her down in one of the chairs. The sergeant stepped forward. "We mean to keep you comfortable, Mistress DeLuca. But if I can't trust that you're not going to assault my men every opportunity you have, I'll have to bind you for their safety."

"Even if I gave that promise, what's to keep me from slipping away as soon as I get the chance?" Antoinette asked.

He shrugged. "If you feel confident about your ability to make it out of this camp without being spotted, then navigating your way through unfamiliar and rough terrain without being tracked by nearly twenty experienced Dominion soldiers, each of whom know this forest better than you know your own home, you're more than welcome to try. But I've never gotten the impression that you were stupid. Just angry, which is understandable."

She considered him, then said, "I appreciate that assessment. I wish I could extend the same in your direction."

The sergeant shook his head. "Don't mistake desperation for stupidity."

"Desperation rarely leads to good decisions. And with every minimal drop of respect due, Sergeant, you have made a truly spectacular poor decision." She held up her hands. "I promise not to beat up any more of your guards unless they lay their hands on me."

"That will not happen," he said, stepping forward to untie her wrists. "We're not animals. We're not criminals. We're just trying to go home."

Antoinette winced at the abrasions on her wrist, and the sergeant stepped over to the table. He took a linen cloth from the bowl, dripping with water, and offered it to her. "There's a local herb crushed in the water. Helps soothe the pain."

"Thank you." She dabbed it on her wrists, and felt a cooling sensation. "Have we reached the point where you tell me what you want, and I explain why you're not going to get it?"

He pulled up a chair, and sat down facing her. "I have to say, Mistress, you seem remarkably calm considering the circumstances."

Antoinette shrugged. "I'm a daughter of one of the oldest families in Vetticci. If you're under the impression that this is the first time that someone has thought that ransoming me was a quick path to a fat bank account, you are sorely mistaken. I've been through this before, Sergeant, which makes me the only person currently in your life equipped to advise you from a position of experience."

The sergeant raised an eyebrow. "Oh? And what would you advise?"

"Cut your throats."

He blinked. "I'm sorry?"

"Each of you, cut your throats," Antoinette said, her voice hard. "If the people coming for me arrive with each of you dead and me waiting for them, they'll be nothing for them to do but to take me back to Westcott and go home. There will be no need to take it further, no message that will need to be sent. That's the best possible outcome for you and your men."

"You can't possibly believe…"

"You can't possibly believe that if you send Toni Deluca, Madame of the DeLuca Family, a ransom demand for her only granddaughter, that she'll send money instead of something much more unpleasant." Antoinette shook her head. "Every so often, people forget. They forget that Vetticci wasn't founded by lords and ladies, by merchants and priests. The very first boots that trod the soil of that bay belonged to pirates. And their descendants have become very good at wearing the costumes of civilized people, but our blood is still that of cruel men and hard women. Occasionally, a reminder of that fact is needed."

"We're prepared for a rescue attempt."

Antoinette shook her head. "A man can stand ten toes deep in the sand and howl to all the gods that he is prepared for the tempest, but he and all he loves will be scoured away no matter how firm his footing."

The sergeant shook his head. "The Tempest are a myth. Stories made up to keep the poor in line."

"Are they." It was not a question.

He took a deep breath. "We're not asking your grandmother for ransom."

"Does that mean you're starting to listen to reason?"

"We were never going to try to deal with one of the Vetticcian families. We're all aware of what little regard you hold the people of the Dominion," the sergeant said. "Besides, we don't want money. We want to go home."

Antoinette frowned, and then stared at him, realizing what he was saying. "You're ransoming me to the duke?"

"He can pardon us. Exempt us from conscription. Let us go back home to our families," the sergeant said. "I'm willing to bet a tidy sum that one-armed captain he has running his home while he's away hasn't sent a message to your family yet. They'll want to clean this up quickly and quietly, because the last thing that Duke Westcott wants to endure is the humiliation of telling Vetticci that one of its daughters under his sworn protection was taken." He tilted his head. "He doesn't have the soldiers available to come after us. He doesn't have the time or money to deal with this. He's a lazy, venal man who fixes his problems with the stroke of a pen, and it's time he put that pen to use for something worthwhile."

"And you think my family will just..." Antoinette shook her head. "I can respect wanting to go back to your families, but this was not the way to do it. You think you can lay your hand on a DeLuca, then just send me back and say, 'We got what we wanted, no harm done, everything is good'? What happens when I'm standing before my grandmother, and she asks me why I stopped sending letters for days or weeks or however long it takes to sort this out?"

He stood. "Are you hungry? Thirsty?"

"I'm fine."

"Spearman!" the sergeant called out. Moments later, a young man with pimples covering his face under shaggy sandy blonde hair stuck his head through the flap of the tent.

"Sergeant?"

"Get some water and some bread, please. I'll stay with the prisoner until you return."

"Right away, Sergeant Saskel."

The flap fell closed as the sergeant winced. "Godsdammit."

Antoinette shook her head. "Your people really don't know how to do this, do they?" *Saskel. Saskel.* She began reaching back in her mind, remembering the stacks on stacks of briefing documents Andreas had placed before her on the long trip north. "Using your name in front of the person you've kidnapped is sloppy."

"He's not a criminal. He's a soldier. Not used to having to hide his actions." Saskel sat back down. "He's nineteen years old. Got married a year ago. She gave birth to his first son three months ago. They were still wiping the afterbirth off of the baby girl when the soldiers came for him." He tugged off his gloves, flexing his hands. Antoinette could see a large star-shaped scar on the back of his right hand, and added it to the list of information she was compiling in the back of her head. "He can read. Write, too. That's always been due an exemption. Gods knows we have few enough scribes in this country. Pits of foolishness to put a bow in hands that know how to hold a pen. That's why he married, why he started a family. Why he worked for hours a day since he was young to learn his letters."

Antoinette didn't say anything, just watched him speak.

"He tried to tell them he wasn't supposed to go. They didn't care. He resisted so much, they took a dagger and pressed it to his newborn daughter's throat. Told him he could leave as a new father or leave as a grieving one, but either way, he was coming with them."

For the first time, Antoinette felt her blank expression fail. "That's barbaric."

"Hoping that's not the last thing you and I agree on." Saskel shook his head. "Every man in this camp has a similar story. The army is fat and swollen. They don't have enough food for every soldier. They conscripted too many, too fast. Men are sleeping on the ground without blankets or tents. They're marching in boots that are falling apart on their feet. The dukes decided to play this little game they're playing without any thought of properly supporting the men they've torn from their families, breaking every promise they've ever made to their people."

He took a deep breath. "I know this seems foolish. But I heard about that little girl with the skinned knee, heard about what you did for her and her family. I'm gambling that you're more than you claim to be, more than just a cold-blooded Vetticcian who'd sooner give me a second smile than the time of day. I'm gambling that when you stand before your grandmother and she asks why you stopped sending letters for the few days you're our guest, you tell her anything other than the truth, knowing that we're just tired, honest men who want to go home. You have the chance to help us do just that. I'm hoping that matters to you."

Saskel stood up, and turned to leave, saying, "If you need anything, just tell the guard."

The last piece clicked into place in Antoinette's mind. "You really think you'll be able to go home to Wedford, play with your children, kiss your wife, and pretend none of this happened, Colin?"

He stopped, and slowly turned to face her. "What did you just say?"

She stood, and tilted her head. "Your name is Colin Saskel. You served two separate conscription periods under Duke Wishmare. You and twenty-three men disappeared from an army camp months ago. Killed a man on perimeter watch as you did. There's currently a bounty on you worth a year's pay for a man of your rank."

"How..." For the first time, he looked at a loss for words. "How do you know that?"

"I'm a DeLuca." Antoinette shook her head. "I'm truly sorry for what happened to you and your men, Colin. But the DeLucas didn't play any part in what happened to you. We would have never cared about your name, your wife's name, your children's name, any of it. But you crossed the only line that can't be uncrossed. What's coming for you won't care about your reasons or motivations, however noble they may be. Run. Leave me here, and run. It won't matter, not really, but it's all you have left."

Saskel stared at her, mouth moving for a moment, and took a deep breath. "Please let us know if you need anything." Without another word, he stepped out of the tent.

As soon as he was gone, Antoinette let loose one silent sob, sinking back into the chair. Her hands began trembling violently, and she felt tears sting her eyes. She closed them, and began taking long, deep breaths, counting back from ten as she collected herself. A memory of long ago swam up, black blades and bloody screams, and she shuddered. "Jaina, please," she whispered. "I need you. Please hurry."

***

The young spearman came back shortly after with some black bread and a pitcher of water. He didn't look at her or speak to her, he simply set everything on the table and turned to flee, as if terrified of her. When she spoke, he froze as if pinned in place.

"Could I have some linen strips, please?" she asked.

"What?" He turned, still not fully looking at her.

"Some linen strips." Antoinette reached down and picked up the hem of her dress, pulling it up to reveal her legs and knees. Her right knee was slightly abraded. "Scraped it on the trip out here. I'd like to clean it, make sure it doesn't go sour."

His already pale face reddened, the freckles standing out in contrast to his complexion. "Ma'am, I... uh, I don't..."

"Calm down. I'm not trying to take your virtue," she said. "I don't play that game. My knee hurts, and I'd like to clean the wound."

"I'll have to ask," he said. "I don't know if we have anything like that."

Antoinette raised an eyebrow, and pointed to the pouch on his belt with two crossed willow branches stamped into the surface. "That's your aid kit, right?"

"What?" He looked down at it as if seeing it for the first time. "Uh, I don't really know. They gave it to me when I got my uniform."

Gods. "That symbol, that's what your anatomists use. It's an aid kit. It should have bandages in it for when you get injured. Could I have one, please?"

He glanced back at the entrance to the tent. "They told me not to talk to you."

She sighed. "Okay. Well, you go ask whomever you need whether or not it's okay to give me a strip of linen. I'll sit here and continue to bleed. Now that we have a good sense of what our jobs are, do you have any questions?"

Somehow his face got redder. He opened his aid pouch, and began pulling out the contents. He found a tightly wrapped leather cord, and stared at it in confusion.

"It's a tourniquet. For when you get so badly injured you can't stop the bleeding," Antoinette said gently. "I'm not quite there yet."

It took a few moments for him to find the strips. He held it up, and when she nodded, he passed it to her. "Do you need... I mean, can you do it on your own, ma'am?"

"I'm quite capable." She pointed. "If you'd bring me that bowl on the table, I would appreciate it."

As she cleaned the wound, Antoinette asked, "What's your name?" She was somewhat shocked when he answered.

"Edley, ma'am."

Gods. "Edley. My name is Antoinette DeLuca."

He swallowed. "Yes, ma'am. I heard."

Glancing up, she said, "Did they tell you who I was before they did this?"

Edley shook his head. "No, ma'am. Sergeant told us he had a plan. Didn't tell us more than we needed to know."

She nodded slowly. "I'm very sorry about what happened to you. Threatening your child like they did was horrible."

Edley stared at his feet. "Yes, ma'am. It was." He looked back up at her. "I'm sorry you're going through this. You must be frightened. But we just want to go home."

"I know, Edley," Antoinette said. "I believe you. And I wish that was going to happen. But it's not."

He shook his head. "The sergeant says..."

"I know what he said. But you and your men crossed a line that no one should ever, ever cross," she said. She set the damp cloth back in the bowl and began carefully wrapping her knee. "There are going to be consequences, and I'm afraid he hasn't been honest with you about that fact."

"Ma'am, if you're about to tell me there's a way out of it, or offer me money, or anything like that, please, don't," Edley said, holding up his hand. "They told me you might try to do that. I'm not turning on my friends."

Antoinette shook her head. "They were wrong. The DeLucas don't do ransom. It's a matter of economics. We don't ever want to place value on someone laying hands on one of ours. The moment you do that, you create demand, and that's a very dangerous thing. So the only thing I have to offer you is something your friends haven't given you all that much of. The truth." She looked up at him. "And the truth is, you're all in terrible danger. Worse than you can know."

The young man opened his mouth to respond, but whatever he intended to say, she never knew. There was an odd whistling sound followed by a deafening crash from outside the tent. Something heavy slammed into the wall of the tent, and the corner pole buckled, the entire structure sagging. Edley's eyes widened, and he spun to run to the flap, pushing through. In the brief moment the flap was opened, Antoinette could see several men running past, shouting.

She took the moment to pull her skirt up higher, revealing her thigh, and the slender black steel stiletto strapped against the front of her leg. Slipping it from its sheath, she tucked it against her forearm, and ran to the entrance, peeking out.

The fire pit she'd seen at the center of the camp was gone, the heavy rocks that ringed it scattered. A chunk of log bigger than her torso had dug a trench in the dirt right through the pit. Antoinette couldn't tell how many men were running about, but she saw Edley about ten feet in front of her, facing away, his head whipping back and forth as he clutched his short sword in his hand. The stiletto fell into her grip, and she stepped forward, eyes locked on the base of his skull, when that whistling sound rose again, and another log came spinning in from the trees on the hill above them. A burly bearded soldier clutching a bow was shouting something when the log struck his shoulder, tearing his left arm from his body with a wet crunch.

Moments later, another log came flying in, crashing into the ground and rolling through camp, scything through the ankles of another man, who folded with a shriek. In the same instant that it struck, a soft hissing sound caught Antoinette's ear, and she heard Edley grunt. He slowly turned to face her, a look of surprise on his face. He tried to open his mouth, a task made impossible by the arrow that had punched through his cheek and emerged, bloody and dripping, from the side of his throat. Edley brought his fingers up to brush the fletchings, coughed once, and crumpled to the ground.

More missiles came raining in. Logs, rocks the size of watermelons, each smashing through camp with terrifying force, and as each crashed to the ground, another arrow came flashing in, finding target after target. It was chaos, and when one log exploded against the side of the steel pot, it shattered, sending splinters of wood whistling merrily in every direction. The barrage paused, and Antoinette saw Saskel helping a man to his feet, bellowing, "Be ready! Be…"

His words died in his throat as Jaina Creighton came bursting out of the treeline, roaring and swinging that black staff of hers through the air. It struck a soldier who had barely had time to lift his weapon in the hip. The man tumbled through the air to vanish into the underbrush. Jaina stumbled, but recovered and charged towards the remaining soldiers. Without hesitation, Saskel lifted the bow in his hands, nocked an arrow, and loosed it, faster than Antoinette could scream a warning.

The arrow struck Jaina right beneath her left collarbone, punching deep enough in her chest that Antoinette knew the point had to have found sunlight on the other side. The ranger staggered, but didn't stop running. She was terrifyingly, impossibly fast, dirt spraying from her heels. Two spearmen moved to meet her, but an arrow zipped in from an unknown spot and struck one of them in the thigh. He didn't have time to scream. Jaina's staff shattered his skull like an egg. Moments later, the second soldier buried his spearhead deep into her thigh, and Jaina screamed, even as Saksel's second arrow found her belly.

Antoinette didn't remember coming up behind Saksel. She didn't remember burying the full length of her blade into his side, right between his ribs where her brother Mattia had taught her, feeling the steel scrape on the ribs and the heart tear itself to bits on the blackened steel before twisting as she ripped it free. She only remembered falling to her knees next to Jaina, who knelt in the dirt, staring dully down at the red soaking her thigh and stomach. The soldier who'd speared her lay dead in the dirt, an arrow sticking from his still open eye. She didn't remember him dying.

She grabbed Jaina, pressing her hand against the wound on her thigh. "No no no..." she kept saying, shaking her head sharply. "We need..." She looked around frantically, and saw the aid pouch on the dead man's belt. She yanked the leather cord out, and pushed Jaina back to a sitting position. "I have to stop the bleeding." The wound in her leg was bleeding in regular spurts, red blood pulsing out. She wrapped the tourniquet around Jaina's thigh, as high as she could, and pulled it tight as Jaina clutched at her arm.

"Hey," the ranger said, her words a bit slurred. She offered a slight smile. "I found you."

Antoinette nodded, feeling the tears sting in her eyes. "You did."

"I think I might be hurt, Antoinette."

"I think you might be right." The tourniquet seemed to be working. The bleeding had slowed to a trickle. Antoinette looked at the arrows in her chest and belly, and let loose a shuddering sob. "Jaina, I don't know how... I don't know how to fix this. Please tell me you brought an anatomist."

Footsteps crunched in the dirt behind her, and Antoinette turned sharply, snatching up the bloody stiletto she'd let fall into the dirt. Boyajian skidded to a halt, holding up his hands, eyes wide, and she exhaled sharply. He stared down at Jaina, who looked up at him, grinned weakly, and said, "Hey. It worked."

He nodded, and Jaina let loose a shuddering breath, and slipped into unconsciousness, slumping against Antoinette's shoulder.

Antoinette looked up at Boyajian. "Where's everyone else? Where's your anatomist?"

He pointed to Jaina, then himself, and shook his head. Antoinette cursed. "I don't know what to do. What do we do?"

Boyajian knelt next to Jaina, his eyes panning over her body, and he swallowed. He looked up at her, his face mournful.

"No. No, I won't..." Antoinette shook her head sharply. "I stopped the bleeding from her leg. We can remove the arrows."

He shook his head sharply. Pulling an arrow from his quiver, he pointed to the barbs at the edges of the broadhead.

"We have to do something!"

Boyajian gritted his teeth, but his expression changed as he looked down at Jaina. Frowning, he reached down and touched the tourniquet Antoinette had tied. He tugged, and it came loose immediately.

"What are you doing?" she shouted, reaching out, but he shook his head, and mimicked tying it the way she had, shaking his head sharply. "I did it wrong?" He nodded. "But the bleeding slowed."

Confused, she looked down at the jagged wound in Jaina's thigh, and her eyes widened. The bleeding had stopped. The tear in her flesh was gaping and raw, but no blood gushed, and as she stared, she saw some of the torn muscles and skin moving and pulsating. "Gods..." she whispered, and for several long, silent moments, the two of them stared as the wound slowly began to knit itself back together.

She swallowed, and looked up at him. "Did you know rangers could do this? Meyers said they could heal, but this..." He shook his head slowly, his face pale. Glancing down at the arrows, Antoinette took a deep breath. "If she can heal that, maybe we should take the arrows out."

Boyajian shook his head again, and Antoinette gritted her teeth. "Can she survive with an arrow in her godsdamned belly? I'm guessing it's going to be really difficult for her to heal with that bastard sticking out."

He made a face, but reluctantly nodded, and reached his hand around Jaina's back, feeling for something. Taking a deep breath, he pulled his hand back, took ahold of the hickory shaft of the arrow that was jutting out of her stomach, and snapped it, breaking the feathered fletching off. Jaina moaned softly, but didn't wake up, and he did the same with the one below her collarbone. He motioned for Antoinette to help him roll Jaina onto her belly. Both arrowheads had punched through. At the range they'd been loosed, Antoinette wasn't surprised. Boyajian got a firm grip of them both, gritted his teeth, and yanked them free with twin spurts of blood.

Jaina screamed into the dirt, her eyes flying open, wildly darting back and forth, her face pressed into the soil. She tried to push herself up, and Antoinette put her hand on the back of Jaina's neck, crying out, "Don't move, please, Jaina, please." Jaina's wild eyes found hers, and she gave a stiff nod as Boyajian stuffed strips of linen into the jagged holes in her back. It had been only moments, but the bleeding had already begun to slow, and as he pressed down on the wounds, Jaina shuddered and passed out once more.

The forest somehow felt very quiet as Boyajian and Antoinette stared down at the supine ranger, seeing the blood slow to a trickle before stopping entirely. Carefully, he pulled the bandages away, and they watched in silent awe as the wounds began to slowly knit themselves back together.

2,076 Hours

J aina woke to bumping wagon wheels and Antoinette's smile.

Overhead, light filtered through tall pine branches overhead. She could hear birds chirping and the sounds of other creatures living their lives within the forest surrounding them, but the sounds felt muffled, as if someone had stuffed cotton in both her ears. Jaina blinked several times, and realized that she lay with her head in Antoinette's lap, the two of them in the back of a battered wagon rattling along an unfamiliar road.

"Where are we?" she asked, and winced at how dry and cracked her voice sounded.

"On the road back to Westcott," Antoinette said. She raised her voice. "She's awake! Can you pass the water?"

From her angle, Jaina couldn't see the person owning the hand that passed back the battered canteen, but she accepted it gratefully. She tried to sit up, and bolts of sharp pain bloomed in her belly. She gasped, feeling beads of sweat burst to life on her brow as she clutched at her stomach.

"Easy!" Antoinette helped her slowly sit up against the side of the wagon. "Please, Jaina, take it slow. You've been..." She paused, and said, "You've had a rough day."

Jaina took a sip of the water, wincing. She'd never felt like this before. Every inch of her body felt raw, exposed, and her limbs were sluggish, leaden things. "How long was I out?"

"A while," Antoinette said. "At least four, five hours. It took Boyajian a while to clear the camp. Even after he had, we couldn't think of a good way to get you out of there. They picked the site to make it difficult to approach. We ended up having to make a litter, and we dragged you out until we found this wagon."

Jaina nodded slowly. She looked up at Antoinette. "Are you all right? Did they hurt you?"

Antoinette shook her head. "I'm fine. They didn't touch me."

Pretty sure she's not the one you need to worry about, Cricket. Jak sounded as if he was sitting right next to her. *Do you remember?*

Do I remember? Do I...

In a flash, images began to bloom into her mind, bursts of blood and screams and crunching bone. She felt flesh tear beneath her knuckles, heard the howls of dying men, and she violently jerked once, then twice as she remembered the tearing sensation of steel carving its way deep into her body. Jaina began to tremble, not just her hands, but tremors rippling from her very core throughout every inch of her frame, and gasped, her breaths accelerating to panicked whoops as she felt herself drowning under the weight of all that had happened.

Through it all, she felt warm arms encircle her, felt Antoinette's breath against her scalp, and heard her soft Vetticcian tones speaking words of comfort. Her hand flew up and gripped Antoinette's, tears rolling down her cheeks as Jaina began to weep. She didn't even realize she was saying something aloud until the words punched through her panic, her own voice sounding alien as she wept, "What did I do? What did I do?"

"Jaina." Antoinette's voice was steady and firm. "Look at me."

She found those deep blue eyes and locked onto them like a drowning sailor clutching at anything that could keep him above water.

"You did your duty. You did your job. You saved me. You and Boyajian. I was lost, and you found me."

"I killed them."

Antoinette nodded. "I know. And I'm so sorry. But you didn't have a choice."

Jaina clung to those words. She didn't know if she believed them, but she knew how important it was that they be true.

She wasn't sure how long she spent in Antoinette's arms, allowing the full knowledge of what she'd done settle into her memories, cheerfully making a home for itself in a place she knew she'd visit every night for the rest of her life. Antoinette simply held her, whispering words of reassurance and comfort. For his part, Boyajian never turned, never looked back at the pair of them. The only proof that the mute soldier knew what was happening just behind him was when he offered another canteen of water once Jaina had drained the first.

Finally, Jaina's fingers found a spot on her belly. "I was hurt."

For the first time, she could feel Antoinette pause, and Jaina sat up, wincing at the pain, so that she could turn to face Antoinette, who nodded slowly. "You were."

"I was hurt badly," Jaina said. "Why am I..." The expression on Antoinette's face was impossible to read, and Jaina lifted the hem of her tunic, exposing hard stomach muscles punctuated with a star-shaped wound the size of a coin. It looked like new scar tissue, sealed over, and it sang with bright pain when her fingers found it, but there was no blood, no red lines of infection. Jaina stared down at it in confusion. "I was struck. With an arrow. I remember..." She shook her head sharply. "I don't understand."

Antoinette shook her head. "Neither do I. Meyers said something once about rangers being able to heal quickly, but I've never seen anything like that. Your bleeding stopped in moments. We could actually see your wounds healing," she said. "You didn't know? They didn't tell you?"

"No," Jaina said. Her fingers began probing the rest of her body, finding two other sunspots of pain in her upper chest and in her thigh. "No, Martine never really said…" She cleared her throat and took another drink of water. "He said I would learn."

"Don't know he meant like this. Probably thought you'd cut your finger or the like."

You always were an overachiever.

Jaina let out a grunt that wasn't quite a laugh, but had some passing familiarity. "I'm going to hire a gods-damned scribe to write a pamphlet called 'Everything you Need to Know About Being a Ranger', and I'm going to make Martine tattoo it on his face." She took a deep breath, clenching and unclenching a fist. "I guess that means I'm going to be all right."

"I'm glad," Antoinette said. "When I saw you lying there, hurt, I…" Her voice had been steady since Jaina had opened her eyes, but here, a slight tremble found its way to her words.

Jaina stared at her for a moment. "How…" She cleared her throat, taking another drink of water. "How are you okay?"

"I wasn't hurt."

"No, that's not…" Jaina took a deep breath. "You're calm. Like this is nothing new, like it's something you've done before."

Antoinette nodded slowly. "That's because I have."

Jaina blinked. "What?"

Antoinette shifted position to sit next to Jaina, their hips pressed against each other, close enough that she could lower her voice. "I was seven. A group of mercenaries ambushed the transport I was in. Killed my guards, killed my teacher. They took me to this rathole in the Nest. I was there for eight hours while they sent a ransom note to my grandmother."

"Gods." Jaina took her hand. "You must have been so..."

"I was," Antoinette said. "I knew it was a possibility, at least academically. It had happened to children of other families. But I always thought my grandmother was somehow... bigger than that. Everyone was afraid of her. Everyone knew who she was, what she could do. But sitting in that dark room, smelling of urine and something rotting, I thought that I'd been wrong about everything."

"What happened?"

A cloud passed over Antoinette's eyes for a moment, so fast it barely registered. "Someone came for me."

"Your family guard?"

Antoinette shook her head. "No." She paused, and said, "Jaina, there are some things that I can't... that we don't speak of. But the families have ways. There are always ways." She squeezed her hand tightly. "But I will say that past the fear of being taken, being in that place, the thing that stuck with me was what happened when they came for me. The blood spilled to teach all who witnessed what it meant to touch a DeLuca. I didn't want that box opened again."

Jaina stared down at the wooden planks of the wagon. "How did you sleep after?"

"Not well."

Jaina let loose a long, shaking breath. "I don't think I'm okay."

"I know." Antoinette lay her head on Jaina's shoulder. "And that's okay."

***

The city of Westcott was undermanned, but the main gate still had a pair of guards standing watch. As their wagon rattled within eyeshot, one of the men peered through the deepening twilight of the evening, and his eyes widened. He barked something inaudible to his companion, who ran back into the city.

"What did he say?" Antoinette asked Jaina, who shook her head.

"No idea. My senses, they feel... turned down. Not like before I was a ranger, but muffled."

"Some side effect of you getting hurt?"

"Your guess is as good as mine."

The guard reached them, huffing as he jogged up. "Gods. You're back."

Boyajian stared balefully down at him, and blinked.

"I mean, yeah. I know."

Boyajian blinked again.

"I sent Tristan to go get the captain. I think you should wait here."

Boyajian stared for a moment, then clicked his tongue. The wagon rolled past the stammering guard and into the city.

They'd made it about halfway to the castle when Poole came galloping up, breathless. He pulled his horse alongside the wagon, and offered his hand to Boyajian, who gripped it. "Well fucking done, soldier." Boyajian jerked his head back towards Jaina. Poole looked at the ranger, and nodded. "You as well, ranger. Wasn't sure how that was going to play out. I was hours away from sending riders."

"You haven't?" Antoinette straightened up, staring at the captain.

"Mistress DeLuca. I'm so grateful that you're safe."

"I can tell." Her voice was cold and sharp. "The sheer number of people you tasked to my rescue speaks volumes to your concern."

"Mistress, I didn't have enough..."

"All things considered, I believe it to be in everyone's best interest that the events of the past few days stay between the handful who know what happened," Antoinette said.

"I have to report this to the duke."

"If that's the case, I have to report this to my grandmother. I have to explain that I was taken under your watch. I have to explain that you sent one man along with my bodyguard to rescue me from defectors from your army who had taken me. I can promise you two things. She will be displeased, and that displeasure will not be silent. Blood will be spilled."

Poole's eyes darted from Antoinette to Jaina and back again, but after a few moments, he nodded slowly. "Perhaps you're right."

Jaina and Boyajian exchanged a silent look. *Your girlfriend scares me a bit, Cricket,* Jak said.

Me too.

Poole cleared his throat. "You'll want to rest."

"I will."

Poole gave a stiff nod, and he fell in alongside the wagon as they finished the trip to the castle in silence. When they arrived, Jaina helped Antoinette down from the wagon. She turned to Poole. "The castle, is it secure?"

He nodded. "I managed to scrape free a half-dozen more men from one of the conscription units coming through. We're putting them on the walls, not in the castle, but no one will get in or out without us knowing."

"Good," Jaina said. "We're going to rest." She paused, and said, "Captain?"

"Yes?"

"Your man here is a hero. Both Mistress DeLuca and I would be dead without him. If there's something I need to sign or fill out to ensure he gets the recognition he is due..."

"I will see to it, ranger." The title had always felt a bit dismissive in the past from Poole. It sounded different now.

"Good."

The castle seemed more empty than ever. The pair walked silently through the cold stone halls that no longer seemed as safe as they once had. They reached their chambers.

"Thank you."

Antoinette cocked her head. "For what?"

"Keeping all this quiet. I don't know what it would mean if the Duke found out, if Martine..." She trailed off, and shook her head. "All I could think about was getting to you. Getting you back. Now that you're safe, I think I'm realizing what it would mean if they learned how badly I bungled this."

"You walked into a camp of nearly twenty men and saved my life," Antoinette said. "Near as I can tell, that's your job."

"I should never have let you be taken in the first place."

"I'm alive because of you and Boyajian. That's all that matters."

Jaina looked down at the bloodstains on her clothing. "I need to change," she said. "I think we both do." She pointed at her door. "I'm going to..."

Antoinette nodded. "Me too."

"I'm here if you need anything."

Antoinette reached out and squeezed her arm. "Same."

Jaina opened her door to find a chambermaid inside. The woman was pouring steaming water from a bucket into the large wooden tub nestled into the corner of the room. She glanced shyly up at Jaina. "Begging your pardon, ranger. When the captain heard you were coming in, he thought you might need to rest up. Change of clothes on the chair over there. We're heating up some stew right now. I'll bring it to you in a bit."

"Thank you," Jaina said. "Could you please make sure Mistress DeLuca has a bath as well? Food, too."

"Madeline is seeing to her right now, ranger."

Once she'd left the tub full of hot water and a bowl full of chicken stew, the woman left Jaina alone. Mechanically, she stripped off her clothing. The blood had soaked through deep enough that it dotted her skin. The wounds on her belly, thigh, and chest had continued to heal, but bruises surrounded each one. She sank into the water, barely feeling the heat, and scrubbed herself, hard enough that it hurt.

She had hoped that the bath and clothes not blotched with the reminders of what had happened would help her feel better. Jaina stared at herself in the mirror for a long time. *Doesn't feel like me.*

The clothes?

Everything that happened.

Jak's voice was quiet and gentle. *Pretty sure that's shock, Cricket. Not much that's going to shift that but time.*

What did I do, Jak? Jaina swallowed. *What do I do now?*

Fuck if I know. But I can promise you, you're not the only one feeling this way.

Jaina stared at the closed door, and nodded. A few moments later, she knocked softly on Antoinette's door. When it opened, Antoinette looked up at her, face scrubbed clean and ringed by wet curls of black hair.

"I wanted to check on you. See how you were doing."

Antoinette gave a half hearted shrug. "That's a question I am in no way equipped to answer right now.

"Antoinette... Are you all right?"

Antoinette chuckled softly. "I don't know if I'm sure what that means right now." She glanced down the hallway. "I also don't know how I'll feel about going back to that throne room tomorrow."

"Doesn't have to be tomorrow. You can take as long as you need."

"I wish that were so. Time is the one thing that even my family has no say over," Antoinette said. She shrugged. "Painful or not, there's still a job to do." She considered Jaina. "What about you? Are you going to be all right?"

Jaina started to nod out of habit, but stopped, and said, "I don't know. I'm so tired. But the idea of sleeping..." She swallowed. "I killed those men. Soldiers. Wearing the same uniform as my brothers. I know that it's different, I know that I didn't have a choice, but they had families. People waiting for them."

"I spoke with them. I know they weren't evil men, but..." Antoinette took a deep breath. "They made their choice when they took me. Forced your hand. I'm not saying that it won't be hard. But if your brothers are anything like you, they would never do that, never harm someone else for their own safety."

Jaina shook her head. "No. But I'm still afraid of what I'll see when I sleep."

Antoinette considered her, and extended a hand. "Come with me."

"What?" Jaina shook her head. "I can't."

"Jaina." Antoinette took a deep breath. "I told you the truth. I've been through this before. But I still..." She swallowed. "This isn't my home, and it doesn't feel safe any longer. The only thing that feels safe is you. Please."

Jaina took her hand, and followed her into her chambers. They didn't speak as Antoinette walked around the room, blowing out candles and dousing the lanterns. The sun had set, and the room was dark. Antoinette came back, and took Jaina's hand once more. "Just stay with me," she whispered. "I don't want to wake up alone."

"You don't have to."

Jaina had been dreading the next moment her eyes shut. The ordeal had clearly drained her body of energy she had thought inexhaustible, and her weariness bore down on her like a millstone around her neck, but the idea of letting dreams find her filled her with a terror she hadn't known since she was young. But as she lay next to Antoinette, their hands intertwined, she listened to this woman's breathing even out and slow, and Jaina exhaled, a long sigh that seemed to carry with it her resistance, and her eyes closed.

***

When she woke, it was dark. The room was quiet, the only sound the heartbeats, her own, and Antoinette's. Her senses had returned to her in the handful of hours she'd slept.

They were no longer side by side. Antoinette had curled into her, her head tucked into Jaina's shoulder, her breath warm and steady against the nape of her neck. Jaina's arms were wrapped around her, having pulled her close sometime in the night. She could smell the lavender from her soap, feel her heartbeat in her skin, and Jaina wanted nothing more than to stay in this moment forever, but something changed. Antoinette's heartbeat began to quicken.

Jaina looked down, her eyes peeling aside the darkness to find Antoinette's blue eyes fixed on her, blinking slowly.

"You came for me," she whispered, so softly it felt like a prayer.

"I had to."

"Jaina."

She didn't know if it was a question or a statement, but it didn't matter. She knew all the reasons they shouldn't, but right here, right now, those didn't matter. There was only one response, and this time, she didn't wait for Antoinette to take the first step. Jaina's lips found Antoinette's. She wondered if Antoinette would pull away. Instead, she felt her sigh and sink into her, felt her heartbeat quicken, felt the shiver that rippled through her body. Jaina knew that the sunrise would cast light upon all the reasons this was a dangerous path, but between the quickening beats of their hearts, everything else melted away, the doubts, the fears, the memories.

There was only her.

2,066 Hours

S he woke to the morning sun filtering through the window. Instinctively, she reached for Jaina, but found only empty space next to her. Antoinette sat up, clutching the blanket to her chest, but the panic didn't even have time to register before the door clicked softly open and Jaina stepped through, carefully balancing a tray of steaming mugs. She saw Antoinette sitting up and her cheeks flushed as she smiled. "It's the tea you brought with you. I found someone in the kitchen to help me brew it properly."

Antoinette shook her head. "I thought you left."

"I mean, I did, but only for a moment." Jaina set down the tray. "I'm sorry. I should have... I haven't really done this before. I wanted to let you sleep a bit more."

"It's okay." *How do I do this?* Antoinette took a deep breath. *Every moment of my life has been planned. Every contingency thought through, every step dictated, and now...* She glanced down, heat burning her cheeks. "I find myself suddenly underdressed."

"I don't mind," Jaina said, smiling shyly.

Antoinette exhaled. "How do you do that?"

"Do what?"

"Smile and burn the reason from my skull. Make everything that I know to be true seem so meaningless." *Make me forget that I'm meant to tell my grandmother every moment of my time here, every word, every breath. If she knew...* She felt her skin grow cold for a moment. "Sit down. Please."

Jaina set down the tray of drinks, and sat on the bed next to Antoinette. "This sounds serious."

"I think we should talk."

Jaina nodded slowly. "Probably a good idea."

Antoinette tried to look Jaina in the eye, but the bloom of heat that her tousled hair and flushed cheeks brought to Antoinette's chest was too distracting, and she shifted her eyes down to the bed. "Last night was perfect." *Impossible.* "Wonderful." *Catastrophic.* She swallowed, shaking her head. "Last night was everything. But I know that things haven't changed, not really. We both still have reasons why you and I would be a terrible idea. Your brothers aren't home, and I didn't wake up with a new last name. Last night, we were both exhausted, and frightened, and worn to our absolute edges, and if we need to pretend that last night didn't happen, I understand." She was surprised that her voice stayed even, that it didn't betray the fear she felt regardless of Jaina's answer.

Jaina considered her. "That's true. Are you still tired?"

"What?"

"Tired. Did you get enough sleep?"

"Yes, I..." She shook her head, confused. "I slept better than I have in some time."

"Are you still frightened? The way you were last night?"

Antoinette shook her head. "Not with you here."

"Good." Jaina leaned forward, bringing her hand up to the back of Antoinette's neck, and pulled her in for a kiss that fired every nerve in Antoinette's body, an explosion beginning in her lips and shivering down to her core. She sighed and sank into Jaina's embrace, and when she finally, reluctantly broke for air, Jaina's eyes were bright and locked on hers.

"Last night didn't happen because of the horrible things that happened over the last two days. Last night happened because of all of the wonderful things that have happened since you climbed down off that horse." She glanced down for a moment. "I have so many voices in my head, all shouting different things. What a bad idea this is. How impossible it is that someone like you could fall for someone like me."

"Jaina..."

She waved Antoinette off. "You're a brilliant, beautiful, sophisticated woman from a world I know nothing about. There's always going to be part of me that wonders why in the gods you chose me. Doesn't make it rational. Doesn't mean I need to listen. I don't know why this happened, why we were brought together, but I can't ignore the way I feel. And I don't want to."

We happened because we're pieces on a board. We happened because my grandmother wanted information on the rangers, and tugged all the strings she has to put me and a novice ranger in the same room. And now?

Now she knew. She knew how strong the rangers were, how fast. How impossibly fast they healed. She knew names. And what's more, in this moment, she knew that there was nothing that Jaina wouldn't tell her, nothing she wouldn't give her, and she knew the lie in Toni DeLuca's words.

It's not our own happiness, our own choices we trade for our privilege and power. It's hers. It's every person we manipulate, lie to, spy on. We treat them as pieces on a board, but Jaina's not that.

I'm not that. Not anymore.

Antoinette nodded slowly. "I wish there was a way for you to see you the way I do." She brushed her fingers over Jaina's face. "I've spent my entire life learning to bring out the beauty in my work. Often it takes weeks or months to discover what makes something special. But it took me exactly half a second after laying eyes on you to realize that you were unlike anyone I'd ever met, and about a full second after that to know I was in trouble. You're loyal, you're funny, you're kind, and yes. You're beautiful."

Jaina smiled. It lit her face up. "I don't know if I believe you, but I'm going to do my best. I have a lot of voices shouting different things. All that's really changed is I've chosen to listen to the right voices."

"And what are those voices telling you?" Antoinette managed to say. Jaina's hand was on her thigh, and even through the blanket, she was very aware of the touch.

"That we may only have a few months, but we get to decide what we do with those months." Jaina shrugged. "I'm a ranger. You're a DeLuca. Neither of those will ever change. But right here, right now, we're here. And we're safe. And we're together. The last time I stepped away from you because I was afraid of how I was feeling, I nearly lost you. I don't intend to make that mistake again." She took Antoinette's hand. "If you want to go back to the way things were, I respect that. But you'll have to make that decision, because now that I've kissed you, I know that I can't."

Antoinette took a deep breath. "You know it's not that simple."

"It never is." Jaina's smile faded. "I can't wipe away what happened in those woods. I can't wrestle the world back on its right course. But you and I, we can…"

Jaina, I'm a spy.

She wanted to say the words. Knew that she needed to say the words. But here, in this moment, watching Jaina tell her everything that she wanted to hear, she couldn't make her lips form them.

I've stopped. Stopped sending information, stopped sharing what I learn about her. Grandmother doesn't know about how strong she truly is, how fast she can heal. I'm not treating her as a source any longer.

Even in her mind, even without being spoken aloud, the excuses rang hollow.

If you tell her, she could be angry enough to tell Poole.

Even that, grounded as it was in the truth, wasn't really honest. Antoinette knew the moment those four words slipped out, they would be a match on an oil-soaked bridge, and nothing could ever be the same. She also knew that no one was pouring that oil other than herself.

Antoinette knew that this was a terrible idea, the worst of all possible choices.

But it's my godsdamned choice.

Jaina had fallen silent, and Antoinette leaned in and kissed her. "You know what a catastrophically bad idea this is, right?" she murmured against Jaina's lips. When they finally broke apart, Jaina let out a trembling sigh.

"It's hard to think of anything being a bad idea that puts you here, with me," she said.

Antoinette sighed, resting her head on Jaina's shoulder. "I don't know if either of us are ready for this."

"Probably not. But I haven't been ready for a single thing that's happened to me this year. This is the first time I've been eager to see what comes next."

"It has to stay in here. Within these walls."

Jaina nodded. "I know."

"Jaina." Antoinette looked her in the eye. "This is so important. My grandmother, she..." She swallowed. "She has people. Everywhere. Definitely in Westcott, possibly in this castle. If she finds out, you become a problem. And she has very little compunction in dealing with problems in very harsh ways."

"Well, does she have anyone in this room? At this moment?" Jaina asked.

Well... "No," Antoinette said, smiling softly.

"Then this, right here, is our place. For however long it lasts."

Antoinette kissed her again. "For however long it lasts."

***

The temptation to stay in bed with each other all day had been a strong one, but the need to maintain proper appearances, combined with Antoinette and Jaina's grumbling stomachs, finally succeeded in seeing them both dressed and back in the throne room. As soon as they stepped through the door, Antoinette's eyes were drawn to the spot on the floor where Meyers had fallen. She took a deep, shaking breath. "Did he..." She swallowed past the lump in his throat. "Did he suffer?" She knew the answer. She also needed to hear anything else.

Jaina rubbed her eyes. "He seemed more concerned about you than anything else. He wasn't alone, though. At the end." She looked over at Antoinette. "That has to count for something, right?" She tilted her head, and quietly said, "Company." A few moments later, Poole and Boyajian stepped into the room.

"Mistress." Poole offered a slight bow.

"Captain," Antoinette said. "Did you consider what I said last night?"

"I did. And, at least for the meantime, I believe you're correct," he said. "Only six people know the details of what happened, not including the two of you. I've impressed upon them all how important it is that circle not expand any further." Poole glanced back at the door before saying, "I've dispatched a courier to the duke with a message, notifying him that four deserters attempted to breach our security, that they were caught by Guardsman Meyers, and that Meyers heroically gave his life defending the duke's home and guests. I've also assured him we're keeping the entire incident quiet, of which I suspect he'll approve."

Antoinette nodded. "Did Meyers have a family?"

"A sister, Mistress. She lives near Havensport with her husband and three children. He wrote her often."

"She'll be notified?"

"She will. I'm not certain when, but I'll see to it."

"If word reaches you that they find themselves in need, I'd like you to let me know."

He nodded. "I'll do that."

"Thank you."

"For the moment, we've locked down the castle grounds," Poole said. "Given everything that's happened, I think it may be a good idea that the next time you leave this building should be when you head home after a job well done."

"What if she needs supplies?" Jaina asked.

"I'll send someone," Poole said. "I don't have the men to give you a full escort at all times, especially now. The best way to be certain that nothing like this happens again is to lock down the castle and keep you inside. Either that, or send you home now. Ultimately, it's your choice."

Antoinette shook her head. "I leave without the job being finished, both my grandmother and the duke are going to have questions. A lot of questions, none of which any of us are particularly eager to answer. I'll finish the work."

"How much longer will you need?"

Antoinette glanced around. "I'm not sure. It's not an exact science, but at least six weeks, maybe as long as ten."

Poole paused, and it was clear he was choosing his next words carefully. "Closer to six would be ideal. Things are happening very quickly in the Dominion now. The political climate is not going to get any simpler, and I know that you and I will both breathe much easier once you're back in Vetticci."

Raising an eyebrow, Antoinette asked, "Is there anything I need to know?"

He shook his head. "No, Mistress. Just..." Poole looked around at the walls. "Just hurry." He gave another bow, and turned to leave.

"Captain, a word?" Jaina asked.

He glanced back, and nodded. "Boyajian, stay here with Mistress DeLuca while the ranger and I speak."

Jaina gave Antoinette a quick glance, and followed him from the room. Once they'd left, Antoinette stepped up to Boyajian. "I haven't had the chance. To properly thank you for coming to my aid."

Boyajian bowed slightly.

"And I'm so very sorry about Meyers. I know you were friends."

His expression didn't change, but she could see the sadness in his eyes as he nodded.

Antoinette considered him for a moment before continuing. "I told the people who took me that my family doesn't do ransom, and that's true. But we do believe in rewarding those who offer service and stand with us. I owe you my life, and I now give you my word as a DeLuca of Vetticci. Should you ever ask of me something I am able to give, it's yours, from now until my death."

Boyajian blinked, and tilted his head in thanks as Jaina came back into the room. As he turned to leave, Antoinette stepped up and took his hand, and kissed him on the cheek. "Thank you for saving me, Boyajian. I won't forget it."

His cheeks flushed red. He swallowed, and nodded once more before turning to leave.

Antoinette turned back to Jaina. The ranger had an odd expression on her face. "Is everything okay?"

Jaina took a deep breath. "I'm not sure." She glanced at the door, cocking her head as she listened for Boyajian's fading footsteps, and stepped a bit closer to Antoinette, lowering her voice. "Poole said they were expecting couriers and a conscription unit to arrive yesterday. They didn't."

Antoinette frowned. "Maybe they were delayed?"

"That's not all. The smith, the one we met?" Antoinette nodded, and Jaina continued. "He's been making spearheads and arrowheads for the army. Every time they'd come to pick up a shipment, they'd have a new order for him, one after another. Five days ago, the last courier came by to pick up the shipment. The smith told Poole that when he asked for the next order, the courier told him that was the last."

"How long have they been having him fill orders for the army?"

"Months. And they gave no indication it would end anytime soon."

Antoinette shook her head. "Maybe the army is being disbanded? Maintaining a force that size is horribly expensive, even for the dukes. There's a reason that they don't usually keep a standing army."

"I hope you're right." Jaina didn't look convinced. Antoinette wanted to reach out and take her hand, but thought better of it.

"Look, you said Martine was going to find the army, right? And that he'd do his best to bring your brothers back through here?" Jaina nodded, and Antoinette continued, "I've seen how fast you move. Martine's probably already reached the Cicerone border. It's only a matter of time before he finds the army, and your brothers are on the way back." She offered a smile. "I'm excited to meet them."

That broke through Jaina's concern long enough for her eyes to widen. "That's a terrifying thought."

"What is? Me meeting your brothers?"

"No, my brothers meeting you," Jaina said.

"You don't think they'll like me?"

"I think they'll adore you," she said. "I also think they're the only two people outside of this room that I've never been able to lie to."

Antoinette smiled. "You're very gifted, but I don't believe dissembling is one of your gifts."

"For both our sakes, I hope you're wrong." Jaina took a deep breath. "Okay. You're right. I'm just... Every day that goes by without knowing is hard." She cleared her throat. "It's been a hard few days."

"Not all of it, I hope?"

Jaina shook her head. "No, not all of it." She smiled.

***

Grandmother,

Something has changed. Expected conscription patrols and couriers have stopped. Recurring military materiel orders have ceased. Indications are that the Dominion army is massed on the Cicerone border, but no further information about their intentions. However, the change in communications indicates two possibilities. Either they have completed whatever goal the army was assembled for in the first place, or they are about to move quickly and can no longer wait for new conscripts or supplies. Given the costs associated with maintaining a standing army of that size and the risks associated with open war with the Confessors, the former feels more likely.

There is no additional information from the ranger.

1,442 Hours

Happiness and fear were strange companions, but the two emotions had both built homes in Jaina's heart in the weeks following the abduction. Every possibility that her mind imagined was tinged with conflict. Every day, she thought about Martine walking through the door, both hopeful it would happen and anxious about what news he would bring. Every day, she thought about Poole learning the truth about what was happening with the army, both desperate to know Jak and Joran were safe, and terrified to hear that they weren't. Every hour they were away from home was too long, bursting with horrible possibilities. Every hour she was with Antoinette was too fast.

After that first night, they had both agreed that spending the entire night together was too risky. When Jaina had closed the door behind them, they both knew she could only be there for an hour, two at most. Despite that agreement, they found themselves wrapped up in each other the following morning. That pattern continued every night, with each morning finding Jaina listening to make sure no footfalls were anywhere near their doors before she crept back across the hall to change.

They did refrain from touching each other while Antoinette worked, both because Jaina found her touch so distracting that her amplified hearing, which had returned several days after her injuries, counted for naught, and because Antoinette insisted that Jaina's hand on the small of her back rendered her incapable of doing anything but shivering. Jaina never thought she could miss someone who sat less than fifteen feet away.

What are you doing, Cricket?

Go away. She didn't want to hear all the reasons she was making a mistake.

You know I'm in your head, right?

Go away. I'm happy.

We know you're happy. We love that you're happy. But we don't like the ticking godsdamned clock that you've tied to your happiness.

Jaina watched Antoinette brush back a stray hair that had tumbled into her face before bending down to the wood once more, shavings tumbling down to join the pile at her feet. *Maybe I don't get happy. Not the way other people do. Maybe this is what I get, this tiny morsel of joy. And if so, I'm grateful for it, for everything I'll be able to look back on and remember.*

Awww. That's beautiful. It's horseshit, but it's beautiful.

I'm not turning my back on her.

If you think that's what we want, you're a bigger idiot than we thought, and that's impressive. She could almost see the scowls on their faces. *You found someone who makes you happy, and you think either of us is going to be okay knowing that you're going to walk away from her for us? Do you honestly think either of us want that?*

I can't turn my back on you two, either. It's an impossible choice.

It's not. Choose the one that lets you be happy. Choose the one that lets you come home to us. Choose the one that doesn't have you lighting your entire life on fire to save us five years. Choose to be fucking happy, you stubborn, mule-headed...

"Are you okay?"

Jaina looked back to Antoinette. "I'm sorry?"

"I asked if you were okay," Antoinette repeated. "You looked upset for a moment."

"I'm all right." Jaina offered a smile that she knew didn't touch her eyes. "Just thinking about my brothers."

Antoinette nodded. "You know what Poole said. Almost no messages are getting through, anywhere. Even if Martine tried to send an update, there's no guarantee that it would have reached you."

"I know." Jaina nodded. "I'm just... It's going to be good to see them. But it's going to be hard to convince them that I'm still on the right path."

"You think they won't approve." Antoinette nodded sadly.

"On the contrary." Jaina chuckled. "They're going to be delighted by you. And they won't want to listen to any reason that keeps us apart."

"Oh." Antoinette smiled. "They sound almost as stubborn as someone else I know."

"I'm certain I have no idea what you're talking about," Jaina said. She took a breath. "When I was little, maybe four or five, I fell into a sinkhole. It was deep. Probably not as deep as I remember, but it felt like I'd tumbled into the Breaking. When I tried to climb out, the sinkhole partially collapsed. Pinned my legs and chest in place. It took my parents and everyone in town almost a full day to get me out."

"Jaina, that sounds horrible."

She nodded. "It was, but Jak and Joran were there. My mother told them it was their job to lay by the edge of the pit and talk to me. To make sure I knew I wasn't alone. So they made up stories, told me jokes, teased me about all the attention I was getting. It was frightening, but being able to hear them helped."

You're stuck with us. Now and forever, Cricket.

Jaina smiled. "A few months before, my dad had gone crazy trying to track down a cricket that wouldn't stop chirping in the inn. Jak told me that while I was down there, I should see if I could find the cricket, ask it to move on so our dad would stop getting so red in the face. And then Joran suggested that since I clearly like hiding in tiny places, maybe I'd actually been the cricket all along." She chuckled. "When they finally got me out, I was giggling. The first thing I did was chirp at my brothers. They hugged me and tickled me, and from that point on, they called me Cricket."

Antoinette smiled as she listened.

Jaina smiled. "They're going to like you. They're not going to be okay with me not throwing you over my shoulder and carrying you back to Lofland Fork, telling the rest of the world to leap in the Breaking."

Antoinette laughed. The sound broke Jaina's heart in one beat and fixed it on the next. "My grandmother would probably have a few things to say."

"Listen, I know that your grandmother is one of the most powerful and wealthiest people in the world, but give my parents five minutes with her, and they'd have her rolling pastry in the kitchen wondering what the gods just happened."

"Honestly, of all the things you've said, that's the strongest case you've made for me to walk away from everything," Antoinette said. "The chance to see my grandmother poking at a pie crust, trying to bribe the dough to rise faster, is now all I want in the world."

"Our family will have the first sourdough starter with an account at the Bank of Vetticci."

Antoinette nodded. "If anyone could buy a shortcut to the laws of nature, it would be Toni DeLuca. Either that or she'd have another starter assassinated, just to really send the message."

"On second thought, she can bus tables."

Antoinette laughed. "I'm excited to meet your brothers."

Jaina's grin faded as she nodded. "You'll love them. They're idiots, but..." She took a deep breath. "Mom and Dad were so upset when I joined. But they just kind of looked sad. They told me I was being stupid, but they never seemed all that surprised, and I think I know why."

"Because they would have done the same?"

Jaina lifted a surprised eyebrow, and Antoinette smiled. "I've gotten to know you fairly well. And I'm guessing your brothers aren't as different from you as you might think."

"That's an outrageous accusation. I demand satisfaction."

"Later." Jaina felt the temperature in the room leap by twenty degrees as Antoinette continued. "You three grew up with each other, for each other. Every story you've told me, every time the three of you got in trouble, it just shows me how eager each of you is to lay down in front of a rampaging bull to spare the others any pain. You love each other, and love makes idiots of us all."

Jaina raised an eyebrow. "Do you think I was an idiot for joining the rangers?"

"You did what you thought you had to."

"That's not an answer."

Antoinette shrugged. "I'm not equipped to answer. I have brothers, just like you. I was raised to watch out for them, to protect them, just like you. But that's where the similarity ends. I would never have sacrificed so much for them the way you did for yours. And the fact that I know that's true makes me deeply sad." She looked back at Jaina. "I dream of loving someone that much, so much that doing something stupid is the only choice you have."

"You've never made a choice that dumb?"

Antoinette looked at her in a way that turned Jaina's legs to liquid, and said, "Just one. The worst decision I could have made, and the best."

Before Jaina could fully process what she'd just said, Antoinette turned back to her work, and as she carved, said, "Do you know what I've been thinking about?"

"What?"

"A cottage."

Jaina frowned, confused. "A cottage?"

"Yes." Antoinette continued to speak as a hummingbird emerged from the oak, its appearance marked by a rain of wooden slivers. "I studied architecture for a year. It was never going to be my specialty, but it helps to have a passing familiarity with many schools of art. I drew so many buildings, but my favorite was from a reference of an Imperial fishing cottage. It was small, only one room. A stove to cook on, a table and chairs, a bed. It was by the sea, but I think I'd like mine by a lake. In the woods."

Jaina smiled. "I'm sure your home is a bit bigger than that."

"It's too big. Empty. Waiting to be filled with people, noise, all talking about me, no one talking to me. Every part of it exists for a purpose, to show our wealth, our power, our influence, but none of it exists just to make us feel at home," Antoinette said. "I've been surrounded by people for my entire life, and I've been lonely my entire life. It wasn't until I came here that I felt actually seen. I don't want to be surrounded by people. I just want to be with the right person."

The rough shape of the wings took form, and she switched to a finer tool, digging the individual feathers from the oak. "I want to wake up when I want to. I want to eat food that hasn't been chosen to ensure my figure remains what it should be, to make sure my stomach doesn't make the wrong noises when I'm meeting with people I don't care about. I want to carve something silly, something pointless, and give it away. And I want to stay up and watch the stars long past when I need to sleep." She paused. "I suppose I'd need to learn how to cook."

"I know how to cook."

She couldn't see Antoinette smile, but she knew it was there. "I believe I remember you telling me your parents didn't trust you to prepare food."

"My mother's standards are quite high, true," Jaina said. "I may not be the best cook, but I know a few dishes."

"Like what?" Grasping feet materialized, wrapped around a branch. "What will you cook for me?"

"I can make beef stew. Brown bread, butter. And peach pie. I could never get the apple or pear quite right, but peach pie I can do."

"Can we sit on the ground by the lake while we eat?"

Jaina nodded, her heart breaking. "We can watch the sun set over the water, listen to the crickets and the owls. Eat the pie with our hands."

Antoinette's blade paused, the curl of wood hanging precariously from the blued steel. "I hate how easy you've made it for me to imagine being happy." Her voice was soft, so soft that Jaina wouldn't have heard it before she woke by the fire. "Sometimes I get so angry. Angry that you've let me see just how easy it is to be happy, and angry that with all I have in the world, I can't have that."

You two are perfect for each other. You're both idiots.

"What can I do?"

Antoinette cleared her throat, and her blade resumed its path through the wood. "Let me be sad. Let me be angry. And when I've finished for today, lay with me and help me forget everything outside my chambers for a few hours. Especially that those few hours bring me closer to having to walk away from you."

***

Jaina could hear both their heartbeats in the darkness of Antoinette's room, hear them both recover from gasping breaths and shivering skin. With the lamps doused, the room was dark enough that she couldn't be sure if Antoinette could see Jaina's face next to her, but she could see the glimmer of tears tumble from her eyes to vanish into the pillow. She brought up a thumb, brushing one away. "Are you all right?" she murmured.

"I forget you can see me so easily." Antoinette brought her hand up to wipe her eyes. "I'm perfect. And terrible." She let loose what was either a quiet laugh or sob. Jaina couldn't tell which. It was probably both. "How could you do this to me?"

"Antoinette..."

"How could you give me a glimpse of what we could be, what we could have? How could you be the kind of person who I couldn't help but fall for, and the kind of person I could never be with?" Her arms came up around Jaina's neck, clinging to her as if she was afraid Jaina would vanish. "I don't want you to go, Jaina."

Jaina opened her mouth, and Antoinette shook her head sharply. "Please. Don't say anything. There's nothing to say. Just kiss me. Please."

Jaina did as she was told. Moments later, when she heard Antoinette speak, it was so soft that she thought she imagined it.

"I love you, and I don't want you to go."

There were a thousand reasons to stay silent. None mattered. "I love you, and I don't want to go."

They clung to each other, and willed the sunrise to wait just a bit longer.

938 Hours

Forty-seven days of paradise and dread.

For over a month and a half, Antoinette had found herself in a bubble, a quiet space away from the realities of the world that seemed determined to tumble on. She'd never known this kind of peace. When she was with Jaina, the world seemed to quiet in a way that let her know that it had always been loud, always hammering her with expectations and demands. Over forty-seven days, she'd gotten a glimpse at what life could be like without the deafening clamor of all that was expected of her, and while she loved Jaina with an intensity that frightened her at times, a very small part of her hated Jaina for showing her what could be.

There weren't many times that the two of them were apart. That was entirely by choice, each of them very aware of the clock ticking behind every shared moment. However, the lack of manpower in the city occasionally meant that Jaina was asked to help with small tasks. After her work helping the smith and her efforts in dousing the fire, the people of Westcott had begun referring to Jaina as "their ranger".

It was while Jaina was helping unload several carts for a woman and her daughter in town that Poole brought Antoinette the letter. He'd been somewhat less withdrawn since the abduction. Five days earlier, he'd sent a note to Meyers' sister, and asked Antoinette if she'd like to include a note. When he knocked softly on the door to the throne room, she stood, dusting wood shavings off her hands. "I gave Boyajian my letter last night. He should have it for you."

"He gave it to me this morning, Mistress. First thing. Sent it off a few hours ago. This is something else." Poole slowly turned to take in the expanse of the throne room, and shook his head. "I owe you an apology, Mistress."

Antoinette frowned. "For what?"

"I overheard the duke tell his advisor how much he was paying for you to come do a..." He shook his head. "What's it called? You living here and doing this work?"

"A residency?"

"That's the one," he said. "How much he was paying for you to do a residency. I was furious. With everything going on, I couldn't imagine spending that much on a frivolity. I didn't say anything, of course."

Antoinette smiled. "Of course not."

"But this..." Poole took a deep breath as he took in the expanse of the mural. A forest now grew from the floor of the throne room, tangled deep with vines, creatures jumping and flying between branches. A pathway wound in and out of the trees, and every time it emerged, a new person strode forth. All told, there were eighteen figures stepping through the trees, each bearing the likeness of a member of the Westcott family. The roads to the left and right of the throne room ended at the back, where they converged on sprawling farmland with the Westcott Sigil formed in twisting vines. Poole spoke in hushed tones, as if he was in a temple. "This is miraculous. I never could have imagined anything like this."

"Thank you, Captain." Antoinette set down her brush and the cup of stain. "It needs a bit of color to bring out the details, but I hope the duke will be pleased."

"Pleased? He'll spend the first few hours not knowing what to say, then he'll never shut up about it." He paused, and said, "I'd be quite grateful if you didn't share that particular comment with His Grace."

"I'm sure I have no idea to what you're referring."

"You're too kind." Poole held out an envelope. "Courier from the border brought this for you. Has your family seal, I believe. Wanted to bring it by before I begin my morning rounds."

"Thank you, Captain." Antoinette did her best to keep the chill that ran up her arms at the sight of the purple wax seal from changing her expression. She took the letter, and glanced down at her grandmother's personal signet.

"Mistress." Poole gave a quick bow, and left, nodding at Boyajian as he did. Once he was gone, Boyajian gestured to the letter and frowned.

"No, it's... I'm fine. It's just a letter from my grandmother. Personally." Antoinette shook her head. "She hasn't written to me since I got here."

Boyajian blinked again, his eyes narrowed.

"That's just her way. I know she's there if I need her." Swallowing, Antoinette broke the seal, and extracted the letter from inside. Her grandmother's precise, angled script greeted her.

Antoinette,

I trust this letter finds you well. The college has shared some of your progress sketches with me, and I'm pleased to see the work proceeds at a satisfactory pace. By my estimate, you should be nearing completion. I'll be glad to see you returned home. I know how eager the Duke was for you to come, but the gulf between us is far too wide for my liking, and the sooner we are both on the same side, the sooner I won't feel so restless. I never liked you being away, not even for two days.

Until such time as you are returned to us, I trust the duke's hospitality will provide all that you need, and that the ranger will give you the peace of mind to see your work to its end. I think once you return home, we'll enjoy your company for a bit, and perhaps take some time without visitors to disturb our reunion.

With pride,

Madame Toni Deluca

Antoinette stared at the letter for far too long, reading it over and over, her skin growing cold. The paper rattled softly, and she realized her hands were trembling.

"Boyajian?" He walked over, and she said in as steady a voice as she could manage, "Please have someone go find Jaina. I need to see her. Immediately."

He raised a quizzical eyebrow.

"I promise, I'll fill you in soon. But I need to speak to Jaina."

Boyajian nodded, and headed to the door.

***

It didn't take long. Jaina walked through the door fifteen minutes after Boyajian stepped out. Antoinette had asked for a cup of tea, and was sitting on the stool sipping it as Jaina came to her side.

"Is everything all right?" she asked, eyes wide. "Boyajian made it pretty clear that I was needed back here fast."

Antoinette took a deep breath, and glanced past Jaina to see if anyone had followed her. "You're alone?"

Jaina nodded. "Boyajian went to go help Poole with something." She crouched down next to Antoinette, looking up at her. "Antoinette, what's wrong?"

She didn't want to say it. She'd gone over the words over and over in the fifteen minutes, and knew what she needed to say, but Antoinette knew the moment she did, the bubble would burst, and the world would thunder into their ears once more. The quiet would be over, and the clock would begin its last few ticks.

She didn't want to say it.

She didn't have a choice.

"The Dominion is at war with the Alddarri Empire, Jaina. Their army crossed the bridge over the Breaking two days ago, and they're marching north."

The room was quiet for an impossibly long few seconds. Jaina stared at her, straightening up to her full height and taking a step back. "How... You can't know that. That can't be true."

Antoinette held up the letter. "A message from my grandmother. We have... There are certain phrases we use, phrases to share critical information with each other. We knew the Dominion was raising an army, so it was important she be able to tell me if the situation changed." She held it out to Jaina.

"I can't read very well."

"Yes. Sorry." She shook her head, and quickly read the letter out loud. "That phrase, 'the gulf between us', refers to the Breaking. The duke being eager tells me that the Dominion struck first. The rest is effectively telling me not to leave the capital for any reason until I finish the job." Antoinette took a deep breath. "She's also telling me to finish as fast as I can so I can get out of the Dominion."

Jaina was shaking her head even before Antoinette stopped speaking. "That makes no sense. We're not at war with the Empire. We don't have any reason to be. It's the Confessors, it's got to be the Confessors."

"I'm sorry, Jaina."

"How can she know this anyway?" Jaina took the letter and stared at it, as if the words would suddenly make sense if she glared hard enough.

"My grandmother is very wealthy. She has a lot of interests throughout the Dominion. Someone must have let her know." Antoinette chose her words carefully, knowing as she did the bridge was crumbling beneath her. "I'm sorry, Jaina."

"Stop. Stop saying that, please." Jaina shook her head again. "It has to be a mistake."

"Martine's had weeks. He must have found your brothers before the army marched," Antoinette said, standing up and gripping Jaina's shoulder. "This doesn't mean..."

Jaina looked up at her. "You're sure about this."

Antoinette nodded, her heart breaking at the naked fear in Jaina's eyes. "My grandmother wouldn't send this message if she wasn't certain."

She watched Jaina begin to pace, back and forth, brow furrowed and eyes wide. "If Martine didn't get to them..."

"There are so many things we don't know, Jaina. We don't know Martine hasn't pulled them out already. We don't know that they were part of the force that went north. I know you're frightened, but they could be perfectly safe."

Jaina shook her head. "I should have done something. Something more."

"You did everything possible," Antoinette said. "Everything you possibly could have done. This isn't your fault."

They didn't say anything for a long while. Antoinette wanted to take her hand, to hold her and make promises she knew had no substance. Instead, she just watched the woman she loved tear herself to pieces with worry.

Finally, Jaina took a deep breath. "Does Poole know?"

Antoinette shook her head. "I don't think so."

Even as she spoke, Jaina's head tilted. "Someone coming. Fast." Moments later, Boyajian ran into the room. He beckoned for them to follow him, and when they didn't immediately do so, he repeated the gesture, pleading in his eyes. Jaina glanced over at Antoinette, muttering, "I think that may have changed." The two of them got up and followed. Antoinette briefly reached out and gripped Jaina's hand. Jaina squeezed back.

Boyajian led them to the courtyard, which was as full as Antoinette had ever seen it. Virtually the entire house staff was there, along with every guardsman remaining at the castle. Everyone was milling about except for Captain Poole, who was having a hushed argument with a man sweating through the dark grey wools of a Dominion army officer uniform. The officer held the reins of a horse, and as they talked, one of the stable hands came out with another horse.

"You have your orders, Captain," the officer said in a raspy voice. "I have four other towns to reach before I can sleep."

"You can't drop this in our laps and ride on without giving us more information," Poole snapped, waving a sheet of paper in the man's face. "People are going to demand answers."

"I have none to give you," the officer said, climbing up on the fresh mount. "You are the senior official left in Westcott. Carry out your orders. More will be forthcoming, I have no doubt." He clucked his tongue, and staffers scrambled out of the way as he left in a cloud of dust.

The courtyard fell silent as everyone turned to look at Poole, who stared down at the page, his face grim. Finally, he looked up. "This is a message from Duke Snowsill. It's signed by seven of the dukes on the council. Our instructions are as follows. We are to lock down the city of Westcott. No travel in or out until further notice. No non-official communications in or out until further notice. We are to identify any citizens of the Alddarri Empire that are currently in the city for any purpose."

"Only Imperials here are with the trade mission," someone shouted. "We counting them?"

Poole nodded. "No exceptions. They are to be detained immediately."

Murmurs rippled through the crowd. "Sir, that's... that's illegal," Sergeant Milla said. "They've got diplomatic protections."

"Not anymore." Poole stared down at the sheet, his lips moving as he came to terms with what he's about to say. "By unanimous ruling of the Ducal Council, a state of war has been declared to be in existence between the Dominion and the Alddarri Empire." He read from the form as the crowd erupted, raising his voice to a shout to be heard. "In response to repeated incursions into Dominion territory by Imperial criminals, and irrefutable evidence of Imperial plots to attack the peaceful people of the Dominion, we have embarked on a campaign to ensure the peace and security of all the peoples of this great continent. Our brave soldiers will not rest until the corrupt leadership of the Alddarri Empire has been brought to justice for their crimes. Already, they have seized the bridge across the Breaking and several Imperial cities, proof of the might of our..." He trailed off, shaking his head. Looking up, he said, "We're at war. We have two hours to lock down the city. Milla, Casper, get to the Imperial trade mission. Let them know they cannot leave, but do not enter. Do you understand?"

"Sir." Milla and another soldier turned and ran.

"The rest of you. We've been ordered to announce this to the people. I'll be speaking in the city square tonight at sundown. Spread out, tell as many as you can. We don't need everyone, but the more we have, the easier this will be. I want everyone back here in an hour, so let's move."

As everyone scattered, frantically chattering to each other, Poole stepped over to Jaina and Antoinette. "How much longer?" he asked with no preamble.

"What?"

"How much longer do you need to finish the job?" He glanced around, keeping his voice low. "Is it days or weeks?"

Antoinette glanced at Jaina. Her face looked as if it was carved from stone. "I don't..." She shook her head. "Days. Two, maybe three."

"You have two." He held up the paper. "These orders specifically exempt you from the travel restrictions. They've already notified The Table. The Iron Eye is sending two fists of soldiers to escort you home. They'll be here in two days. I don't know if they're willing to wait for you or not, but if the next orders that come tell us that you can't leave, I do not want to have to deal with two dozen angry Iron Eye bastards who take exception with those orders. I appreciate your work here, but I don't know what's coming for any of us, and I think it's best that you find your way back home sooner rather than later."

"Two days?" Antoinette swallowed. "Surely Jaina could escort me to the border..." She trailed off as Poole was already shaking his head.

"The Table doesn't want anyone from the Dominion responsible for your security. Besides, this was included in the orders." He held up another sealed note. "It's for you, ranger. My guess is that you have new orders."

Jaina took the note, but made no move to open it. She was at a loss for words.

"Do what you can until the Vetticcian escort arrives, and I'll call the contract fulfilled," Poole said. "If you'll excuse me."

The old captain turned and walked away, leaving Jaina and Antoinette alone.

***

They walked back to the throne room in silence, their footfalls echoing through the empty stone walls. They reached the room, and Antoinette stood and stared down at her tools while Jaina slowly turned, taking in the room.

Antoinette gestured at the sealed note in Jaina's hands. "What does it say?"

Jaina looked down at it, as if surprised it was there. "I should have had the captain read it for me." She offered it to Antoinette. "Would you?"

Antoinette nodded. Tearing the letter open, she let out a long breath. "You're instructed to hand over my security to Captain Poole and report to Lofland Fork as soon as possible to meet with someone named Edmund Shakkar." She handed it back to Jaina. "Do you know who that is?"

"He's the ranger assigned to Lofland Fork." Jaina scowled, crumpling up the letter. Glancing around, she asked, "Can you finish in two days?"

Antoinette wanted to say no, wanted to say anything that would change what was about to happen. "It'll take me a day, day and a half. I just have to apply the..." Her words died in her throat. "This isn't fair."

Jaina chuckled. There was no humor in it. "It's not like we didn't know this was coming."

"Yeah." Antoinette picked up a brush, turning it over in her hands. Tapping it against her palm, she walked over to stand next to Jaina.

"This room is beautiful, Antoinette. It's so much more than someone like the Duke deserves. It's so much more than I expected."

"What did you expect?"

Jaina smiled down at her, and Antoinette could see the tears in her eyes glimmer with reflected lamplight. "Not this. Nothing like this."

"Jaina..."

"I know I was the one who said it was better to take the time we had, to look at this time as a gift." Jaina cleared her throat. "And it's been..."

Antoinette took her hand, and Jaina looked down, blinking.

"Someone could see."

"I don't care." Antoinette was stunned to hear the truth in those words. "I don't care, not anymore."

Jaina squeezed. "There is a part of me that is so angry at you."

"Why?"

"Because I didn't know," Jaina said, her voice raised for the first time as she stepped back. "I didn't know that this could be..." She wiped her eyes in a rapid movement, as if angry at the tears. "I could have stood here, watched you, thought about you, fantasized about you, dreamed about you, and it could have stayed nothing more than that. And that I can take with me. That can fade on its own time, if it ever does. But now, I know what a pale imitation that would be, and what a pale imitation my life is without you, and I'm so angry, because there's nothing ahead of me but knowing what I had and will never have again."

"If you think for a moment that I'm not..." Antoinette stepped forward, narrowing her eyes. "You think this is easy for me? I should have finished this job three weeks ago. Every day, I went as slowly as I could, because every cut I made was another step closer to this godsdamned moment. I've spent every moment torn between thinking about you and thinking how we could just disappear, from the rangers, my grandmother, the war, everything, just find a place where we get to hold onto this. I would burn my world to the ground to stay with you, Jaina, and if it were only about us, I'd already have lit the match."

Jaina stared at her, cheeks wet and face flushed. Finally, she said, "I've been thinking a lot about what happens when Martine gets here. What happens when I hear a voice at that door and turn around to see Jak and Joran grinning at me. After the hugs, after the ton of shit that they'll have carted down to give me, after all of that, I've been thinking about the moment that I introduce the two of them to you. About how long it would take them to realize that I'm in love with you."

Antoinette didn't say anything. She didn't trust herself to say anything.

"It would take Jak a few moments. He's always been the slow one. Joran, though…" She shook her head. "He'd spot the way I looked at you right away, and then he'd get so very angry."

"Why?" Antoinette asked.

"Because the two of them would politely but clearly tell Martine to go fuck himself, and they'd walk their ass back to the army, informing them that the exemption doesn't apply anymore because they're not going to let me do this. They're not going to let me walk away from you."

"You think so?"

Jaina tilted her head for a moment, almost as if listening to someone, and she nodded, smiling softly. "Doing something stupid and self-destructive to spare those we love any pain isn't just my game. It's a Creighton trait."

"You three love each other so much you're just scrambling over each other to throw yourselves onto the fire just to keep the others from getting singed." Antoinette shook her head. "What a stupid, destructive, pointless fucking thing love is."

"Yeah." Jaina took a deep breath. "And that reality, that certainty has me questioning what the actual fuck I'm doing."

"What do you mean?"

"There are two possibilities. First, that Martine found them before the army marched north. If that's the case, they're already on their way here. Even if something were to change, even if they were to be called back for some reason, they're not going to walk north on their own, cross the Breaking on their own, just to find the army. They'll have to wait, and by the time they do, this entire disaster will be done, one way or the other."

Antoinette had never felt this blend of hope and despair begin bubbling in her chest as she did listening to Jaina in that moment. "But you don't know that he found them."

"I don't." Jaina took a deep breath. "And if that's the case, they're far away from me, far away from Martine, and well beyond his reach. And I don't know how to handle that. I've spent months living with a question that I was terrified to know the answer to, and now I do, and I don't know how to handle spending every day knowing that Jak and Joran are in danger at every waking moment. The only thing I do know, the only thing they're screaming at me right now, is that whether I hold to my oath or not won't change where they are. Martine can't bring them back if they're on the other side of the Breaking. I can't bring them back. Which means that everything I did to bring them home was for nothing."

"Jaina…" Antoinette stepped forward, gripping her forearm.

"So when you talk about running, talk about finding some place where our fucking lives and this fucking world isn't hanging over our head like a bloody scythe, I'm finding it harder and harder to see that as anything other than the best idea I've ever heard," Jaina said. "Because if the alternative is letting go of you, knowing that it won't do a damned thing for my family..." She raised red eyes to meet Antoinette's. "Could it work?"

In that moment, the part of Antoinette's mind that had been molded since she was a child to connect the dots of everything laid before her burst into frantic life. She saw the weak security in this place they knew so well, saw the woods that had been her prison but had also done such a job of hiding so many for so long. She thought about the accounts she had access to, the sources she could tap, every way her family would come searching for her and all the ways she could avoid them. She thought about waking up next to Jaina, not rushing to break apart before someone could see, but spending her days wrapped up with someone who had no agenda for her, no plan for her future, wanted nothing more than to see her happy, and for a moment she could see that life so clearly that it stole the breath from her lungs.

But that part of her mind couldn't stop there.

She saw all the ways she would evade her grandmother, and all the ways Toni DeLuca would step around them. She saw the two of them waking up in the night to black blades and black bags, the nightmare that would come when Jaina tried to stop her family from bringing her home. She saw the fear, the anxiety that would come from spending every day wondering how long it would be until they found them, and even with that, Antoinette wanted to grab Jaina's hand and run, to see just how far they could get together.

And then she saw two shrouded bodies, brought home from a war they should never have been a part of, and the dream cracked like cheap porcelain.

She saw Jaina break as she realized what their love had cost.

She saw grief and rage consume them, consume any life they could build, consume even the memories they'd made in the all too short weeks they'd had together.

She met Jaina's eyes, and said in a trembling voice, "No. No, it couldn't."

"Antoinette..."

"This has been lovely, Jaina. This has been..." Antoinette shook her head. "This has been everything. It's been everything I never knew I wanted, and everything I will hold onto for the rest of my life, but if you and I run, if we turn our back on the rest of the world, the world won't simply spin on without us. It will come for us. It will come with teeth and rage, and it won't just be you and I that pay the price. You know this. You've known it since before we met."

"And what if I don't care?" Jaina asked, eyes flashing. "If we're on borrowed time, if we're on stolen moments, then I want to steal as many as I can. And if the world comes for us, I'll be there to stand between the world and what we found in each other."

Gods, please, don't do this.

"I've done nothing my entire life but throw everything I want, everything that makes me happy into the forge for those I love," Jaina said. "But I've never had something I was so willing, so eager to fight for. What we have..." She stepped forward and took Antoinette's hands. "This is worth fighting for, isn't it?"

"Jaina..." Her voice broke. *Please. Please don't make me do this.*

"I love you, Antoinette. I know that my family would never want me to let go of someone like you," Jaina said, pulling her in close. They were back in that moment outside their doors, Antoinette looking up into Jaina's eyes, feeling like she was falling, knowing how close she could be to giving into everything they both wanted, both needed. "The world is on fire, and we can't stop that, but maybe we can..."

"I'm a spy."

The moment the words were out, Antoinette wanted nothing more than to claw them back in, to reach out and yank them from Jaina's perfect ears. Instead, she picked up the jagged pieces of her breaking heart, and dug them deep into the only person who'd ever made her feel seen.

Jaina blinked. "What?"

"I'm a spy, Jaina." She kept her voice steady. She was so desperate to keep her voice steady. "I was here to gather information. That's what my family does, that's why we have the wealth and power we have. My grandmother didn't train me to be an artist because she wanted to nurture my gift. She trained me to be valuable, to be invited into the homes of the rich and powerful, and she trained me to listen."

Jaina stepped back, shaking her head. "But..."

Antoinette couldn't let her speak. She was terrified that Jaina would once again say the perfect thing to break down all her defenses, to remind her how she felt when this woman held her, spoke to her, kissed her. So she pressed on, relentless. "We didn't know why the Dominion was raising such a large army. The duke had been after me for years, ever since he was told I didn't do residencies outside Vetticci. It became an obsession, one that we cultivated, teased, allowed to flourish, until we had something we needed. This was the perfect time, and so I was sent to learn everything I could about the Duke, the Dominion military, and..." As much as she knew she needed to say it, she couldn't make the last word come out.

She didn't need to. "And what?" Jaina said, her tone a knife into Antoinette's guts. "And rangers? And me?"

Forgive me, Jaina. "We didn't know anything about the rangers. The opportunity was just too valuable to let pass."

Jaina stared at her. "Too valuable?" She swallowed, turning away. The crumpled orders crinkled as her fist closed around them. She stared at the floor for a long time before speaking. "Every day. Every day, that fucking voice in my head asked me how someone like you could fall for someone like me. It didn't make sense. It never made sense. But I pushed it aside. Convinced that was just my insecurity, my fear talking." She turned to meet Antoinette's eyes. Her expression tore Antoinette's guts out. "I suppose this explains it."

Everything inside Antoinette howled with fury, desperate for her to say the truth, tell Jaina what she truly meant to her, to rip that expression of betrayal and sadness from the ranger's eyes. It was all she wanted. *But I don't get what I want. I'm a fucking DeLuca.* Antoinette gritted her teeth, and twisted the knife. "You came here to do a job. So did I. You had your reasons for being here. So did I."

Jaina's head lowered, and her shoulders sank. It was as if something had been yanked from inside her, hollowing her out. She didn't say anything for a long time.

"Jaina..."

"I'm so fucking stupid."

Antoinette swallowed. "I'm so sorry."

"Why?" Jaina turned, and the expression in her eyes showed just how thoroughly the bridge had been burned. They were empty and hard. "You did your job. I hope you got plenty to share. I hope it's fucking useful."

Antoinette had trained as long as she could remember to keep her feelings from her face. It took everything she had to do so now. She knew, right now, in this moment, that she would never forgive herself for the words she had to say. "It was never personal, Jaina. It was my job."

Jaina shut her eyes for a few impossibly long moments. When she opened them, they were cold. "Thank you for your honesty, Mistress. But..." She held up the crumpled orders. "You're no longer my charge. And I'm no longer your source."

Jaina turned on her heel, and was gone in moments. Antoinette stood, surrounded by beauty she'd coaxed from bare wood over months, and she began to cry, quietly and alone, in the ruins of the world she'd just set aflame.

920 Hours

There was a long-standing tradition that when a ranger asked a town to provide them a mount, the town did so. While it had never been documented into law, there was an understanding of the role rangers played in society, and no one wanted to be the one responsible for delaying them on their way to whatever lay ahead. When Jaina had asked Poole for a horse, he had offered no objection, only a quick nod and a quiet, "You did well, ranger."

It had been all she could do not to burst into laughter. Or tears. Out of uncertainty as to which would emerge, she kept things locked down as best she could.

The Dominion was a massive country. Easily the biggest of the four nations on the continent, it stretched for thousands of miles from the Breaking to the Myre. When one looked at a map, the two cities of Westcott and Lofland Fork were only separated by a few fingers. The road between the two was well kept. It was as easy a journey as one could find in this country, but it still would take Jaina over a day to reach her home.

She declined several invitations to travel with convoys, ignoring the nervous expressions of men and women hopeful to have a ranger ride alongside them while they traveled. Whenever they got close, she could pick up snippets of conversation as worry burned its way through the roads and communities of this country. She was not alone in the constant simmer of fear that had settled on her shoulders since learning of the invasion. Jaina knew the constant chatter of speculation and rumor was a way to hold that anxiety, that fear at bay. But when they saw the blackthorn staff strapped to her back, they would pounce, certain that she would know more, have some tidbit of information.

It was exhausting. And Jaina was already exhausted.

You could try getting some sleep.

She ignored them. Since she left Westcott and everyone in it behind her, she had tried to focus on nothing more than the road in front of her, the steady hoofbeats punctuating the sounds swirling around her. It had not been particularly effective.

I know that seems obvious, you know, actually sleeping. But that's why they'll never see it coming.

She shifted on her saddle, gritting her teeth. *Go away.*

Again, in your head, Cricket. Only here because you want us here.

You know that's not true. I want to be alone.

Jak snorted. *You've never wanted to be alone. Not once, in your entire life, have you been comfortable alone. That's why we showed up in the first place, remember? Why it was so important that you keep us with you?"*

I'm not a child anymore. Not stuck in that hole, not scared and alone.

You sure about that? Joran's voice wasn't cruel. It was even and calm. *Far as I can see, you're still stuck in a hole. You're still alone. And you're exhausted. You need to sleep.*

I'm a ranger. I can go days, maybe weeks without sleep.

You're a woman with a broken heart. I don't think that ignoring that is part of your particular collection of abilities.

I'm fine.

Hear that, Jak? She's fine.

Makes perfect sense, Joran. Why else would we be here unless she was completely, unquestionably fine? The picture of fine? The textbook image of fine stored in a college vault to reference in case anyone was ever confused what the word meant?

"Why won't you leave me alone?" she moaned aloud. The road stretched ahead and behind her, mercifully empty. "I was an idiot. I know I was an idiot. And I know that I'll spend the rest of my life knowing what an idiot I was."

Well... yes.

Jaina's shoulders sagged. *I never should have trusted her.*

That's not why you're an idiot. She could see Joran rubbing the bridge of his nose in his tone. *Take a breath. Think. Actually think, don't just cheerfully pummel yourself for some imagined error in judgement. What did she gain?*

I told her everything.

You don't know anything, Cricket. You've been a ranger for eighteen seconds.

She knows I can heal. How strong I am.

The intelligence coup of the century, I'm sure. Stop whining, and think about it. What did she gain by telling you that she was a spy?

For a brief moment, Antoinette's face swam up in her memory. It hurt worse than the arrow punching through her guts, and she shook her head. *I don't want to think about this.*

Afraid it's not that easy, Cricket. We don't get the choice of what haunts us.

Jaina shut her eyes, and took several deep breaths. When she opened them once more, it was quiet. She knew they were still there. They were always there. But for now, they left her to her misery.

It was nearly sundown on the second day when she reached the western gates of Lofland Fork. She heard the chaos long before she saw it. Dozens, hundreds of wagons and horses milled in the woods surrounding the gates, countless people sprawled on the ground or leaning up against their mounts. As she rode through, questions bombarded her from all sides as people realized who and what she was. By the time Jaina reached the gates, it had taken her nearly an hour to navigate through the mass of impatient people.

Twelve guards were posted before the gates. As she approached, one of them, an older man with an eyepatch and the red markings of a sergeant jogged up, hand outstretched. "The city's locked down. No one in until further notice. So turn that nag of yours around and..." His voice trailed off as his eyes flicked to the staff sticking out above her shoulder. He cleared his throat, and offered a quick bow. "Begging your pardon, ranger. Didn't realize."

"Why is the city locked down?" she asked, climbing down off the horse.

He shrugged. "Orders. Got 'em a few days ago, after the announcement of the war. No one in or out. Way we hear it, it's the same way with any city bigger than a handful. They said hold for further notice. So we're holdin'."

She looked around, frowning. "There are hundreds of people here. Shipments, food for inside the city. What are they supposed to do?"

"All respect, ranger, but I don't know. I just do what I'm told."

Jaina exhaled slowly. She knew she should be angry about this, but she struggled to care. "I'm looking for Shakkar. Local ranger."

"Last I heard, he was in Duke Gaille's home."

"With the duke?"

The sergeant shook his head. "Duke ain't been here for months. Wife and son went with him. Lord Callow's in charge."

Jaina nodded. "Can you see this horse to the stables? It needs food and water." The sergeant nodded, and without another word, Jaina walked through the guards and into the city.

She had been thinking about coming home for some time. Imagined what it would feel like to see the pale blue cobblestones beneath their feet, hear the shouts of the vendors in the Autumn Market, smell the blend of woodfires and rendered fat. Jaina had wondered how it would feel, whether she'd be happy or apprehensive. But she just felt numb. She didn't realize that she'd taken the side roads until she'd actually done it. She knew it was to avoid getting anywhere close to the inn in which she'd grown up.

Duke Gaille had never been nearly as ostentatious as Duke Westcott. His duchy was smaller, lacking the mineral deposits that had made Westcott so wealthy. The only thing the Gaille Duchy really had was Lofland Fork, the crossroads of the Dominion. The road connecting Vetticci to the Breaking passed through south to north, and the road connecting Westcott to Havensport went through west to east. It was important, but never important enough to warrant a castle or even an estate. Instead, his home was a relatively simple walled house, three stories tall, on the west side of town.

Jaina found Shakkar in the large dining room, along with several guards with officer markings. The guards were arguing while Shakkar leaned against a wall, arms folded. As she entered, he straightened up, grinning at her.

"Jaina Creighton. Long way from spending your days at the forge," he said, sticking out his hand. The skinny man was a full ten inches shorter than she was, the pair of blackthorn staves hanging from his belt the only sign that he was a ranger.

"Yes, sir."

"Nice work with the Vetticcian."

Jaina frowned. "Sir, no disrespect intended, but how could you possibly know that?"

Shakkar considered this, and shrugged. "She alive?"

"She is."

"Her job get finished?"

"It did."

"I mark that as nice work." He gestured to the other men in the room. "You remember Watch Sergeant Greaves, I trust."

One of the men looked up, and nodded. "Miss Creighton. Come up a bit since I saw you last."

"Yes, sir."

He shook his head. "You don't call me sir anymore, ranger. Understand you're going to be taking over for the old man here."

Shakkar raised an eyebrow. "Old man?"

"Compared to Ranger Creighton here, we're all old men."

"Good thing, too," one of the other soldiers muttered. "Otherwise we'd be up in that mess."

"Mess?" They all turned to see the thin man who'd just entered the room. Even if Jaina hadn't recognized him as Lord Edwin Callow, the senior advisor to Duke Gaille, the way that everyone else suddenly made a face as if smelling something unpleasant would have been a strong first hint. "I hardly think that the proper description." He glanced at Jaina. "Who are you and why are you here?"

"This is Ranger Jaina Creighton," Shakkar said. "She's going to be taking over for me here in Lofland Fork."

"The novice." Callow raised an eyebrow.

"No longer," Shakkar said. "As of today, her novice period is complete. She's a full Ranger of the Sylvan Order." He glanced her way. "Sorry we don't have more pomp and celebration, but it's just not our style."

The news should have resonated with Jaina in some way. It didn't. "Are you leaving soon?"

Shakkar shook his head. "No, Lofland's a big city, and there are a lot of frightened people here. We're both going to hold station until this little adventure of the Duke's plays out."

Jaina glanced at Lord Callow, but other than a scowl, he made no comment to Shakkar's phrasing. "The people of Lofland Fork are, as always, grateful for the dedicated service of our rangers. However, given that you have no authority to make strategic decisions for this nation, perhaps it's best that you two go wander somewhere?"

Shakkar grinned. "Come with me, Jaina. I'll tell you what you're going to be doing."

Once they'd exited the building, the older ranger said, "The dukes floated the idea of the rangers joining in with the army. Few months back. They're still a bit put off that we cheerfully told them to fuck off."

"You don't think that might have repercussions?"

Shakkar shrugged. "It's healthy for them to remember where the line is every now and then." He glanced at her as the pair turned onto the cobblestone street. "You been to see your parents yet?"

Jaina shook her head. "I just got into town."

"I can spare you for a day."

"No." Jaina took a breath, and said, "No, I... I want to be able to tell them something when I see them. Right now, it's just old wounds and nothing new."

"You sure about that?" Shakkar asked. "Lofland Fork's a big town, but it's not that big, and your pa knows everyone and their dog. Word's gonna get back to them that their daughter is frowning her way across town."

"Just... I'll give it a day or two." Jaina glanced over at him. "It'd help if I had anything I could tell them. I don't suppose you know if Martine found the army before it moved."

Shakkar stopped, and turned to face her. "I'm sorry, Jaina. Last I heard, Martine was still on the western borders. And as I said, the rangers didn't go north. He didn't find your brothers before the army moved. But I do have a bit of news. Some bad, some good."

Jaina stopped, trying to keep her face even. "Okay."

"So. Bad news." He took a breath. "Your brothers were assigned to the 4th Gaille Archery Battalion, in the First Dominion Army, under the command of Duke Westcott. And we have confirmed that the First, Second, and Third armies were the ones that marched north."

Jaina shut her eyes for a moment, trying to ignore the pit of lead quickly forming in her stomach. "We were too late."

"Not necessarily," Shakkar said. "Martine knew there was a possibility that he wouldn't find them before the army marched to wherever it was headed. So he sent out messages to every ranger he could think of, asking them to register your family exemption if they came across the soldiers. One of our rangers in Galen's Crossing ran into a military courier group heading north, and had them carry those orders north. So even if we can't go north and find those armies ourselves, they're going to get the orders."

"They're not going to stop in the middle of an invasion just to send two boys home," Jaina objected.

"No, but there are going to be groups heading back into the Dominion. Casualties, messages, that sort of thing. It's an easy thing to send Jak and Joran with them." Shakkar reached out and squeezed her arm. "It's not over."

We're basically immortal.

Jaina ignored her brother. "All right. Do we know anything about the war?"

"Is that your polite way of asking if we have a single solitary clue as to why the Dukes would do something like this?" Shakkar shook his head. "They claim there were border violations. How the Empire managed to violate our borders when there's exactly one crossing over the damn Breaking is something no one has managed to figure out. Whatever the reason, virtually every Duke in the Dominion supported the invasion. Last time they all agreed on something like that, this country stopped being a kingdom and became a Dominion, and the king got a haircut about eleven inches too short."

Jaina shook her head. "It doesn't make sense. First few years after the bridge finished, all anyone talked about was how fearsome the Empire was, how much trouble we'd be in if they decided to cross."

"Things change." Shakkar fell silent as a pair of women walked past, giving the rangers an odd look. He gave them a polite nod in return, and waited until they were out of earshot to speak again. "There's not a lot of information that we're getting, but we know the Dominion army was able to seize control of the bridge in less than an hour. We also know that after that, they marched west long enough to clear the mountains, and then turned north. The reports we've gotten back down here have spoken of scattered resistance, no real organized defense. From all accounts, the Empire had no idea they were going to be attacked."

"Do we know anything else?"

Shakkar shook his head. "Not that many pigeons left. There are a few the army took with them, but given their scarcity, they're holding those for military communiques. Means we have to wait for couriers, and it's a long, long ride from The Breaking down to here."

"So we have to wait." Jaina shook her head. "I hate this."

"You're not alone," Shakkar said. "Look, seeing your parents, the choice is yours. But it's going to be quite a while before we have any idea what's happening up there, and even if your brothers are headed our way right now, we're talking weeks, maybe even months before you get word. That's a long time to avoid them."

"I know. I just…" Jaina swallowed. "I don't know what I'd say."

"Well, my folks have been dead for twenty plus years, so I have zero advice on the topic." Shakkar raised his hands. "Like I said, it's your choice. For now, I need you on the eastern gates. We're trying to convince Lord Callow that locking down the city like this is idiotic, and I'm fairly sure he's going to lift that order within the next week or so, but for now, we have a lot of people angry they can't get in."

"I saw the mess on the western gate."

"Eastern's worse. Havensport, the mines in Walshire and Bruget, all of them are cut off if Lofland stays locked down." Shakkar shook his head. "Damned foolishness. In any case, what's left of the city's guard force is barely enough to keep those gates manned. I want you out there, keeping things calm as best you can."

"Understood."

"Good."

***

It took less than three days.

Jaina had made her way to the eastern gates of Lofland Fork, and was immediately overwhelmed by the hundreds of people who had effectively set up camp in the plains leading into the city. It hadn't taken her long to understand why Shakkar had sent her there. People red with anger who screamed abuse at the stoic city guard were more reserved with her. Whether that was due to their respect for rangers or the fact that many had watched her lift a wagonload of clay bricks out of a mud puddle, it gave her the ability to diffuse many unpleasant situations well before they became hostile.

She slept in a tent outside the city walls. Initially, she'd tried to convince herself she was doing so to be close to her duty station, but deep down, she knew it was because she thought it less likely for her parents to learn about her being back home. But less than seventy-two hours had passed before Jaina, walking an injured man to the gates to grant him passage to see an anatomist, heard her voice.

"How long have you been back?"

Jaina shut her eyes for a moment.

Oooooooh, you're in trouble....

Shut up.

She turned to find Gail Creighton standing with one of the guards, who took one look at the expression on Jaina's face and promptly decided a tactical retreat was in his best interest. Jaina met her mother's eyes, and immediately felt like she was ten years old again, standing in front of her parents waiting to be admonished. "Hi, mama."

"How long?"

"Just a few days," Jaina said. "I got orders to help keep a lid on things here at the gates."

"If you tell me Shakkar told you not to come see us..."

"No. No, he didn't. I just..." Jaina swallowed, and found herself looking at her feet as if she was being scolded for stealing from her brothers' room. "I didn't know what to say."

"Hello is a good start." Gail smiled. "We missed you, Jaina."

Jaina was a full head taller than her mother. It never mattered when her mother folded her into her arms. Jaina felt the lump form in her throat as she smelled the cinnamon and yeast that was so familiar, and hugged her mom back. "I missed you too." Pulling back, she said, "I just wanted to be able to tell you something good the first time I saw you."

Gail nodded. "Times like these, good news is more scarce than coin. If you wait for the perfect time to see the people you love, you're likely to be waiting for a long while."

"Does dad know?"

"That you're back?" Gail shook her head. "No, I wanted to be sure first." She looked Jaina up and down. "Your hair is longer."

"Not much chance to cut it," Jaina said, running her fingers through her hair.

"I've always thought you'd look good with it longer."

"Long hair's not a good idea in a forge."

"Well, you're not working a forge any longer, are you?" Gail said. "I don't suppose there are rules about how rangers wear their hair, even for novices."

Jaina shook her head. "There aren't that many rules for rangers, period. And I'm not a novice. Not anymore."

"I thought it was going to take a year."

"So did I," Jaina said. "Strange times."

Gail's eyes widened. "Does that mean your brothers..."

"We're working on it. It's complicated, especially with everything going on."

The pair sat on a large rock jutting out of the dirt at the side of the road and talked for a while as Jaina told her mother what was happening. Finally, Gail held her daughter's arm as Jaina said, "I really hoped it would be over by now, that I could come tell you and dad that I didn't do this for nothing. That I brought them home."

"You are bringing them home," Gail said. "We just have to wait."

"I hate waiting."

"Everyone does." Gail nodded at the hundreds of people sitting in the dirt, leaning against wagons, or milling about in muttering groups. "We're all waiting right now. Waiting to find out what comes next. And most of these families don't really have any idea what's coming, but we have some hope. Makes us luckier than most."

"I suppose."

"You didn't tell me much about your training," Gail said.

"Nothing to tell. I had the ritual, then they gave me my first assignment." *Please don't ask what it was.* Jaina hadn't wanted to admit the other reason she'd been so hesitant to see her parents.

They're going to ask how it went, Joran said. *You're going to try to say something benign. Dad's going to buy it, but ma's always been able to see right through you.*

I can't tell them.

Tell them what? That you fell in love, or that you let it slip away because you were too stupid to see how much she loved you back?

Gail squeezed her arm again. "Where did you go?"

"Mmm?"

"You did that thing you used to do," Gail said. "You get all quiet, like you're somewhere else."

"Sorry." Jaina offered her mother a wan smile.

"What was your first assignment like?"

"Mom, I really am glad to see you," Jaina said, extracting her arm and standing up. "And I'm sorry I haven't been by. But I have to..." She gestured at the crowd, and Gail nodded.

"I know." She stood up, and walked up to Jaina. Reaching up, she brushed a lock of hair out of her eyes. "If you're going to have your hair this long, you need to at least keep it in order."

"I know, mom."

Gail smiled. "When can you come for dinner?"

When Jak and Joran come home. When the war's done and dad doesn't look at me like that anymore.

Aloud, Jaina said, "I'll ask. I promise."

"All right, Cricket." Gail leaned up and kissed her cheek. "I love you."

"I love you too."

She watched her mother tighten the shawl around her shoulders against the wind as she headed back to the gates, and took a deep breath. *I really, really need you two to hurry home.*

Joran grunted. *Pretty sure that's out of our hands. Yours too. And that's not going to fix the reason you don't sleep, Cricket. Not going to change how much you're hurting.*

She's gone. By this time, she's either on her way back to the city, or home already. Filing her report on everything we did.

If you honestly believed that, I wouldn't be here, telling you that you are a steel-plated, master-rated, absolute champion-level idiot. He sighed. *Why did she tell you?*

It's done.

If it was, you wouldn't still be thinking about her.

Jaina didn't respond. She watched her mother disappear through the gates, and turned to do her job, hoping it would keep the memories at bay.

It didn't.

782 Hours

Antoinette's heels clicked against marble tile as she nodded to the young woman who held the door open for her. "Thank you, Lily."

"It's good to have you home, Mistress."

Antoinette offered her a smile and a nod. She had been home for nearly twenty-four hours, and had yet to be able to find itself within her to return the sentiment. "Is my grandmother here yet?"

"No, Mistress. She's been delayed, but she should be here shortly."

Antoinette nodded and stepped into the library. The three-story room had no floors in the center, just a set of balconies stretching to the greenhouse ceiling overhead. The walls were lined with shelves, each groaning beneath the weight of more books than any family could read in a lifetime. In the center of the room, a large oak table surrounded by chairs housed only one occupant, who rose to his feet with a broad smile.

"Welcome home, Mistress," Andreas said, bowing deeply. "It's so good to see you."

She smiled. "I wondered when I'd be seeing you. I confess to some surprise that you didn't join the Iron Eye escort to bring me home."

"That would have been my preference, but things have been quite busy in the last few weeks," he said, waving his hand over the dozens of papers neatly stacked in various files on the table. "Your grandmother has kept us all quite occupied. I trust your trip home was uneventful?"

Antoinette nodded. "The gods love the Iron Eye. They're not much for small talk, but they do their job. Was it really necessary to send quite so many?"

"Technically, you were traveling home through a country at war," Andreas pointed out. "Prudence seemed wise."

"You sent sixty soldiers."

"See? Prudent."

Antoinette shook her head. "I really have missed you."

"And I you, Mistress," Andreas said. "So tell me, how did you find your time in the bustling capital of the Dominion?"

"Wasn't much bustling about it, I'm afraid," she said. "I'll confess, I don't know how much she expected me to get with the duke and his entire staff gone the entire time I was there."

"We cast a wide net, Antoinette." Andreas came to his feet at the voice from behind her. Antoinette turned to see her grandmother walk into the room. "Andreas, I have a fair amount of correspondence that needs to go out with the next courier. Could you see to it?"

"Of course, Madame." He bowed, and offered Antoinette a wink before disappearing through the door, which was shut behind him.

Toni DeLuca gestured at the table. "Sit. I'm having tea and pastries brought in."

"Yes, grandmother."

Glancing up at the sky through the glass panels, her grandmother pursed her lips. "Storm coming in today. Should be here soon." She sat in a chair across from Antoinette. "In response to your comment earlier: This was your first foreign residency. I didn't expect it to be particularly taxing, and I suspected the duke would take his staff with him." She fell silent as a porter stepped through the door, setting down trays of tiny cakes and steaming cups of tea. Once he was gone, she continued. "The point was less to gather a wide range of information, and more to establish several connections that I believe may prove valuable in the future."

Antoinette nodded, picking up a pastry. She stared down at it, realizing she wasn't hungry, and set it back down, brushing the sugar from her fingertips. "Will I be home for a bit?"

Toni took a bite, waiting until she swallowed to answer. "I believe so. The war has everyone a bit on edge. Our position of neutrality keeps us out of combat, but this city has a lot of investments in the Dominion. Depending on which way this war goes, those could very much be impacted, and that could have a dramatic effect on our futures. I don't believe many families will be looking to pay out the kind of sums we expect for your services."

"From what I've heard, there may not be too much to be worried about," Antoinette said. "Everyone I've spoken with says the Dominion achieved complete surprise with their attack. This war might not last long."

"Yes, well, your reasoning may be valid, but your conclusion might be flawed," Toni said. "The Dominion attack was well executed. They've managed to advance very quickly inside the Empire. The last information we have places them nearly halfway to the city of Y'Shah, which is much further than I would have expected."

"That's what I was trying to say."

"Don't mistake speed for strategy, Antoinette." Toni shook her head. "They're on a single supply line over a single bridge. They're moving so quickly their forces are spreading out. The majority of their men don't have mounts, so this pace has to be grueling. And they have yet to encounter organized resistance. Sooner rather than later, the

Imperial Army will recover from the shock and respond, and none of us know what will happen then."

"Do we know anything about the Imperial Army?" Antoinette asked.

"Very little," Toni said. "As you know, I've been trying for years to establish sources inside the Empire, with little to no success. We know the Empire maintains a standing army, but we're not sure of the size. We know that army is supplemented with the Chorale, but no one's quite sure what they can do in battle. And we know who will be in command." She shook her head. "That, perhaps, is the Dominion's greatest miscalculation. The Dominion army has nearly 130,000 men, but led by dukes with little actual battle experience. That is not the case with the Imperial Army." She selected a sheet of paper, and slid it to Antoinette.

Picking it up, she scanned the first few lines. "I don't know this name."

"Outside the Empire, he's not well known. Within the Empire, he's a bit of a legend." Toni took a sip of her drink. "General Greenleaf is an experienced battle commander. He was a major at an age that most soldiers are still figuring out what end of the spear to hold. He's a graduate of the Imperial War College. He's known to be ruthlessly pragmatic, strategically insightful, and he's wildly popular with his soldiers. If he hasn't struck back yet, it's because he's waiting for the right opportunity to do so. A man like that doesn't throw a punch until he's got a rock in his fist."

Antoinette felt her stomach twist slightly. *Gods, I hope she got them home before they crossed.* She did her best to keep her face even. "If the Empire can defeat the Dominion army in the field, what happens after that?"

"Theories abound." Toni shook her head. "Some think they'll cross into the Dominion and conquer as much as they can. Others think they'll cross and head right for Havensport."

"Why Havensport?"

"There are strong rumors that the Dominion has a fleet there. Thirty troopships. They've also assembled fifty thousand men as an auxiliary force, with the idea of sailing them up to the eastern coast of the Empire," Toni said. "We don't believe the Empire maintains a strong navy. In fact, the only report I have are several rumors of a single small ship sailing south from the Imperial coast. Much too small to be a troopship. Most likely reconnaissance. If they're going to stop them, marching their cavalry towards Havensport would be an option."

"Wouldn't the better choice be to go through the Shadowed Path, have their forces ready to meet the Dominion at the coast?" Antoinette asked. "That's a much easier task than fighting their way through the whole of the Dominion to get to Havensport."

"True, but that's a lot of coastline to defend. And from what we do know about General Greenleaf, he prefers aggression in battle, a decisive blow that ends the fight as fast as possible."

Antoinette nodded. "If you're right, the Dominion had best hope that he doesn't defeat their army in the field."

"You may be more right than you know." Toni shook her head. "The Empire has been peaceful since they built the bridge. I don't believe the Dominion's claims of incursions whatsoever. The Dominion convinced themselves that peace was a sign of weakness. I worry they've woken up something that's been sleeping since the Unification War ended, and none of us can predict the chaos that may follow."

"How can we prepare?"

"Chaos breeds opportunity. We don't know what will happen next, but we know that both nations will be shaken, and that may present us with chances to expand our influence," Toni said. "However, this is not all I wished to discuss. I know that you didn't have any opportunities to connect with the duke. But I wanted to learn more about your time in Westcott."

Antoinette kept her face even. "You've received all my messages."

"I have." Toni reached for another stack of paper, sliding it close. "I have a few areas that could do with some clarification, however."

"Such as?"

"Well, there's precious little information about your abduction."

The temperature in the room dropped ten degrees, and Antoinette knew she had failed to keep the shock from her face. "My..."

"If we could dispense with the dance of denial, I would appreciate it. There's much to do, and I don't have an excess of time to spend on this." Toni's face was unreadable, her voice calm.

Shit. Antoinette cycled through various denials in her head before giving it up as a lost cause. "How did you know?"

"I sent you into a country on the brink of war, alone, with no family escort," Toni said. "I do hope you realize I wouldn't do so without having several sets of eyes on you."

"You had someone watching me."

"Of course I did."

"Who?"

"You tell me."

Antoinette gritted her teeth. "You didn't trust me?"

"You're my only granddaughter. I didn't trust anyone else."

"So you knew." Antoinette shook her head. "When no one came, I thought we might have succeeded in keeping it quiet."

"Part of this job was to see how you handled yourself without your family there to pick you up when you stumbled," Toni said. "If I sent in the Iron Eye, or even your brother and his friends, every time you run into a spot of inconvenience, that accomplishes little."

"And if I'd been killed?"

"I arranged for you to have a ranger as your personal bodyguard. I was confident between her capabilities and your resourcefulness, you would be able to manage." Toni raised an eyebrow. "Speaking of the ranger."

Antoinette didn't respond.

"You certainly seemed to abandon the idea of Miss Creighton being a viable source of information," Toni said. "From what I've heard, the two of you got along quite well."

She had thought carefully about how to respond to this. Antoinette knew the challenge wasn't figuring out how to explain herself. It would be keeping her face even when talking about Jaina, when remembering her face before she turned her back on Antoinette forever. "Part of the challenge we've had in establishing any solid details on the rangers comes directly from the rangers themselves. Whether as a security precaution or simply because they don't know any other way, the rangers seem to have no real sense of command structure, organizational structure, any of it. Creighton and I got along fine. She spoke of her family, her home. But she seemed genuinely unsure about whom she reported to, or how many rangers there actually were. Even if I believe it likely that she would be amiable towards working for us, which I don't, the amount of information she could provide would be limited at best, and not worth the time and expense."

She couldn't tell how long her grandmother considered her. Antoinette didn't know what would happen if Toni realized the truth of all that had happened, but a lifetime of experience spoke to how disastrous that would be. Those grey eyes fixed on her were carved from ice. Finally, Toni said, "You were on the ground. I defer to your judgement."

Antoinette did her best to keep her relief from showing. "With that said. I would like to ask for your help with several things."

"Go on."

"A guard died defending me during the abduction."

Toni nodded, plucking a sheet of paper from the desk. "Ethan Meyer. I heard."

"He has a family. A sister, with several children. He was providing for them. I'd like to ensure that they continue to get that support."

"Could you please pass that quill?" Toni asked, pointing at a quill and inkpot on the other side of the table. Antoinette did so, and Toni made a note on a piece of paper. "What else?"

"Creighton was not alone in coming to get me. Another guard, Boyajian, was instrumental in bringing me home safe. I don't know his first name."

The quill scratched on the page. "I do. You'll want him rewarded, I assume?"

"If that's what he wants," Antoinette said. "He and Meyers were close. He may prefer a change of opportunity rather than to continue to serve without his friend. If so, I'd like to offer him a position in our house guard. I promise you, he has the capabilities."

"Interesting." Toni nodded slowly. "He'll need to be properly vetted, but should that be his choice, I believe we can make that happen. Anything else?"

"Yes." Antoinette swallowed, and said, "Whether it was her job or not, Creighton fought hard to see me rescued."

"One could argue that were she doing her job properly, the abduction wouldn't have happened."

"One could argue that, if one was taking an overly simplified view of what I know you understand to be a much more complicated situation," Antoinette said, a bit too harshly. Her grandmother's expression didn't change, so she continued. "Creighton has two brothers serving in the Dominion army. They shouldn't be." She quickly explained the exemption policy. "The rangers have been trying to get a message to the army command to have her brothers separated and sent home, but last I heard, they were encountering some difficulties."

"I believe the term for those difficulties is open warfare."

"Yes, well..." Antoinette cleared her throat. "Anything we can do to help the rangers find her brothers would go a long way towards repaying her service. Even if she didn't know that we were involved."

"I hesitate to agree, not because I don't approve, but because I don't know that such action would be possible." Toni considered this for a moment. "I will ask Andreas to make some inquiries. Quietly, but if we see an opportunity to help expedite the return home of the Creighton brothers without exposing our network, I don't see a reason not to do so."

"Thank you."

Toni was quiet for a few moments. When she spoke, her voice was softer than it usually was. Antoinette found it disconcerting. "Cultivating possible sources is always a complicated affair. It's not unusual for the role you're playing to bleed into reality, to find yourself feeling personally invested in this person you've come to know so well. That's not a failing. That's part of being human. It would not be unexpected, particularly after spending so much time together, that you might begin to view Jaina Creighton as a friend."

Antoinette didn't respond. She didn't trust herself to do so.

"Well." Toni nodded. "You're home. We'll have dinner one night later this week, you and I."

"Yes, grandmother."

Toni DeLuca stood and walked from the room, the heavy oak doors to the library closing behind her, leaving Antoinette alone in the yawning expanse of the massive room. She looked up at the first taps of raindrops falling on the glass panels high overhead, and quietly shut her eyes, listening to the rain, trying to think of anything but Jaina's heartbroken face.

733 Hours

"I understand," Jaina said for the nineteenth time. The first time that she'd said it to the red-faced caravan master, her tone had been sympathetic, and she'd been determined to keep it that way. By the fifteenth time, she realized that ambition was going to die unrealized. The most recent iteration of the sentiment had been communicated between gritted teeth.

The caravan master was a tall man, slightly taller than Jaina, and seemed to try to elongate his spine every time they spoke in order to maximize the difference. While no one in the chaos bubbling at the eastern gates was particularly pleased with their current circumstances, this man seemed to possess a reserve of entitlement and indignation that was, by all appearances, inexhaustible. In the absence of an actual target for his irritation, he had settled on Jaina as the next best thing.

"Thousands of ducats. Not Dominion tin, coral. My backers know I'm reliable, and they pay me accordingly," he said, his finger poking at Jaina but stopping just shy of touching her breastbone. She didn't know if he understood the action she had already settled upon should he touch her, but he'd yet to cross that particular line. "And now my cargo sits, rotting in the sun, because you don't know how to do your godsdamned job."

You should hit him.

Shut up. "Sir, as I've said, I'm not responsible for the lockdown. I have no authority to let you in the city."

"Oh, but you have the authority to keep me out of the city?" He rolled his eyes. "Excuses are the purview of the coward, woman."

You should absolutely, definitely hit him.

Shut up. Jaina shook her head. "Everyone here is waiting. Once the lockdown is lifted, you'll be able to get into the city."

"And when will that be?!"

"I have no idea, sir."

"Well, either you're lying or you're stupid." His lip curled. "Which is it?"

Antoinette would have stabbed him by now. Not fatally, but you know, somewhere he'd remember for a while.

Please, for all the gods, shut up.

If you punch him, I will.

"Here's what's going to happen," the man said, his cheeks red under the patchy beard that grew like a fungus from his face. "You're going to turn around. You're going to walk me to the gate. You're going to open that gate. I'm going to take my caravan through, and then you're going to fuck off to whatever you were doing before you ruined my day." His finger jabbed into her chest one time, then another. He didn't have the chance to do it a third time.

Jaina's fingers wrapped around his hand. She smiled at him as his eyes widened. He tried to yank his hand back, but it may as well have been encased in the side of a mountain. Jaina spoke in a low, calm voice, quiet enough that no one else could hear what he said. "Do you know the penalty for assaulting a ranger of the Sylvan Order?"

"What?" He brought his other hand up to try to pry her fingers open, failing miserably. "Let me go, woman!"

"That's Ranger Creighton to you, and I asked a question." She tightened her grip, only a bit, and the color poured out of his face in a heartbeat. "Do you know the penalty for assaulting a ranger of the Sylvan Order?"

"I didn't..." Her grip tightened a bit more, and his eyes grew wide. "No."

"Neither do I." Jaina felt bones start to shift beneath her hands. "I understand your frustration. It's shared by everyone else here. But your cargo is ore. Not fruit, not livestock, not something with a shelf life, ore. Even before your childish temper tantrum, you were at the bottom of my priority list. Now you're three feet in the dirt." A bit tighter, and he gasped in pain. "If you lay a hand on me again, I will dramatically increase the number of bones in that hand. If you raise your voice to me again, I will physically drag every wagon in your convoy the half mile to the river, and leave them axle deep in the mud. If you do anything other than sit and wait like everyone else here, I will make it my life's purpose to ensure that crossing the Breaking would be a simpler matter than you getting into Lofland Fork. Am I clear?"

He nodded frantically. "Please. It hurts."

"I'm sure." She let him go, and he stumbled back, cradling his hand to his chest. "Thank you for your input, sir. I'll be sure to take it into consideration."

He stared at her, mouth opening and closing like a beached fish, before turning and stomping away.

I still think you should have punched him.

"Excuse me, ranger?"

Taking a deep breath, Jaina turned to face the person speaking behind her. The guard waiting for her was well into his sixties. His right eye was covered with a cloth patch. "What is it?"

"You're needed. Back at the ducal residence. Lord Callow asked that you come immediately."

Jaina nodded. "Did they send relief to help manage all of this?" She waved her hands back at the crowd behind her.

"Ayuh, they did," he said, nodding. "Me and four others. We'll keep the lid on, promise you that."

"Fine." Jaina pointed at the retreating caravan leader. "That one's already gotten a warning for his behavior. If he steps out of line again..."

"Both feet, ranger," the guard said.

"Good." With that, Jaina headed to the gates.

She hadn't spent much time in the city. Late in the first day she'd been there, she asked one of the guards to bring a tent for her to sleep in. Jaina had explained to them that she wanted to be close in case trouble erupted. She knew that wasn't the reason. As she wove through the streets, she kept her head down, not wanting to look up and see her father staring at her from the crowds.

Lofland Fork wasn't as big as Westcott, but it was big enough to always have had a general hum of activity filling the streets, particularly as one got close to the sprawling Autumn Fair at the center of town. But in the ten days since Jaina had arrived, the city was muted, as if a smothering blanket had settled over the residents. Part of that was the lack of goods moving in and out of the town. But Jaina knew the bulk was the worry that had wrapped around nearly every Dominion subject like a choking scarf.

Rumor burned through the city like an inferno. Even outside the walls, Jaina had heard the theories. Kaani, the Imperial capital, had fallen. Kaani was under siege. The army had stopped because they'd run out of food. Ships sailing south on the eastern coast. The Empresses had surrendered. The Empresses were dead. The dukes had surrendered. The dukes were dead. Each rumor was delivered with an ironclad certainty. She'd already broken up several fights by people absolutely certain that their information was correct.

Even considering the atmosphere of anxiety that Lofland Fork had been simmering in, the crowd surrounding the ducal residence felt different. Jaina saw faces lined with fear, murmured conversations. Her ears picked up snippets as she wove through them.

"... don't know that uniform..."

"... did you see his bodyguard?"

"... not one of ours..."

That seems bad.

Jaina tried to ignore the growing lump in her stomach as the guard at the entrance nodded at her and held the door open. "They're upstairs, in the map room," he said.

"Thanks." She jogged up the stairs. Two more guards stood by the door to the map room. "Lord Callow's on his way," one of them told her. "Wait inside with the others."

Stepping through, she spotted Shakkar immediately, along with the watch sergeant. They stood against a wall, quietly speaking to one another, and glancing at the pair of guests standing stiffly against the far wall. One of them was a burly man in an unfamiliar uniform, snow white wool with red strips on the sleeves. The cut was severe, and his brow was beaded with sweat. His forearms were bare except for the pair of dull grey bracers wrapped around them. He stared at Jaina as if dissecting her.

The soldier's companion was smaller and thinner. His uniform was a similar cut, but dark grey. There were a series of piercings hanging from his nose, and his face was a mask of stone. He didn't look at anyone, but instead stared down at the leather tube he held in his hands.

"Jaina." She turned as Shakkar stepped up to her. "Thanks for coming so quickly."

"What's going on?" she asked, keeping her voice low.

"Not sure. They got here an hour ago. Won't speak to anyone but Lord Callow."

"Who are they?"

Shakkar's jaw tightened. "Imperials."

"What?" Jaina stared at him. "How?"

"Don't know. But they came through the south gate. Up from Vetticci."

The door opened, and they all turned to see Lord Callow step through, breathing heavily. His eyes fell on the two Imperials, and his already flushed face grew red. "Sergeant, there are standing orders to detain any Imperial citizens. Why have you not followed those orders?"

Sergeant Greaves stepped forward. "They claim to be envoys, sir. With a message from the Empresses. Ranger Shakkar thought it best to bring them here."

"Did he." Lord Callow stared daggers at Shakkar. "On whose authority do you countermand ducal orders, ranger?"

"Lord Callow, with all due respect, maybe we should hear what our guests have to say before we clap the irons on them?" Shakkar said.

"Something for your consideration," the big Imperial soldier said, consonants sharp with his northern accent. "Before you decide to arrest us."

"And what might that be?" Lord Callow said, his lip curling.

"If you touch Sub-Archeron Ivanovich, I'll kill every man in this room."

Silence slammed down with an almost physical force. The soldier hadn't sounded particularly threatening. It had been as if he'd simply been sharing an interesting tidbit about the weather. Callow's eyes looked as if they were about to bug out of his head, but before he could start yelling, Greaves stepped forward.

"You had a message for Lord Callow, I believe?" He spoke quickly, eyes darting between the Imperials and Lord Callow.

The smaller man nodded. "My name is Erik Ivanovich, Sub-Archeron of the Greymare district, and duly appointed envoy of the Alddarri Empire. I speak on behalf of the Empresses, at their command. I was instructed to deliver this message to the senior royal official in Lofland Fork. Is that you, Lord Callow?" His voice was thin and reedy, and Jaina could hear the tremble in his words.

Someone's nervous.

"You have no authority..."

"Gods, shut the fuck up, Callow," Shakkar snapped. "Let the man deliver his message."

"Ranger, I..." Callow gritted his teeth, eyes darting from Greaves to Shakkar to Jaina. Finding no support, he turned and snapped, "Go ahead then."

Ivanovich nodded, and untied the leather cord wrapped around the cylinder. As he did, the entire cylinder unrolled. Several sheets of paper with immaculate script had been sewn to the leather, and Ivanovich began to read in a flat, hard tone.

"Imperial Proclamation 77567: In response to the barbaric, unprovoked, and ruthless attack on Imperial citizens by the forces of the Dominion, the Alddarri Empire has declared a state of war to be in existence between our two nations. This state of war will continue until the unconditional surrender of every surviving member of the ducal council, as well as the immediate surrender of all individuals responsible for planning this criminal attack on our people and sovereign soil. The Alddarri Empire intends to conduct unrestricted warfare upon the government and people of the Dominion until said surrender." He flipped the page. "Imperial Proclamation 77568: Any Dominion subject who has set foot on Imperial territory forfeits any protection under Imperial law. Any Dominion subject who has set foot on Imperial territory is subject to any and all retaliation. Any Dominion subject taken prisoner on Imperial territory will be treated as a prisoner of war, and will not be entitled to any protections afforded other prisoners."

Jaina looked down. Her hands were trembling.

Another page. "Imperial Proclamation 77569: The Alddarri Empire lays claim to all territory within a ten mile radius of the southern termination of the bridge across the Breaking. Any violation of this territory will be met with deadly force." He rolled the papers back up, and tossed them on the table. "I have witnessed your receipt of these proclamations."

Callow's face was a shade of red Jaina had never seen before. "Bold words. We'll see if your tone changes after our colors fly over our capital. Our army has already marched..."

"Your army has been defeated." Ivanovich said, his voice hard. "Two days ago, the Imperial Army engaged the invasion force just south of Y'Shah. The battle lasted less than ten hours. Your forces were soundly beaten, and no longer pose a threat to the people of the Empire."

"Impossible." Callow shook his head. "It would take over a week to travel down from the Empire to Lofland Fork. Unless you flew..."

"We are the Alddarri Empire," Ivanovich said. "We have our ways." He pulled a pouch from his belt, and tossed it on the table. "We thought this might convince you."

Shakkar stepped forward, picking up the pouch, and frowning as he felt the contents. He upturned it on the pale wood of the table. Six rings came tumbling out. They would have made a merry sound when they hit the wood were they not still around fingers.

Through the dull roaring in her ears, Jaina watched as Shakkar picked one up, inspecting it. Swallowing, he said, "This is Duke McElroy's signet ring." He pushed it aside, looking at the others. "Duke Snowsill." He picked up one of the fingers. The nail had been lost at some point, the pale dead flesh still stained with blood. Shakkar brushed the dried blood off the ring, and muttered, "Duke Westcott."

The room fell deathly silent. Jaina felt as if she was going to throw up. *Gods, please. Please not this.*

"We have prisoners. More than a few," Ivanovich said. "Aside from the immediate consequences should you try to detain or harm us that my kaviak friend here specified a few moments ago, should I not report back to the Imperial Embassy in Vetticci within one week's time, they will all be executed."

"How many?" Jaina asked the question at the same time as Lord Callow. She idly wondered if he would take her to task for speaking out of turn, but if he'd heard her, he gave no indication.

"We will permit one person to travel to the new border between our countries. Ten miles south of the bridge, a representative from the Imperial Army will wait to meet this representative from the Dominion," said Ivanovich. "Your representative will be unarmed. At that point, we will hand over the casualty report, so you may begin to let the families who will now be mourning know the cost already exacted by your nation's barbaric actions. Choose your representative."

"We don't..." Lord Callow shook his head. "I can't leave Lofland Fork."

"I'll go."

Everyone in the room turned as Jaina spoke. She tried to keep her voice even as she repeated herself. "I'll go. I can travel fast. I don't need to... I can travel fast."

Shakkar stepped over to her. "Jaina, are you sure? You don't have to be the one to do this. I can go."

She shook her head. "I'm sure." She met his eyes, and whispered, "Please."

He didn't look convinced, but took a deep breath and nodded to Lord Callow.

Ivanovich looked to his guard, who considered Jaina for a few moments, then nodded. "She'll do," he rumbled.

"Your name?" Ivanovich said, withdrawing a pencil from his pocket.

"Jaina Creighton."

"Are you a guard or a soldier?"

"I believe she's a ranger," the Imperial guard said. Ivanovich glanced at him, and looked back to Jaina.

"Yes. I'm a ranger."

"Very well." Ivanovich scribbled a few notes on a piece of paper. "Ranger Jaina Creighton is granted leave to approach the border and receive the casualty report from the battle. Anyone else approaching will be treated as hostile." He folded the paper and slid it into a pocket. "Will you be attempting to detain us?"

Everyone looked at Lord Callow. After a few moments, the nobleman shook his head wordlessly.

"I should escort you to the south gate," Sergeant Greaves said. "There are a lot of angry people out there."

Ivanovich nodded. "That would be acceptable." Without another word, the three walked from the room.

Callow sat down in a chair, his eyes fixed on the severed fingers sitting on the table. "How is this possible?" he muttered.

Shakkar ignored him, turning to Jaina. "I'd ask you again if you're sure, but I think we don't have a choice any longer," he said. "You should have asked me first."

"You might have said no," Jaina said.

Shakkar grunted. "There is that." He thought for a moment. "All right. We'll get you set up with a pack and a horse." He looked at Callow. "My lord, we need a pen and paper."

Callow didn't respond. He just stared.

The older ranger shook his head, and went over to a drafting table upon which sat a stack of maps. He picked up a charcoal stick and nodded, flipping through the maps. Finally, he pulled one out. "You'll take the Duke's Road north. It'll take you right to the bridge. These towns..." He circled twelve towns dotting the road north. "The rangers keep horses in the stables in those towns, pay the local groom to keep them healthy. Get to these towns, switch horses, and keep moving. If you need to sleep, do it on the road. Don't stay long enough to be asked questions." He folded the map, and handed it to her. "Follow me."

When they emerged into the afternoon sunlight, the crowd outside had grown. Questions were shouted at them as they pushed their way through, but they easily made their way out of the crowd. They moved quickly, weaving through the alleys and streets of the city until they reached the northern gates. Each of the four gates into the city had a stable built right near it, and Shakkar walked inside.

After speaking with the groom for a moment, he came back out. "He's getting your first horse. If you leave now and push, you can make it to Meadowbrook by morning." He scowled. "I don't like this."

"I'll get it done," Jaina said. He didn't look convinced.

"Jaina, whatever happens at that meeting, whatever that casualty report says, you can't…" He took a deep breath. "This is bad. This is very, very bad, and you are in a very unique position to make things so much worse. I should have said something in there, should have overruled you. As things stand…"

He's right. This is not a good idea, Cricket.

I have to know.

"I know the stakes," she said. "I'll get back as fast as I can."

"If I could, I'd order you to keep that report sealed until you get back here," Shakkar said as the young groom came out of the stables, leading a grey stallion by the bridle. "But I do my best to not give orders I know won't be followed. Just…" He gripped her shoulder. "Please. For your own sake, don't open the damned thing until you're back home. Until you have the space to deal with whatever it says."

"Shakkar, I'll do my job," Jaina said. She climbed up on the horse. "I give you my word."

He didn't look convinced, but he nodded. "Go."

Jaina nodded, and dug her heels into the horse's flanks and rode, the eyes of her brothers on her.

***

Days thundered past on an impossible number of hoofbeats. The Dominion sprawled. The largest nation on the continent, Jaina Creighton had never been more than twenty miles north of her home. By the third day, she may as well have been in another country.

If it hadn't been for the map, she wouldn't know what kind of progress she was making. Every time she rode into one of the marked villages, Jaina rode directly to the stables, pounding her fist on the door if no one was there. Once, she had to knock on a neighboring home, find out where the groom slept, and wake them to get her next horse. She said little, just quick instructions to care for the horse and a warning she'd be back soon to trade out again. Questions were asked. None were answered. Jaina just shook her head, and said she had nothing for them.

Fear was spreading through the nation like a raging wildfire. Every place she went burned with worry. Town after town, village after village, already hollowed out by the hunger of the swelling army. People had lived for months fighting to keep the worst scenarios from their minds about their sons, their fathers, their brothers, their friends. As news of the war reached them, those scenarios bloomed into vivid reds and blacks. They were desperate for someone to tell them anything that might offer a bit of hope, and a ranger seemed like the best option.

But if Jaina told them the truth, everything would come crashing down around them, just as it had already begun to crumble around her.

Each day, she rode until she either reached the next waystation, or until foam flew from her horse's lips, its chest heaving. As much as every bit of her wanted nothing more than to keep pushing, she knew on foot the journey would take months, and so she would rest. No fire, no shelter, she would simply find a grove of trees or a hidden saddle between several of the rolling hills dotting the countryside, make sure her horse could drink, and wait. She did her best to take these breaks at night, staring up at countless stars speckling the midnight blue sky.

You need to sleep.

They had been in her ear every step of the way. Jaina shook her head slowly. *I'll sleep when I know.*

You're not invulnerable. You do have to sleep sometimes, no matter what they did to you.

I don't want to sleep.

Cricket, you need...

If I sleep, I'll dream. Jaina felt a tremble shiver through her for a moment. *And if I dream, I don't know what waits for me there. I don't know if I'll hear that sound, that awful sound that man's jaw made when I hit him. I don't know if I'll feel what it was like to have steel punch through my belly, actually feel it scrape on my spine as it came out my back. I don't know if I'll taste the blood in my mouth. And the worst part? I hope, I pray that's what I dream of.*

She raised her eyes to look into the dark night. *I don't want to think it. I can't think it. If I think it, it becomes real, and I don't know how to live in a world where that might be a reality, so if I have to stay awake to keep those thoughts at bay, that's what I'll do.*

You'll drop. Joran's voice was thick with frustration and worry. *You have a limit. The gods only know where it is, but you haven't slept in five days. You've eaten nothing but dried meat.*

I'm a ranger. Maybe it's time I find out what that really means.

He snorted. *Please. You've been trying to figure that out since you took that bloody oath in the first place. Trying to figure out if you're a victim, or a hero, or a guardian, or a soldier. Thinking that if you figure out what it actually means to you to be this person, you could wrap that meaning around your shoulders and keep all the doubts at bay.*

This has to mean something. This choice, this thing that I've done has to have made a difference.

That's not how it works, Cricket. Jak said. *You aren't big enough to stop everything bad from happening. Sometimes the dice come up wrong. Sometimes it happens over and over, and you being able to lift a wagon or heal your wounds doesn't change that. Bad things happen. People make choices, and others pay the price. That's how it's always been. And I know what's really hard for you, what's really keeping your eyes open.*

She didn't answer. He didn't need her to.

You've been clinging to this belief that you had the ability to change what happened. Maybe, in another world, you could. Maybe in another world, Martine found the army before it marched. Maybe in another world, his message got to our commanders, and we walked south while everyone else walked north. But every time the dice came up wrong, you realized more and more that whatever was going to happen to us, it was out of your hands, and the moment you heard about the battle, you knew that illusion of having any control over what was coming was gone.

An owl hooted mournfully from a tree off in the distance. She could hear voices too, but knew they were miles away. Jaina couldn't make out what they were saying. *Funny. I've been thinking about dice lately.*

We know.

In the Battle of Snowsill, the one dad fought in. He told us one out of every six men died in that fight. One out of six. She took a deep breath, trying to steady herself. *That seems almost laughable. That your lives could come to the same thing as the dice we played as kids.*

Five out of six are pretty good odds, Cricket.

I don't want to dream about the one.

Joran's voice softened. *Maybe you'll dream about a different one.*

Jaina shook her head. *That might be worse.*

I thought you two had this grand plan. This rationale for how you justified everything you shared, Joran said, annoyed. *You knew there was a clock, and you still clung to each other. You wanted to be happy when you could, and whether you want to admit it or not, you were.*

I also didn't know she was spying on me.

The pair chuckled. *Jaina, our dear sister, we've been trying to be nice, trying to consider all that you're going through, but if you don't drop that bullshit, we're going to beat the stupid out of you.*

You're not really here. You're in my head.

Just means we can do a hell of a lot more damage. Also means deep down, you know what we're saying is true, Jak said. *You're not an idiot. You know damn well why she told you what she did.*

Shut up.

Fuck you.

Tears stung Jaina's eyes. *She wasn't lying.*

Of course she wasn't lying. But while I can't claim any time as a spy in my history, I'm pretty sure that "Don't fucking tell people you're a spy" is at the top of the godsdamn rule book.

Doesn't change what she did.

You have no idea what she did. You only know what she was supposed to do. And I'm pretty sure she wasn't supposed to fall into bed with you. Antoinette loves you. You know that, no matter what she said.

Even if that's true...

I swear to the gods I'm going to kick you.

Even if it's true, it's done. It's over.

You knew it was going to be over. But that doesn't mean the memories have to be gone too.

Jaina didn't answer. She just looked back up at the stars.

***

It took her eight days to make the journey.

Her endurance had found its limits. The night before, she'd fallen asleep on the ground, hidden by a cluster of greenery. She had a blanket, but never had a chance to use it. Jaina slept for six fitful hours, and dreamed of Antoinette.

When she saw the soldiers, she realized just how close she'd been to her goal when she had fallen asleep. There were five of them, but her eyes tracked movement to the east and west, and she spotted mounted soldiers a half mile away in each direction. Listening carefully, she could hear the faint hoofbeats of still more soldiers, stretching in a line for miles in both directions. A series of yellow pennants had been driven into the soil. Twenty feet apart, they drew a sharp line, on the other side of which five soldiers waited for her.

Far in the north, she heard the rumble of thunder, and frowned. The sky overhead was clear and bright.

She dismounted, and began walking forward, keeping her hands visible. Jaina left the blackthorn staff strapped to her horse.

Probably a good idea, Jak said. *Those fellows don't look particularly happy.*

Joran spoke. *Be so careful, Cricket.*

She watched the Imperial soldiers carefully. A hundred feet away, Jaina stopped, staring at the biggest soldier. "That's not possible," she muttered.

Uh, Cricket? Not sure you should stop.

She shook her head sharply, but continued walking forward, eyes fixed on the same soldier that had stood in the ducal residence with her in Lofland Fork, idly promising to murder them all. *He can't be here. How could he get here before me? They went south.*

Maybe by ship?

Don't be an idiot. Joran snapped. *We're nowhere near the coast.*

Well then he must have fucking flown.

Jaina got within twenty feet, and the soldier stepped across the line, walking up to her. He looked her up and down, and nodded. "You got here faster than I expected."

She swallowed. "You did too."

"Bit different, I suspect." He tilted his head. "Captain Elash Bluewater. Kaviak of the Imperial Army. Didn't have the chance to properly introduce myself earlier."

"Jaina Creighton."

"No rank?"

"Just ranger."

He grunted. "Always been curious about the rangers. Not the time, though. Follow me."

She fell into step beside him. When they reached the flags, she paused before stepping over into their claimed territory. When they reached the others, one of the soldiers stepped forward. His uniform was a different cut, more formal, and two red bars were sewn onto his sleeves.

"Ranger Jaina Creighton, designated envoy of the Ducal Council." Bluewater gestured at the other officer. "Captain Ian Saunussi, Imperial Cavalry, aide-de-camp to General Tomas Greenleaf. He speaks for the military command here."

They do like their titles.

Jaina offered her hand. Captain Saunussi stared at it for a moment. "That's not why we're here, ranger."

Jaina let her hand drop. "I suppose not." Her eyes fell to the rolled parchment in his hands, and her heart began to thump in her chest. "I'm here at your government's request. To receive the report, and take it back to my people."

Saunussi didn't move to hand her the parchment. "Why?"

"Why?" Jaina frowned. "Your envoy asked us to..."

"Why did you attack us?" Saunussi's voice was flat, his eyes hard. "It's the one thing that none of us can understand. We have never spoken so much as an angry word to your people. What could have possibly justified this madness?"

The fuck am I supposed to say to that?

Say something. I don't think he's the patient sort.

"I'm not part of my government," Jaina said. "I didn't know what the dukes were planning. I wasn't part of that decision. I'm just a ranger."

The other soldiers scowled. One of their hands fell to the butt of the sword at their hip. Saunussi glanced back at them. "Hold fast." He looked back to Jaina. "That's a wholly unsatisfying answer, ranger."

"It's the only one I have, Captain."

His jaw worked. "My sister was a merchant. Working one of the hundreds of tents we built on the bridge. It was practically a market. Hundreds of Imperial and Dominion citizens, working together, trading..." Saunussi swallowed. "Do you know what they did? What your countrymen did? They rained arrows down on them. Pulled their citizens out in the night, while everyone was sleeping, and fired arrows until no one was left breathing. Pushed their bodies off the edge." His eyes were hard, and his hand was now resting on the hilt of his weapon. Jaina didn't think he realized. "I'll never be able to bury my sister."

Jaina took a step back, and every one of them tensed.

Don't do that, Cricket.

"I grieve for your loss," she said slowly. "If our soldiers did that, it's unforgivable. But I wasn't there. I didn't hurt any of your people. I don't want to hurt any of your people. I came to do a job. I just want to do my job."

Saunussi shook his head. "Your job." He spat in the dirt. "Whether you were there or not, none of that matters. The flame has been lit, and this fire is going to spread to every corner of the Dominion. A clock began ticking when the first boot landed on our soil, and when it reaches zero, the blood spilled to this point will seem like a drop in an ocean." He thrust the roll of parchment into her hands. "Go home and tell your people. You began this fight. We will finish it."

Jaina's eyes fell from him to the casualty list in her hands.

Don't do it.

Saunussi was saying something else, but a dull roar filled her ears.

Cricket. Please. Don't do this.

The cord tying the bundle together fell into the dirt at her feet. The Imperials fell silent as she unrolled the papers. Names were written in sharp, precise letters. She wasn't a strong reader, but she knew what their names looked like. She scanned the first page, terrified to see the familiar marks. *You're not here.*

The second page. *You're not here.*

Her heart began to beat faster. Third, fourth, fifth pages. *You aren't here!*

The fifth page was the last. She reached the end, and let loose a long, shaking breath. "Okay," she said, her voice trembling. Letting out a long, slow breath, she looked back up at Saunussi. "The people responsible for this war deserve all that you bring to them. I'll not say different. This list is shorter than I thought it would be, and for that, I thank you."

Jaina.

"Could you tell me where the prisoners are being held?" she asked. "Can messages be sent from their families?"

Jaina.

"I don't know which dukes are left, but if they surrender, how long before you release..."

Jak's hand fell on her right shoulder. Joran's fell on her left. They weren't really there, but for this one quiet moment, it felt as if they were. *Listen to him, Jaina. He's talking to you.*

"I'm sorry, I'm just..." Jaina shook her head. "You were saying something."

Saunussi's anger was still in his eyes, but there was something else as well, something sadder. "Ranger, you misunderstand."

We're so sorry, Cricket.

"That's not a casualty report."

We love you.

"That's a list of survivors."

Jaina stared at him. She heard the words he spoke. Heard the heartbeats of every soldier. Heard the wind blowing through the grass, the creak of leather as they watched her.

She didn't hear Jak. She didn't hear Joran.

She was alone.

637 Hours

The only sounds in the studio were her own breathing, the musical *tink tink tink* of the hammer tapping at the base of the chisel, and the soft clatter of stone chips tumbling to the ground. Antoinette had very few places in which she could be alone in the DeLuca estate. When she was twelve, her grandmother had this small room converted to a private studio. There were no windows, but cinderstone blocks were inlaid into the ceiling, bathing the entire room in an odd pale light. Small chips of the glowing stone were common in medical tools and jewelry, but large slabs were extremely rare and expensive. Toni DeLuca hadn't balked at the expense.

She didn't look behind her when the door clicked open. The person who had entered waited until she finished the section she was working on before speaking. "I thought you'd given up marble as a medium." Andreas stepped forward, examining the fingers emerging from the stone.

Antoinette nodded. "I did. Takes too long. Too many ways for it to go wrong."

"What made you change your mind?"

"I didn't." She brushed marble dust off her lap. "Still don't think it's the right choice for residencies or submissions."

"Then why...?"

"I just wanted to do something for me. Something that didn't have a purpose." She glanced at him. "Think it's a waste of time?"

He shook his head. "I could make all the arguments about how it still counts as practice, how you're developing your skill, all that kind of thing. But at the end of the day, it might not be the worst thing for you to remember that you love this."

Antoinette stared at the sculpture. "Not sure that's true any longer," she said. "Not sure it really matters, though."

Andreas pulled a second stool forward and sat on it. "So are you ready to talk to me about it?"

Antoinette opened her mouth to repeat the same denial she'd been repeating to herself for days. That's not what came out. "It doesn't matter."

"Fine, we've established all the things that don't matter." Andreas raised an eyebrow. "Well done. But this time of quiet, while everyone's waiting for the hammer to drop up north? It's not going to last. Sooner or later, this house will be full. You'll have people demanding your services, and you'll have your next assignment," he said. "This is a rare opportunity where you can work on things you want to work on, and maybe figure out how to pull yourself out from beneath that cloud you've been under."

Antoinette didn't look at him. "I've done as I've been told. What more would you like me to do?"

"Lorenzo's been here for nearly a full day," Andreas said. "You've been in here since he arrived. I would have thought that you'd appreciate the chance to see your brother."

"Why?" Antoinette set down her tools. "I've seen him four, five times in the past two years. I'll see him at dinner tonight. We'll exchange the same pleasantries we always do. He'll compliment my work. I'll ask how the family fishing fleet and canneries are doing.

We'll speak the same way I do to Mattia. With courtesy, kindness, and absolutely gasping beneath the weight of how little we actually know about each other."

Andreas chuckled. "How long have you wanted to say that?"

"Enough, all right?" Antoinette heard her bitterness creep into her words for the first time. A voice in the back of her head pointed out that it most likely was not the first time. "I go where I'm sent. I do as I'm told. I smile when I'm supposed to smile, make what I'm supposed to make, be who I'm supposed to be, and I don't argue. I don't complain. I'm perfect. I'm always exactly what I'm meant to be, exactly how I was fucking built!" The last words flew from her mouth as if propelled, and without thinking, her arm shot out and pushed the half-finished sculpture off the stand. It struck the stone tile floor, the fingers shattering and skittering across the floor.

The room was silent for a long few moments. Antoinette felt something wet on her cheeks, and angrily brushed the tears away.

Andreas plucked a fragment of marble off of his sleeve. "It's a good thing that was just for you. Feels like you needed it."

She didn't respond. All the walls she'd spent the last few months carefully building around everything roiling around in her heart were cracking, and she was afraid that speaking would send them tumbling.

Andreas considered her. "You know, I made sure that all your progress sketches found their way to the college of masters as well. I got to see each of them. They're lovely, by the way. I have no doubt you'll be adding a new leaf to your arm," he said. "My favorite thing about seeing those sketches, reading the messages you nestled within them, seeing these tiny glimpses of what was happening in that throne room, is how easily a picture came together, how easy it was to see the journey you were going on."

He offered a handkerchief. She took it, and wiped her eyes. "Isn't that the point?"

"I read all your letters too." He smiled. "They were short. To the point. Really just tiny glimpses. But look at them all in total, and a picture comes together." Andreas waved when she offered the handkerchief back. "Keep it."

"And what does this picture show you?" she asked dully.

"A harder life than most people can know, lived by a woman who for too long has labored without a word of protest," Andreas said. "I've seen you grow up from a quiet little girl to one of the most remarkable women I've ever known. And you've rarely complained, rarely questioned your role in this world. So if there's someone that forced you to ask that question, to wonder what else might exist out there for you other than the duty and responsibility that's been clamped around your neck since you could speak, that person must have been truly remarkable."

"Does it matter?" Antoinette was too tired to deny what he said. She felt wrung out, like someone who'd been tasked with holding a heavy weight aloft for an impossible amount of time. "It's done. She's gone."

"It matters." He shrugged. "I told you I have a picture. But that doesn't tell me most of what happened between you and this ranger. And I don't need to know. You came home. You did what you were meant to do. Your grandmother will continue to pretend as if nothing untoward happened."

Antoinette shook her head. "So you think she knows."

"Of course she knows. She's Toni DeLuca."

"Gods. She can't even be a person when I fuck up," Antoinette said. "Where are the lectures? I crossed the line, the one I've been told over and over I can never cross. She's the closest thing I have to a mother, why isn't she here telling me how disappointed she is?"

"Two possibilities. Either she really is as dispassionate as you think, and she's determined that the cost of doing so isn't worth it, particularly considering that you clearly ended whatever was going on with you and Miss Creighton."

"And the second?"

"That she may not be as unsympathetic as you might think." Antoinette scoffed, and Andreas said, "You don't know everything your grandmother has been through in her life. Is it so hard to believe that she might have faced a choice similar to the one you just made? That she might know from personal experience just how difficult making that choice can be?"

Antoinette didn't know how to respond to that. She was spared from doing so by a soft knock on the door. Andreas hopped off the stool and walked over, cracking the door. Someone spoke softly and handed a slip of paper to the family attaché, and he shut the door as he read. Slowly, he turned back to Antoinette. "News from the Empire. From one of our sources." He handed her the paper. "It's over."

Antoinette read the three short sentences, and shut her eyes, a trembling breath slipping past her lips.

Oh, Jaina. I'm so sorry.

397 Hours

Jaina knew it had taken her longer to ride south than it had taken her to ride north. Ten days had passed since her world cracked in two. Some distant part of her brain knew she had still made good time. She rode to each waystation in silence, shutting off everything around her. Her eyes were fixed on the road before her, every stride of the hooves beneath her pulling her closer and closer to the end, to her home, to the last place she wanted to go.

She ate silently, mechanically, chewing dried beef and cheeses without really thinking of what she was putting in her mouth. She hadn't slept. When her horses needed rest, she sat by the stream while they drank and slept, her blackthorn staff across her legs, eyes fixed on the dirt and grass beneath her. Jaina had braced for the grief and recriminations to thunder in her head, but for the first time that she could remember, there was nothing. She was truly alone, and that knowledge tightened around her throat like a collar that would remain for the rest of her life.

When she rode through the north gate of Lofland Fork, it was late, well past midnight. She spoke only what she had to, a few words to the guards seeing her past. Jaina had braced herself for the memories that would accompany seeing the places where her brothers had stood, had laughed, had fought, had lived, all before they were chewed up by a machine indifferent to every piece of herself she'd thrown upon the gears. There was nothing.

She knew where she meant to ride. Her orders were as clear as a summer sky, and Jaina had every intent of riding to the ducal estate, of reporting to Shakkar the disaster that had befallen their country. Jaina didn't remember changing her mind, didn't remember making the decision to turn right at the dark and quiet Autumn Fair instead of left. It felt as if she had blinked, and found herself standing in the empty dining room of the Oak's Shade.

Jaina sat down at a table. Her eyes panned over the room, waiting for the grief to find her, idly wondering if it ever would, or if that part of her heart had burned away. She was tracing her fingers over the pine surface, and found a long scratch, nearly worn away from time and use. A memory cracked through. Jak and Joran wrestling, falling on the tabletop, the buckle on Jak's belt digging a deep furrow on the table, the argument of who would take the blame. Jaina could feel herself skitter back from the memory like a sleepwalker who woke on the edge of a precipice.

"Who's there?"

She didn't look up. "It's me, Evan."

"Jaina?" Her father's brewer blinked the sleep from his eyes. He gripped a lantern that he'd been holding aloft, sending flickering orange light across her face. "What... When did you get home? What are you doing here?"

"I need you to wake my parents. Please."

Evan stepped closer, frowning. "Jaina, are you all right?"

"My parents, Evan."

He nodded, backing out of the room until the darkness fell once more. Jaina sat, counting the heartbeats she could hear throughout the building. Guests, staff, and two that she wondered if she'd recognize.

She listened to the footsteps upstairs, the creak of door hinges, a whispered conversation. She listened to the rustling of clothes thrown on in a hurry, to stairs taken a bit too quickly. Her eyes stayed fixed on the tabletop until the hinges squeaked on the dining room doors, and her father spoke her name.

Rising to her feet, she turned to face her parents. Gail and Paul Creighton were still in their nightclothes. Her father's thinning hair stuck out at an absurd angle, but they both lit up when they saw her. "Jaina!" Paul exclaimed, rushing forward to throw his arms around his daughter's neck. "When did you get back?"

She hugged him back, out of instinct more than anything else. "Hi, dad."

"Sit, sit! We'll get some food, something for you to drink. Can you stay? We can have a room ready in ten minutes. How long are you here for?" The words tumbled out of his mouth. Behind him, Gail Creighton looked at her daughter's face, and Jaina heard the pewter bracelet on her wrist tinkle softly as her mother's hands began to tremble.

"Dad."

"Shakkar said you might be stationed here," Paul said, as if she hadn't spoken. "I don't think he was supposed to tell us, but he said you might be assigned to Lofland Fork. Do you know where you'll be staying? If they haven't picked quarters, maybe we could set your old room aside."

"Dad."

"When was the last time you ate? The ovens are cold but we can get some bread. There's still pie left over..."

"Paul, stop talking." Gail's voice was shaking, the blood draining from her face. Her husband looked back at her, confused.

"Honey, what's wrong? Why..." He looked back to Jaina. "What's going on?"

Jaina opened her mouth, and stopped. She could hear both her parent's hearts going faster and faster.

Jak. Joran. How do I do this?

There was no answer.

The silence grew heavier and heavier. Jaina could see her father open his mouth, about to demand answers, to ask her again. She didn't remember speaking, only heard the words after they'd slipped past her throat to shatter three lives.

"They're dead."

The moment she said it, she wanted to take it back. Wanted to tell her it was a lie, a mistake, a bad joke. She got to hear their heartbeats change, got to hear the sharp exhalation from her mother as she sank into a chair. Her perfect senses made sure to capture every hideous detail of that moment, to carve it into her very bones in flawless detail.

"What..." Paul shook his head as Gail buried her face in her hands, her shoulders beginning to silently tremble. "That's not right. You can't know that."

"I do." Jaina shook her head. "I do, dad. I know."

He stepped back from her, eyes wide and unblinking. "They're... You can't know that. They're far. They're far, but they can't be... No." He shook his head. "Mistakes happen. They always happen. I know. Saw it all the time, over and over. They're not dead."

"Dad..." She reached out to grip his shoulder, and he knocked her hand away.

"Stop saying it, Jaina. Stop it."

A wail emerged from her mother's hands, a broken howl that echoed through the dining room. Paul turned and dropped to his knees, wrapping his thick arms around his wife. "It's not true, love.

It's not true." He kissed the side of her head. "We would know. We would feel it. It's a mistake, I promise you."

"Please, dad…"

"You're upsetting your mother," Paul said, not looking up at her. "No one knows what's happened up north. You can't know. Someone told you something, and you brought it back to us without taking the time to actually be sure that it's true." He cupped his wife's chin, bringing her tear-filled eyes up to meet him. "Remember? Remember when everyone heard that there'd been a battle in the Moors? Everyone was running around, trying to find out whose sons had been there. We heard fifty dead, then a hundred, even two hundred." He offered a smile. It was somewhat less convincing with the tears carving paths down his ruddy cheeks. "A battalion got stranded there when their horses ran off. That was all. Four days of eating terrible food before they were found. Worst injury was a sprained ankle from a gopher hole. That's all this is. It's just a bad rumor that will be a story we tell once they're home."

Jaina's hands were shaking. Her stomach was a pit of acid. "Dad. You need to listen to me. This isn't a rumor. I didn't hear this from a trader or some retired sergeant." *Please, Jak, Joran, how do I make him see? I have to make him see.*

"I don't care." Paul shook his head, sharply. He still wasn't looking at her. "I don't care who you heard it from. I don't care who told you this. It's not possible, it's not."

"It is."

"We would know." He shut his eyes, shaking his head back and forth. "We would know." Paul kissed his wife's cheek, her tears glistening on his lips. "Remember? When they got sick, when you were in Havensport? You said you felt it. You knew something was wrong.

You couldn't sleep, left two days early because you knew something wasn't right. You would know."

Gail turned to look at Jaina, and whispered, "Please. Tell me that it's not true."

"You don't need her to tell you, Gail!" Paul's voice was breaking, desperation clinging to every syllable, still refusing to look at his daughter. "It's not true! It can't be true!"

"Tell me." Gail's voice was so low Jaina would never have heard it before waking up by the fire. "Jaina, you're my daughter, my baby girl, and I'm begging you. Please, by all the gods, just tell me that it's not true. Tell me you're not sure, tell me there might be a chance. Just give us something. Anything."

More than she had ever wanted her brothers to come home, more than she had ever wanted to wake up with Antoinette in her arms, more than anything she'd ever wanted as far back as she could remember, Jaina wanted to tell her mother what she so desperately needed to hear. She wanted to tell her there might be a mistake, that she needed to go check. Every part of her soul beat at her chest screaming for her to lie, to say anything to tear that expression off her mother's face, to spare her this pain if only for a few days.

I'm so sorry, momma. I'm so sorry, dad.

Her hand came up. Somewhere in the back of her head, she was surprised it wasn't shaking. The leather-wrapped casualty list was clutched in her fist. "I went north. All the way to the border. To meet with the Imperial soldiers, to get the list of survivors."

Paul began to shake. "Please."

"I don't read well, but I know their names."

"Please, Jaina, don't do this."

"They aren't on the list."

Something in her mother's eyes broke.

"I tried. I tried so hard," Jaina said, her voice trembling. "I gave up everything. I turned my back on everything. I just wanted them safe, and home, and to keep this family together, and none of it mattered."

The dining room she'd grown up playing in was quieter than she could ever remember. Paul's shoulders sank. It was if he'd been hollowed out, and was collapsing in on himself. "They're dead."

Jaina took a step forward, but came to a halt when she saw his eyes. "Dad..."

"Please. Leave." His voice was thick.

"Dad, I can't leave you."

"You already did." Paul Creighton's eyes were pointed in her direction, but it was as if he was looking through her. "You already walked away from us.."

"You have me," Jaina whispered.

Paul's eyes fell to the floor. He wrapped his arms around his wife. His eyes found his daughter one last time, and his voice broke as he whispered, "Please. Just... just go."

She ran.

She ran through the streets, fist balled, feeling the crushing weight of everything doing what it could to bury her. Her tears had dried on her cheeks by the time she stalked through the door of the ducal residence. Shakkar was waiting.

"The guards said you came through an hour ago. What..." He saw her face, and the color drained from his own. "Jaina?"

She stalked up to him, pulling the casualty list from her bag. It crushed in her fist, and she shoved it into his chest. "Here."

He looked down, swallowing. "What happened?"

"I failed."

"Your brothers..."

"They're dead. They're all dead. All the brothers and sons and fathers, all of them. This fragment is all that's left, and nothing we did made a godsdamned difference," she said. "We sent them north to be butchered. Martine failed. You failed. I failed." She felt like she should cry, but there was nothing left.

"Jaina, sit down. Please."

"No. I just..." She shook her head. "I'm done. I'm just fucking done."

Jaina didn't wait for him to say anything else. She pushed through the door into the night, and walked away.

319 Hours

Her pencil skittered over the sheet of paper tied down to the board on Antoinette's lap. A glass of wine sat on the table next to her, untouched since it had been brought out to her over two hours ago. Thunder rumbled overhead, and she looked up to the gathering clouds overhead. The first drop had yet to fall, and she returned to her drawing. She heard the footsteps behind her but didn't turn.

"How many do you need to draw?" Her pencil paused, and she glanced back at the burly man standing next to the table. He'd reached down to the stack of drawings, virtually identical renderings of the sculpture of a crow that stood in the garden in front of where Antoinette sat.

"Enough to get them right," she said.

He snorted. "These look pretty gods-damned right to me."

"They're not perfect."

"Didn't think perfect was possible."

She set her pencil down and turned to face him. "What do you want, Lorenzo?"

Her older brother sat in the other seat next to the table. "Can't a guy check on his baby sister?"

"I don't need checking in on."

"You were at dinner for a grand total of three minutes the other night," he said. "Since then, you've barely spoken to anyone. People are starting to talk."

She shook her head. "I just want to be alone."

He nodded. "I get that. I do. It's not really possible for our family, but I get the urge." He leaned down and plucked a few blades of the brilliantly green grass at his feet.

"Grandmother hates when you do that."

Lorenzo chuckled. "Why do you think I do it? We have to find some way to rebel. Sure, I go where she tells me, do what she tells me. I'm at sea for seven, eight months a year. I barely see my wife. But I'll be damned if I can't make this perfect lawn just a bit imperfect."

Antoinette shook her head. "It's foolish. It'll just make her upset without any purpose."

"Oh, I don't think she'll notice. She's too busy being annoyed with you." He dropped the blades of grass in a pocket on the vest he wore. "She won't tell me why. Don't think she's even told Andreas." He leaned over and elbowed her gently. "Want to clue me in?"

"Go away, Lorenzo."

"Oh, come on!" He grinned, showing the flashing gold tooth that had replaced one of his front incisors. "The perfect granddaughter did something to get under her skin. We're all dying to know what."

She shook her head. "You don't want to know."

"That's categorically untrue."

"Fine, then I don't want to say."

"Please? It's my name day."

"It's not."

"It could be."

"Drop it, okay?" A fat drop of rain landed on her page, smearing the charcoal, and she muttered a curse. Standing up, she began to gather up her belongings. Lorenzo took off his vest and wrapped the sketches up to protect them from the rain. "You don't have to do that. I'm just throwing them away."

"Can I have one?"

"Why?" The pair ran inside as thunder rumbled and the rain began to fall in a steady downpour. A chambermaid was waiting for them with a blanket. Antoinette waved her off. "I told you, they're not quite right."

Lorenzo pushed a lock of wet hair out of his face. "And I told you, they look wonderful to me. I want to show Layla."

"Fine." Antoinette shook her head. "When do you head back out?"

Lorenzo shrugged. "Next inspection tour is supposed to start tomorrow, but the weather might push that back." He leaned over and nudged her with his shoulder. "Hey, whatever's going on with you, if I can do anything..."

Before he could finish his thought, they were interrupted. "Antoinette." She and her brother turned to see Andreas approaching. "Your grandmother wants to see you in the foyer." He wore a strange expression.

Antoinette felt a flash of anger, but pushed it aside. "I need to change. I got caught in the rain."

Andreas shook his head. "I wouldn't keep her waiting."

"Fine." Antoinette handed her supplies to the chambermaid. "Put those in my studio, please."

"Yes, mistress."

She nodded at Lorenzo, who offered her a sympathetic smile, and fell in behind Andreas, who set a brisk pace as they navigated the halls and stairs of the sprawling estate. She had barely spoken to him since the moment in the studio. To be fair, she hadn't spoken to virtually anyone. He didn't say anything as they walked, his face giving nothing away.

They emerged at the top of the twin staircases to find Toni DeLuca waiting for them. The matriarch's eyes took in Antoinette's wet hair and clothing, and she arched an eyebrow.

"Andreas suggested that you wouldn't want me to delay," Antoinette said, doing her best to keep her voice even. She didn't know why she was angry at her grandmother. She just knew she was angry. No matter what she did to push past it, she was angry. It had become her companion for the last few days, from the moment she woke until she shut her eyes, and that bitterness was evident in every word, no matter how hard she tried. "Apologies for my state of disarray."

Her grandmother didn't react. She never did. Toni DeLuca expressed her distaste in the microscopic shifts of her stone face, every twitch of her eyebrow carrying more disdain than any other person's rant. "You have a visitor."

"I'm neither in the state or the mood to entertain, grandmother," Antoinette said. "And why someone would come out in this weather is beyond me. Whoever it is can..." She trailed off as Toni DeLuca took a step to the right, and Antoinette looked down at Jaina Creighton, standing on the marble tile, hair matted against her face, water pooling at her feet.

She didn't think, didn't consider the eyes of her grandmother or Andreas. One moment, she was staring down at the ranger, the next she was rushing down the stairs, her wet slippers squishing on the floor. Antoinette ran up to Jaina, coming to a halt before her, her heart drumming in her chest.

Jaina's eyes met hers, and the big woman began to tremble. Her voice was barely above a whisper as she said, "I didn't know where else to go."

Antoinette threw her arms around Jaina's neck. "Oh, Jaina. I'm so sorry. I'm so, so sorry."

Jaina didn't move at first, but after a few moments, her arms came up to wrap around Antoinette, and she began to cry. Antoinette held her as tightly as she could. She knew the eyes that were on them. She could hear her grandmother's heels clicking as she came down the stairs. It didn't matter. Nothing mattered but her.

When Toni DeLuca spoke, her voice broke through the moment, and Antoinette felt a flash of anger. They both turned to face Toni, Jaina wiping her eyes.

"Miss Creighton." Toni tilted her head. "Welcome to Vetticci."

Jaina stared at her, at a loss for words. "Madame DeLuca. I apologize for the intrusion, I just…"

"Not at all." Toni glanced back at Andreas, who had followed her down the stairs. "Andreas, please see the room next to Antoinette's prepared for our guest."

"Yes, Madame." Andreas nodded to a nearby chambermaid, who bowed and headed upstairs, Andreas falling in behind her.

"Antoinette, perhaps you and your… friend would be more comfortable in the sitting room." Toni extended a hand. "I'll have Andreas bring tea, as well as something to dry off with. I'm certain you two have much to talk about."

Antoinette nodded. "Yes. I… Yes, please."

"Miss Creighton. I look forward to speaking with you later." She stared at Jaina with hard eyes for a few moments, then turned and walked away.

"This way." Antoinette took Jaina's hand, leading her down a hallway past several doors before stepping through one. Inside, several plush chairs surrounded a low slung table. A fire burned in a large fireplace carved from a single massive piece of granite, and several small bookcases lined the walls. Antoinette sat on a long sofa, and said, "Sit. Please."

Jaina looked down at her clothes. "I'll get everything wet."

"I don't care." Antoinette pulled her down to the sofa.

Jaina was still trembling slightly, but whether from cold or emotion, Antoinette couldn't tell. She took a few deep breaths, and said quietly, "I suppose you know."

Antoinette took her hand. "I know about the battle. I know how bad the casualties were. I held out some hope that at least one of your brothers..." She trailed off as she saw Jaina's face. "Oh. Gods. I..." She took Jaina's hand. "I don't know what to say. I'm so sorry."

A soft knock at the door. Andreas stepped through, holding several towels in one hand and a tray with steaming mugs in the other. He set down the tray and the towels, and said, "I'll see to it that no one disturbs you for a while, mistress." He turned to Jaina. "Please accept the condolences of myself and our entire staff on your recent loss, Ranger Creighton. The resources of this house are at your disposal during your stay."

Jaina nodded. "Thank you." The door closed behind him.

"How did you get through the Myre Road?" Antoinette asked. "The last I heard, they'd restricted movement because of the war."

"I don't know." Jaina shook her head. "The border guard stopped me. They told me to wait while they spoke to someone in charge. I was ready for them to turn me back, to figure out another way down here, when they came back and let me through. They knew my name."

Antoinette shut her eyes for a moment. "Of course they did." She shook her head.

"Is that a problem?"

"No, it's..." Antoinette took a breath. "It doesn't matter." She took Jaina's hand. The ranger looked dully down at it.

"I didn't know how you'd feel. About me coming down here," Jaina said. "After the last time we spoke, I mean."

"Jaina." Antoinette shook her head. "I didn't want to hurt you. I promise, that was the last thing I wanted. But I didn't know what to do. I knew..."

"I get it." Jaina nodded slowly. "I do. Didn't make much sense otherwise, you telling me that you were a..." She gestured at Antoinette, and water dripped onto the couch. Jaina winced. "Sorry."

Antoinette shook her head, handing her a towel. "There's not a world in which I care less about the furniture getting wet." Jaina dried her hands and arms, and Antoinette carefully said, "Your parents?"

Jaina looked at her, and shook her head. "They know. It didn't go well." She told Antoinette of everything that had happened in the Oak's Shade. She didn't cry, just spoke in a hollow voice. "After that, I just couldn't keep going. I didn't know what else to do. There was only one thing in my mind." She let out a long, shuddering breath. "Antoinette, I'm sorry."

"Sorry?" Antoinette gripped her hand. "What could you possibly have to be sorry about?"

"I'm sorry that I walked away."

"I didn't give you much of a choice."

"I had a choice," Jaina said. "I always had a choice, right from the beginning. From the moment I saw that red chit in..." She choked on the name, and swallowed. "I've made choice after choice, and in that moment, I could have made the choice to say what I really felt, to see what you were trying to do."

Antoinette reached up and brushed a tear from Jaina's cheek. "Pushing you away broke me. I didn't realize how badly until I was standing in that room alone, knowing that I wouldn't see you again. I had to do it, but it broke me." She locked eyes with Jaina. "I won't do it again."

Jaina's eyes widened. "Antoinette, things have changed for me. Everything has changed for me. But you're still..." She waved her hand all around them. "All of this."

"I am." Antoinette nodded slowly. "And as much as I want to run off to our cottage, to live that life we spoke about, being back here, surrounded by what my family is, reminded me how impossible that truly is. We can't disappear. The world will find us."

"I know."

Antoinette gripped her hand tightly. "So we have to find a way within this world."

Jaina shook her head. "I don't understand."

"I can't go back. Not to how things were before I knew you. I'm not the same. My life isn't the same. The moment I took your hand, I made the first cut in reshaping my life into something I never thought possible, and I told you once, once you put blade to wood, there's no going back," Antoinette said. "I can't put the world back in the shape it was before we met. And I no longer have any intention of doing so."

"So what does that mean?" Jaina asked.

"I hid so much from you," Antoinette said. "What I felt about you, what I still feel about you, none of that was a lie, but I never let you see who I truly was. And as much as I might choose to fight it, the truth is, I'm a fucking DeLuca." Her voice was hard. "And DeLucas don't ask the world for permission. We grab it by the throat and drag it into its proper shape." She looked up at Jaina. "Do you want to be with me?"

"Yes." There was no hesitation, no question in Jaina's voice.

"Then I'm done lying. Done running, done hiding. Done pretending that my future has any shape at all without you in it. I watched you walk away once. I will not do it again." Antoinette leaned forward, and softly kissed Jaina. She felt the big woman tremble and tasted the tears on her lips. "I am Antoinette DeLuca, scioness of the DeLuca family, master artisan of the Vettician College of Artisans. And I am yours, Jaina Creighton, from now until the end. That is the truth of who I am, and should my grandmother, the dukes, the rangers, or anyone else take exception to that truth, I will use all that I know and all that I am to cut them into the proper shape."

Jaina stared at her, light from the cinderstone lanterns glittering in her forest green eyes, as if she was seeing Antoinette for the first time. "You mean that."

"I do."

"I've lost so much," Jaina said. "When I walked away from you, I didn't really understand what it meant to have a piece of who you are torn away." Her voice broke slightly as she spoke. "I won't lose you too. I love you, and I'm yours, Antoinette, from now until the end."

They kissed again, and Antoinette brushed Jaina's hair back. "When was the last time you slept?"

Jaina chuckled dully. "The night before I reached the Breaking."

Antoinette's eyes widened. "Jaina, that's almost two weeks."

"Yeah." Jaina shrugged. "Rangers don't sleep as much."

"Ranger or not..." She shook her head. "You need to sleep."

"I've been afraid," Jaina said. Her voice was very small. "I didn't know what was waiting for me if I did."

Antoinette nodded. "Come with me."

"Where are we going?"

"To my room. So you can sleep."

"Are you sure?"

"I told you." Antoinette stood up, and took Jaina's hand. "I'm done hiding."

310 Hours

J aina woke from a dreamless sleep. She had fallen asleep with Antoinette curled next to her, her raven hair spilling over Jaina's chest, their fingers entwined together. The dreams she had feared didn't come. As she blinked her bleary eyes awake, she felt a stab of grief bloom in her chest. She'd been terrified to see Jak and Joran in her sleep, but their absence reinforced the reality that they were truly and forever gone.

Antoinette wasn't next to her. Jaina had barely begun to register that fact when there was a soft knock at the door. Jaina glanced down to be sure she was dressed. She had changed into some simple, soft cotton clothes the night before. Satisfied, she said, "Yes?" Her voice was raw and croaking, and she cleared it before repeating herself.

The door cracked open, and the man who'd introduced himself as Andreas stepped through. He offered a bow. "Apologies for the intrusion, Ranger. Mistress Antoinette was called away. She wanted to be sure you knew she would not be gone long. I suggested she leave a note, but she insisted I deliver the message in person."

Jaina sat up. "I can't read very well." She rubbed her eyes.

If that statement surprised Andreas, he didn't let it show. "Are you hungry, Ranger?'

Jaina nodded. "I am, but don't call me that. Please."

"Pardon?"

"I'm not a ranger. Not anymore."

If he had questions, he didn't let it show. "Very good, Miss Creighton." Andreas gestured at a stack of folded clothes. "I took the liberty of having some fresh clothes brought up for you. If you'd care to follow me once you're dressed, we've set aside some food in the garden. It's a lovely day, and Mistress Antoinette will meet you there once she's done."

Jaina quickly dressed, and stepped out into the hall where Andreas was patiently waiting. They began walking, and Jaina said, "I'm sorry for the inconvenience. Coming here unexpected, I mean."

"It wasn't." Andreas glanced at her. "Who do you think made certain the border guards knew to let you through?"

Jaina's eyes widened. "You? But how did you know..."

"I didn't. Not really." The older man shrugged. "But I knew it was a possibility. Should you have decided to come to Vetticci, I knew there were several obstacles in your way. I also knew how important you are to the mistress. Removing one of those obstacles was a minor matter."

"Are you..." Jaina tried to think of the right words. "I don't know your role here."

Andreas smiled. "I'm the family attache and chargé d'affaires. I help manage the family affairs, the business, and act as an advisor to the DeLucas."

Jaina nodded slowly. "So Antoinette told you? What happened up there?'

"Absolutely not." He shook his head. "Mistress Antoinette has been very discreet about what happened in Westcott. But I've known her since she was born. And I can tell when something is weighing heavily on her."

They came to a long hallway, one entire side of which was floor to ceiling windows looking out on a sprawling expanse of carefully manicured grass nearly the size of a city block. Hedges taller than Jaina lined the borders, and a table was set up. Andreas held a door open for her, and Jaina stepped through. "May I ask a question?" Jaina said.

"Of course."

"How much trouble have I caused? Coming here, I mean?"

Andreas shook his head. "I couldn't say. But I can promise it's well within our means to manage. You are a guest of this family. We take that very seriously. The rest can be dealt with later." He gestured at the trays of pastries, cheese, and fruit. "Please. Eat. I don't believe Mistress Antoinette will be long."

Once he'd left, Jaina sat and began to eat. She was mid-bite when she heard the sound of hooves on grass. Through a gap in the hedges on the other side of the garden, a soft braying sound drifted out, and the snout of a donkey peeked around. Its fur was patchy, the color of grey mud, and Jaina could swear the animal was glaring at her. The donkey stopped, staring balefully at her, and Jaina glanced down. "Do you want some food?" she asked.

"Please do not feed that godsforsaken creature anything." Jaina turned at the voice from the door, and swallowed. Toni DeLuca stood at the entrance to the garden, hands folded in front of her. Her expression was unreadable. "He has an unfortunate habit of biting if people try to feed him. Or look at him. Or exist within several miles of him."

Jaina came to her feet. "Mistress..." She winced. "Apologies. Madame DeLuca." She glanced back at the donkey. "Not the kind of animal I would have expected here."

"Stuart came to us years ago. No one likes him, and he generally feels the same way. But I admit to having an odd fondness for the animal," Toni said. "There's something to be said about a creature who gives not a single solitary damn about what the world thinks of it. I admire that."

"Is the feeling returned?"

"Absolutely not." Toni sat down. "We should talk."

Jaina nodded, returning to her chair. "I owe you an apology. Coming to your home like this, I know that it must have caused some difficulties."

"Indeed." Jaina blinked at the matter-of-fact tone, and Toni said, "Are you aware there's a warrant for your arrest?"

"I wasn't."

Toni reached into the hidden folds of the shawl she wore around her shoulders, and produced a sheet of paper. "Issued by a Lord Callow. Charges of desertion and refusal to obey orders." She set the paper down. "If it helps, I doubt anyone is all that eager to expend resources tracking down one wayward ranger. The Dominion has much bigger problems at the moment. But that doesn't change the fact that you came to my door as a fugitive. That presents no small degree of difficulties, in addition to the other complications that you bring with you."

Jaina took a deep breath. "I'm sorry. I didn't consider what coming here would mean for you and your family."

"That much is clear."

"So what happens next?"

Toni considered her. "You know, I haven't the slightest idea." She reached out and picked up a cloth napkin and a small pastry with a dollop of chocolate on top. "Have you tried these? A specialty of one of my cooks. I'm quite fond of them."

Jaina shook her head. "Madame DeLuca, I don't want to cause trouble, but I..." She fell silent as Toni raised a hand.

"I'm certain your rationale would have been interesting, but we can dispense with that part of the conversation. It serves little purpose."

She took a bite of the flaky pastry. After swallowing, she set it down on the napkin. "You are an interesting problem, ranger."

"I'm not a ranger anymore."

Toni raised an eyebrow. "I'm fairly certain you could throw Stuart there onto the roof of this estate. And that any bites he would be certain to inflict would be healed before we could find a way to get him down. If you're not a ranger, I'm altogether uncertain what that makes you." She dabbed at her mouth with the napkin. "Should it make you more comfortable, I'll call you Miss Creighton. Or Jaina."

"Either is fine." Jaina glanced at the door. "Do you know if Antoinette will be long?"

"Long enough that we can speak. I made certain of that." Toni tapped a manicured fingernail on the wooden table. "As I said, you're an interesting problem. On the one hand, no matter how distracted the Dominion is at the moment, sooner or later they will begin to ask questions about where you might have disappeared to. Should word reach them that the DeLuca family is sheltering you, that crosses the line from problem to diplomatic incident. That's a headache I'm not eager to experience."

"So you want me gone." Jaina did her best to keep the irritation from her voice.

"Jaina, I said before that you are still a ranger. I believe that it's important to be honest about who we are, no matter how we feel about it. You're a ranger. I'm a prickly and cold-blooded bitch." Toni shrugged. "But the advantage of being a prickly and cold-blooded bitch is that I don't feel the need to couch what I say. If I wanted you gone, you never would have reached my front door. But you are a problem. And the biggest problem you present has nothing to do with an ineffectual warrant issued by a nation that is currently occupied with losing a war quite badly, and more to do with the fact that my only granddaughter is in love with you."

Jaina didn't know what to say. It seemed safest to remain silent.

"The warrant is an administrative problem. You and Antoinette..." She shook her head. "That's potentially existential. The smart thing to do would be to send you away. Disappear you before things get worse."

"So why don't you do that?"

"Several reasons, not least among which is the fact that this family owes you. You saved Antoinette's life in those woods, and you endured a significant amount of pain doing so. That puts me in your debt. I don't like being in debt."

Jaina shook her head. "I was doing my duty."

"You'd make a terrible Vetticcian," Toni said. "Never give up positioning in a negotiation."

"Is that what this is? A negotiation?"

"Everything is a negotiation."

"She's your granddaughter," Jaina said in disbelief.

"I'm aware." Toni considered Jaina. "Duty or not, you bled for this family. That's not something I take lightly. So that puts me here, in the position to ask you a question." Leaning forward, she said, "What do you want?"

Jaina took a breath. "That's a complicated question."

"I think you know quite well it's not," Toni said. "And you also know that what you want is the one thing that I can't allow."

"I think that's not your choice."

"Don't be a fool," Toni snapped. "Antoinette is more than just my granddaughter. She's the only heir to this house, a house that stretches back over eight hundred years. The first DeLucas stood on the beach when there was nothing here but white sand. This family directly employs over four thousand people. We contract with nearly ten times that number. We are part of the lifeblood that keeps the greatest city on this continent breathing. That's more than legacy. That's obligation. That's responsibility." She shook her head. "You say that it's not my choice, and in that, you're right. None of us have the choice, the ability to toss that aside for the sake of a dalliance that's lasted less than two months. Even if I was inclined to allow this, I couldn't."

She expected to feel anger, but Jaina was just tired. "I'm not surprised to hear you say that. She's told me how you feel. What she is to you. But she's more than that to me. She's everything."

"Infatuation is not a rationale for chaos."

"If you think this is a simple infatuation, you don't know me at all."

"Think on what you want, Jaina." Toni considered her. "And you're wrong. I understand more than you know."

The anger began to creep through the exhaustion. "If this is where you tell me that you were in love once, that you made the hard choice to do the right thing, you can spare me."

"No. I've never sought out such things," Toni said. "My late husband was a political choice. A decision made to advance both our families. I won't pretend to have ever felt what you and Antoinette feel for each other."

"Then you can't understand."

"That's not what I'm speaking of." Toni looked up at a pair of seagulls wheeling overhead. She was silent for a long few moments before she spoke again. "Has Antoinette spoken to you about her mother?"

Jaina shook her head. "Only that she passed a while back."

"In childbirth. With Antoinette's younger brother, Mattia," Toni said. She began fiddling with the corner of the napkin. "Carmen was a light in this world. She laughed, always. I still remember hearing her giggle from another room as Andreas teased her. She loved everyone in this house, and they loved her. I loved her. She didn't have Antoinette's gifts. No one does. But she was kind, and she was thoughtful, and I knew from the moment I first held her that I would burn this world to the ground to keep her from knowing a single moment of pain."

Toni didn't look at Jaina as she spoke. Her voice was quiet. "I have wealth. Influence. Power. I have done great and terrible things, and I will do even greater and even more terrible things. But none of it made a difference. None of that wealth or influence mattered when she began to bleed. I sat, and I held her hand, and I threatened and bribed and promised every anatomist that came into that room. I looked into Carmen's eyes and I promised her it would be all right, and I watched utterly helpless as my baby girl begged me to save her. Watched as those laughing eyes closed forever. So yes, I understand. I understand what it is to be willing to give up everything for someone you love, and to watch the world tear them away for no other reason than random and vicious chance. In that, I understand you better than Antoinette ever will."

Jaina felt as if she couldn't breathe. But she didn't say anything, only listened.

"People will offer you platitudes. Priests and clerics will promise your brothers and my daughter are in a better place. Others will praise their valor or their kindness, all while knowing nothing about the people they were or how they died. Everyone, my granddaughter included, will search for any lie or empty banality to make you feel better. They'll believe they do it out of consideration for your grief. But in truth, they do it because they can't bear the look in your eyes, the glimpse they get at how easily this fucking world can tear the very guts from our belly with no rhyme or reason." For the first time, Toni DeLuca's even tone broke. Her fingers balled into fists. "And you'll tell them what they want to hear. You'll pretend it helps. Not for you, for them. But there will always be a part of you angry, angry at everyone who somehow made it this far in life without hurting the way you do."

Jaina felt the tears on her cheeks. "I don't know how to talk to her about this."

"That won't change." Toni met her eyes. "This kind of thing, it hollows you out. Takes something away that will never come back. Day by day, you'll get better at hiding it, better at convincing everyone, most of all yourself, that the wounds are closing. But it's been over twenty years, and they still bleed inside me."

She came to her feet. "Jaina, I am truly sorry that your brothers died. There is nothing I nor anyone else can say that will make it feel any better. It was cruel, and it was pointless, and it was undeserved."

The words struck Jaina with an almost physical force, but it was almost welcome, as if this fearsome woman was giving her permission to feel all the grief and rage that made a home inside her heart. "Thank you," she whispered.

"You are welcome to stay as long as you choose," Toni said. "There are hard choices ahead, and more pain in your future. But you have earned the protection of this house, and you deserve to have a chance to mourn." She nodded at Jaina, and left her alone with her grief.

Ten Minutes

"**Y**ou know this can't last, don't you?"

Antoinette didn't turn at her grandmother's voice. She stood at a window on the second floor, looking down at Jaina and her brother sitting together and talking in the garden. Jaina had taken to spending most of her time outside, in the sunlight. "She and Lorenzo get along quite well," Antoinette said as Toni came to stand next to her. "Ever wonder why that is?"

"Jaina's a very impressive woman. I would imagine there are several reasons."

"She is. He also knows it annoys you. It's no different than him plucking the grass."

"I'm glad he thinks me so easily distressed," Toni said. "Keeps his rebellions to a very manageable level. Whereas you, on the other hand..."

"We're not sending her back."

"They know she's here." Antoinette glanced over at her grandmother, who nodded. "I don't know how. I promise you, I had nothing to do with that. Probably one of the border guards. Allowing a ranger through isn't exactly something that happens every day."

"Have they filed an extradition request?"

"No, but they will. And when they do..."

"You'll clap her in irons and send her back north?"

"Of course not," Toni said. "But it will alter this situation somewhat. And sooner rather than later, you're going to have to come to terms with reality."

Antoinette nodded slowly. "I've been giving that reality a great deal of thought these last few weeks. Since I came home, really."

"I'm glad to hear that."

"Are you." It was not a question. "Do you remember the Aldano contract?"

Her grandmother nodded. "You did six stone carvings. I believe that was the job that led to your distaste in stonework."

"They were keystones for a new library their family was building. I got particularly annoyed when I discovered that one wouldn't even be visible to the public. Felt like the most absurd display of wealth imaginable, spending that much to create a work of art that would be hidden in the rafters where no one could see it," Antoinette said. "It wasn't until the architect explained its purpose that I understood. It was hidden, but it held the weight of all the other stones in the arch. The Aldanos thought it fitting that the piece that held the rest together get the same attention that the rest of the building did."

She turned to face her grandmother. "I didn't understand until I saw her again. Not really. I knew my heart was broken in two. I knew that I mourned those brief moments that we'd had together. But I didn't understand why I felt so unmoored, so fragile, until I looked down and saw her again. She's my keystone. I love Jaina. I walked away from her once, and it nearly brought me crumbling to the ground. I will not do so again. And should the Dominion decide that it wants to press the issue, I'll use every tool at my disposal to bring them to ruin."

Toni watched her, unblinking. "You and she together would mean a disruption to this house and this family like we haven't seen in centuries. You are the only daughter. If you marry a foreigner, let alone a woman who cannot bring this family an heiress, there will be chaos. The DeLucas will be vulnerable, and being vulnerable in this city of sharks is a very risky thing."

"We're always vulnerable," Antoinette said. "Always at risk. You've taught me that since I was young. It's the reason that Lorenzo learned ledgers and shipbuilding and all the things he did when other children his age were playing. It's the reason Mattia has come home bruised and bleeding since he could barely walk, why he vanishes for months at a time. You told each of us that our role in this family was critical, because the sharks were circling. They're always circling, and we've always survived."

"Because every member of this family does their part."

"And what if I'd died in that forest?" Antoinette asked. "You plan for everything, calculate for everything. You knew the risk. You knew that you were sending me off, alone, with no family guard." She shook her head. "I inherited your distaste for gambling, but I'd be willing to wager a not insignificant fortune that there's a file in that bare and empty office of yours with plans for what to do if one of those deserters had been a bit too eager to send a message. A way that this family could continue, could move on."

She turned away. "You plan for everything. I'm telling you that it's time to plan for this. I will not walk away from her. Not again."

"You would put at risk a legacy of centuries for her?"

Antoinette looked back. "I will go to war for her." She shrugged. "I always hoped that should I need to go to war, my family would stand beside me. But my place is with her. It always will be, and may the gods help anyone who stands against us." With that, she walked away, praying to those very same gods that her grandmother hadn't seen her hands trembling.

You're out on a very high and slippery ledge now.

Antoinette would not be the one to speak her greatest fear into reality, but it sat at the front of her mind as her heels clicked off the stairs. *My grandmother sees everyone and everything in terms of assets and liabilities. If she decides Jaina's a liability...* She swallowed. Every moment she hadn't been with Jaina, she'd been pouring over every document, every message, every slip of paper she could get her hands on. Everything she asked for Andreas produced, without ever asking her why. *I have to make the cost too high. And that means that cost must be very, very high indeed.*

She stepped out into the garden. Jaina had already come to her feet. The ranger rarely smiled these days, but when she saw Antoinette, the tightness around her eyes relaxed for a moment, and Jaina's lips twitched in the smallest of smiles. Antoinette was always taken aback at how much she treasured those tiny moments. She lay her hand on Jaina's chest, and kissed her. "I'm sorry I was delayed. Did you wait to eat?"

"She did," Lorenzo said around a mouthful of cheese and bread. "Better breeding."

"He was hungry," Jaina said. "I told him it was all right to go ahead." She paused, and said, "I saw you. In the window, I mean."

Antoinette nodded. "Did you hear?"

"A bit." Jaina took a breath. "I know me being here is..."

Antoinette shook her head. "If you heard, then you know. I meant what I said. I'll not let you walk away again."

"Not much point in arguing with her," Lorenzo said, swallowing a bite that would choke a python. "She was always stubborn."

Antoinette glanced at him. "A gentleman would excuse himself to let us share a quiet morning together."

"One of the many reasons that I'm so very pleased to not be a gentleman." Lorenzo shrugged. "Besides, I like Jaina, and did you ever think that you might be interrupting our lovely morning together? Hmmm?"

"Isn't it time for you to head back to sea?"

"Storm season. Very unpredictable."

"It hasn't rained for four days."

"Maybe I'm just lazy," Lorenzo said. "Or maybe, just maybe, I'm relishing the opportunity to stand with my baby sister."

Antoinette frowned. "What?"

"It's truly tragic how slow she is," Lorenzo said to Jaina. "I hope you're able to love her despite her limitations."

"You're an ass."

"I am. A very stubborn ass that happens to control the entire fleet, canning operations, and manufacturing wing of our family's assets. A very stubborn ass who may have made it clear that anything that brings my sister heartbreak would almost certainly have side effects that would cost this family dearly." He leaned back in his chair. "I told grandmother I wasn't leaving until this was resolved. She's quite upset with me."

Antoinette stared at him. "Lorenzo, I..."

He shrugged. "She's spent every moment of our lives shoving the idea that nothing was more important than family down our throats. But the moment you have the chance to actually find something that makes you happy, she's ready to cast that loyalty aside? I call that a special grade of bullshit. You and I don't know each other as well as I'd like, but you're still my sister, and you deserve to be happy." He grinned, his gold tooth glinting in the sunlight. "Consider it a giant fistful of grass."

Antoinette was dumbstruck, but she stepped forward and wrapped her arms around her brother's shoulders.

"What are you doing?" he squawked.

"I'm hugging you."

"It's weird."

"It is." She kissed his cheek. "Thank you. I don't know what to say."

"Just let me go. You're supposed to be hugging her."

Antoinette laughed. Turning back to Jaina, she said, "He's not usually…" Her voice trailed off. "Jaina?"

The ranger was staring into the distance, frowning. "Something's wrong."

Lorenzo came to his feet as Antoinette reached out to touch Jaina's arm. "Do you hear something?"

Jaina nodded. "Birds."

"Birds?"

"There." Lorenzo was pointing to the sky in the east. The sky was dotted with the black haze of a flock of birds. "Starlings."

A flutter of motion from the willow tree in the garden, and they watched as three birds exploded from the branches, darting into the sky. Moments later, they heard screeching. Overhead, a seagull flew past. First one, then ten, and then the sky darkened under the shadows of countless sea birds from the massive city taking flight, all screeching, loud enough that it could be heard everywhere. The door flew open, and Andreas and Toni came outside, followed by several members of the house staff, all with their heads craned upwards.

The birds numbered in the millions, all flying west as fast as they could. The day grew dark as the impossibly huge flocks blocked out the sun. Antoinette's eyes tracked one that split from the rest. It tumbled down towards them, striking the table with a thud, its broken wings twitching. Another fell, then another, and Antoinette felt Jaina grab her and Lorenzo, pulling them back to the shadow of the house as thousands of birds began to tumble from the sky, crashing against the roof, the lawn, splashing in the fountain.

"What is this?" Lorenzo shouted over the din. "What's happening?"

Before anyone could answer, the ground beneath their feet lurched, hard, as if someone had taken hold of an impossibly huge rug they all stood on and yanked. The cracking of windows raced down the length of the estate as Antoinette was knocked to the ground, her grandmother falling next to her as shattered glass rained down upon them. They scrambled to their knees. A piece of roof tile cracked loose, tumbling down towards Lorenzo. Jaina was faster, her fist darting out to shatter the tile before it could strike his head.

Antoinette turned to her grandmother, and was stunned by the look of fear on Toni DeLuca's face. Before she could say anything, she heard Jaina cry out. The ranger clapped her hands to her ears, falling to her knees. "Jaina!" Antoinette scrambled to her feet, but the ground lurched again, and as she fell once more, the sky screamed.

It was deafening, high pitched and discordant. What few windows had survived the earthquake exploded under the sonic onslaught, and Antoinette pressed her hands to her ears so tightly she feared she would break something. The sound dug past flesh, vibrating the very bones of her skull, and she felt hot blood trickle from her ears to smear on her palms. Antoinette turned wide eyes to the sky, and her blood ran cold. The clouds were being shoved aside by some unseen force, and the pale gentle blue that had been there before was replaced by a violent, hideous purple.

She felt Jaina wrap her arms around her, and Antoinette buried her head in Jaina's chest as the shrieking went on and on, impossibly long, battering the city with waves of deafening sound as a torrent of dead birds rained down upon them, carpeting the lawn and tables in bloody eyes and broken wings. She didn't know how long it lasted, but when it finally died down, she was weeping into Jaina's tunic.

For a long moment, there was silence. Slowly, Jaina rose to her feet, then Lorenzo, who helped his grandmother stand. The city was quiet. Antoinette looked around at everyone. They all had blood trickling from their ears, and it took a moment before sound returned to their world.

"What..." Andreas was trembling. He wasn't the only one. "What was that?"

Toni DeLuca wiped the blood from her ears. "I don't know."

Together, they all stood, ears ringing, in a city struck mute with fear.

Event + 33 Hours

"It's a nightmare."

Jaina nodded at Antoinette's words as they stared up at the massive map of the continent of Alddarri that hung in the DeLuca library. They were not alone in the room. Andreas stood in charge of various staff that ran in and out of the house with messages clutched in their fist. Jaina had given up trying to count them. The family attache stood bent over the table, sorting through the slips of paper, mouth moving silently as he worked.

Toni DeLuca had been a force of nature. Before any of the rest of them had truly recovered from the screaming sky and shaking earth, she was barking orders, sending runners in all directions. For twelve hours, they knew little to nothing of what had happened. There was fear that the event had killed every bird for miles, which would have crippled the courier pigeon network that was the fastest way to send messages. But late into the evening, the first of the black-throated birds began to arrive in the city, messages strapped to their legs, and within an hour, dozens arrived at the large dovecote at the top of the east wing.

Each of those messages came to Andreas. As he read them, he plucked a small pin with a blue flag from a bowl, and pinned it to the map. Minute by minute, hour by hour, a picture emerged. Flags were placed in Westcott, Sansbury, Vorchese, Galen's Crossing, and the map began to fill with these cerulean markers that someone was still there, still whispering in Toni DeLuca's ear. Jaina had nearly burst into tears of relief when a flag sprouted in the heart of Lofland Fork. But as the cities to the west of the Dominion responded to the call from Vetticci, those in the east stood silent. A massive section of the Dominion's eastern coast was empty, not a single flag filling the space. Birds were sent to the larger cities in that region. None returned.

Jaina pointed to the map as she spoke. "Walshire. Havensport. Breguet. Thousands of people live there. Tens of thousands. How can there be nothing?"

Antoinette shook her head. "I know we have people in those cities. There's a full Vetticcian guild house in Havensport. We trade there constantly. At any given time, there have to be fifteen, twenty ships in that harbor."

"How long would it take them to get back?"

Andreas answered as he walked up to them. "It depends on the ship. A trade galleon moves like a drunk spotted whale. But sloops, frigates? They're much faster."

"It's only been two days," Antoinette said. "They couldn't get back this soon."

"No, but..." Andreas glanced at Jaina, and swallowed. "We sent sixteen sloops from the Merino and DeLuca fleets east to meet whomever came back from Havensport. By now, they will have reached the halfway point. Each of them have a dozen messenger doves on board." He held up a slip of paper. "From one of our captains. They've seen no ships coming south."

"That doesn't make any sense."

"There's more." He handed another slip to Antoinette, who read it quickly. Jaina could see the way her lips tightened, heard her heartbeat quicken.

"This is confirmed?"

"It matches other reports we've gotten. All from farm communities about halfway between the coast and the Duke's Road."

"What is it?" Jaina asked.

Antoinette swallowed, and read. "East is dead. Many wounded. Water poisoned. Plants dead. Send help."

Everyone in the room had stopped speaking as she read. For a few moments, the library was silent, the quiet only broken as someone stepped through the door. An aide muttered an apology as he walked over to Andreas and handed him a bowl of black flags. Andreas slowly began pinning them into the map.

Jaina felt sick. "I need..." She swallowed. "I'm sorry. I need some air."

"I can come with you," Antoinette said. The slip of paper was still clutched in her fist.

"No, I..." Jaina shook her head. "Please. Stay here. Keep working. I just need to collect myself."

Antoinette frowned, but she nodded, and kissed Jaina on the cheek. "I'm here. Whenever you need me."

"I know."

Jaina had not set foot outside since it had happened. The dead birds and broken glass had been cleaned up, but the wooden boards nailed over the broken windows and the jagged edges to the estate's stonework still held a reminder of how bad it had been. Jaina stumbled out on to the grass, and stood in the sunlight, taking long deep breaths. She kept trying to wrap her head around what the messages were saying. It didn't fit. She heard the flutter of wings, and watched as one, then two pigeons appeared over the northern wall of the DeLuca Estate.

Are they carrying blue flags?

Or black?

"Jaina?"

She didn't turn. Jaina had come to know those precise footfalls quite well. "Madame DeLuca."

The older woman came to stand beside her. Her dress today was a deep, inky black. It seemed appropriate. "We got a message from one of our contacts in Lofland Fork. Your parents are safe. I thought you might like to know. "

"Thank you." Jaina gestured back to the house. "Andreas marked Lofland Fork with a blue flag, but I appreciate the confirmation."

"Of course."

"I don't suppose I'm allowed to ask what the Table said." The silence that had hung over Vetticci in the moments following the event didn't last long. Almost immediately, panic choked the city, riots breaking out in hundreds of neighborhoods. The great houses and guilds poured every guardsman and mercenary they had into the streets, restoring order with boot heel and spearpoint when necessary. Six hours ago, Toni had been summoned to an emergency meeting of the ruling families of Vetticci, to brief them on what she knew about the event that had plunged the city into chaos.

"Asking costs nothing. Answers are always the expensive part." Toni shook her head. "The Table is postponing any action pending more information. They wish to fully evaluate the circumstances before deciding which investments are best to allocate to a response."

"I suppose that makes sense."

"You're not well versed in politics, are you?" Toni asked. "That's a very formal way of saying that they're not going to do a godsdamned thing. The only concession made was that they would not lock down travel outside the city. If individual families or guilds wish to send aid north, they can, but the Table will not back such actions financially."

"Do you think anyone will?"

"Doubtful. Without Table support, any meaningful aid would be prohibitively expensive." Toni scowled. "Godsdamned shortsighted fools."

Jaina glanced at her. "You disagree."

"I think allowing the nation that provides over half the food that feeds this city to its own devices is idiocy."

Jaina felt a flash of anger at the callous and mercenary tone. *That won't help. She might.* "You could help."

Toni shook her head. "I told you, without Table support..."

"But you could," Jaina said. Toni lifted an eyebrow. "I'm sorry. I don't mean to interrupt."

"I'm quite certain you did."

"Well... yes." Jaina swallowed. "I apologize. But you could help. You have the resources. The funds. And if you were to send aid north, show that you believe that it's worth the cost, isn't it possible others might follow suit?"

"This is important to you," Toni said.

"It's my home. I know you said my parents are all right, but things have to be chaos up there. People hurt. People without homes, starving. And with so many of the dukes dead, I don't know what's going to happen." Some small voice in the back of Jaina's mind muttered a warning. She pushed it aside. "You have the ability to help. What does it say about you if you choose not to do so?"

"It says I am a practical woman not given towards shoveling money into a pit with no possibility of return," Toni said. "Our wealth was not handed to us, Miss Creighton. It was earned through generations of struggle and effort. I would be a poor steward of that legacy should I simply place the fruits of those labors onto a pyre that offered no return on our investment."

It's not going to happen. Jaina tried to keep the scowl from her face. She knew she had been wholly unsuccessful. "So my people suffer while you remain a good steward of your accounts. That's the legacy you choose."

"Do not presume to know my mind, ranger."

"I told you, I'm not a ranger."

"Keep saying it. Perhaps one day you'll even believe it." Toni's hard grey eyes remained locked on her. "It could be done."

"What?"

"Lorenzo's temper tantrum about you and his sister has been an annoyance, but it has also meant that we have six warehouses full of preserved fish and seaweed." Toni tapped her fingernail against the large gem adorning the ring on her middle finger. "Shipments north will be resuming soon, but they were halted for nearly two days. That means wagons, hundreds of them, waiting for cargo that will take some time to be made available, wagons that could easily be repurposed. We donate no small amount to the Pallia Clinic; it would not take much convincing to have them spare a few anatomists."

"Even two or three would make a difference," Jaina hurriedly said. In the back of her head, that small voice was struggling to push past the hope she was beginning to feel.

Toni scoffed. "Two or three would be an insult. Two or three dozen would be more commensurate with our investment. Andreas could arrange for medical supplies, tools. We've not mobilized such a large group before, but Lorenzo is quite good at coordinating operations on a large scale. He would be ideal to take the convoy north, direct its efforts, and begin to stabilize things where he could. Given my approval, I believe we could have such an aid convoy heading north within a day."

"Are you saying you'll do it?"

"I am." Toni glanced at Jaina. "You appear surprised. Is this not what you wanted?"

"It is, but..." She shook her head. "You just said that it was too expensive."

"With hearing as good as yours, you have little excuse not to listen," Toni said. "I believe I told you I would not throw money on the fire without a return on that investment. This isn't a donation, this is a negotiation."

"The Dominion's in no position to offer you..." Jaina trailed off, the voice in her head finally breaking through. "Oh."

"I'm not negotiating with the Dominion. I'm negotiating with Jaina Creighton," Toni said. "I will invest as much as is needed to see a full aid convoy sent north. This convoy will be supported by anatomists from the finest clinic on the continent. It will carry enough foodstuffs to feed a small city for a month and enough medical supplies to treat that city's population. It will be escorted by a guild guard force, and will include enough manpower to deal with whatever the situation may be up north. And I will order it to proceed north on the Myre Road before the sun sets tomorrow evening. I will do this under one condition." She locked her hard grey eyes on Jaina. "You will go with them, and you will not return to Vetticci."

Jaina took a step back, a pit in her stomach. "You would use the suffering of my people to drive a wedge between me and your granddaughter?"

"I will use any tool I have, any tool whatsoever, to ensure the future of this family. If that's my wealth, so be it. If that's blades and blood, so be it. If that's the pain of those foolish enough to lose a war, so be it," Toni said. Her voice was carved from ice. "I once told you that it was important to be honest about who we are, ranger. And I have never lied to you, to Antoinette, to anyone about exactly who I am, and I promise you, if I believed that you disappearing in the dark of the night would see my granddaughter back to her proper place, you wouldn't have time to scream."

"You're a monster."

"I'm a DeLuca."

"Antoinette's nothing like you."

Toni's eyebrow twitched north. "So certain of that, are you?"

"I won't leave her."

"Then Lorenzo stays here. The wagons stay here. Your people suffer without aid, and I continue my work to find a way to deal with you." Toni shrugged. "I've made my offer, ranger. I've made it quite clear what type of person I am. All that's left is for you to decide what type of person you are."

Event + 36 Hours

The library was quiet. The sun had gone down hours before, and Andreas had finally ordered the exhausted staff to get a few hours rest. After they'd left, he'd asked Antoinette if perhaps she should do the same, but she had wanted to wait for Jaina to return. But the more the hours slipped past, the more the pit in her stomach grew. She had seen the expression on Jaina's face as she left the room. She had also seen her grandmother follow her.

It was well past midnight when the door opened and Jaina stepped through. Antoinette was sitting at the huge table in the center of the library, a stack of messages before her on which she'd long since given up the battle of keeping her attention. Instead, she'd begun sifting through dozens of possible scenarios, dozens of outcomes that could result from Jaina and Toni meeting. She took everything she knew about Jaina, everything she knew about Toni, and when she saw the expression on her love's face, the pit in her stomach made itself a home.

"Ah." Antoinette nodded slowly, and set down the pen she'd been fiddling with. "Long conversation?"

Jaina's jaw was set, but her eyes gave away the pain she was feeling. "I needed to take a walk. After she…" Her voice trailed off. She took a few steps forward, then stopped. "Antoinette."

"Andreas told me about the Table's decision," Antoinette said quietly. "I'm going to guess that my grandmother has decided to send aid despite that. Am I right?"

"How did you know?"

Antoinette offered a smile, not because she felt like smiling, but because she knew Jaina needed it. "I know her. And I know you. And I know what she wants most in this world, and I know what you need more than anything in this world."

"I need you."

"I know," Antoinette said, rising to her feet. She walked slowly over, her bare feet padding over the soft rug, and took Jaina's hand. "But it's your home. People you know, people you care about."

"I don't even know if anyone from Lofland Fork was affected," Jaina said. "But I can't stop thinking about it." She met Antoinette's eyes. "I hate this."

"I know," Antoinette said again. She took a deep breath. "Do you know why I pushed you away? Back in Westcott, when we found out about the war?"

Jaina nodded. "You knew we couldn't be together. You didn't want me hurt."

"It was more than that. I knew that it would be hard. That outrunning those who would come looking for us would be a daily struggle, that we'd never be able to rest." Antoinette laid a hand on Jaina's chest. "But I still believed that you were worth it, that we were worth it. I would walk through fire with you, Jaina, just for the paradise of falling asleep in your arms, and if I fell asleep in a different place each night so we wouldn't be found, I'd mark myself fortunate."

"Antoinette…"

"Please, just let me say this." Jaina fell silent, and Antoinette continued. "I know you, Jaina Creighton. I know the woman who spent weeks helping everyone she could in Westcott. I know the woman who spent two sleepless days making spearheads just so a weary old man could get a moment to miss his sons."

"I never told you that," Jaina said softly.

"I'm a DeLuca, my love," Antoinette said. "I know you. And I know that you don't have it in you to turn your back on those in need, and if our choice led in any way to people you love coming to harm, it would break you in ways that can't be fixed." She brought Jaina's hand to her lips and kissed it. "I have never met anyone so determined to throw their own happiness on the fire for those in need. It makes me so angry at you in the same breath as it reminds me why I love you. And the unfortunate truth was that it was only a matter of time before my grandmother realized that as well." She paused, and asked, "She's sending help north, isn't she?"

Jaina nodded, her face breaking. "I'm going with it."

Antoinette nodded. "Of course you are."

"She made me give my word…"

"I don't care."

Jaina blinked past the tears. "What?"

"I don't care what she made you promise." Antoinette took a step back, but didn't let go of Jaina's hand. "I told you that I know you, and I do. If you had said no, if you had walked away from her offer just so you and I could be together, you wouldn't be the woman I love. And it wouldn't have stopped there. She would have pushed harder, pushed further. She would have pulled strings and pushed pieces until your parents were in the fire, and offered you a bucket of water in exchange for turning away from me. This moment was inevitable from the moment she saw me in your arms."

She squeezed Jaina's fingers. "But I gave my word. I will not walk away from you again, Jaina. I will not give up on us. She found a way to make it far too expensive for you to stay with me, because that's the way a DeLuca handles a problem. But I'm a fucking DeLuca too, and I give you my word, I will twist her world on its head and find a way to make it impossible for her to keep us apart. I am yours, and nothing in this world will keep me from finding my way back to you."

Jaina stared at her for a long breathless moment, and tears began to stream down her face as she let out a choked sob. "Gods, they would have loved you."

"Your brothers?"

Jaina nodded. "They are... they were so stubborn. And they would have kicked my ass for even thinking about walking away from you."

"They would have walked right beside you," Antoinette said, reaching up to brush the tears away. "Part of them always will."

"I hate this."

"I know. There's never going to be a moment that you walk away that I'm happy about it," Antoinette said. "But I give you my word. I will tear her world out by the roots to find a way for us to be happy together." She leaned up and kissed Jaina. "You do what you need to do. And I shall do what I need to do. And we'll find each other at the end. Always."

Event + 84 Hours

"Three... two... one... LIFT!"

Jaina gritted her teeth, and tried to straighten her bent legs. The wooden edge of the wagon dug into her forearms, and she felt the blood begin to trickle down her forearm as a splinter tore the skin. She made a mental note to pull her sleeves down, not wanting to draw any attention from the others when the wound was gone in a few minutes.

She had, several times, idly wondered what the upper limit of her strength as a ranger was. The wagon she had been trying to lift for the past ten minutes had provided her first benchmark to that effect. The convoy had nearly three hundred wagons, but two of them were unlike any Jaina had ever seen, massive oak platforms rolling on thick slabs of round wood, carrying four massive sealed casks full of clean and boiled water. One of those slabs of wood had cracked, canting the wagon to the side and leaving it immobile, and try as she might, it wouldn't budge. She released the edge, breathing heavily and shaking her head.

"I don't know that this is going to happen."

Lorenzo stood next to an older man in blue robes, a senior anatomist from the Pallia Clinic who wore a constant expression of irritation. He was shaking his head back and forth heavily. "This won't do."

"You have another," Lorenzo said, gesturing at the wagon's twin a few hundred feet away. "We've been working at this for an hour before she got back here. If a ranger's not going to do it, I'm not sure what other option we have."

"A lever of some sort, perhaps?" the anatomist suggested. "We don't know how many wounded we'll encounter, and we have no way of knowing if we'll be able to get sanitary water there."

Lorenzo glanced around them, eyebrow raised. "You see a lever that wouldn't crack the moment she tries to use it?" They were in the Moors, a barren area of sagebrush and stiff yellow grass to the east of Lofland Fork. The wagon train had moved quickly, far faster than was probably advisable. Once they emerged from the Myre Road, they cut east on smaller roads to avoid the chaos. They'd come across several groups of refugees, carrying whatever they could coming out of the moors in Gaille. They all told the same story: Ears bleeding, animals panicked, and crops dead.

"If we'd taken the main road from Lofland to Havensport, this would never..."

Lorenzo didn't give him time to finish. "That road's choked with so many refugees that you can't get a weasel through. Lofland's in chaos. Biggest city close to the event, and every survivor that can still walk is heading straight there. You really think it's a good idea for us to be moving against that particular tide?"

"Let me give it one more try," Jaina said. "From a different angle."

"Jaina..."

"He says we need it, we need it." She shifted over until she was gripping the wagon right over the back axel. She exhaled once, twice, and grunted as she tried once more to lift it. For several long moments, nothing happened, but to her shock, the wood creaked and groaned as it suddenly lurched upwards. Confused, she almost lost her grip, but held it as Lorenzo shouted instructions. It took the crew less than a minute to replace the wheel, but by the time they shouted for her to lower it, her muscles were screaming and sweat was pouring down her face. It took all she had not to drop the wagon, and as she slowly lowered it, she saw the face of the man on the other side of the wagon lowering it with her, and her stomach lurched.

The wagon settled into place with a final thump, and she released it as Lorenzo walked up to the other man, extending his hand. "Thank you, ah…"

"Shakkar." The ranger shook Lorenzo's hand. "How long will it take your men to get the wagon ready to move?"

Lorenzo glanced between Jaina and Shakkar, eyebrow raised, but said, "Twenty minutes. Maybe thirty."

"Good." Shakkar gestured at Jaina. "Mind if I borrow Miss Creighton for a quick hello?"

Lorenzo gave Jaina a questioning look. "It's all right, Lorenzo," she said. "We won't be far. Call us if there's a problem."

Neither said anything until they'd walked out of earshot. There was a twisted log half covered in moss, and Shakkar gestured at it. "Want to have a seat?"

"If it's all right, I think I'll stand," Jaina said. "My arms and legs still hurt from…"

Shakkar waved her off. "We both probably tore the hell out of our muscles doing that. Be fine in a bit, but I get it." He stared out over the long column of wagons stretching far off into the distance. "Didn't think you'd come back."

Jaina nodded. "Didn't expect to."

"Knew you were in Vetticci."

"Figured you'd reasoned that out when I heard about the warrant."

Shakkar snorted. "Callow. Overheard me asking about you. Suppose it made him feel like he was only mostly worthless instead of completely worthless."

"So what happens now?" Jaina asked. She didn't know what she would do if he tried to detain her.

The older ranger chuckled. "Question every damn one of us has been asking for the past week. And if you've got any clue, you'd be the first." He shook his head. "I'm not going to arrest you, Jaina. Even if I thought that would go in any direction other than catastrophic, there's no point."

"I broke my vow."

"You did. More than once, from what I hear." Jaina glanced over, and he shrugged. "Spoke to Captain Poole. Being short an arm doesn't make him blind, and you and the Vetticcian woman weren't quite as subtle as you might have hoped."

Jaina closed her eyes for a moment, and sank down onto the log. "I didn't realize."

"Young people never do." Shakkar sat next to her. "I'm not going to arrest you, Jaina. When I said there was no point, I meant it. No one's looking for one ranger in the midst of all this shit. And in four days, that warrant's not going to be worth the paper it's scribbled on."

"I don't understand."

"That's when the surrender is signed." Shakkar gestured to the west. "That's where I'm headed. Westcott. Two of the Empresses have been there for the last two days, meeting with Duke Walshire."

"Why Duke Walshire?"

"He's the only one left alive," Shakkar said. "And he's agreeing to whatever they say. Tough to blame him. Not really in a position to negotiate when your guts have been ripped out. Empire doesn't want a trace of the Ducal Army left. Ordered every part of it disbanded.

And while we've tried over and over to convince them that the rangers aren't part of the Ducal Army, seems the Empire isn't much interested in the rangers still being a going concern. Soon as that surrender is signed, the Sylvan Order of the Rangers ceases to be, and that warrant is worthless."

Jaina stared at him. "What happens to all the rangers?"

"We find other paths." Shakkar shrugged. "We'll still be what we are. But there won't be any more novices. You're the last ranger, Jaina."

She shook her head. "No more rangers. I can't even imagine that." She ran her fingers through her hair. "I just wish the last ranger could have been a better one."

Shakkar shrugged. "You made mistakes, I'll not deny that. But if you think you're the first ranger to fall in love, the first to question whether the vows they took were worth giving up a person that mattered to them, you're wrong. And you took a hit. More than one." A pained expression came over his face, and when he spoke again, he was very quiet. "We felt it, you know."

"What?"

"Doesn't happen often," he said. "But sometimes, when one of our number is hurt, really hurt, we all feel it. It's fast. Doesn't last more than a heartbeat. But I felt it."

"When I took the spear in the woods?" Jaina asked. Part of her knew that wasn't what he meant. The rest of her didn't want to think about what he meant.

"No." Shakkar stared out into the distance. "Loss like that, I can't imagine. But I figure it changes a person, changes them in ways that you can't know until you find yourself staring down the throat of that kind of pain. Don't know anyone would have it in them to keep going after something like that."

Jaina didn't trust herself to speak for a long few moments. The walls that had been holding back her grief and pain had been cracking more each day, and it felt that speaking their name would shatter them like glass. "I'm sorry I let you down. All of you."

He sighed. "Jaina, do you know why I said yes? When you asked to become a ranger?"

"I was desperate."

"That's why I nearly said no." Shakkar looked over at her. "I've known you your whole life. Seen the kind of person you are. You throw yourself into saving others. Stupidly, even recklessly sometimes, but you came to me willing to burn your future on the chance to keep your brothers safe." He gestured out at the wagons. "And here you are, back in a country that threatened to arrest you, with all of this."

Jaina shook her head. "I had to come."

"I know. You're a ranger, Jaina. You were a ranger before you set foot in the Myre, before your brothers got those slips, and you'll be a ranger long after we've been burned at the alter of this fucking war." Shakkar nodded at Lorenzo, who was waving at them in the distance. "I think it's time to go."

They both stood, and Jaina waved back. Turning to Shakkar, she said, "Will you look in on my parents? Make sure they're..." She trailed off, the lump in her throat threatening to choke her.

"I will." Shakkar glanced back at the convoy. "You know, I've never met a Vetticcian who'd give you the time of day without a deposit. And I've met Toni DeLuca. She's not the type who'd spend this kind of coin without getting their value back. So tell me. What did all this cost you?"

Jaina fell silent for a moment before finally saying, "No more than I promised you."

"So far too much." Shakkar shook his head. "Good luck, Jaina. I hope you can find some peace. And I hope there's enough left of you to enjoy it." He shook her hand once more, and walked away.

***

The convoy lost four wagons by the time they reached the dust cloud. The pace that Lorenzo had set was relentless. Every time they debated pausing to rest, they ran into another cluster of fleeing refugees. None of them had been close enough to the event to be able to provide any clear details, but all were panicked and desperate to put as much distance between themselves and whatever catastrophe had befallen the east Dominion. But after nearly eighteen hours, Lorenzo rode up next to Jaina.

"We're going to have to stop soon," Lorenzo said, peering up at the sun trying desperately to pierce the haze. They'd entered the huge dust cloud hours ago. They had hoped the wind would blow it clear, but the air was stagnant, and it hung over them, lending the sky a reddish hue. Men and women spat into the dirt every few minutes, trying to clear the grit from their mouth. "Take ten hours."

"That's a long time," Jaina said, shaking her head. "People have been resting in the back of the wagons, trading off."

"The horses can't do that," Lorenzo pointed out. "The donkeys can go for a long time, but we need to rest the animals."

Jaina scowled. He was right, but she didn't want to admit it.

"Not all of us are rangers, Jaina." His tone wasn't cruel, just matter-of-fact. "Look, we're over two hundred miles from any major settlement. It's likely going to be days before we find anything. We've got to make sure our people are in the right condition to help those we're coming to help."

She nodded. "Maybe I can scout ahead. See what I can find, come back and report."

"On foot, maybe. But your mount needs rest too." Lorenzo was going to say something else, but they both turned at the shouts from the front of the convoy.

"Anatomist! Anatomist!!" They couldn't see who was screaming, but the pair both dug their heels into their mounts, stirring them on. Ahead of them, two men and a woman in the pale blue robes of the Pallia Clinic were climbing down from their wagons, running forward. Jaina and Lorenzo passed them quickly.

The haze in the air kept them from seeing what was happening until they were nearly on top of them. Several Vetticcian drivers flanked a man in his early forties. They were gripping his arm, as if holding him up. He wasn't struggling. He just stood there, staring forward. It wasn't until they were less than twenty feet away that they could see why.

"What in the gods..." Lorenzo muttered as Jaina leapt down from her horse. She ran forward, swallowing as she slowed to approach the man. He was weaving back and forth on his feet, almost as if drunk. Black streaks marked twin paths down his cheeks. His eyes were open and sightless, dotted through with inky black that formed droplets on his dry and open eyes like morning dew. "Sir? Sir, can you hear me?"

"He's not speaking," one of the Vetticcians said. "Hasn't said anything since we spotted him."

One of the anatomists reached them, gently pushing Jaina to the side. Her fingers pressed against his throat, and she nodded. "Bring him to the closest wagon. I want to lay him down to examine him."

"What the fuck happened to him?" Lorenzo said, having come up beside Jaina. She wasn't listening. Instead, she frowned, peering into the haze, her eyes tracking movement.

"There are more," she said, quietly at first, then louder. "I see more!" She pointed at the two other anatomists. "With me!"

They ran into the haze. An older woman emerged. She was carrying a piece of tattered green fabric, stumbling forward. An eight-year-old child was sitting on the ground, chin down, lap covered in vomit streaked with inky black. A young woman stood idly, a baby in her arms. Neither child or mother made a sound. They simply stared through sightless eyes weeping black.

The progress of the convoy came to a halt as anatomists and workers poured into the haze, finding clusters of two, three people at a time. Over the next hour, they found nearly sixty survivors. Most were mute. Some were speaking, muttering or screaming over and over. One girl, less than five years old, just stood stock still, as if paralyzed, weeping and screaming the same words over and over. "I can't breathe. I can't breathe! I can't BREATHE!" Her voice was raw, her throat ruined from the constant litany.

The anatomists checked her over, the same as all the others. And just like all the others, the report was the same. She was breathing fine. Her heart was fine. With the exception of their eyes, they were all fine. They had no injuries, no evidence of illness. They were each perfectly fine up until the point that they began dying.

The baby died first. The mother lasted a bit longer. She wouldn't let go of the child, not until her heart stopped. Jaina carried their bodies to an empty wagon. They had brought twenty wagons with nothing in the back to transport injured people back to the city for treatment. They filled the first ten with corpses in less than four hours.

The movement of the convoy slowed to a crawl. Any talk of rest died the moment the baby did. Hundreds of Vetticcians walked in all directions into the haze. They returned leading mute victims. A strange silence had fallen over them, the horror of what they were finding leaving them struck dumb, a silence only punctuated by the occasional mad screaming of the few still able to speak. Each of these few said the same thing, shrieking about not being able to breathe, and breathing just fine until their heart gave out.

"Ranger?" Jaina turned to see a heavyset wagon driver approach her. He spat into the dirt. "Apologies. The dust." His eyes were red. Whether from crying or irritation, Jaina couldn't know. "Something you should see. Can't find Master DeLuca."

She nodded. *What next?* The first few victims had left her horrified. She realized how quickly she was growing numb to it. *I'm getting good at being broken.* The thought rooted in her head. "Show me."

Jaina followed the man east. The haze had only gotten worse. They passed clusters of people trying to help those who would be dead soon, laboring furiously at a task they knew to be pointless. A young Vetticcian man ran from group to group with a pitcher of water. Still others brought linen bandages, though they hadn't seen any wounds. They passed all of them, and walked for nearly twenty feet.

"We haven't found any past this point," the man said. "But something's not right." He pointed at a dagger driven into the dirt, a strip of red cloth tied to it. "That's mine. Past that point, we start feeling..." He shook his head. "Sick. Bad, too. But soon as we come back, it's okay."

Jaina stepped forward, and he grabbed her arm. "I'm not lying, Ranger. It's bad."

"I believe you," she said, nodding. "But I need to see."

He released her, but made no effort to follow.

Her boots crunched in the soil as she drew closer to the dagger. There was nothing to indicate that anything was amiss beyond what they'd already seen. She stepped up to the dagger, paused, and stepped across it.

At first, there was nothing. Jaina frowned in confusion, but a prickle tingled at the back of her neck, and nausea began to bloom in her stomach. She grunted, and a wave of dizziness rolled through her. Gritting her teeth, she took another step forward, and gagged, gorge rising to the back of her throat. She looked around, but there was nothing. Leaning forward, she spat into the dirt, and her eyes widened. The spittle was red, as it had been since they entered this haze, but among the red was a dot of black.

Her hair ruffled as the wind picked up, blowing out of the north, sending grit and dirt flying from the ground. Jaina stumbled back past the dagger, bringing her arm up to block her eyes. As soon as she backed past the marker, the sickness vanished. The wind picked up even more, and she could hear shouting as anatomists threw blankets over their charges. The haze began to thin out, and Jaina felt her skin grow cold as she stared ahead. She heard the big man whisper, "Gods protect us." Every bit of conversation fell silent as the dust in the air was finally pushed aside enough to see what lay before them.

Two hundred yards ahead of them, a shimmering wall hung in the air, distinct enough that Jaina could see where it stretched to the north and south, towering into the sky. She couldn't see where it ended. It looked like the surface of an oil-slicked stagnant puddle shivering in the breeze, impossibly huge, and beyond, everything was ruin.

The landscape was scoured. There were no trees, no buildings, no life. The ground was broken, looking like a shattered piece of ceramic, slabs of rock and ground canted wildly in all directions. A strange grey dust coated the ground, and while the wind whipped through Jaina's hair and sent grit into her unblinking and horrified eyes, everything within this ruined area was motionless. From where they stood until it vanished over the horizon, all was dead, broken, and desolate.

***

In the three days since they discovered the border, wooden posts with bright strips of fabric had been hammered into the soil about two hundred yards away. Jaina had heard different terms for that thin strip of land between the edge of the event. The area struck people immediately with brutal nausea and cramps, and had earned the name "noxious zone", "black area", and "last chance".

But one name had been spoken early in reference to the impossibly massive event that had devoured such a massive swath of the Dominion, and once it had been spoken, no one called it anything but.

"The Desolation," Jaina muttered to herself. Even as she spoke, she felt her stomach seize up, gorge rising in her throat. She doubled over, vomiting black bile onto the worn wooden floor.

She wiped her mouth clean. *That's three times you've thrown up. Two more, you have to leave.*

She stood in what had once been the tavern area of an inn. There was a battered bar, a shelf stocked with a dozen various spirits in glass or wooden bottles, and several tables. Both the bar and one of the tables had been neatly bisected. Eight feet away from where Jaina spat the last of the bile from her mouth, the edge of the event shimmered, having halted halfway through this building.

She'd been in the noxious zone for nearly twenty minutes. No one else could last more than two, maybe three, but she could feel her body fighting to repair the damage being done every moment. They had found several settlements like this one, split in two by the point in which the Desolation had finally come to a stop. The border was now fixed in place, a shivering delineation between where she stood and utter devastation.

It had been days since they'd found a survivor. Nearly all of the stumbling, broken souls they'd encountered had died. Lorenzo had told her that one child had lasted long enough to be taken back to Vetticci, but the four anatomists who traveled with him didn't believe he'd make it to the border. For those who had been within several miles of the Desolation's edge, the effects had shattered their minds and left their bodies barely able to function. Of those who had been within, there was nothing left.

She knew there weren't going to be any survivors within the wreckage of this tavern, just as there hadn't been any survivors in the countless other homes dotting the edge. Still, Jaina searched. She was the only one who could last long enough this close to the Desolation to be able to finish the search of a building before she stumbled back out, shivering and cramping in the dirt, gulping water, waiting until her guts were no longer tied into knots and her head was no longer splitting in two. Once she'd recovered, she hauled herself to her feet, and wearily walked back to the next building.

Why am I doing this? She'd asked herself that question over and over again. Jaina couldn't remember what hope felt like. Even the thought of getting back to Antoinette was a distant echo, driven from her mind by the relentless parade of horror she'd seen since arriving here. *You'd think by now, I'd be getting used to pain.*

She paused for a moment. She didn't admit that she was waiting to hear one of them reply, one of them to say something to help her keep moving forward. She didn't admit it, but Jaina also knew it was true. But they were silent now.

But you know what they'd say. She swallowed back the gorge. *You're here because you can. Because after everything, after all of this, you still are trying to fix things that can't be fixed.* She gripped a heavy pine joist that had tumbled through a wall when it had been split, lifting it easily and peering beneath. There was nothing.

I know there aren't going to be survivors. She dropped the joist. This close to the Desolation, sounds were oddly muffled. *But I'm going to keep going. I can. I can keep trying. It's all I can do.*

Movement caught her eye, not from the wreckage, but from a hill less than a quarter mile from the edge of the Desolation. She saw light glint off the armor of the two men on horseback. She felt a brief pang of anger, but even that had been drained from her by the exhaustion. The Imperial Army had arrived yesterday, less than a week after the unconditional surrender of the two surviving dukes. Lorenzo had told her they had brought massive aid tents, supplies, equipment.

They did this. She shook her head. *And now they come down here and patch us up after they rip out our spine.*

She started to walk towards a back room, but her stomach seized again, and she spat out more bile and black onto the dusty wooden floor. *Four.*

Jaina straightened up, and her eyes widened. One of the Imperials was riding. Hard. He was leaned tight against his horse, animal and man hurtling down the hill at a reckless pace. The other stood fast, shouting something. *What in the gods is he doing?* The soldier rode hard, almost in her direction, directly at the edge of the Desolation. For a brief moment, she wondered if the sight of what his people had done had driven him to madness, but her ranger's eyes caught a glimpse of hard eyes as he flew past, and she stared in horror as his horse leapt, carrying him past the flags, past the wreckage she stood in, and through that shimmering barrier.

The horse struck the ground, and screamed, its legs buckling beneath it. The rider was thrown, and she could hear the muffled clattering of armor as the man rolled across the ground. He staggered back to his feet, and began moving further into the Desolation, leaning forward as if struggling into a heavy gale, but the dust inside the border didn't move. Behind him, his mount convulsed, thrashing in the dirt, and before Jaina's horrified eyes, the horse was torn apart, bursting into a black and red mist. The soldier didn't look back. He was covered head to toe in a strange, dull grey armor, and Jaina could see it begin to coruscate, color and light pouring off of it. She could hear a sharp keening noise, like nothing she'd ever heard.

What in the gods' name is he doing?! She stepped closer to the edge, staring at the man doggedly marching forward. A loud crack issued from one of his pauldrons, and light poured forth from the new fissure in the shoulder piece. He didn't stop. He just drove one armored leg in front of the other, eyes fixed on...

Jaina felt her stomach drop, and she followed the direction he was heading. Her eyes locked on a slumped figure thirty feet ahead of him. The figure had been blocked from her view by the bulk of the tavern until now. The haze and the distance made it difficult, but she quickly realized two things as the soldier fell to his knees and began to crawl. She was a child, maybe ten years old.

And she was breathing.

She would never remember making the decision. Jaina didn't think about the consequences of what she did, but then again, she never had. She burst into movement, leaping forward so hard that the pine boards of the ruined tavern cracked beneath her heels. She knocked aside a ruined table, and took one step, two steps, and Jaina Creighton ran at full speed through the shimmering barrier of the Desolation, her boots coming down on cracked and ruined

brother holding a red token mother crying Antoinette missing the jaw
exploding beneath her fist spear driving through her guts tearing organs
and flesh scraping on her spine arrow punching through her shoulder
blood in her mouth list in her hand heart breaking in two screaming at
her father

Jaina screamed as her head exploded with a thousand shrieking images. She couldn't see anything around her, but howled as something stripped the flesh of her bare arms away as if dragging an invisible grater over the skin. As soon as it ripped away, the muscle and skin began knitting back together, but she could feel her face, her throat, even her eyes, being torn apart piece by piece, even as her ranger healing fought desperately to hold her body together. It was pain beyond reason, an onslaught that tore at her flesh and mind, and every fiber of her body that wasn't being flayed howled for her to turn around.

She didn't.

She never did.

Jaina Creighton ran as the Desolation tore at her. The cacophony in her head was blinding and deafening, memories of pain and loss buffeting her, and beneath it all, a voice, screaming with madness, the same words over and over.

can't breathe can't breathe can't breathe can't BREATHE!!!

She didn't know if she was going in the right direction. Her vision was clouded with more than dust now, some distant part of her brain registering that whatever was shredding her flesh must be doing the same to her eyes. But through the bloody fog that had settled over her sight, she saw that flashing, keening armor, and drove towards it. The soldier had reached the girl, wrapped her in his arms, and was trying to make his way back, but whatever protection had been provided by the armor couldn't last. The backplate cracked with a sound like thunder, and he fell to his knees.

Jaina came up behind him, and wrapped her arms around him. He stiffened, and his hand came up, not to strike at her, but extended out before him. The four fingers on his hand danced a staccato rhythm, and the bracer on his hand exploded into liquid movement, filling his fist with the haft of a long spear. The weapon settled into its form, and immediately began trembling and vibrating like a tuning fork, waves of violet light pouring from it, but he still tried to bring it around, and she tightened her grip.

"Stop fighting me!" she screamed in his ear, and hauled him to his feet. They stumbled forward a few steps, and fell to their knees. She didn't know if he could hear her over the howling chorus of voices screaming at them. "Use that fucking spear! Hold yourself up, godsdammit!"

He shook his head. "Arm's jammed! Armor's broken!" As he spoke, the spear vibrated hard enough to fly from his fingers. It struck the cracked and broken ground with an oddly dull sound, and shattered, exploding into countless fragments that skittered over the ground.

Jaina screamed as a long tear opened along her bicep. Her body started to heal, but she realized to her horror that it wasn't healing as fast as it had been. "Then dig, you Imperial bastard. DIG!"

Together, they staggered forward. She dragged him, he clung to the child, and inch by inch, they stumbled forward. Jaina could feel blood pooling in her eyes. She clenched her teeth so hard that one cracked in her jaw. She had no idea how much further, but as the world darkened around her, a bleak realization settled over her.

It didn't matter how much further.

I'm sorry, Antoinette.

She wasn't going to make it.

Fuck that, Cricket!

The voice punched through the shrieking, the pain. She blinked past the blood. Jaina couldn't see anything, but she saw them, standing beside her, always beside her, and felt them grip her shoulder and speak to her.

This is what you do. You tear yourself to pieces to fix the world. Joran wasn't shouting. He was smiling. *You ignore every bit of advice, of common sense, of simple logic, and you tear yourself to pieces to make the world just a little better.*

I can't. Jaina sobbed, tears of blood pouring down her face.

You can. Jak nodded. *You can move forward. Not because it will fix what's broken. But because you're not the type to ever stop trying. You couldn't save us. You never could. But right here, right now, you can save this man and this child.*

You took the vow without really understanding. But now you do. You lift up those who cannot walk, those who cannot continue, and you do it not because it will fix the world, but because you are who you are. You wanted to know what it means to be a ranger. This is what it means. And you're not alone. Joran squeezed her shoulder. *You'll never be alone.*

Each step was agony. With each of the infinite seconds she spent in that place, Jaina was taken apart, bleeding from a thousand wounds, feeling her bones actually creak beneath her skin. But the howling voices were gone. The only ones left were theirs.

Never alone.

Jaina stepped through the edge of the Desolation, and silence crashed down upon them as she fell to the dirt. Her head tilted back, and she choked and screamed, blood foaming on her lips as Imperial soldiers ran up. They grabbed the general, a young girl, and the broken and bloody ranger who had done her duty, and dragged all three away from the nightmare.

She shuddered, knowing she was free, and darkness swallowed her.

Event + 135 Hours

When her riding boots hit the ground, Antoinette could feel every eye locked on her. She had been trained from the time she was a child that it was crucial that whenever she was seen outside the walls of her home, that she present the perfect image, hair, paint, clothing, all immaculate and intentional.

In this moment, she wore the simplest riding dress she could find, a dress that was now statistically likely to be made up more of sweat and road dust than fabric. She wore no makeup. Her hair was bound behind her head, tied up in a simple ponytail, and as Lorenzo ran up to her, his eyes widened, but he said nothing about her appearance.

"Follow me," he said, and she fell into step beside him.

"How bad?"

"No real change from my message," Lorenzo said, his tones clipped and even. Even Toni DeLuca had always begrudgingly admitted that when faced with a crisis, Lorenzo DeLuca was ruthlessly efficient and focused. His message to Antoinette had arrived two days prior, and had been similarly efficient.

Jaina badly injured. Not recovering.

No further details were given. None were needed.

Andreas had been the one to bring her the message. It was late, nearly midnight, and he had knocked on the door. When she opened it, he was carrying the slip of paper and her riding clothes. He'd brought her to the stable, and promised to delay her grandmother as long as possible, and Antoinette had ridden north, accompanied by two guardsmen who wordlessly flanked her on the hard ride through the dark Myre Wood.

"It won't take her long, you know." Lorenzo weaved through a series of tents, glancing at a pair of armored Imperial soldiers tying up a horse nearby. The aid camp had swollen to massive proportions, and hundreds of the canvas tents were set in neat lines. Hundreds of armored men and anatomists filled the camp, the low din of chatter and the stink of shit from man and horse alike filling the air. "You two haven't been speaking all that much, but she almost certainly knows you've left by now."

"I'll deal with that when I have to." Antoinette felt something squish beneath her foot, and shook free the horse manure, not pausing in her stride. "What can you tell me?"

"They've had anatomists in and out on the hour, every hour. She's breathing. Her heart's beating. But she's not healing."

They split off from the main approach, and Antoinette came to a stop. Her eyes widened at the quartet of armored Imperial soldiers standing watch around the tent. "Is that...?"

"That's where she is."

"They're guarding her? Is she in trouble?"

Lorenzo shook his head. "They're not here for Jaina." He waved her on. "Come on. They know we're coming."

Antoinette glanced at the hard faces of the guards, who did not return her stare. Lorenzo lifted up the flap of the tent, Antoinette stepped through, and her hands flew to her mouth. She had trained her entire life to mask her feelings, hide her true emotions. That training shattered like cheap glass at the sight that greeted her.

Jaina Creighton lay naked on a cot, covered by a thin linen sheet dotted with spots of red. Her scalp had several large patches of hair missing. In their place were the angry weeping abrasions, deep gouges of the flesh that dotted her bare shoulders and arms as well. What skin remained was a mottled bruised purple. Her lower lip was split wide open, and her eyelids were rimmed with blood. Crouched next to her was a woman in pale blue robes with a bowl of water. She was gently squeezing drops onto Jaina's lips.

Antoinette felt her legs go weak beneath her, but Lorenzo was there, gripping her by the shoulders and holding her up. "Hey. Stay with me, Antoinette." His voice was kind but firm. "She's alive. The gods only know how, but she's alive."

At his words, the anatomist looked up. She rose to her feet. "Mistress DeLuca. Senior Physica Alana Paotti, at your service."

Antoinette nodded, not trusting herself to speak for a few moments. She finally tore her eyes away from the battered body of the woman she loved, and said, "Apologies. I was unprepared."

"No one could blame you." Paotti offered a kind smile. "I've been directing the ranger's care for the past day. We've been trying to find someone familiar with treating injured rangers, but as far as we can tell, the very term "injured ranger" seems to be a bit of an oxymoron up until this point." She nodded back at Jaina. "And while I know her condition is alarming, I want to assure you. She is healing."

Antoinette shook her head. "You don't understand. I've seen her recover from wounds in moments. This..."

"I don't know what kind of wounds you witnessed her heal, but I promise you, they were nothing compared to this," the anatomist said. "I've never seen trauma on this scale in a living person. To be honest, I couldn't say that I've seen it in a cadaver, either. But in the past day, she's lost enough blood to fill three people. The only way she could still be alive is if her body is producing enough to replace the loss at a commensurate rate. And those wounds were actively bleeding until four hours ago. They've slowed. She's healing. It's just taking much longer than I think we hoped for."

"Any update on her?" Lorenzo asked.

Antoinette was confused at the question for a moment until she spotted the other cot in the tent. She had been so focused on Jaina that she hadn't seen the young girl sleeping.

Paotti shook her head. "She's fine. She was dehydrated and malnourished, and suffering from exhaustion. But we've managed to get her to eat and drink, and she let us examine her. No wounds worse than an abraded knee."

"Is she..." Antoinette had been briefed on the nature of Jaina's injury on the way north.

Lorenzo nodded. "The mystery child. And the reason four kaviaks are standing guard outside."

Antoinette's eyes widened. "Those are kaviaks?"

"They are. Under direct orders from the Empresses, from what I hear," Lorenzo said, rubbing his tired eyes. "You'd be better off attacking a Table member in their home than trying to touch that child."

"Why haven't they taken her somewhere more secure?"

"She won't leave Jaina," Lorenzo said. "They tried. She became incredibly agitated, panicking, nearly went into shock. She won't speak, but Jaina's the one who pulled her out, along with that general. Since the child woke up, she's only been calm with Jaina. I've been around enough that she'll leave for short periods with me, but only if we stay close, and for no longer than ten minutes."

"If I may?" Paotti said. "I'll return in a few hours to check on you." She handed Antoinette the bowl. "If you can get her to drink more, it will do a world of good."

"Of course. Thank you." Antoinette took the bowl, and sat on the stool next to Jaina. She dipped the cloth in the water, and squeezed it just over Jaina's cracked and broken lips. Jaina's eyes were still closed, but her mouth moved as the drops struck her tongue.

"Good. Just like that."

"How much should I give her?"

"As much as she'll drink," Paotti said. "Dehydration is my biggest worry. It's difficult to give those who fall unconscious for this long enough water." She nodded to both of them, and slipped out the door as Lorenzo settled onto another stool.

"I'll make arrangements to have another cot brought in here," he said. "You can stay with her."

Antoinette glanced up at her brother. "How long has it been since you slept?"

He chuckled. There was no humor in it. "I got a few hours this morning. Not by choice. Just kind of passed out eating." He shook his head. "Things I've seen over the last five days... Don't much fancy the idea of letting them into my dreams."

Jaina murmured softly in her sleep, and the tip of her tongue came out to lick a drop off her lips. Antoinette rested her hand against the most undamaged part of Jaina's shoulder. "I'm sorry, Lorenzo. If we'd known what was waiting for you..."

He waved her off. "No one could have. No one knew this was even possible, let alone that the Empresses were the kind of people who could do something so unthinkable."

"Do we know how many were killed?"

"I honestly don't think they ever will. It covers too much territory, countless villages, towns, cities. But the best guess I've heard is over a million dead." He swallowed. "A million dead, and one child walks out unharmed."

Antoinette glanced over at the sleeping girl. She was young, perhaps eight or nine, and she slept curled into a tight ball. "They have no idea how?"

"None. And believe me, they want to know," Lorenzo said. "They haven't sent any resonants down here. After what they did, that would be a recipe for riots, but they've had a dozen or so anatomists and artificers come mutter over the kid. Rumors are they want to take her back to the Empire, keep watch over her, but they can't figure out a way to basically abduct a Dominion child without catching six holds worth of shit."

"They won the war. They can do what they like."

Lorenzo shook his head. "They won the war, but everyone, even their own people, are horrified at how they did it. Rumors are that Imperial soldiers are deserting en masse. That general, the one who helped Jaina rescue the kid? He walked away. He's an Imperial hero, a legend, and he left the broken pieces of his armor behind and just walked away. I've even heard some of the Imperials talking about riots and protests back home. They're going to be walking a fine line for a long time, and dragging a screaming and traumatized child north of the Breaking isn't going to be accepted."

"Not... happening."

They both whipped their heads around at the weak muttered words, and Antoinette gasped as she saw Jaina looking at her with eyes bloomed through with dark red. "Jaina!" She waved at Lorenzo. "Find the anatomist! Hurry!" Her brother was already moving, bursting through the front of the tent shouting. She leaned down over Jaina, and her eyes widened. There was a deep gouge in Jaina's cheek right below her left eye. As Antoinette stared, she saw the edges twitch and begin to move.

"They're not..." Jaina coughed, wincing in pain.

"Here." Antoinette brought the bowl to her lips, and Jaina took several sips. She coughed a few times, but her hand came up and gripped Antoinette's.

"They're not taking her," she said, her voice cracked and thick. Jaina blinked, and a tear of blood tumbled down her cheek. "I won't let them."

"I know." Antoinette leaned down and kissed Jaina's cheek as softly as she could. "We'll figure it out. Together."

***

Once the healing had begun to be visibly apparent, it had progressed quickly, and within five hours of Jaina waking, nearly all the open wounds had closed before several anatomists' astonished eyes. Food was brought, and Antoinette sat with Jaina as she methodically demolished several trays piled high with dried meats and boiled potatoes. In between bites, the two of them spoke quietly.

They were alone in the tent with the exception of the young girl. She had woken a few hours after Jaina, and when she found her upright and awake, quietly climbed out of bed, clambered up onto the cot next to Jaina, and leaned against her. Her eyes were hollow and weary, and she said nothing, staring into the middle distance. Jaina was able to convince her to eat a few bites, and while she was chewing, she looked up at Antoinette, who stuck her tongue out. The faintest of smiles ghosted over the girl's expression, and she kept watching Antoinette, even as they spoke.

"Do you think it will work?" Jaina asked, wiping grease from her mouth with a napkin. "Is it enough?"

"I don't know," Antoinette said. "But it's what we have." She swallowed. "Almost all we have."

"Almost?"

Antoinette nodded. "I have one more card to play. But..." *I don't want to lie to her. Never again. But this...* "I found something. Something big. It's enough to force my grandmother's hand if we have to. I don't want to use it. I don't even want to speak it. But it's there if things get out of hand."

"What is it?"

"Jaina." She reached out and took her hand. "I told you I would never lie to you again. But I need to ask something of you, and I need you to trust me and say yes."

Jaina frowned. "What's that?"

"Don't ask again. Ever."

Jaina stared at her. "I don't understand."

"I know," Antoinette said. "But please believe me. Nothing good can come of you asking more. Hopefully, we won't ever need to bring it up. But this..." She shook her head. "Some secrets are poison. They will ruin everyone they touch."

"You know it, though."

"I'm a DeLuca. I was poisoned a long time ago."

"Antoinette..."

"I love you, Jaina. I will never lie to you again. But I need you to believe me, and I need you to trust me." Antoinette met those green eyes. *Please.*

Finally, Jaina nodded slowly. "Okay."

The relief Antoinette felt was nearly a physical thing, and she let out a long exhalation. "Thank you." She looked down at the girl, who was quietly eating a piece of bread. "And the rest? Are you sure you're good with it?"

"I'm sure." Jaina looked down at the girl. "She's alone. I've had moments where I know what that's like." She looked up, and said, "Someone's coming. Fast."

Moments later, the flap to the tent flew open, and Lorenzo burst in, breathing heavily. Before he could speak, Antoinette said, "She's here?"

He nodded. "Not alone."

Shit. Antoinette had expected this, but she had hoped she might be wrong. "Okay. Jaina?"

Jaina nodded, and leaned down to the little girl. "Honey? Lorenzo here is going to take you to go get something sweet." The child clung tighter to Jaina's arm. "I promise, it won't take long. He'll take care of you, and he'll bring you right back to me."

Lorenzo crouched down. "Come on, little bit. I think I know where some honey candy might be hiding. We can bring some back to Jaina and Antoinette. I'll bet they'd like that."

Slowly, the girl released Jaina's arm, and slowly took Lorenzo's hand. She stared back at Jaina, who nodded and said, "Bring me back a big piece, okay?" The child nodded, and she and Lorenzo left the tent. Antoinette could hear the boots of the four kaviaks fall into step behind them, and swallowed.

"Might have been better to have those soldiers close."

Jaina shook her head. "We have a plan. But it won't work if we can't speak, and we can't speak with them in earshot."

"I know, but..." Antoinette fell silent as Jaina rose to her feet.

"It's her," Jaina said. "I can smell her perfume."

Together, they turned and faced the entrance to the tent. It seemed to take forever, but when the flap opened, Antoinette reached out and took Jaina's hand.

It was not Toni DeLuca who stepped through first. The man was tall and rangy, and was dressed head to toe in black. Antoinette could see several blades strapped to his tunic. She knew there were more she couldn't see. A second black-clad soldier stepped through. When the third came through, the pit in her stomach became a yawning void. Mattia's red hair was shockingly bright against the black clothing. Her little brother's face might as well have been carved from stone. "Mattia..." she said, but he didn't respond.

Seconds later, Toni DeLuca pushed through the flap. There were very few times in Antoinette's life that she could remember seeing her grandmother lose composure. She had seen a few instances of surprise, even fear when the city rocked beneath their feet and the sky screamed. But she had never seen the cold rage that poured from every inch of Toni DeLuca as she stood before them, fists clenched at her side, eyes burning at the two women standing before her.

She spoke. "Ranger." Her voice was cold and hard as iron. "You broke our contract."

"I didn't return to the city."

"Don't play the fool with me, child," Toni snapped. "You knew the price. I fulfilled my side of our agreement, and you spat in my face." Her jaw worked. "Do you know the price in Vetticci for violating a deal?"

"Stop it, grandmother," Antoinette snapped. "She did nothing. She was unconscious when I left the house."

Toni's eyes tracked over to her. "I am aware. And rest assured, I will deal with you shortly."

"That sounds like a threat," Jaina said, her eyes narrowing.

"Good."

"Grandmother. There's a way out of this. For all of us to get what we want. If you'll just..."

Toni held up a hand. "I will not. I've tolerated this childishness for far longer than was wise. I let it infect your brother, infect Andreas to the point that they act against me. This is no longer a dalliance. This is a cancer in the heart of this family, and I will do what I must to cut it out." She raised her voice. "Captain."

"Madame DeLuca," the tallest of the soldiers said. His voice was cold.

"If my granddaughter does not walk out of this tent with me in the next thirty seconds, you will cut the ranger down."

Steel whispered against leather as three black blades slithered out of scabbards. Mattia's eyes were locked on Jaina, his face a blank mask.

"Grandmother," Antoinette snapped, moving between them and Jaina. "I will not let you touch her."

"You can leave this tent heartbroken or you can leave this tent grieving, Antoinette. It's entirely your choice," Toni snarled. "Twenty seconds."

The soldiers dropped into identical combat crouches. Jaina stepped forward.

"Another step, ranger, and I put this blade through your heart," Mattia said.

Jaina's eyes were storm clouds, her fists closed. "Do it. I'll rip it out and give it right the fuck back."

"Jaina, please."

"If she threatens you again..."

"Ten seconds." Toni's voice was unflinching. "Make your choice, Antoinette."

The soldiers spread out, surrounding Jaina.

Jaina lowered into a crouch.

"So be it." Toni turned her back on Antoinette. "Captain..."

"Hasan Amin."

Toni DeLuca spun on her heel, faster than Antoinette thought her capable of. "HOLD!" She stared at Antoinette, shock painted over her face. "Captain. Take your men and go outside."

"Grandmother..." Mattia started to say.

"I will not repeat myself. Get the fuck out. Now." She said nothing until they were gone, but stared at her granddaughter, who did not quail from that hard expression.

Okay. Time to deal, Grandmother.

"You as well, Ranger," Toni said.

"She stays," Antoinette said before Jaina could speak.

"If you're telling me she knows..."

"She doesn't. Not yet." A soft rattling sound drew Antoinette's eyes. Her grandmother's hands were shaking.

"Where did you hear that name?" Toni asked quietly.

"I'm your granddaughter," Antoinette replied. "You've trained me my whole life to find the truth. Is it so surprising?"

Toni's eyes locked on Antoinette's. "Do you know what that name could do?"

"I do," Antoinette said softly. She gestured at a chair. "I don't want that to happen any more than you do. So let's deal."

"Deal." Toni shook her head. "Holding a blade to someone's throat isn't negotiating. It's extortion."

"You'd know," Jaina growled.

Toni glanced at her, and shook her head. "I suppose I do at that." She slowly sat down. "Speak."

Antoinette squeezed Jaina's hand, looking up at her. *Trust me,* she mouthed. Jaina gave the smallest of nods, and Antoinette sat down.

"You have a problem, grandmother," she said.

"I should say so," Toni said. "If this becomes public…"

"Hasan Amin is not your biggest problem."

"Please stop saying the name." Toni rubbed her forehead. "If not that, please, enlighten me. What is my biggest problem?"

"You have a blind spot," Antoinette said. "You have no eyes or ears in the Empire."

"This is not a new situation," Toni said.

"Oh, I disagree. I think it's completely new. I think it went from being an annoyance to a catastrophe the moment the Desolation wiped out a million godsdamned people," Antoinette said. "Because a few hours after the city stopped shaking, you had to stand in front of the Table as they demanded answers, and you had to tell them you knew absolutely nothing."

She leaned forward, locking eyes with her grandmother. "You had no idea. You had no idea this kind of attack was even possible. You had no idea this kind of attack was coming. You had no idea that the Empresses were even capable of ordering such a thing. I saw you. You stood in that yard, and just like the rest of us, you had no idea what had happened. But the only difference is, you're the person that has to know. The person Vetticci depends on to know."

Toni watched her speak, silent.

"Three questions, grandmother." Antoinette said. "Can the Empire do that again?"

"I don't know."

"Did the Empire intend for so many people to die?"

"I don't know."

"Could the Empire do the same thing in Vetticci?"

Toni visibly blanched at the question. "I don't know." She bit the words off as if they tasted unpleasant.

"You don't know." *Here we go.* "Would you like to?"

Toni scowled. "Explain."

"You know about the child?"

"Of course."

Antoinette nodded. "You know about the Empire's desire to bring her north, and the difficulties they've experienced in doing so?" Toni nodded impatiently. "Good. We've made an offer to the senior Imperial official here. His name is Sub-Archeron Ivanovich. He's accepted."

"What offer is that?"

"To adopt that girl." Antoinette took Jaina's hand again. "The two of us."

Toni tilted her head. "Explain."

"The girl doesn't like to leave Jaina's side. Give it ten, maybe fifteen more minutes, and she'll insist on coming back. So what if she didn't have to?"

"Why would the Empire agree to a Dominion ranger and a Vetticcian scioness adopting the child they're so determined to bring north?" Toni asked. A heartbeat later, her eyebrow lifted. "Oh."

Antoinette nodded. "That's right. We've agreed to raise the child in an Imperial city. The Dominion won't object if she's with a Dominion citizen. The Empire will be satisfied that she's within their borders. And you..." She tilted her head. "You get to put your granddaughter, the woman you've trained since childhood, within the borders of the only place you've never been able to build a network."

Toni's eyes widened. "You're offering me eyes and ears? In the Empire?"

"You can't afford to be blind to the Empire anymore," Antoinette said. "I'll make sure you aren't. I'll use everything you ever taught me, everything I am as a DeLuca, to give you eyes everywhere. Ears everywhere. You'll know how their people traveled so fast. You'll know what their leaders are thinking. You'll know." She shrugged. "The only thing you have to do is say yes, and you will accomplish what no DeLuca has ever been able to do, at a time where we need it the most."

Toni sat silently for several impossibly long moments. She glanced up at Jaina. "And you? You're all right with this?"

"Is it my first choice?" Jaina shook her head. "Of course not. But I give you my word. I will watch over your granddaughter, and I will watch over this child. And I will never speak of what was discussed in this tent today."

Toni looked back to Antoinette. "And when I die? What happens to the DeLuca legacy then?"

"It lives on. In me and my brothers," Antoinette said. "We will find a way to keep this family moving forward. I am your granddaughter. But hear me, and know the truth of what I say. I will not leave Jaina's side, and if you attempt to push the issue, I will burn that legacy to the ground."

Toni sat for a long time before she rose to her feet. "This won't be easy."

"No."

Toni nodded slowly. "I think, my dear, you have been paying better attention than I gave you credit for." She paused, and said, "Jaina, would you please give me and my granddaughter a moment?" Jaina hesitated, and Toni said, "I agree to your terms. But given what I'm agreeing to, it will be some time before I see her again."

"It's all right, love," Antoinette said. "Why don't you go find Lorenzo? Let him know we're safe."

Jaina nodded, and left the tent.

"She knows the name," Toni said quietly.

"She doesn't know what it means," Antoinette said. "And she's not going to ask."

"Were I you, I would pray every day that she keeps that promise," Toni said. She looked over Antoinette, and said, "You'll need to be more presentable. I'll have your wardrobe and anything else you need sent north."

"Yes, grandmother."

Toni hesitated, and said, "I don't know what to say. You've always come home."

"I know." Antoinette lowered her head. "But things change."

"They do." Toni reached out, took Antoinette's hand for a moment, and then released it. "Goodbye, Antoinette." Before Antoinette could respond, she was gone.

Epilogue

The wagon they were in wasn't of particularly high quality. The first hour of their journey had been over open country, and the rattling had made it uncomfortable. Once they'd reached the road heading north, it smoothed out somewhat. The bed of the wagon was loaded with supplies, clothing, and a pair of very special inkwells. In the back, a long bench was occupied by Jaina and Antoinette, the girl sitting between them. Antoinette had given her a bound notebook and some pencils, and the child was quietly drawing.

"She's good," Jaina said, looking down at her progress. A cat had peeked its way out of the blank page, the scratch of the graphite pulling one whisker after another from the page. "She might follow in your footsteps."

Antoinette nodded. "It would be nice to know there was something I could teach her."

Jaina reached over and gripped Antoinette's shoulder. "You nervous?"

"I am." Antoinette shook her head. "I know how to do what I need to do, but raising a child?"

"We'll figure it out. Together," Jaina said. "I just wish we knew her name."

"Elia." They both looked down in shock at the soft words. The girl didn't look up from her drawing. "My name is Elia." She leaned her head on Jaina's arm, and fell silent once more as the three of them rode north.

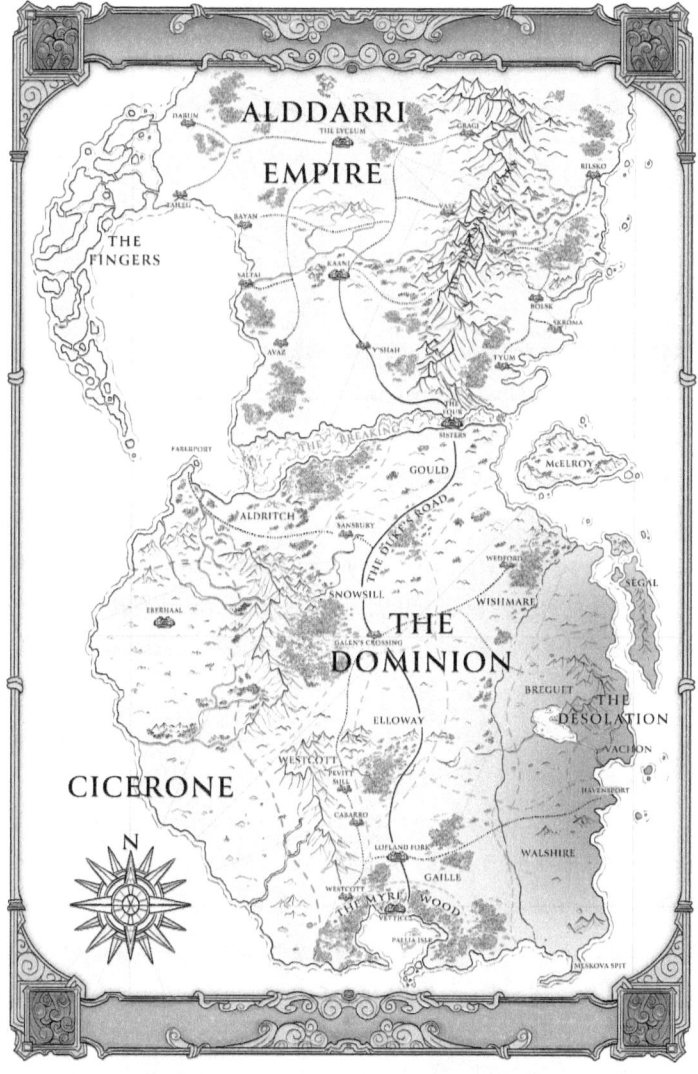

Acknowledgements

This story, the story of Jaina Creighton and Antoinette DeLuca, is one I've had in my head since late 2020. It was part of the backstory I put together for the characters of *Resonant*, which has been drafted but not released. And that story, of two people who absolutely should not be together and yet have no choice but to be drawn to one another, stuck with me for a long time. I always knew I wanted to write this book, and that made it pretty terrifying. It's my first multiple POV. It's my first romantic subplot. And it would have been fairly easy for me to absolutely screw this up, and I have no doubt I would have if it were not for some truly wonderful, amazing people.

There are few certainties that I have in this life, but one of them is that none of the books I've released would be even close to as good as they are without the exceptional work of Cee Taylor, my incredible developmental editor. I found Cee in the wilds of TikTok three years ago, and knew I wanted to work with her, but I could not have expected to find such an incredible colleague and friend to help me bring this world and these characters to life. Her fingerprints are all over Alddarri, and if you're curious which parts you can thank her for, just assume that it's the best parts. You're the best, Cee. Thank you.

Writing a book is terrifying in the best of times, and I honestly think it would be close to impossible without someone to talk through every step of the process. If you're a writer, and you don't have a good critique partner, get one. They won't be anywhere nearly as good as Libby Webber, but that's a very high bar to reach. Thanks for helping me reach the finish line, Libby, even from the other side of the planet.

Writing a romance between two women was something I knew I needed to be intentional and respectful about, at least if I didn't want to be just the biggest ass in the world. There was never a doubt that I was going to engage a beta reader. I didn't expect to get the chance to work with an author like Rebecca Thorne. Thank you so much for dedicating your time to make sure that I gave Jaina and Antoinette the kind of story they deserve, without getting my dude stink all over it. It's genuinely annoying that you can simultaneously be one of the most gifted authors I know AND a truly decent and thoughtful person. Pick a lane, dammit.

One of the weirdest things about the writing community I've been lucky enough to be part of is that I somehow manage to trick some ridiculously gifted authors into being friends with me. I don't know how it happens, but Paula Lafferty has spent a half-dozen FaceTime calls with me helping me dig this story out of the muck, and having an author of her caliber in my corner is as wild as it is wonderful. Thank you, Paula.

Taylor Vaughan: You've become like family. Specifically, that weird cousin that writes fantastic books, lives in my sink, and occasionally pops out to give me mountains of shit. Please never stop.

Adrienne Renick: You're going to win a Hugo Award one day, and on that day, you'll find me in the audience, grumbling that I don't know why it took them so damn long. One day, I'll find something you're bad at. But I don't expect it to be soon.

Cate Page: You're kind, funny, and thoughtful. You are also unquestionably the most ferociously talented writer I've ever been able to call my friend. When the world sees what the rest of us have already realized, it's going to be wild.

Cassie Corbin: I always hoped this series would have a fan like you. I'm so proud to know you, so proud to see how far you've come as an author, and I'm so excited that *Ranger* gets to be the first time the world hears your voice bring a book to life.

Mellody Stout: Thank you so much for sending me a message asking if I liked working with my editor. That led to some of the best things in my life, not least of which is you becoming one of my dearest friends. You're brilliant, you're kind, and you're an amazing storyteller.

People have been putting up with me rambling about my stories for a long time, but no one longer than Josh Mauthe. Thank you so much for always being there to help me get just a bit better as a writer, thank you for being the friend I can't wait to talk about books with, and thank you for standing with me at pretty much every major moment of my life. You're a hell of a good friend, even if you did argue the cinematic merits of Pootie Tang at one point.

Toni, you got the dedication. Don't be greedy. Love you.

Every book in this series has been written with two very good boys curled up at my feet. At this point, Pickle, Charlie, and Patton might need a coauthor credit.

Emi, I love you so much, and I'm so happy you found someone who makes you as happy as your mom makes me. Jae, welcome to the family.

Hannah, I will never stop marveling at what a capable, determined, and thoughtful woman you've become. I'm proud of you every morning when I wake up, and I go to sleep excited to see what lies ahead for you.

And to my wonderful wife, Jen. Thank you for loving me. Thank you for inspiring me. Thank you for being my person.

Dietrich Stogner was born in Fayetteville, North Carolina, and spent his childhood bouncing around military bases reading anything he could get his decidedly non-athletic mitts on. His father was a decorated paratrooper in the 82nd Airborne, and his mother was a brilliant academic and professor. After graduating high school with an impressively mediocre GPA, Dietrich served in the United States Navy, during which time he ignored the advice of those more intelligent and experienced and volunteered not just for the nuclear pipeline, but also for submarine duty, serving on the USS Pennsylvania ballistic missile submarine. After leaving the navy, Dietrich returned to college on the Post 9/11 GI Bill, earning degrees in journalism and economics, and working as a freelance journalist for several years.

Today, Dietrich lives south of Nashville, Tennessee with his wife, two lovely daughters, and two wonderful dogs. He spends his time reviewing books, filming content on writing and indie publishing, and plowing his way through the Alddarri Archive series. He's the author of 72 Hours, Frostbitten, Extraction, and Ranger. When he's not writing, he enjoys cooking, photography, and hiking.